The B...

Conte Barretto di Rienzi... cast long shadows into the candlelit room, as he moved toward the bridal bed.

Allegra lay rigid with tension, aware of the rose petals someone had scattered on the bed—as though, her heart whispered bitterly, this were a true and happy wedding night....

Now the Conte stood at the foot of the bed, his dark eyes appraising her slight figure. She stared at his strong dark hands as they unfastened his robe. "*Ebbena*, Contessa," he said coldly. "You and I will now fulfill our duty to the house of di Rienzi."

The last Allegra...

As Renaldo's hands caressed her cheek, the fine di Rienzi eyes shone in the startlingly handsome face. He pulled her closer. His hands, gentle but insistent, turned her face to his.

Allegra's will failed beneath the warm exploration of his lips. His kiss grew more urgent and Allegra was aware only of the call of her body and heart.

But the next moment he roughly thrust her away. His eyes probed hers. "So, you do not push me away as you do my brother. What, then, do you offer to me, Allegra?"

About the author...

Catherine Kay is — are — Catherine Dees and Kay Croissant. Close friends and writing collaborators for fifteen years, they live just across the street from each other in Pasadena, California, in 1920s Spanish-style houses. Together and separately they have traveled to Asia, India and Europe. Most recently they were in Egypt, where they worked for three months as researchers for an archaeological film project.

Kay, the widow of a college professor, has no children, but is kept company by her literary cat, brought as a kitten from Egypt in an empty Perrier carton. Cathy is divorced and has two daughters.

Kay and Cathy were educated at prestigious colleges in California (Kay at Occidental, Catherine at Stanford) and share a lifelong love for history — evident in all their fiction. Although their tastes differ in personal matters (Kay is a gourmet cook, Cathy eats when necessary; Cathy sews well, Kay would rather not; Kay is a talented artist, not so Cathy), they are in total agreement on one thing: as long as they can sit upright before a typewriter, they plan to keep turning out a steady stream of good romance fiction.

The way the two collaborate is unusual: they begin by discussing the story until they know exactly what they're going to write, then they work every day of the week in their library office at Kay's house. Incredibly, they are able to keep a consistent tone and style in both narrative and dialogue, no matter which one is writing. Each writes a section of the book, with input from the other.

Their work is carefully supervised by the Perrier cat, Nabi Daniel (Arabic for "the prophet Daniel"). Kay insists that she isn't comfortable about their work unless the cat has sat on it. Judging by the quality of their writing, he does — often.

CATHERINE KAY

Legacy of
PASSION

TORONTO · NEW YORK · LOS ANGELES · LONDON

Published November 1982

ISBN 0-373-97002-1

Printed in Canada

I stood in Venice, on the Bridge of Sighs
A palace and a prison on each hand:
I saw from out the wave her structures rise
As from the stroke of the enchanter's wand....

from *Childe Harold's Pilgrimage*

This book is for Bud Kay, a long time lover of
Venice, past and present, with grateful affection
for his help and encouragement. May the world-
wide efforts to preserve the beauty of Venice for
the future be successful, and may it always bring
its magic to the hearts of lovers.

Byron kept voluminous diaries, but his most personal memoirs he left to be published only after his death. These were burned by his executor at the request of his relatives, who feared personal disclosures about themselves from his shockingly honest pen. Scholars have regretted the loss of those papers ever since.

Perhaps in those burned pages a woman was mentioned...a woman unknown to history, whose life he touched and whose tragedy was too real for Byron to speak openly of it in his other journals. And this is her story....

BOOK I
THE BYRON
SECRET

CHAPTER ONE

VENICE, 3 DECEMBER, 1817

CONTE BARRETTO DI RIENZI'S imposing figure cast long shadows into the candlelit room. He stood for a moment at the heavy carved doors and then walked slowly and with authority toward the bridal bed. His rich brocaded robe glittered with silver sheen, the finely wrought silver lion's-head clasps seeming to spark and flare with each step he took.

Allegra lay shivering with tension. Her eyes focused upon small details of his dress, as if what she saw now was a last glimpse of life before all things changed.

Only silver, she thought distractedly . . . only silver for the master of the Ca' d'Argenti, the House of Silver. For others the hot sunlit gleam of gold, but for him the cold sharp blaze of silver. His face was no warmer than the bold lions on his robe.

She was rigid under the red velvet bedcover and painfully aware of inconsequential things—the lavender fragrance of the cool silk sheets with their silver monogram, the rose petals someone had scattered on the bed. As though this were a true and happy wedding night, her heart whispered bitterly.

The *conte*'s shadow moved before him until he stood at the end of the bed. His dark eyes appraised the slight figure beneath the bedclothes.

"Ebbene, contessa," he said in a harsh yet strangely compelling voice. "You and I will now fulfill our duty to the house of di Rienzi." A flicker of a smile was on his lips.

She looked up into his deeply lined dark face. Beneath a crown of thick silvery hair his aquiline features had a look of vigor, his tall body was straight. Coolly handsome for his age, she had thought three months ago when she first met him in her father's study. Older than her own parent, courteous with the true manners of an aristocrat, he had watched her carefully that day, as she poured wine into the delicate Murano goblets for them. How innocently she had served him, never in her most insane imaginings thinking that he would be her husband. Her husband! It could not have happened to her. . . .

She stared at his strong dark hands as they unfastened the clasps of his robe. Deliberately he opened it and threw it on the prayer stool near the bed. "You need not be afraid. I know that you are a virgin," he said in a practical tone. "I am a man of experience. I will not hurt you."

With unwilling fascination she saw his body. The lean hard figure was like the trunk of some vital tree, which had weathered many storms, and the growth of white hair on his chest was like snow on dark winter limbs. She closed her eyes, and then, feeling him come into the bed beside her, she silently sent up a small painful prayer.

His hands began to touch her intimately, and her body drew itself tighter. She could not respond to his devouring kisses. She sensed that he was trying to arouse her, and dutifully she hoped to fulfill her promise to him—but her body refused.

Sounds of impatience came from his throat. "I see that you will give me no pleasure, *madonna*. Let us hope that it is the problem of virginity." After that he wasted no gentleness on her. She wanted to cry out with the pain, but couldn't. . . .

HER MIND FLED from the pain and saw again the large dreary nursery room of the Ca' d'Argenti. He had taken her there only a few hours ago, after the wedding guests had departed. In that lifeless room the tall narrow windows were shuttered and heavily draped, and the bare walls echoed with their footfalls. To one side, near the raised hearth, was a very old wooden cradle set within a darkly tarnished silver frame. The *conte* had lighted a candle in the wall sconce and pulled Allegra to the cradle.

"We shall fill the di Rienzi cradle, my dear. Many times." H placed her hand on the side of it and started it rocking. It shoul: have been a moment to cherish, but she felt frightened. Barretto's large hand enveloped hers, forcing her to push the cradle again and again as they stood in the shadowy cold nursery. . . .

FINALLY IT WAS OVER. He lifted himself from her. She gasped a deep breath of relief and opened her eyes to find him gazing at her intently. "Poor child." He spoke more gently. "It will be easier after this. You have a good body and you will bear me good sons. I am not ungrateful, Allegra, but you must remember above all things that you belong to the house of di Rienzi. I will tolerate no young *cavaliere servente* dancing attendance on you. I am not as other husbands."

He rose from the bed, threw his robe around himself and went to the door, turning to her with his hand on the latch. "Good night, *contessa*. Sleep well."

SHE WAS ALONE. Slowly and uncomfortably she moved her hands over her body, the body that had always belonged to her only. Now it was strange, all of its privacy gone, and burning tears welled up in her eyes. She wept in futility, wincing as she saw the streaks of her own blood on the silk beneath her.

She remembered the niche before the statue of Santa Chiara in the convent in Faenza, where until last spring she had been a student. Her knees had ached from the hard stone floor, as she prayed in complete faith to the sweet saint to bring her true love—that one face whose smile would waken her heart to joy. The other girls there had been amused by her prayer vigils. "Be practical, Allegra," her friend Nadia told her, "our fathers will try to find good husbands for us. Just be glad if you get one with money and a good house—one who lets you have your own way in little things."

But she secretly continued her prayers. Surely the good saint, who had so loved San Francesco, would understand. What a stupid girl she had been so few months ago! She hadn't known then that prayers were useless, that her fate was being shaped by the politics of Napoleon and the wars, and that her father was desperately trying to salvage the ruined fortunes of the noble Lamberti family.

Allegra turned her face into the rose-scented pillows to escape the odor of Barretto's lovemaking. She wanted to blank out everything that had happened today, but the pictures battered against her mind.

It was not possible to forget the curious faces of the Venetians who had gathered in the gray chapel of the Ca' d'Argenti for her wedding, silent in their furs, silks and jewels—like a tableau. The light of the great buttery candles failed to cut the gloom of the damp December morning. It was a half dream of beauty and ugliness.

Her younger sisters Lipia and Gemma had fussed endlessly over her, arranging the creamy satin wedding dress, chiding her for not smiling. They were so pleased with her for bringing wealth to the family again. What good is it to be an aristocrat, they asked, if you have no money? Her father's face was alight with pride, too. She shivered under his firm grip on her arm as he led her to the altar, as if he feared she might break and run before the final words could be spoken. *Poor father,* she had thought, *I won't shame you in front of all Venice. I'm not a coward.*

She didn't need to raise her eyes to know that Barretto's lips were spread into a thin smile watching her being brought to him. She knew what everyone in the chapel was thinking: she was the young mare that Conte di Rienzi had purchased to bring forth a son with a good bloodline—a legitimate son.

The voice of the priest intoned the wedding ritual, and she heard her own whispered replies to questions that should have been spoken from her heart. Small uncomfortable bits of gossip about Barretto's past had reached her ears, but her mind had run away from stories of the misfortunes of his first two wives. They had both died young. One thing she knew: his hope for a son went beyond desire into obsession.

When she left the chapel on Barretto's arm she sensed looks of pity from some of the watching eyes. The reception in the great ballroom afterward was a blur, except for the pleased faces of her father and sisters and her own growing awareness that her life was no longer safe or understandable.

SUDDENLY SHE COULD NOT STAND the feel of the luxurious bed. Her body ached from Barretto's urgencies. The need to cleanse herself from his touch overwhelmed her. There were only embers in the deep marble fireplace, and cold was creeping into the room from the heavy stone walls.

As she tried to rise, her body had a terrible and unfamiliar stiffness. She found it painful to move to the door of the bathroom. A small brazier on the marble floor was cold, and the water in the jeweled silver pitcher seemed near to ice, but she was past caring. She dashed water into the silver bowl beside it and furiously tried to work the hard cake of rose-scented soap into suds.

The white lace gown was damp and smelled of Barretto. She stripped it off and flung it away from her. Her delicate skin recoiled from the touch of the icy wet bath cloth, and she rubbed her body hard to erase the hot feel of Barretto's hands and lips. Areas of redness on her milky body began to glow in the wake of her urgent purifications.

"May I help you, *madonna*?" a quiet voice spoke from the doorway. Allegra whirled around to see her new maid, Gina, watching her. The woman did not wait for permission but came toward her with a gentle smile. She took the cloth from Allegra's shivering hand and poured fresh water into another bowl, proceeding to rinse and dry her as though she were a small child. Her hands were comforting and warm.

Allegra looked at the composed and steady face. Gina was neither young nor old, but there was beauty in her dark coiled hair, and the pure lines of her cheek had the look of one of the patient saints. She picked up a jar of soft lotion and stroked it soothingly over Allegra's skin. In a graceful motion she plucked a fresh nightrobe from a Byzantine carved chest and wrapped her in it.

The silent communication of sympathy began to ease Allegra's shocked nerves. She was led to one of the heavy oak chairs by the hearth, and Gina quickly set the fire burning again. She went to the bed and pulled away the damp sheets and ornate cover, shaking off the crushed rose petals and bringing out smooth linens. The bed was transformed to a fresh comfort.

"How can I thank you, Gina?" Allegra whispered, feeling a rush of gratitude.

'There need be no thanks between us, *madonna*," the calm voice replied. "I have lived more years than you, my lady. I know that the convent does not well prepare us for life itself. Also, I served the last *contessa*, Lucia, may her soul be happy." From the dressing room she took a silver brush and began to smooth Allegra's dark disheveled hair back into glistening waves. In the low flickering light of the room, Gina spoke of the house of di Rienzi. "They say that Conte Barretto resembles his old merchant ancestor who built the Ca' two hundred years ago."

"The one who named it the House of Silver?"

"*Si*. Renaldo, the beginning of the present di Rienzi line. He was a strange man, they say, who took his payments in silver only, and when he traveled, many guards were needed because he always took his silver with him. He was forgiven his little madness because he was so rich."

"What about the last *contessa* . . . Lucia? I have heard stories . . . ." Allegra felt compelled to ask.

The brush hesitated in its even stroke. "My lady, I could tell you a honeyed lie, but the truth is that she died from too many miscarriages—year after year. Finally she bore a live girl child, a frail *bambina*. The *conte* took her away to a wet nurse in the country. He was angry that the girl survived while the males had died. The *contessa* never saw the child except twice—once at birth and then at its christening. I think it was too much for her. She was ill and feverish, and all the will for life went from her. It has been about a year now. But this is a sad conversation. You are not she, and she is not you. God alone wills these things. It need not be an unhappy time for you, *madonna*. The marriage bed is but a small part of life, and Venice is still the most beautiful city in Italy. A lovely woman can have anything she wishes. Each day will be better, I promise you." She bent to give Allegra's cheek a gentle reassuring kiss. "Now, you must sleep."

SHE LAY ALONE in the shadowy, unfamiliar room and heard t. bells of the campanile in the Piazza San Marco, ringing from f. off down the Grand Canal. Their penetrating rhythmic tones became words in Allegra's distraught mind, calling out "Blame

Na-po-leon! Blame Na-po-leon!'' The same words that her father had spoken five months ago, on the night he told her she would have no dowry and no hope for a husband.

"Blame Napoleon," he said, shrugging. "I did not make these infernal wars. The Austrians are impossible to deal with, and now that Napoleon is sitting on his miserable little island my contracts with the French are just so much paper." He looked up at her from his desk in the study. "My line of credit is used up, all the Lamberti family capital is gone, except for this house. . . . In a short time I will be ruined—nothing left . . . ." His voice was toneless and resigned.

Allegra was about to tell him that it didn't matter to her whether they had money or not, that she would be happy in any circumstances, when he spoke again. "At eighteen you are old enough to understand what this means for us all. You must prepare yourself to enter the religious vocation—your sisters, too. No man of position will marry a poor woman, and I won't consent to an alliance outside of our class. My grandchildren will be noble Venetians or there shall be no grandchildren!"

He turned back to his account books and poured himself a full glass of cognac. "In these times the only safety may be within the cloister walls," he murmured. "God knows what our future will be . . . ."

THE BELLS OF THE CAMPANILE stopped, and Allegra remembered one particular night a few weeks later when she was called again into her father's study. He was entertaining a visitor, Conte di Rienzi. Recently there had been many men coming to discuss finances and politics, but this was the first time she had seen the Conte di Rienzi here. She knew of his reputation as a powerful ？ ？ who had survived the stormy times since the fall of Venice ？？？ years earlier, multiplying his fortune in spite of everything. "I compliment you on your charming daughter, Lamberti," the old *conte* said. Allegra felt his speculative eyes on her. "What have the nuns taught you in the convent, my dear?"

"I speak some French, sir, and a little Latin and English," she said, not used to being addressed by her father's associates.

"Her handwriting is very well formed," her father added eagerly, "very fine."

Their visitor smiled. "A satisfactory list of virtues. It isn't wise to stimulate young girls with too much learning. It makes them restless." He raised his fragile crystal goblet and looked at Allegra for a long moment through the tawny liqueur. "I am a man of the old school."

His words carried authority and sureness. Allegra thought how much she preferred her own father to this uncomfortable man. She would not have been happy as the daughter of Barretto di Rienzi. Conte Lamberti was neither a strong nor a powerful man, but he was not severe. For that she was grateful. She easily forgave her father the quick rise and fall of his emotions. He had been deeply pained by the loss of his wife and hadn't really known what to do with three small daughters, except to send them away to school with the nuns.

She thought no more of their harsh visitor until late that night, when her father came to her room to tell her that he had arranged their marriage. In three months' time she would be the Contessa di Rienzi and go to live in the Ca' d'Argenti.

His eyes avoided her astonished face. "I had no choice, Allegra, I had to be practical. He is rich. He has an old name and is willing to offer you protection. And he made a very generous offer for your hand." He said more, attempting to make the arrangement seem a desirable one, but Allegra could hear only the laughter that flooded into her ears . . . the laughter of the girls in the convent, who were so amused by her childish belief in a marriage for love.

BARRETTO HAD NOT BEEN an unkind husband-to-be. He was lavish with his gifts for her and her sisters. At fourteen and sixteen they were becoming dazzled by the prospect of their own marriages. They were too young to see beyond the excitement of great wealth.

The large, run-down, old Lamberti palazzo was kept in a state of constant uproar by the deluge of invitations to honor the future bride. Allegra didn't enjoy the teas and luncheons, where the older ladies whispered behind their fluttering fans. She was acutely aware that they were savoring bits of well-worn gossip about the aging *conte* and the financially needy father of the bride. What could she do except hold herself in dignity and pretend she didn't notice?

There was nobody to confide in. Many of her school friends lived in Florence and were swept in their own marriage plans. Her older cousin Elletra lived in Vienna now with her husband and would not be at the wedding because of advanced pregnancy. Allegra had never been close to Lipia or Gemma, who danced upon the surface of life like two young lambs. They were delighted to be wearing their new gowns and baubles and to be sipping tea with the most fashionable ladies. She could not begrudge them their pleasure in it. After all, just a short time ago they were expecting to spend the rest of their lives in nuns' habits behind locked doors.

SHE TRIED to pull her mind back, but one memory stung more bitterly than all the rest—the pearls. The beautiful double strand of pearls she had worn around her throat that morning in the chapel. It was Venetian custom that every woman of good family be given a gift of jewels by her mother three days before her wedding, but Allegra's mother had been dead for many years. The presentation would be made by her father.

Her mother's pearls were magnificent ones, perfect, large and very old. They had come to Venice from Constantinople in the sea chest of a merchant ancestor in the early eighteenth century and were given from mother to first daughter in each generation that followed. They glowed with the soft creamy luster made by the warm breasts of the women of her line. Allegra knew the pearls well and loved them, because they had belonged to her mother and because of the aura of expectation and romance she had always felt around them. She had never thought of them as objects of value. They were beyond that.

"Father is giving you the pearls tonight," Gemma had

whispered. "I heard him telling Conte de Rienzi. Aren't you excited?" She gave her elder sister a quick embrace and ran off to dress for supper.

Conte Lamberti made a little ceremony out of the presentation and told Allegra to close her eyes. She heard her breath come faster and felt the cool weight of the necklace as it was pulled around her throat and fastened from behind by her father.

"These pearls will make you even more lovely on your wedding day," he said, bending to kiss her cheek. She put her fingers to the heavy double strand, and as she did her father's voice continued speaking close to her ear. "Of course these are not your mother's, but Barretto has made this fine gift so that you would not be without your bridal pearls."

She had no need to hear the words. Her fingers quickly told her the truth: they had been sold to pay debts! She was unable to speak.

"She is shy to express her gratitude, Barretto," her father explained, not seeing the expression in her eyes or the red fire of her cheeks.

"An admirable quality," the *conte* half smiled from across the table, "if that is what it is. Allegra, my dear, are they not to your taste? I can arrange for others . . . ."

She pushed back her chair and ran silently from the room so that her tears would not make it all the worse.

Now, FROM HER COOL BED in the Ca' d'Argenti, she silently smiled at the innocence of Allegra Lamberti and all the wrenching tears that flowed before the wedding, for all the many reasons. She didn't really blame her father or Barretto. There wasn't anyone to blame—not even Napoleon. She turned her face into the pillows and let darkness and sleep carry her away from the House of Silver. . . .

"YOU WILL LOOK BEAUTIFUL with a great belly, *contessa*. I will be very proud," Barretto laughed softly. Allegra opened her eyes to see her husband seated upon the edge of her bed. "I didn't want to start my day without a visit to my sweet young bride." He leaned

.o kiss her on her lips, running his hand down over her breasts. In her drowsiness she responded to him a little. "Ah," he whispered, "you will learn soon enough to welcome my caresses. I will be an eager lover for you tonight. Until then, my dear . . . ."

Allegra was fully awake as he pulled the door closed behind him. Her body and her mind were tired, and she realized slowly that this new day would end for her with another night like the one just past. The thought made her shudder. She had heard that some women drank brandy before their husbands came to their beds.

She couldn't believe that this painful act of their bodies was what poets wrote about in their rapturous lyrics. Why would the Holy Church bless such an act as a divine gift from God? The lovers of all times knew a great secret, which she had been denied, but someday she would know it, too, she promised herself.

Barretto was gone from the Ca' during the days, and she had endless hours in which to prepare herself for his overpowering presence at night. When he came to her bed there were no gentle preliminaries, no loving words. He demanded that she open her eyes and watch their lovemaking, as if he could force a response from her body. But the very texture of his skin repelled her senses. She thanked God that he left her alone afterward. She had never felt so wretched in her life.

Obedience was something that had been trained into her from childhood, but obedience had never before gone against every desire of her being. She had not been a fearful child, so why should she feel this cold dread of her husband? *Because,* she answered, *I am his possession. He does not care what I think or feel.*

She thought about writing in her diary. It had lain untouched since Gemma had presented it to her on the wedding day. But she didn't want to put any words onto the clean linen pages, because the very act of writing would give permanence and reality to her situation, and her fingers refused to write Allegra di Rienzi. The name was alien to her. Gemma's breathless inscription was like a mocking joke: "May each day of married life be more beautiful than the last for my adored sister." The red velvet cover had a finely painted miniature set into it, showing a man and woman dancing in a ballroom, lightly touching with gloved hands and gazing at each other with lovers' eyes. They were supposed to be she and Barretto, but the artist had idealized Barretto, making him young and his hair dark.

Each morning she awoke wanting to believe that she had just had a disturbing dream, and she was still in her own bed at the Palazzo Lamberti. She was like a stranger here, cut off from anything familiar. Barretto expected her to become an accomplished hostess when he entertained his business associates, and she would have to learn quickly how to be the mistress of his house.

She explored the labyrinth of rooms and hallways while her mind wrestled with its terrible problem. Except for Gina, the servants never spoke unless spoken to. Most of the staff were older, and Allegra felt very young and inexperienced.

The silence of the Ca' d'Argenti made her feel more alone than she really was. It was as if Barretto had given orders that no voices were to be raised above a whisper and, above all, there should be no laughter. Instinctively, she found herself walking almost stealthily through the high-ceilinged rooms, making no sound in her passing. Once she entered one of the unused guest chambers and surprised a parlor maid, who was taking a light nap in the comfortable chaise longue. The terrified woman went completely white. "Please, *madonna,* I meant no harm! Please! I beg you not to tell the master. . . ." Tears streamed down her face as she stood next to the chair like a cornered animal.

"Of course not," Allegra smiled, alarmed at the intensity of the woman's fear. "I shan't tell a soul. I am only sorry I startled you."

The maid rushed up to her and kissed her hand swiftly before fleeing the room. Allegra turned to see her disappear down the hall. A man's face showed itself around the corner of the adjacent hallway and withdrew again instantly. It was a peculiar face, which she had not seen before in the house. For the first time she had the thought that she was being watched.

She said nothing to Gina about the man. She didn't want to appear childish, imagining things that were not there. That evening Barretto asked her to join him for supper in his rooms. The message was delivered by a footman, who added that the *conte* wished her to be punctual.

SHE CONSIDERED WEARING her best dinner dress for him. It would please him. But she stopped herself. *Why should I wish to appear alluring,* her unhappy inner voice asked. *It would be better if I came to him looking as plain as a washboard.* There were still sore places on her body, where he had held her too tightly as he claimed his rights each night, and she chose to wear a loosely falling brown woolen gown and no jewels. The pinch of a close-fitting seam or the chafing of too many underskirts could only remind her of Barretto's rough use of her.

"You have an odd sense of style, *contessa*," Barretto said as he entered. "For a bride of less than one week you are intent upon seeming matronly . . . almost like a nun. But we shall not speak of that further. Sit down. I wish to give you instruction for your new role in the House of Silver."

Allegra could not fathom his mood. Was he angry, or was the thin smile a customary one? In the candlelight of his study his face took on a threatening aspect, which she tried not to notice. She knew she was young and prone to emotion, and she was trying to become a woman of strength.

"We shall dine here while I tell you some important rules of conduct." He rang for his personal servant, who brought a tray. A footman had set up a table for dining.

"I wish to be well versed in the running of this house, my lord," she said deferentially beneath his steady stare.

"Indeed," he remarked, and said no more until the servants had left the room. Allegra's hands clasped each other in her lap, fighting down the tremors in them as the silence deepened.

He picked up his heavy silver fork and began to spear the food on his plate, chewing vigorously as Allegra watched him. "Eat," he motioned and followed his word with a swallow of red wine.

She picked at the pieces of lamb and aubergine and wished he would get it over with—whatever it was that he called her here for.

"I may have made a mistake," he said at length. "The convent was not the best training for you . . . you are too artless."

"Ar . . . artless?" she said in a small voice.

"Yes. I find you unskilled in the manners of our class. For example," he dabbed at his lips with his napkin, "today you found a servant doing something inexcusably lax and then begged *her* forgiveness. I will not tolerate such absurd behavior by my wife."

Color rose quickly into her cheeks. "But she had only fallen asleep. There was no crime. . . ."

"Do not plead her case. The woman was discharged with no references. My point is this: the Contessa di Rienzi behaves at all times like a *contessa* and not a kitchen girl. Sentiment is not to be a part of your life . . . you left that behind when you married into the house of di Rienzi. Sentiment will not be a part of our personal relationship. Schoolgirl emotions will only cause your existence here to be painful, believe me. Your duties are simple: dress well, behave with proper dignity, obey me in everything. Beyond that, you are free to pursue your small interests. Your life should be reasonably happy as a result." He regarded her with a look that said, *there now, it is settled. Go back to your rooms and leave the important things of life to your husband.*

By the end of the first week as Barretto's wife Allegra was unable to think of anything except escape. She could not possibly become the wife he demanded. Longing thoughts came to her of the convent of Santa Chiara. At least it was a sanctuary, but the remembrance of the pale, patient faces of the sisters told her that there was no happiness there, either. She would have to see her father. He was the only one who could help her now. Barretto must not know.

She sent one of the servants rushing to the Palazzo Lamberti with an invitation for her father to come that afternoon for tea. She worded it carefully, lightly—flattering him as her first guest at the palazzo. There had been no callers at the Ca' since their wedding, out of respect for the privacy of the newly wed couple—surely that was the worst of ironies. The servant came back to say that Conte Lamberti was honored to be the first visitor to call on the new *contessa*.

It was a gloomy gray day with constant drizzling rain. There had been rain every day since the wedding, and as she stood at the windows of her sitting room she felt as cold and stricken as the windblown waters of the canals. "The bride of rain is the wife of sorrow," her old French nursemaid Odile used to say. It was difficult to lift herself from such morbid feelings.

A simple dark blue gown would be best, she decided. *Father must not think me frivolous . . . he must believe me*. She knelt at her prayer stool for a long time collecting her thoughts, gathering courage, then pulled a heavy wool shawl around her small shoulders and left the room.

The Ca' was a cold place, the floors all marble and the ceilings high. In the *galleria* outside her rooms she stood and looked down to the magnificent foyer. She had stood there many times at the pink marble balustrade, thinking about the beauty of the graceful curved stairway, the blue-and-cream flowered patterns of the Aubusson rugs and the elaborate marble maze inlaid upon the entrance floor. Beyond that, two great carved doors shut away the outside world.

Today she looked at the dancing flecks of silver and gold suspended in the many arms of the huge Venetian glass chandelier below her and felt nothing but emptiness and exhaustion. Who was she, this person standing and waiting for the sight of a familiar figure to enter the door? If she didn't belong in this fine house, where did she belong? Would there ever be such a place as *home*?

Why was her father taking so long to come here? She started to imagine Barretto preventing him from entering but dismissed the thought at once and continued to watch the closed entrance doors.

Behind her she sensed the somber presences in the dark paintings that hung on the *galleria* wall. The di Rienzi *contes* and their *contessas.* She didn't turn around. She had already studied their faces enough to imagine what their lives had been. The Ca' had not been a place of joy for a long time.

There was a portrait of Lucia. She looked very sad and frail, almost a shadow of a woman, engulfed by a heavy black-and-silver brocade gown and a wide collar of pearls. It was a disturbing picture, and Allegra didn't like to look at it. She avoided the gaze of all the dead di Rienzis.

Far below, one of the liveried servants was responding to the sound of the visitors' bell. Allegra watched her father enter and remove his coat and hat. She took a deep breath for courage and called down to him.

"Ah, there you are, Allegra," he said jauntily. "Shall I come up?"

"We'll have tea in my rooms, father."

He embraced her, then held her at arm's length for a moment. "You look very well, my dear. Full of color. Marriage agrees with you." She turned from his smiling eyes and led him along the hallway. He looked admiringly at the di Rienzi portraits. "Your mother would be so happy to know that you are safely under the protection of this great house."

Allegra's sitting room was a cheerful place, with bright yellow curtains at the tall windows and comfortable furniture—not at all in the formal style of the rest of the Ca'. The sad Lucia had decorated it for her times of waiting for the birth of an heir.

Gina set a lively fire in the flower-tiled fireplace. Over tea Allegra and Conte Lamberti talked of inconsequential things. Her father spoke of politics and the economy as if they were games. He was delighted with his recent speculations in the grain markets.

"Eighty thousand profit, imagine it! And I have your Barretto to thank. He is a genius with investments." He didn't read the expression on her face as he rambled on happily. "I'm going to Vienna next month to meet Barretto's bankers. All we have to worry about now is the foolhardy hotheads who press for overthrow of Austrian rule. They will ruin us all. I can't understand what they—"

"Father," Allegra said softly, but with such force that he cut his words short. "Father, I want to come home."

He slowly lowered his cup and looked at her. "What are you saying?"

"I can't stay here. Not one more night." She tried to hold his eyes with hers, to force him to see her misery. "He doesn't love me. He only wants a woman's body that can give him a son."

Conte Lamberti looked at her incredulously. "Is that what you think marriage is—love? What have those nuns filled your head with? People in our position make alliances, arrangements, and a fortunate one this was. I don't know where we would be if it were not for Barretto's very generous settlement for your hand!"

"He bought me," she whispered, her strength suddenly flowing out of her.

"Don't be dramatic, child. I want what is the best for your happiness, believe me—but when you are young you don't really understand what happiness should be. He is not such a heartless fellow, I'm sure. You are overwrought."

"Father, I can't . . . ."

He took her in his arms. "There now—many inexperienced women have your complaint, I am told. Give it time, my dear."

She pulled away in tears. "I can't spend another night here. . . ."

"I disagree," he said with an impatient edge to his voice. "It is not too much to ask that you pull yourself together. You are not the first woman to have her childish fantasies bruised. Venetian women are strong. Bear with your situation like a lady, and realize that it could be much worse. And for the love of God, give him a son!" His face softened a little. "Have lots of babies, Allegra, and then your life will seem happier. There will be time for romance. Barretto isn't young, you know. When you are older you will laugh at yourself for making such a scene."

He went to the door and stood awkwardly for a moment with his hand on the heavy silver latch. Almost apologetically he said, "These are not easy times for any of us. . . . We must make the best of things. *Addio.*"

She turned away from him and waited for the sound of his departing footsteps in the hallway. The room was silent except for the soft crackling sounds of the fire. She walked slowly to the hearth and stood motionless, watching the golden licks of flame. The room began to fill with a familiar sound—the older girls at Santa Chiara were still laughing at her. *Well,* she smiled grimly, *they were right and I was wrong. I didn't understand the world at all. And the nuns were right, too. This life is for suffering and enduring. The joy will come after I am dead.* At that moment she envied Lucia, who was free.

When Gina's gentle knock sounded at the door it was almost full dark outside, and the small logs in the fireplace had fallen into a shapeless pile of embers. Tears of loss and resignation moved down Allegra's face. She checked them with an effort of the will. If there had been a dream, it was now locked securely away in the corner of her heart, where it wouldn't torment her any longer. As Gina pulled the curtains closed over the windows, Allegra went to her desk and lifted a silver-sheathed pen from its holder, slowly dipping the tip into the inkpot. She opened her diary to the first page and wrote: "Allegra di Rienzi."

CHAPTER TWO

MARCH 1818

BARRETTO SAT at the far end of the dining table and raised his glass in a silent toast to Allegra. She saw the sparkles of ruby light shimmer in the red wine and felt nausea creep slowly into her body. Through her dizzied vision Barretto's face was smiling, showing for a moment what a handsome young man he must once have been.

"I am more than pleased, my wife." His usually harsh, peremptory voice was softened. Allegra tried to smile back at him. Only a moment earlier she had told him in a formal voice, "*Signore*, I believe that I am almost two months with child."

Now that the words were out she sat clutching the edge of the table, fighting faintness. Dimly she was aware that Barretto was moving swiftly toward her, then a comfortable blackness took her into its welcoming depths.

When she awoke it was to see Gina waving a vial of salts for her to breathe, and Barretto hovering nearby.

Almost immediately Allegra's pregnancy isolated her. Barretto intended to take no chances with his unborn child. The trauma of his earlier stillborn sons was still strong in him. Mercifully, he removed his presence from her bed for fear of causing a miscarriage.

He saw to it that the best of medical care was brought to her. Dr. Aglietti was a specialist in women's problems, a discreet older gentleman whose large imposing body gave a sense of assurance and whose eyes were habitually sympathetic. He had been attending the beds of the ladies and mistresses of Venice for more than twenty years, and yet Barretto mistrusted even him—never allowing him to be alone with Allegra.

During the first six months of pregnancy the nausea and headaches were constant. She was barely able to eat and grew gaunt and listless. Even the effort to pick up her pen and mark off

the passing days in her diary was too much. The doctor worried
about her and patiently administered drafts of drugs and plant
tinctures, but nothing seemed to help. She wept uncontrollably
when she first felt the quickening of life within her.

Dr. Aglietti finally spoke to Barretto. "She must have a change
of air, perhaps go to one of your villas for a few weeks. In cases
like this the lady often benefits from a complete change of situation. *Complete*," he ended.

Barretto's response to the hidden meaning was swift. "That
will not be possible. The *contessa* is young and strong. She is not
one of those pale hypochondriacs who have you wrapped around
their fingers. No. She cannot be separated from her life at the Ca'
d'Argenti. I know from experience that a prescribed routine will
produce a live infant. She must be here under my supervision."

"Some outings, then, my dear *conte*. Something to take the
thoughts from the coming birth." Allegra heard him whisper to
Barretto, "It is a malady of the nerves . . . melancholia."

"Perhaps," Barretto had answered, ending the discussion. He
spoke no more of the doctor's suggestions, and Allegra retired
into her endless time of waiting—just like Lucia, she thought
hopelessly.

She began to write sporadically in her diary, sitting at her curved
French desk, which faced the window. For 7 May:

> I have been taking Gina's special medicine—*teriaca*—a bit-
> tersweet black potion, which makes me feel eased for a few
> hours at a time. Thank God. The rest of the time I suffer as if I
> have committed dreadful sins—but what sins? I have only
> dreamed of being free of Barretto. Surely my sweet Lord does
> not punish me for this!

On one of Conte Lamberti's visits late in May he was slightly
out of breath from haste. "I have an invitation for you, my child,
from Elletra! She has just arrived in Venice to find a school for
her eldest daughter."

Elletra Clodio was Allegra's vibrant, witty older cousin, who
lived in Vienna with her husband Umberto. The remembered im-

age of Elletra in Allegra's mind brought with it the fragrance of fine perfume and the sound of impulsive laughter. Umberto was attached to the Venetian trade mission at the imperial capital and had long been intimate with the nobility of Vienna.

"She delegated me to tell you," Conte Lamberti continued, 'that she will not visit an invalid in a sickroom. You must come to her. She has a storehouse of pleasant gossip for you, she says, and she wants you to spend the day with her at the Palazzo Clodio. She meant today, and I could not say no to her when she presented herself at my door this morning. She is quite a whirl-wind of a woman," he smiled, exchanging a swift worried look with Gina.

Allegra sat up from her couch by the French doors and asked Gina to help her to dress. Color appeared in pink patches on her cheeks. "Bring me some *teriaca* and my cambric dress—the one with the bright green ribbons at the hem. Elletra mustn't see me like this," she said, reaching for a hand mirror to examine the state of her hair. Gina was smiling broadly.

Conte Lamberti's face bore a look of fatherly relief. He retired from the room, stopping at the door. "The gondola will be here for you in an hour. I told Barretto that your cousin was better medicine than all the rest and assured him that you would be in good hands. It would be wise if you returned before dark," he ended with a conspiratorial wink. If Allegra had had the strength she would have thrown her arms around his neck from happiness. She had no intention of arousing Barretto's anger by overstaying her visit with Elletra.

The Palazzo Clodio was not far away—near the Campo Morosini. Allegra hadn't thought anything could rouse her from the hypnotic sameness of her quiet rooms, but Elletra's summons was like a bracing breeze that set the blood flowing again. She had come and gone in Allegra's life over the years—whether arriving from a dazzling trip to Paris, or entertaining the entire troupe of the Viennese ballet, Elletra brought excitement with her always. Allegra had not seen her since before the wedding.

She swallowed a large dose of *teriaca* for strength and shakily followed Gina's efforts to dress and coif her. The white linen

frock hung easily over her form, making her seem younger than
she was. Her ankles showed like a child's beneath the hem,
wrapped in the ribbons of dainty green slippers. She was terribly
thin, except for the small round bulge under the high waistline.

The gondola was waiting at the water steps. Allegra swayed
unsteadily then caught herself, as she emerged from the entrance
door of the Ca'. The air was stifling because of a sirocco wind,
and the sunlight was intense. Gina was with her on the pretext of
visiting one of the servants in the Palazzo Clodio, but it was clear
that she was there in the role of nurse.

The gondolier poled them silently onto the Grand Canal and
eased his black boat into a narrow side *rio*. Venice gleamed with
reflected light from the faces of the palazzos and the restless
windblown ripples on the water. It suddenly looked like a land of
delights. Even in decay the old stone walls managed to arrange
themselves into crumbling patterns of beauty. Light and shadow
moved artfully upon the stones of Venice, calling attention to tiny
votive niches where the faithful had placed fresh flowers. Gondola landings were guarded by grinning stone lions.

"I had forgotten how beautiful Venice is!" she said to Gina.
"Do prisoners feel this way when they are let out of their cells, I
wonder?" She closed her eyes and took a deep breath, as if to in-
hale and hold the precious feeling.

Gina laughed. "Things are always more beautiful when there is
something to look forward to. Your world has been too small for
too long, only watching life from the windows of your rooms.
Maybe that will change now. . . ."

THE PALAZZO CLODIO was in cool shadows at the end of a short
canal, black-and-white awnings flapping in the hot breeze. Elletra
Clodio was standing at the little dock waiting—a tall slender
woman with shining black hair swept into a cluster of curls at the
back of her head. She ran to the gondola and gathered Allegra
into her welcoming arms.

"I knew if I could lure you here you would be better!" she
said, holding Allegra in a tight embrace. "I know that old Ca'
of yours . . . silent as a tomb . . . a beastly place for a girl. It's

nough to give anyone the vapors, at the very least! Come up ow, I've opened the chambers on the top floor, and we have the most delicious flow of pleasant air." She spoke a moment to Gina nd graciously showed her to the staff quarters where she could isit and lunch with her friend.

"I wouldn't have known you, Allegra, you're so changed. Should I say grown up? But you know what I mean . . . we must alk over good food. I brought my wonderful cook from Vienna."

She wove a soothing mood of small talk, while leading Allegra o the airy salon where they would spend their afternoon. Allegra vas grateful; she hardly had to speak. Elletra's cheery voice was a balm to her tired nerves. She knew that her dear cousin vas aware of exactly what she had been going through. Elletra always was.

She helped Allegra to a comfortable sofa chair and perched on an ottoman next to it. "How did you hear that I was ill?" Allegra asked. "I haven't talked with anyone for so long. . . ."

"Your maid told me, I must confess. I like her courage. She is a friend of my head parlor maid, and she discreetly arranged for me o receive a letter. It is here if you wish to read it. She wrote only nough for me to realize that you could do with a day away from our stuffy old *casa*—and I lost no time speaking to your father."

Elletra took Allegra's hands in a gentle clasp. "Your husband has behaved Hunnishly, hasn't he? Did you know that many peo-ple stayed away from your wedding because they couldn't bear to ive their approval to such a match?"

"I didn't . . . ." Allegra whispered.

"You know me . . . I don't mind speaking out. So I wrote your father as much when I heard of the betrothal, but he was blinded y his financial worries. You have been in my prayers every day. The churches near my home in Vienna are filled with candles for ou," she grinned. "And now," she bent to press a light kiss on Allegra's forehead, "I have you here in my clutches, and I will do anything in my power to make you happy. What would you think f coming to Austria with me as soon as the baby is born?" She gnored Allegra's slight gasp and the quick flash of her eyes

"There are men there who will make you feel like a Greek god-
dess, believe me. You need to spread your wings. I could thrash
your husband for intimidating you. He has, I know it. You look
like a frightened little bird, all shivering in her nest and afraid to
see what is in the next tree."

"Elletra . . . ." Allegra interrupted. "I couldn't go. You don't
know Barretto—he would never let me go."

"Who will ask him? We shall simply do it." She stood up and
looked out of the high windows. "Where would half the women
of Venice be if they waited for permission to live their lives? But,
let's talk of other things over lunch."

An inner door flew open with a great noise and barking and
scuffling. A flock of small wiry black-and-white dogs erupted into
the room ahead of two servants bearing trays, almost causing an
accident underfoot. Elletra scooped up two of the eager yelping
animals and gave them a hug, letting them tumble from her arms.

"Now, it's your turn to tell me news. It seems ages since I was
here in Venice. Tell me about Byron. . . . I hear he's taken over
part of the old Palazzo Mocenigo with a menagerie of animals
and women. Now there is a man!"

"I have only heard his name. I'm afraid . . . ."

Elletra interrupted. "And what a poet he is! No wonder he only
has to lift a finger and the ladies swoon around him! I met him the
year before last in Milano. A fascinating creature—even his
lameness makes him seem romantic. But you must have heard
something about him, Allegra. I would think his name would be
spoken in all the salons."

"I haven't been out for so long, it's no wonder I don't know
about him."

"How many cities can claim to have Byron living there? I have
a little book of his poems. Take it home and read it, and then tell
me what you think about our scandalous English milord." She
reached into a writing desk and picked up the book of poems.
"There's no one who writes as romantically."

OVER A DELICATE FISH ENTRÉE Elletra continued to probe
Allegra's situation. She had an irresistible good-heartedness,

which made her a beautiful woman in spite of her long narrow
nose and thin face. Allegra laughed at the bits of silly gossip and
forgot that she couldn't eat anything but broth. After lunch
Elletra became serious, and Allegra knew that the subject of Barretto was being brought up again.

"What have you heard about your husband's past? I have a
reason for asking," she said.

"Just little things. I know that his other wives died and that he
married me to get a son. I know that he is a jealous man, and he
would do something violent if I gave him cause for suspicion."

Her nausea was starting to return, and she shivered in the warm
room. There was enough *teriaca* in her purse for one dose, which
she quickly drank.

"My poor dear cousin, forgive me. That is precisely why I want
to take you away from here. It pains me to see you like this. That
is what he did to his last wife. Lucia was sweet and sensitive, like
you, and look what happened to her . . . no friends called on her
for fear of having to deal with the *conte*. Is that not your situation, as well? You need to know how that man uses people. You
must gain heart and not let him use you. My Umberto would be a
beast if I let him, but I don't, and he gives me freedom. That is
what I want for you, so you must listen to me!"

Allegra tried to control the spasms in her stomach and waited
for the medicine to lay its calming energy over her. She might as
well know about Barretto, and there was no stopping Elletra
anyway.

"Your husband wasn't always like this. When he was younger
he was married to the first *contessa*—I forget her name. The one
before Lucia. He was in love with her beauty and airs. She was
hauntingly lovely. They made a nuptial contract that permitted
her to have four *cavaliere servente* at her beck and call. It was
nothing unusual—many women had three and four, and their
husbands thought nothing about it. But Barretto was jealous. He
knew that jealousy was frowned upon but he couldn't stop those
impulses. He hid them until they were like a poison in him.

"He was handsome then—virile and demanding. When his wife
started to ignore him, he took a series of mistresses. He tried to

force his wife to be faithful—at least until they had a son—but she laughed at him. One day, when she was several months pregnant, she went riding on their estate with one of her lovers and took a fall during a hunt. She lost the baby—a boy—and then she refused to take Barretto to her bed again. He was beside himself with anger and after a few months she became ill and died. There was some question about it, but Barretto di Rienzi was a powerful man, and it was not investigated. Then Napoleon invaded, and everyone was preoccupied with politics. Barretto stayed to himself and multiplied his fortune. Along the way he took another wife—young, quiet, and docile.''

"I know about Lucia," Allegra said, hoping to forestall another long tale of abuses.

"But do you know about Placidia?" Elletra's tone was solemn. "She is probably dead by now, too. It has been a few years and women like her don't last long. She was well known. While Lucia was having one of her fruitless pregnancies, Barretto was amusing himself with Placidia. He lavished jewels and rich gifts on her in return for her faithfulness.

"But once she did a very stupid thing and refused to see him, because she had another man in her bed. You can imagine his reaction. He plotted a terrible revenge and invited her to the Padua estate for a few days of amusement. He gave her wine and food and then took her to bed. After he had enjoyed her he opened the door to six of his drunken friends, who took their turns with her. They were not very pleasant in their manners, I heard. They did unspeakable things in the name of masculine fun. Later the story was that fifty men claimed Placidia's favors that night, but I doubt that even Barretto di Rienzi would plan a revenge on such a grand scale. Anyway, Placidia was ruined as a desirable woman, and she left Venice. That same night her other lover was castrated, by a gang of men in masks.

"That is the kind of man you married, Allegra, and that is why I had to tell you. You must not feel obligated, even by the sacrament of marriage, to stay with him. He is not entirely sane. Unless you are another Lucia—and I don't think you are—you will suffer someday at his hands.''

"Ellétra . . ." Allegra said and then stopped, looking away for a long moment. "I already suffer. But I cannot leave him. I don't know what I shall do yet, but I live each day as I can. First I will have this child, and then I will think about what to do. My father would be ruined if I did anything rash. My sisters would never make good marriages. Barretto would punish them somehow and hunt me down, I know. There aren't any happy alternatives. At least when I am pregnant he doesn't dare come to my bed." She managed a wan smile. "Meanwhile, keep lighting your candles for me."

She wanted to leave. Everything had been said, and she was unable to stop the churning feeling of sickness. She had to go back to the yellow sanctuary of her rooms and sleep away the painfulness of her body.

Elletra held her close for a quick embrace. "Next time we will go to tea at Florian's and watch the pigeons in San Marco. Maybe we'll catch a glimpse of Byron while we're at it. My dear little Allegra, don't forget. . . . I'm here if you need me. I return to Vienna in a week."

Gina helped her into the gondola, giving a questioning look to Contessa Clodio, who responded with a shrug of her shoulders.

Alone again in her boudoir, Allegra looked at her pale reflection in the fine Murano mirror. *Dear Elletra,* she thought, *I won't be seeing you again in Venice, because you are too strong, and I would find myself caught between two great tides. I haven't the strength now. Maybe someday . . . .*

DURING THE SUMMER MONTHS Barretto spent much of his time visiting his farms and vineyards near Verona. While he was away he left the Ca' in the hands of his steward, Zeno Bartolo. His was the sly furtive face that often watched Allegra from dark doorways.

Allegra asked Gina about him one evening, when she was preparing to retire.

"Phah! That one!" Gina gave some vigorous strokes to Allegra's hair, which made her head bounce. "The *conte*'s watchman . . . the eyes of the master, you understand? He will report

anything the servants do that he disapproves of and will give a full
account of your activities to the *conte*. He is new here and tries
too hard to make a good impression on his master."

Allegra remembered the man's eyes, like bits of brown polished
stone, hard and cold. "Well, surely there is nothing to report. I
am a prisoner of my pregnancy and this palazzo."

SHE FELT EVEN MORE LETHARGIC when the hot months of July and
August came, seemingly endless. Allegra grew to welcome the
times when Barretto returned from his travels—at least then
something was happening. He seldom entertained at the Ca' now,
but he was accepting of Allegra's family.

He smiled indulgently when he saw Gemma and Lipia drinking
tea and talking of the latest fashions and scandals. The two girls
were coquettish with him, to Allegra's irritation, but Barretto
seemed to enjoy their flirtatiousness. In their presence he grandly
told Allegra to buy all the new dresses she needed. She had to
smile. Dresses for what? She was forbidden to go out into society.

"I wish I could have new dresses," Gemma whispered to her.
"Then I would try to meet the wicked, charming Lord Byron."

"I'm sure that he would find you a silly little girl," she said
sharply, growing tired of Gemma's affectations.

AS AUTUMN CAME Allegra was having more days of feeling well,
and the Conte Lamberti's visits were more often to Barretto, with
whom he would sit, wine at hand, discussing business. He assumed
that her adjustment difficulties were over. Every time he took his
leave he patted her hand and winked affectionately, as if to say,
*now aren't you glad all that fuss is finished with? Life goes on,
my dear emotional child. . . .*

One welcome visitor was Aunt Adriana, an elderly relative on
the di Rienzi side. Allegra liked this gossipy comfortable woman,
who was the widow of a younger brother of Barretto's father.
Many people in the old society were her friends. It was lonely in
her small villa near Mestre, and old Adriana eagerly came to visit
for a week at a time in the Ca' d'Argenti.

"Give Barretto a boy, Allegra," she chuckled, "and after that you can make your own life in Venice. You seem . . . so locked away, my dear. Not even one *cavaliere*! Well, after the birth I'll see to it that you are introduced to everyone. Barretto can be terribly ignorant about these things. . . ."

Allegra looked up from her embroidery with a doubting smile. Adriana was a dear old soul, full of memories of Venice and eager to spin an aura of romance around everything. It would be cruel to tell her the truth of her life with Barretto.

The warm yellow room had a strong atmosphere of patient waiting impressed into its walls. In the many quiet hours, she turned her attention to the little diary and began to write every day. It became the other self who listened, observed and understood. The friend to whom everything could be told.

Allegra could not bring herself to speak to the priest who was attached to the chapel of the Ca'. He was well paid by Barretto, and even the sanctity of the confessional did not cover the uneasy feeling that secrets might be in jeopardy with him.

The diary grew full of nonessentials, but once in a while—when the child kicked strongly in her womb, or when she had had a difficult encounter with Barretto—then she cried out her frustration onto the pages.

"Is this to be my life?" Her pen pressed sharply on the question. "Is there nothing but this place, the child? So I am a *contessa* and I have jewels . . . I would rather be one of the women in the food market selling fish. At least then I might have a husband and children chosen with love. I resent my baby when it moves in me, because it was planted against my will and without love, and I cannot spend my life bringing forth children for the Conte di Rienzi."

When she reread the page she thought about destroying the diary and its pitiful shouts into the darkness of the world. Instead she placed it gently into the far corner of her writing-desk drawer. She planned to hide it entirely when she had filled its pages. Perhaps someday the diary would be read and understood by sympathetic eyes.

ONE DAY IN LATE SEPTEMBER Allegra unexpectedly met another of Barretto's close associates. Coming into the large library room near the grand salon, she was startled to see a young man seated at a table, copying from a book. He rose quickly with a flourish of his well-kept hands, while his bright and bold eyes stared at her.

"Excuse me, *contessa*," he said in a soft deep voice. "Allow me to introduce myself. I am your husband's assistant, Luciano Antonino. He does not need me just now, and so I am stealing some time to learn in his library." He stood at ease, his figure having an air of careful elegance. But something in his voice was unpolished, despite his well-controlled aquiline face. He smiled, showing fine teeth between thin mobile lips, and a shiver went over Allegra's nerves. His brilliant eyes were disconcerting. They had in them a challenging glint of masculine energy. He knew that he was attractive.

Allegra tried to acknowledge his greeting with her usual dignity when speaking to a stranger and a servant of her husband. She didn't care for his proprietary tone.

"May I assist you, *madonna*?" His voice had the caressing note that men use with a pretty woman.

"Go on with your work. I only wish to find a book to read this afternoon." She turned away toward the shelves along one wall. She heard him sit down again. Surely his eyes were still on her. She concentrated on the books, running her hand over the titles.

His pleasant voice spoke to her stiff back. "It must be hard for women to pass the long time of pregnancy." Without turning she agreed. After a moment he spoke again. "I know that the *conte* is often away, but when I am here it would give me pleasure to just sit for a while and speak to you." He paused, and Allegra's mind raced to think of a suitable answer. "Forgive me, *contessa*, but you are such a lovely woman . . ." he ended on a sigh.

She turned to face him, a book in her hand. A flash of intimate smile flowed over his face. "I am sure that sometimes you want to hear and feel a younger man's point of view of things." A hot spark burned in the darkness of his deep-set eyes, and he rose quickly and came to her side.

She moved away from him toward the door. "Good day, Signor Antonino." She felt trapped by his energy and hated the trembling that began inside herself. There was raw power in him that plucked at her nerves. He would not easily be deflected from his desires.

Her hand reached for the latch, but his was there first. She felt his hard fingers possess her hand. With a slight bow he bent to kiss her fingers. It was a hot kiss, and she felt a swift tiny flicker of his tongue against her skin. Then he pulled open the door and bowed her out, as if he had done nothing wrong. "You are far more beautiful than Veronica Bardolini . . . fortunate Conte di Rienzi . . ." she heard him whisper as the door closed.

Back in her own rooms she scolded herself for being weak. She must be careful never to be alone with him. His urgent masculinity burned like a fire.

Gina brought tea. "Luciano said you met him in the library."

"Yes, by chance. He says he is my husband's assistant. How little I know about things. . . ."

Gina nodded, laying out the dainty tea things and opening the doors onto the balcony. "He says you are the loveliest woman he has seen in Venice." Her voice was noncommittal.

"I don't like him," Allegra replied sharply. "He is too quick with compliments. I don't want to see him again."

"Was he impolite?"

"Not really, but he is too sure of himself. It is not what he says, it is his manner."

Gina gave a perceptive look. "He has been with your husband for two years. He likes women, as you have seen. He comes from the lower class of Rome and has risen by his wits to some acceptance in society. My lady, you are wise to avoid him. He is one who would be cruel with a smile on his lips."

"I want nothing to do with him. Please let me know when he is here so that I won't be surprised to find him." She took the teacup that Gina offered. "Who is Veronica Bardolini?"

Gina's startled hand clattered the cake plate against the teapot. "Who has spoken of her—Luciano?"

"Yes. He said that my husband was fortunate to have both of us."

"*Dio mio,*" she said on a sigh and put the plate back on the table with a thump. "*Madonna,*" she finally said, choosing her words slowly, "it is best that you hear from me about the Bardolini. She is the mistress of the *conte* for the past three years. She is a vigorous woman with a beautiful body. She comes from impoverished people who hang on the edges of society. Your husband keeps her in a small home here in Venice. There are no children, but it is said that her sensual appetites are strong, and this is her value to your husband. Many men keep women like this. Do not be disturbed, my lady."

Allegra looked up with a tight ironic smile. "It does not disturb me, Gina," she said, surprised at her own coolness. "I think she is to be pitied."

A pained expression flowed over the older woman's face. "*Cara mia*, you must not think that all men are users of women. There are those who truly love. . . . You are young and have had to meet the most difficult part of being a woman, but in your life there will be more than this. The *conte* is not a young man. . . ." Her voice trailed off. It was the echo of Allegra's father's words.

"If I wait long enough I will be free. Is that what you are telling me?"

Gina's usually calm face twisted with a shared despair. "I want you to be happy, *madonna*, but happiness is a shy thing, which must be waited for patiently."

Allegra's eyes were shadowed. "When I was a child I was so foolish. I prayed to Santa Chiara for the love of a true man . . . but Gina, the dear saint must have wanted me to see reality. She could not answer an impossible dream."

THAT NIGHT SHE FELT RESTLESS and on a whim picked up Elletra's little book of poems by Lord Byron. She was disappointed to find it in English and not Italian. The small green volume was entitled

The Corsair, almost fifty pages long. Perhaps it would not be too difficult to read with her convent English. She turned to the first canto and read aloud to herself:

> O'er the glad waters of the dark blue sea,
> Our thoughts as boundless, and our souls as free,
> Far as the breeze can bear, the billows foam,
> Survey our empire, and behold our home!

Even though she understood only part of the meaning there was a powerful energy in the rhythm, a euphoria . . . .

> Ours the wild life in tumult still to range
> From toil to rest, and joy in every change . . .

No wonder Elletra found him fascinating. His words spoke of daring and headlong adventure.

After a while she grew tired of trying to unravel his poetic meanings and started to close the book. A loose page slipped from the center onto her lap. It was a separate poem written in Elletra's handwriting—a short work also by Byron. She read its title, curious to discover what would interest Elletra enough to copy it for herself. . . . "She Walks in Beauty." A quick shiver seized her nerves, as if a man's beautiful voice spoke the words. Her eyes eagerly read the first stanza . . .

> She walks in beauty, like the night
>   Of cloudless climes and starry skies;
> And all that's best of dark and bright
>   Meet in her aspect and her eyes:
> Thus mellow'd to that tender light
>   Which heaven to gaudy day denies.

Is that what lovers say, she wondered, as she returned the page to the book and closed its cover. She felt an edge of irritation in her thoughts, that Elletra would give her this to read. Byron was a great genius, she was sure, even if a little mad. But his world was one of danger and emotion, which she wanted no part of. Elletra should have known better. . . .

MONTHS PASSED in dull succession, until finally there was the confusing disturbing day, when she at last gave birth to Barretto's child. The labor started hard and stayed that way until the end. But always Gina's steadfast face and soothing hands were near.

Allegra resisted being carried to the coldly regal bedroom of Renaldo, the builder of the Ca', but Barretto's sharp voice cut across her protests. All di Rienzi children—legitimate ones—must come into the world in the ancestral bed.

She shut her eyes and shouted out against the high-canopied monstrosity. Couldn't Barretto understand?

"I hate that gruesome piece of furniture!" she cried out.

Even Barretto smiled at this. "You will not need to sleep in it," he said on a note of indulgence, "only give birth there." Her continued pleadings to stay in her own room fell on deaf ears. "The bed must be prepared," he said with finality.

DURING HER TIMES of intensely painful labor the inlaid silver bands on the thick spiral bedposts seemed to take on life and writhe like serpents. Anxious faces swam into her view and out again. Finally she was beyond thought, her whole being taken up with the overwhelming necessity of birth.

Very faintly she heard a child's cry, and then exhaustion took her into a kind of sleep—the laudanum she drank for pain had clouded her mind. Time drifted away into a floating sensation of relief. *I should know about the child,* she thought, *is it a boy? . . .* But even this seemed not to matter very much.

She awoke to feel Gina rinsing her face and placing a goblet to her lips. Candlelight made fiery flashes in the wine. She sipped weakly, and then her eyes were drawn beyond Gina to the beaming smile of the midwife, who held a richly wrapped velvet bundle in her arms. Her flushed broad face drew nearer, and Allegra saw Barretto immediately behind. He too was smiling—more widely than she had ever seen. Careful hands folded back the blankets to show a red little head and two tiny waving fists.

It was the first time she had seen her son. The midwife put him into her arms for a few moments, while she touched the warm round head with its growth of dark hair. She made the right gestures, but she felt a sense of deep sadness for this small life. It was not the rush of love that should have come. Inwardly she wept that she could feel so little. The child was taken to a waiting wet nurse, and Allegra was not unhappy to see him go.

Barretto came closer to her bedside. *"Madonna."* His voice was respectful. "You have done your duty well. My son is a fine child, perfect in every way. I am grateful."

He held out a velvet-covered box to her. It had a familiar look, even through the haze of the laudanum, and her hands shook with expectation as she lifted the cover from the old box. Inside, glowing with the patina of age, lay her mother's pearls.

She raised her eyes slowly to his smiling ones. "But how . . . ? These were sold. . . ." Her fingers moved over their cool silky surfaces.

A look of satisfaction deepened on his face. He spoke quietly. "I knew that you felt their loss very much, and so I sent out my agents to find them for you. I have had them since shortly after our marriage, but I was waiting for our son to arrive. They are a token of my gratitude." He leaned down and placed a kiss on her forehead. "Sleep now, my dear, you deserve your rest."

Gina took the pearls from her hands and called to one of the footmen, who came and easily lifted the weary *contessa* from the huge bed. He carried her to her chambers and laid her down on her own soft sheets. A fire glowed and sang in the fireplace. After that, she remembered little as sleep came like a healing cloud around her.

For a day she slept and awoke and dreamed. In those dreams she was filled with joy. Unburdened and free, she ran across a flowery meadow, like those she had known in her childhood at the Lamberti villa near La Mira. Someone waited for her. . . . Tantalizing glimpses of a man's beautiful face wove in and out of her vision, and a voice called her name. He loved her, truly loved her, and she was completely happy. Barretto was not a part of the dreams, nor her baby, nor the Ca' d'Argenti. She resisted leaving that dream life to return to the world of the di Rienzis.

Her body was slow in recovering from the effort of giving birth. Each day she dutifully held her baby and played with him. Barretto named him Renaldo, after the first prince of the House of Silver. Once she whispered into the tiny uncomprehending ear, "I am so sorry, so sorry. . . ."

WHEN HER FAMILY CAME for the christening her sisters were, as usual, very much preoccupied by the treasures in the grand salon. Lipia whispered to her, "You have everything, Allegra! How I would love to live in such a beautiful palazzo as this. . . . You must find husbands for us!"

After Barretto excused himself and retired to his study, Allegra showed her father the box with the pearls. For a moment he stood holding them, and when he looked up, tears were in his tired brown eyes. "I am glad you have them, *cara mia*. I hated to cause you grief, but we needed the money. You understand."

She nodded and returned the pearls to their box. He put a light hand on her shoulder and turned her to him. "Allegra, Barretto has no hold on me now. . . . All the debts are paid, and I want to give you something."

"I have everything I need," she said, looking at Renaldo di Rienzi's dark portrait on the wall and wishing for the hundredth time that her baby did not have the same name.

"Please, my child, I am not blind. I am going to speak to Barretto about you. I intend to do something I was powerless to do when I consented to your marriage. The fault was mine for not arranging a contract for you, as other women have with their husbands."

"It won't do any good. He would never sign a contract, why should he? You have already given me to him without strings attached. . . ."

"But you have a right to certain freedoms: to go out to the theater, the opera . . . to have you own little pleasures. I cannot stand to see you so unhappy. You have a right to a *cavaliere servente.* . . ."

She swung around at the last words. "No! Father, now *you* don't understand. I could never have another man near me. Barretto wants to know that any child I bear is his. Believe me, he is not like other husbands. For the love of God, I beg you not to mention this to him. He will think I already have a lover." The fear in her eyes silenced him.

"Is it that bad, my dear, even with the baby here?"

"Why should my life now be better than it was?" she replied flatly.

AFTER HER FAMILY HAD GONE and she was alone in her rooms, she thought long and painfully about the world of men. She refused to believe that her vows to Barretto bound her to him for eternity. It had to be possible that love would come, full of joy—that two souls could seek each other from across time, finding in their union the completion of themselves.

Allegra protected this fragile dream like one of her Florentine pictures of the saints, the kind that had small carved doors to fold over the precious faces.

That night as she prepared for bed Barretto appeared in her room ready for siring. Everything in her body cried out in rejection. She could not be invaded so soon! She could not, so soon, go through the nausea again, the dragging weariness of pregnancy, the wrenching frightening work of giving birth.

Gathering up her courage, she spoke in a shaking voice, "*Signore*, you must give me more time. Please, I have only just borne your son." As he stared at her she looked directly into his icy eyes. "I am not well enough. . . . I cannot."

He looked down at her with one hand on the lion clasps of his robe. A shadow of indecision moved across his face. Then he shrugged the robe more securely around him. "I will be lenient this time, but the next time I will not be patient with you. I will have more children. I will secure the house of di Rienzi. Make no mistake, *contessa*, you have not ended your duty to me." His measured words sent ripples through her nerves. "I cannot be as distasteful to your sensibilities as you pretend. But, considering the birth, I will give you some time. You must see the doctor tomorrow if you are ill.'' He suddenly smiled. ''You misunderstand me, Allegra, I am a gentle man. Sleep well.''

Barretto was present the following day when Dr. Aglietti examined her. ''There is still a low fever, my dear *conte*. She is correct.''

''What does it mean?'' Barretto demanded.

''An infection is still working in her. If she can have complete rest for some time, there is every reason to think she will be able to conceive a child again. If not . . . .''

''How long?'' he pressed. ''Two, three weeks?''

''As long as her body requires for recovery. It was not an easy birth.''

Barretto grunted skeptically, as if he suspected a conspiracy between Allegra and Dr. Aglietti. ''How will I know when . . . ?''

The doctor smiled easily. ''The *contessa* will let you know when she feels ready to resume her marital obligations.'' Allegra sent up a quick prayer of gratitude.

CHAPTER THREE

DECEMBER 1818

ALLEGRA'S VOICE was barely a whisper, as she walked alone down the great curving staircase. . . . "Have I been married a year? Is my Venetian blood so strong that I have been able to endure until now?"

Three months before, Barretto had commissioned a portrait of her, and the workmen had just finished hanging it in the formal reception room beyond the foyer. Allegra caught a glimpse of herself through the open doorway and felt a shock of unreality. The portrait had nothing to do with her own life. It belonged to some other strange existence, which the elegantly gowned woman represented.

It was meticulously painted to show the myriad points of light on the copper beading which cascaded down the full amber satin skirt. The waistline was high, caught with a sash of golden satin, and clusters of pale rosebuds gathered the sleeves into little puffs just below the shoulders. In the portrait her shoulders were white and fragile looking, the only sign that she had been in the eighth month of a difficult pregnancy.

When she sat for the nervous middle-aged artist, he had seemed fearful to have more than a hesitant polite conversation with her, since they were always watched by someone who reported everything to Barretto. But often his perceptive artist's eyes spoke to her of admiration and pity.

Allegra hadn't cared how the likeness turned out. The Contessa di Rienzi was another person—a face to show the world. She was even a little annoyed when she saw a hint of sorrow painted into the dark eyes on the canvas. Barretto wanted his wife's portrait to hang in the large and impressive grand salon, where it would be seen by his wealthy visitors from the emperor's court, who were no more gentle than Barretto. She wished the picture had never been painted.

On impulse she walked into the grand room. Dark red velvet curtains reflected the primary color of the Oriental rugs scattered on the black marble floor. A portrait of Renaldo di Rienzi, builder of the Ca' d'Argenti, dominated the room from the wall opposite her own portrait. There was indeed a resemblance to Barretto, she thought. The face smiled coldly from its heavy silver frame.

Her eyes were drawn in fascination to the treasures of the first di Rienzi merchant prince, whose talent still lived in the cleverness of his descendants. Two massive silver armchairs were placed beneath his portrait. Barretto had told her how many coins had been melted down to make the pretentious ugly chairs. Throughout the room silver glittered from inlays, bowls, artifacts of all kinds. Two heavy silver candelabra stood upon a table of intricately inlaid wood and silver chasing. Tapestry woven with silver threads hung against another wall, alive with brilliant colors.

She looked across to her portrait. Barretto had received his money's worth, as he always did. The double string of pearls at her throat glowed lifelike from the canvas, and the creamy silk rose, which filled the deep cleft of her breasts, looked fresh-picked from some happy garden.

From somewhere above her came the sound of a child crying. Little Renaldo was a fretful two months old. She heard the crooning voice of his nurse, and his complaints grew fainter. "Am I really the mother of a child?" she asked the pensive image in the portrait. It was difficult to feel a real warmth for the son of Barretto, whose miniature face already resembled his father's. *Mother of God*, she thought, *why cannot I love my baby? Such a poor little thing . . . I pity him, but that is not the same as love.*

When she thought of him it was with regret that nothing could change the ice around her heart. Her morning and evening visits to the cavernous old nursery were only a duty. How many women would he cause to suffer when he grew to manhood? She knew he would become fashioned into the mold of his father's wishes . . . another Barretto. The di Rienzi cradle, now gleaming and polished, was still an ugly thing, squatting in the nursery as if it demanded to be filled again and again with sons of Barretto.

She sat down in one of the silver chairs, running her fingers along the deep etching of its cold silver arms. It had been a long year in her life.

She heard shuffling steps outside the salon door. Zeno's small gargoyle face suddenly appeared and then drew back, and his steps faded away. Allegra smiled to herself. The prison guard could report that the prisoner was safely within the walls.

She would never be comfortable with Zeno. He rarely spoke and was fastidious about accounting and record keeping, constantly scribbling notes in the dirty yellow book that he always carried. For the *conte*, only one thing in the world was more important than his financial dealings, and that was his son.

Unable to free herself from tension she rose from the silver chair and continued to walk through the salon, pushing open the high double doors that led to the little winter garden. She wrapped herself in a heavy white woolen cape against the crisp cold air, and it felt good to her tired mind—like a caress that was pure and clear.

Two stone griffins stood at each end of the low wall that separated the garden from the busy traffic of the Grand Canal. A climbing vine made a lacy pattern along the wall. She watched the small gray birds, which pecked hopefully at the cold soil, and drew her diary from the pocket of her white karakul hand muff.

The pages were nearly filled with the record of her year in the Ca' d'Argenti. She wondered what some far future di Rienzi woman would think of the life of Allegra. Perhaps she had it in her power to warn a distant granddaughter of the hard truth of being a woman.

She opened the soft red cover with its miniature of the waltzing man and woman, and reread the entry for this day:

3 December
Our wedding anniversary. One year. My body is stronger each day since Renaldo's birth and Barretto knows it. I wish I were

one of the clever women who know how to deal with men . . . make them believe they are the conquerors, but not let them conquer.

Tonight Barretto and I are having supper alone, Zeno informed me. I pray he doesn't have a gift for me. There is never a gift without something painful in exchange.

Gemma came early and presented me with a new diary—a perfect match to this one, except that the miniature painted on the cover has no happy couple dancing in each other's arms. At least this time Gemma had the tact to commission a more suitable scene . . . a man and woman alighting from their gondola at the water steps of the Ca' d'Argenti.

As I read these pages back to the beginning of my marriage I cannot find even one time when Barretto and I laughed together over a little amusing moment . . . or shared anything at all except our names.

Aunt Adriana cannot understand my reluctance to venture outside my prison, but I think Gina can. I am afraid to see what is out there . . . it could only make my life with Barretto more difficult.

Allegra closed the diary and walked to the low crumbling wall. She planned to conceal the full diary within the inner pocket of an underskirt and pack it in one of the attic wardrobes.

She stood looking out over the canal, letting her eyes drift over the golden facades of the palaces across the way. She knew their names and many gossipy stories about the people who lived in them. What stories had Venice enjoyed exchanging about the newest Contessa di Rienzi, she wondered.

She was not eager to sit with Barretto tonight over supper and have his appraising eyes on her body. She was not ready yet.

Aunt Adriana's cheerful face appeared in the door to the garden. "We'll have to hurry to get to the Redentore. The new music director starts the afternoon concerts on time. He was trained in Vienna," she laughed. "The gondola is ready for us, my dear."

Allegra tucked the diary into the inner pocket of her muff.

Adriana had insisted on taking her to a concert at the orphanage of the Redentore, as an anniversary gift. It would probably be a pleasant way to spend the day, and the young girls at the orphanage did have a reputation for exquisite musical performances.

The Ospedale Redentore was a dark, four-story building with black shutters over its windows. Someone had hung a canary cage from one of the small balconies to catch the winter sun, and its happy song mingled with the pianofortes, violins and voices in the music rooms inside.

A quiet young nun opened the tall iron-strapped door to lead them into the small concert hall. The building looked as if it had once been very rich. Now it badly needed paint and patching on its plaster, and repairs to the marble inlay on the floors, but it still had dignity.

The program featured a girl named Giovanna, who sang Alpine shepherds' songs, accompanying herself on a lute. She was charming with her simplicity of voice, her soft rounded figure and appealing warm eyes. The audience of perhaps one hundred guests was predominantly young Austrian officers in their uniforms.

Allegra remembered that Napoleon had confiscated the endowment of the orphanages like this one. They were very special because of the fame the young girls had achieved for their music.

"Some of them are extraordinary," Adriana whispered between songs. "Later we will hear a chamber quartet that comes straight from paradise. You know, before the French came, the girls from the Redentore found husbands because of their glorious music. And who knows . . . maybe some of these handsome young men today will lose their hearts. Even if they *are* Austrian," she huffed.

After the performance Allegra was eager to know more about the orphanage. There was something so lovely and poignant about the girls she had seen. Adriana reluctantly agreed to stay a while to allow Allegra time to meet the directress of the institution, Signora Nicolo. "Barretto won't be pleased if I keep you too late," she warned.

Signora Nicolo was a loving woman of middle age, who spoke softly. "I have had no babies of my own, and yet I am the mother of dozens. It is a wondrous gift of God." She walked with Allegra and Adriana back to her office. "I am familiar with the di Rienzi name, *contessa*. Your patronage here will benefit us. . . . You see, we are just starting to rebuild our conservatory of music, and we can now give training and shelter to forty girls."

"Would you allow me to visit you again?" Allegra asked. "I wish there were something I could do to be of use here. . . ." Adriana's mouth opened in surprise.

Signora Nicolo studied Allegra for a moment before speaking. "If you came here to work you would be sharing much grief and need . . . and joy as well. Poor women, desperate women, come here to bear their infants, and because they cannot give them a home they leave them with us. It puzzles me that you would wish to be a part of this life, considering your own state in society."

"The *contessa* means to give a donation to your orphanage," Adriana said. "Her husband would not be pleased to have her do more that that."

Allegra spoke quickly. "I feel I belong here, *signora*."

"It should not be something that conflicts with your obligations, *contessa*. I would not ask such a sacrifice," Signora Nicolo added.

"You are most kind," Allegra said. "I do want to come again." She stood and reached out her hand.

"If it is right for you, you are very much needed here." The woman smiled warmly, and Allegra felt as if she transferred a loving energy into her hand as she clasped it.

When they were again outside the doors of the Redentore, Adriana was bursting with indignation. "I couldn't believe my ears, Allegra! What are you proposing to do?"

"Signora Nicolo is a charming woman," she laughed at the bluster.

"Well, I'm sure she won't be seeing us again. Filthy work it would be, anyway. Still, that girl did sing like an angel. . . ."

Allegra kept silent. She had every intention of returning. Who at the Ca' d'Argenti had any need of her? At the Redentore there was true need. Her heart felt full with pleasant anticipation.

SUPPER WITH BARRETTO was strained. He ate silently, wrapped in his own thoughts. From time to time he looked up, and a thin smile cracked the stern lines of his face. Allegra was used to him now, and his silence was almost welcome.

After the sweetmeats and liqueur, the servants departed and Barretto cleared his throat to speak. "A very special occasion, my dear—our first year together." He raised his glass. "A toast to our marriage . . . to our son."

She took a sip of the rose-colored liqueur as he continued to speak in measured words. "You have had difficulties in adjusting to your new life, but I am not an ungrateful man, as you know. I have a token of my love that I wish to present to you."

Barretto reached into a pocket of his coat and drew out a folded paper. He opened it ceremoniously and spread it before him on the table. "Your father has reminded me that we are without a nuptial contract . . . an oversight I wish to correct. He suggested that you are feeling confined, shut away from life," he laughed dryly, "but I assured him you were as free as a bird. And you *are* free, my Allegra . . . within certain limits. I knew you would be happier to have those boundaries clearly defined—and so I have written our contract." He rose from the table and held out the sheet of paper for her to take.

She quickly ran her eyes down the page. The writing was divided into two columns. She raised her eyes to his face with a wave of apprehension and turned the paper so that the light from the candelabra brought the words into clarity.

"Read it aloud," he prodded, smiling at her. "I want to be sure that you understand it perfectly."

"3 December 1818," she started. "I, Barretto di Rienzi, bind myself by my signature to perform certain duties as husband to Allegra, Contessa di Rienzi:

I will provide a gondola for her exclusive use.

I will provide a box at La Fenice for the season, and a country house near Padua. A coach-and-four for her use there.

I will give her the freedom to move about Venice and its environs at times when I do not require her presence.

I will provide monies for clothing and personal adornments according to her desires."

She stopped at the end of the first list with a sense of relief in her heart. "Read on," he pressed. She turned to the words he had written in the second column. They were a list of her own obligations to him:

"I, Allegra . . ." her eyes went quickly to the lines below . . .

I will be docile and obedient and ready to follow all the directions of my husband.

I will not go out alone from the Ca˟ d'Argenti, and only with companions chosen by my husband.

I will be faithful and have no appearance to the contrary.

I will accept any punishment he may take against me as fair and justified, should I break this contract.

In exchange for this, I will be be cared for in the manner described above."

"Simple rules for our life together," he said softly, as he brought an inkstand from the sideboard and offered her his pen. "I give you my fortune and good name, and you must only maintain the modesty that you already possess in such overwhelming abundance. It merely assures me that there will never be children in my house that are not mine—although I doubt that you have the capacity to give yourself up to passion under any circumstances. The *cavaliere servente* is not a tradition that will enter our lives, I promise you. The law will find me justified in any punishment I bring down upon you, should you betray me with another man."

The cruelty in his eyes was something she had seen too often before. She held the pen over the contract. Why shouldn't she sign it? These were old issues—only a formality for what already existed between them. She wrote her name in a swift scrawl and pushed the paper away from her. As she returned the pen to Barretto's hand, she was compelled to speak.

"My lord, did all of your wives agree to this contract—even the first one?" The words hung in the air as Barretto's mouth twisted.

"I will ignore that ill-advised question."

"But I wish to know . . . is it only for me to be tied to you thus . . . like a bond servant?" she said softly, determined to make her point. Strangely, she was not afraid of him. It was more than the wine at dinner, it was a sudden rising up of her sense of justice.

"Watch your tongue, *contessa,* it is not for you to judge. Your lack of gratitude appalls me." His voice cut at her like a knife. "The rights of a husband are the only rights in this house, and I promise swift retribution if you should forget that. Good evening, *contessa.* I pray that you come to your senses, for your own sake!" He coolly refolded the contract and turned his back to her and left the room.

Had she pushed him too far? She had to let him know that she was not a docile child he could abuse without opposition. A shiver of apprehension moved through her body, but she did not regret her words to him.

As she stood alone in the dining room, she was oddly amused by it all. Whenever she thought about her situation, there were strange twists of logic. Just that morning Adriana had told her that after the first year of marriage all noble Venetian husbands welcomed the *cavaliere servente* into their menage . . . to accompany the lady to the opera, the gambling casino, to await her in the boudoir. Adriana rambled on about the delicious frivolities that were in store for Allegra. She smiled to herself.

Barretto speaks of honor, but where in the contract does it say he will not dishonor me between the legs of another woman? . . . Is it only for me to remain undefiled?

Where was the answer for her? She knew that she was capable

of feeling—she was not by nature cold; Barretto had made her so.

As she prepared for bed she noticed Elletra's book of Byron's poetry and reminded herself to have Gina return it to the Palazzo Clodio. The presence of the slim volume in her room made her uncomfortable, as if Elletra were still prodding at her to take action against the restraints of marriage. But only Barretto's women knew how dangerous it was to deny him his wishes.

She fell into a heavy sleep. The touch of a rough hand on her breast woke her with a jolt. In the dark the strong, sickening sour odor of wine enveloped her. Her mouth was covered by a hard, invasive kiss, and she was held down by the heavy weight of a man's body.

Terror flooded into her, and she writhed against the silent intruder. Fear made her struggle desperately against the exploring hands.

"Ahh . . ." Barretto's husky voice said in her ear. "You have caught fire at last. I knew you would one day!"

Allegra wrenched away from his drunken face, almost wild with loathing. Her voice was a thin shriek. "No! Don't touch me! Don't ever touch me again!"

The air around the bed was thick with his heavy emanations. In the blackness of the room she could feel his fury. He put a hand over her throat and held it there in an iron grip. His breathing was labored as his fingers pressed down around her throat.

"You would be better off dead," he growled.

"Santa Chiara!" she gasped.

"Go to your saints . . . go to hell . . . I don't care! But I will make you have my sons!" His other hand ripped the covers from her, and he clumsily tore at her gown.

She looked at the darkness where his face would be and painfully choked out "No!" On the last of her breath, as the feeling was leaving her body, she said, "Never again . . . !"

He did nothing for a moment and then released her. She lay still, waiting . . . then felt him lift himself from her and heard his footfalls leave the room. "Never is a long time, *contessa*," he said from the threshold, "we shall see." The door clicked shut and she was alone. She ran to the door and bolted it, pushing a heavy chest against it.

She lighted a candle and studied herself in her heavy silver hand mirror. Her eyes stared at the eyes in the mirror.

"Never," she whispered. . . .

CHAPTER FOUR

SHE STAYED AWAKE for the rest of the night, until she saw the winter dawn light push along the edges of the draped windows. The room was cold, but she didn't notice it. She had thought until she couldn't think anymore.

She was amazed at her courage in finally refusing Barretto. She had done it, and she was still alive, and she didn't want to wait passively for his reaction.

Gina knocked lightly at the door as she always did when bringing the morning tray. Allegra sprang from her bed to push aside the chest and unbolt the lock. She took the tray from Gina's hands, ignoring the questions on the quiet woman's face.

"Quickly," Allegra said to her, "run to Aunt Adriana's room and tell her I wish her to join me here. Help her old bones into a dressing gown, Gina, I want to her to come right away. And find out where my husband is!"

Gina hesitated, but Allegra insisted. "Go, I'll explain later."

She reached for her heavy woolen robe and pulled open the double curtains at the windows to look out at the gray water of the Grand Canal. Around the great S-turn of the canal the bells of La Salute were sounding for early Mass. Other bells from churches all over the city were calling their faithful. Shafts of sun were starting to peek through the clouds, bringing out the ocher and pink colors on the palaces along the water.

Allegra felt a shivering light-headedness, a sense of freedom. If Barretto came to find her she would be gone on her own business today. If he wished to murder her for no reason at all, then she could be no worse off by doing whatever she wished. Death was death, after all.

She and Adriana would pay a call on Signora Nicolo's orphanage. She was eager, almost urgent, to walk out into the winding narrow streets of Venice again, as if she were any other woman. The Redentore was not far . . . near the gondola pool, behind the Piazza San Marco.

Gina reentered the room silently. "Signora Adriana will be here shortly, but she is not happy to be awake so early. As for the *conte*, he did not sleep in his quarters. It is assumed by the servants that he is with the Bardolini woman. I am sorry, *madonna*." She looked at Allegra's animated face and kept further comments to herself. "What do you wish to wear this morning?"

"Something warm and simple, Gina. I am going out into the city to call on a lovely woman at the Redentore, and after that Adriana and I will feed the pigeons in San Marco and look at life! The rain has stopped and it is beautiful outside. I feel so well!"

Gina's face clouded. "Is everything all right, my lady?"

"Perfectly. You may tell my husband that he will find me among the other free citizens of Venice, doing something useful with myself." She held her hand mirror poised in the air. "No, don't tell him that. Say that I am visiting the orphanage with Aunt Adriana. He cannot object to that."

She began to feel a lessening of her courage as Gina helped her into her hyacinth-blue street gown. Its high neckline was edged with silver braid and clusters of seed pearls. Her blue gloves had pearls sewn in florets on the backs of them. She tried to cling to the euphoric feeling of emancipation, but the grim shadow of Barretto reached around her heart, constricting it with fear again.

"You did not sleep last night," Gina said as she stood behind Allegra at the dressing table. "I understand the difficulties of living in this house, my lady, but you must be very careful with the actions you take. Some may not be worth the pain that comes later."

"You are telling me I should take care not to be reckless," she said to Gina's reflection in the mirror. "But I have already done a reckless thing, and now my cowardly self doesn't know what to do about it."

"You cannot live in fear of your husband, *cara*. You have an immortal soul that must not fear anything but your Creator. I sense what you have done—why you locked the door—and now you must gather your strength and dignity so that the *conte* will think of you with respect. If you tremble and shake like a cowering animal, he will enjoy whipping you—that is how he is. Hold yourself in dignity . . . it is your best protection.''

Allegra's eyes filled with tears and then emptied again, as she gathered her nerves into a better state. "Thank you, Gina.''

The older woman said nothing more, but her presence was comforting. Allegra looked out at the gondolas and barges in the canal and wished Adriana would hurry. She longed to have Gina's faith and Adriana's innocence. Then the world would be a beautiful place indeed.

GINA BUSIED HERSELF pouring Allegra's cup of Turkish coffee. It came out thick and black, wreathed in a fragrance that filled the room with hints of far places. What law of God decreed that some of His children would see exotic places of the earth, while others would be confined to a tiny corner of it? How restricted she was! Was it written somewhere that Allegra di Rienzi belonged in the Ca' d'Argenti and no place else? At the age of nineteen she was already living the life of the elderly women who dress in black and sit on their doorsteps all day long.

She told this to Gina, who sighed. "You should not go out today, *madonna*, you should rest. I do not like the color of your thoughts. You worry me.''

Adriana appeared in the doorway. Her eyes were puffy, and her face was without makeup. "If the Pope himself had called me, I would not have stirred myself this morning,'' she said with slurred speech and a petulant expression on her pale lips. "What is so important that you shake me from my warm bed? I was at the casino until two o'clock with Bernardo Giulini. He would have taken me to his *casa* after that, except for his ogre of a wife.'' She chuckled to herself and took a steaming cup of coffee from Gina's hand. "Ah, I feel revived. Satan must have invented this naughty sweet brew to keep his workers alert. What a night, Allegra . . . don't believe that older men lose their vigor . . . but, then, you already know that,'' she winked.

Allegra motioned to the window. "It's a beautiful day and I thought we should go out. I want to visit the Redentore, and after that, do something foolish—anything we can think of!"

"Oh, my, you do sound urgent. But the Redentore . . . you still have that silly notion. Well, I won't keep you waiting. Give me a few minutes to put on a new face, and we shall go out exploring."

ON IMPULSE, Allegra slipped upstairs to the nursery, surprising the two nursemaids, who were not used to seeing her there so early in the day. Little Renaldo was at the breast of one of them, a large blond young woman with an amiable face.

Allegra recalled how her own milk had begun flowing in the days after the birth, and how she had used all of her will to try to stop it from coming, so that she would have no reminder of giving birth to Barretto's son. She bent and kissed his forehead and left the room. The impulse that brought her there was a sudden rush of warm feeling for life, but when she confronted the tiny face, which already had such an unsettling resemblance to Barretto's, she grew cool again.

Adriana met her on the nursery staircase. "First you tell me that you cannot wait another moment to leave the Ca', and then I have to search for you. I have sent a message to Bernardo to meet us for lunch at Florian's. Heaven knows we shall need cheering up after visiting your orphanage."

Allegra wanted to walk and waved aside Adriana's plea for a gondola. "It's only a short way, and we both need to breathe some clean air. The one time that Barretto took me to the casino there was so much smell of tobacco and wine soaked into the fabric of my gown that it had to be aired for a week."

Adriana's eyes widened in objection. "But that is the delightful aroma of the male! Fine tobacco and well-aged cognac. At my time of life, any reminder of men and virility is welcome, I assure you."

Allegra smiled and pulled her cloak closely around her. By the time they had gone as far as the Campo San Fantin, Adriana was out of breath. "I had forgotten how far it is to cross Venice on foot," she puffed, as they stood in front of the elaborate closed doors of La Fenice theater. "I must stop for a rest." She sat down on the steps of the theater. "Did you know that Barretto gave a small fortune to rebuild this place after the fire in '73?"

"No, he never spoke of it." Allegra wondered why, since he often boasted of large expenditures of money.

"I remember when the old Teatro San Benedetto burned to the ground, right on this spot. Barretto thought his wife—the first one—would be pleased if he became one of the sponsors of the rebuilding project. What a perfect name for something reborn: the phoenix—*la fenice*. I can tell you this—when Barretto's wife was at La Fenice with him, at least he knew where she was!" she laughed. "The grand opening was the high point of the year. It had to be, what with Napoleon coming just months before and ruining the old Venice. . . ."

Allegra listened with half an ear, while Adriana replayed her usual complaints against the French and the Austrians. Elletra's story of Barretto's passion for the beautiful first wife took on an added dimension. She reached her hand to her throat where the flesh was still bruised from last night. How had the first wife died, she wondered with an involuntary shudder.

"If you are getting a chill standing there, I'll never hear the end of it from Barretto," Adriana chirped. "Let's get on with your charity visit and then relax at Florian's." She stood and shook out her cloak. "Antonia Bianchi is dancing here tomorrow night. I think I shall demand that Bernardo escort me. Bianchi is a passable dancer, but it's her lover Paganini that everybody wants to see. What a fascinating man! They say he must have sold his hands to the devil or he wouldn't be able to play the violin the way he does. . . . He is supposed to be in Venice just to watch her perform."

Allegra was thoughtful for a moment. "Let me take you tomorrow. Barretto has given me my own box."

"What a delightful idea, but I'll let you know after we have lunch today. Bernardo . . . you understand."

A pleasant middle-aged nun met them at the door of the Redentore orphanage and led them upstairs to a sparsely furnished waiting room. Allegra gave her calling card to the nun, who disappeared down a broad hallway.

Adriana thrust her hands into her fur muff. "We must leave them a few coins. They don't seem to have enough to purchase coals."

Allegra noticed the empty grate in the finely carved marble fireplace. "It's supposed to be good for the soul, Aunt Adriana," she smiled, "and if you want to wait here, I won't be long inside."

A door opened partway down the hall, and a man strode past the waiting room. Allegra's smile evaporated. What was Luciano doing here? Without seeing them, he hurried past and down the stairs.

"Wasn't that Luciano?" Adriana said. "What a strange place to find him! He probably has his eye on one of the young girls here, if I know men."

Signora Nicolo appeared in the hallway with her arms extended. "My dear Contessa di Rienzi . . . what a pleasure! I hoped you would come."

Adriana stayed behind, obviously enduring the situation and not very happily, as Allegra walked with Signora Nicolo into the office.

The directress poured coffee and regarded Allegra with kind-faced shrewdness. "I have thought of you many times since yesterday, *contessa*, and last night I prayed that I had not been too discouraging to you."

"Nothing you said to me was a discouragement, *signora*. This place has a special quality, which I want to be a part of. I really want to help if I have any talents you can use."

"I am sure you do. I have asked the Holy Mother to send me people with good hearts to help here . . . not ladies seeking an amusing diversion to speak about over tea. Your kind offer is accepted. When do you wish to begin?"

Allegra stood and reached out her hand. "Tomorrow, if I may."

"Tomorrow, *contessa*," she replied, again holding Allegra's hand with a loving clasp.

ALLEGRA SAT THROUGH LUNCH at Florian's with Adriana and her elderly admirer. An Austrian military band was playing just outside in the Piazza San Marco to scattered applause. The Venetians in the alcoves of the restaurant went about their gossip and ignored the music.

Bernardo loved to talk almost as much as Aunt Adriana. He paid gallant compliments to Allegra's beauty, and Adriana's. Allegra let her mind wander from the conversation. She recognized a woman at a table nearby. She had been a guest at one of the teas Allegra attended recently. Today she was with two men, neither one her husband, and she flirted outrageously with them.

Allegra recalled the lady's husband as an occasional visitor to Barretto's study—a man of middle age, who had made pleasant conversation with her as he left one evening. A good-hearted man—hardly a tyrant. *If he were my husband,* she thought, *I wouldn't give him double horns.* But maybe he had his own mistress. What a game they all played!

She didn't want to return home after lunch. She knew that Adriana and Bernardo were making their own plans for the afternoon, and she would not be missed.

"I have shopping to do. You don't mind if I leave you?" she said offhandedly.

"Of course not," Adriana smiled, "but I don't want Barretto angry with me. He's so worried that somebody will carry you off."

"I'll find my way home safely, and I shall deal with Barretto," she said with a confidence that she didn't really feel.

She walked directly to a dressmaker's shop and ordered a soft gray day dress with white collar and cuffs. She would wear it while working at the Redentore.

As she left the shop and joined the crowd of afternoon strollers in the lanes behind San Marco, she thought about Elletra and wished she could tell her that she had finally stood against Barretto. But Elletra was still in Vienna and would have to hear the news by letter. Allegra wanted to tell her to keep lighting candles for her.

Clouds blew over the sun, and light rain was falling in little flurries. She was suddenly very tired. She walked swiftly back to the Ca', to what she hoped was not a confrontation with Barretto.

Zeno met her at the door with a servile expression. The *conte* wished her to come to his study immediately upon her arrival. She moved reluctantly across the wide marble entrance hall toward the heavy doors of the study.

Barretto stood with his back to her as she entered. He let her stand unacknowledged for a long moment before he turned to face her. In spite of the fatigue of her body and nerves, her mind was clear. She saw that his face was taut and white, and his eyelids drooped in slants over his impenetrable black eyes.

He walked two steps to his desk and picked up a sheet of paper. "It took less than twenty-four hours for you to break your contract with me. What will you be guilty of by the time the sun sets today?"

"My lord, I have done nothing except go with Aunt Adriana to the orphanage of the Redentore," she said with a steady voice that surprised her.

He crushed the paper roughly in his hand and threw it at her feet. "You don't think I am fool enough to accept your word and let it go at that."

She flushed at his innuendo. "I have done nothing to cause you to suspect me. I only plan to offer my help at the . . . ."

"I already know that," he barked impatiently. "If it is some game you are playing, I will know that, too. For now, you have my permission to visit that place."

He watched her with his hooded eyes and then cleared his throat. "One more thing . . . there will be no further opportunities for you to refuse me your bed. It is clear to me that you are not a normal female and have not the least spark of warmth in your body. While our child lives and is healthy, I have no more need to go through the futile exercise of sex with you. Your father assured me that you were capable of your duties to me . . . he will regret it if he willfully misled me. I should have chosen another of his daughters; Gemma would certainly not be averse to my attentions." He smiled punishingly at her.

Even as he was speaking the words that set her free, a feeling of outrage burned through her. How dare he threaten her with the possibility that he would take some revenge on her father! And then to suggest that he might be intimate with Gemma . . . .

"The stakes are high, Allegra," he continued in an icy tone. "We shall not make another contract, but let my words sear into your soul like the fires of judgment: one hint—just one—of disloyalty, and your fate will be sealed. That is all." He drew a careless hand along the line of her cheek. "It is now up to you to decide what shall happen to your pretty face."

He held the door open for her to leave and pulled it closed behind her. The swirling pattern of the marble maze on the floor made her feel dizzy. Barretto had given her freedom and threatened her life at the same time. But he had given her the one thing that meant the most to her—her body. It would never again be invaded by his hard flesh. She smiled through a mist of tears and walked slowly up the curved stairway to her rooms.

ALLEGRA LEFT THE OFFICE of Signora Nicolo feeling comfortable in her gray woolen work dress. It had been arranged that she would tutor the older girls in Latin. By the end of February her life was assuming a reasonably pleasant routine, visiting her students several times each week. She found that she loved her work. Her simple dress and quiet ways caused amusement among the nuns, who called her their *contessa monacale,* the nunlike *contessa.* But they said it with love, and she was as happy as she could allow herself to be.

Elletra and her husband had returned to the Palazzo Clodio, and Allegra looked forward to lunches with her good friend and cousin. Elletra refrained from pressing to know too much about Allegra's situation with Barretto. She understood that Allegra had finally asserted herself with him, but she also knew her young cousin well enough to recognize the fragile structure of contentment that Allegra had erected around herself. She would not probe at it.

Aunt Adriana was no longer in Venice. She had returned home at Twelfth Night. Barretto was gone much of the time on business, and the Ca' had become a quiet place again.

The year 1819 was starting on a peaceful note; the colors of her life were soft and muted. She was not unhappy. She had come to an understanding with herself about her life. She would not expect more than was given by God, and she accepted the gift of the Redentore with gratitude.

Barretto's unloving presence did not intimidate her any longer. He would never have cause to think her unfaithful with other men—it was the farthest thing from her mind. The children of the Redentore had begun to fill the empty parts of herself so fully that she was immune to the shallow invitations of Venetian dandies. It made her smile to think how impossible that would be.

The past few months had given her something to write about in her diary, beyond the usual teas and fittings and complaints about her life at the Ca' d'Argenti. The foolish dreams of her youth were put to rest at long last—nothing could disturb this new serenity, which she clung to so earnestly.

CHAPTER FIVE

March 1819

IT WAS A SLOW SEASON that spring in Venice. Influenza had caused many events to be canceled, and Barretto insisted that Allegra discontinue her visits to the Redentore until the danger was past. He didn't want her to bring home infection to his son, he said, but she suspected that he was finding a way to punish her for having found contentment there.

The days blended into one another in dull repetition, until it was mid-March. Barretto had gone on an extended visit to his mainland holdings, taking Luciano with him. Since Zeno was ill with influenza, it was arranged that Aunt Adriana would come to look after Allegra and the staff. It was the best he could do on short notice, even though he had no confidence in her abilities as a taskmaster in the Ca'.

Allegra looked forward to having a cheerful companion for a few weeks. But the old aristocrat was restless with the slow pace of events. Too many theatrical performances, Adriana's favorite evening activity, had been canceled. She had hoped to see some of Goldoni's comedies, which she dearly loved, from her favorite box at La Fenice.

"Imagine, my old friends telling me they are afraid to go out because of this influenza thing? What am I supposed to do to keep sane—pace the halls of this drafty place?" Allegra smiled noncommittally. "And you . . . how many evenings do you plan to spend with your embroidery, my dear?" she quizzed. "You can't retreat from society. You should make friends of your own kind, not just nuns and waifs . . . and I need a companion. I want you to go out with me."

She grinned like a child. "And don't say no, the way I know you are about to. At least we can accept Marina Benzoni's invitation to a *conversazione*. Goldoni's *The Lovers* has just been canceled for tomorrow night, and Marina is having an early salon. There might be some interesting people . . . she always attracts them, heaven knows.''

Allegra's first thought was to refuse, but her own boredom had made her restless, and Adriana deserved a little amusement. Barretto's spies were either ill or traveling with him, and so he would never have to hear about it. Still, she felt uneasy about accepting the invitation.

"I'll go with you—" she conceded guardedly "—but these affairs make me uncomfortable. Promise me you'll not complain if I just sit in a corner somewhere while you talk with your friends."

"Who are you hiding from? You must let things happen . . . you are much too shy. But do whatever you wish, my dear. Thank God for Marina or this old city would be a dull place indeed!"

THE DRAWING ROOM of Contessa Benzoni was blazing with candles, and the scent of warm perfume, tobacco and wine engulfed them as they entered. A large soprano was filling the room with song. She and her piano accompanist played to an indifferent audience, which buzzed in low-voiced comment. Venetians, it was said, always found it hard to be absolutely silent.

Allegra had a strong urge to turn to the door again and leave. A kind of shaking excitement moved in her for no good reason, yet Adriana's pleased and eager face made her continue into the crowded room. There were a few women whom she knew from society teas, but most were strangers. There were laughing greetings—what a surprise to see the *contessa monacale*—while their eyes assessed her critically.

She did not realize how much her quality of simplicity stood out. Her softly draped gown in pastel tones was without the usual decorations. Dark wavy hair drawn back into a gentle knot at the neck emphasized the wistful beauty of her eyes. Tonight she had pinned a white spring rose on her dress—it grew in the lonely orangery on the roof of the Ca'. Adriana saw the envious glances of some of the women and smiled to herself—*the little one has a true sense of elegance*.

Allegra did not feel at ease, but she smiled quietly and took the proffered hand of the effusive Contessa Benzoni, who made a special point of greeting her. Marina Benzoni's bold eyes were watching Allegra curiously, but not unkindly. The hostess was outspoken, nearly sixty, with bright blond hair and a more than ample body. She zestfully enjoyed her position as one of the most colorful women in Venice. There were rumors that she was about to marry her lover of thirty years.

Adriana was already chattering with friends near the refreshment table, and Allegra found herself alone for a moment. The hubbub of the crowded room and the close contact of so many welcoming masculine faces set her nerves on edge. If one of them secretly reported to Barretto for a price, she would never know.

Long double doors were open onto a balcony, and she moved through them into the brisk night air. She looked up at the flickering stars with a sense of relief and sighed . . . but then a shiver of foreboding touched her again.

Suddenly a deep soft voice spoke from the shadows. "Can it be possible," it said, "that two women can have the same unearthly beauty? My God, do not mock me with this!"

Allegra's heart began a swift uneven rhythm, as she turned slowly to find intense, gray hazel eyes probing into hers. The face and eyes were so arresting that she could only stare.

The man reached to take her hand, and the touch of his caressing lips sent a stabbing, strange fire through her veins. She could not speak; her eyes were locked to his gaze in an exciting dread and fascination. She wanted to escape, but she couldn't move.

He stood cradling her hand while his eyes filled with tears. "Forgive me—" his low voice woke vibrations deep in her body "—you remind me of someone whom I love very much . . . more than I have a right to love."

He paused, searching her face, and still she could not move from him. "It is incredible. The same sweetness and simplicity, and yet a strength . . . ."

His voice trailed off, and they gazed at each other without words. The fine lines of his face were pale against his dark auburn, crisply curling hair. In the silence between them she saw that a frost of gray gleamed at the temples. All of Allegra's senses were absorbing him. There was an aura of strength and tension in him. His compact figure radiated vitality. His elegant dark satin evening coat sat well on broad shoulders, and his white loosely tied cravat was held by a single gold pin . . . on it, a small coat of arms with magical looking horses rampant.

Strange and miraculous thoughts flew through her mind. She knew this man's face! His voice was as familiar to her as her own. *He is the one I have dreamed about, the one for whom I whispered my prayers!* her heart cried out. She could not stop staring at him.

He spoke again. "You say nothing, *bellissima.* I beg you tell me, are you real? Surely you have a name as sweet as your person. . . ."

"Allegra," she said in a whisper, caught in the force of his energies.

"Good Lord! I must be dreaming. Allegra!"

His amazed tones lifted her into a little more reality, and she removed her hand from his warm grasp, remembering her social manners. In a small voice she said, "*Signore,* I hope I have not caused you pain by my resemblance to a loved one."

His lips moved suddenly into a smile that lighted his face with dazzling charm. A delicious weakness flowed in her. No one had ever looked into her eyes or smiled at her in that way. Her heart ached against its chains. "And my name is Allegra di Rienzi." She drew a steadying breath. "I am the wife of Barretto di Rienzi."

He was still smiling. "So, you are the little nun. Marina told me that there was a virtuous woman coming here tonight. I might have known. She made me promise to be a good boy." All at once his face was serious, almost tragic, and his mobile mouth drew down. "My sweet lady, you remind me of my sister Augusta, one of the beings on this earth most dear to me." He put out a gentle hand to her hair. "Yes, it is the same—like touching a night shadow. And the name Allegra is dear to me, also. It is the name of my small daughter."

He made a slight bow and took her hand again. His Venetian

accent was light and musical, not the speech of one born in Italy.
"I am remiss in my manners, Contessa di Rienzi. I beg to introduce myself. I am Byron."

Her heart lurched. It couldn't be—not the scandalous English
lord—the dangerous poet—it must be a mistake. . . . She didn't
want this beautiful being to be Byron. "I am honored, my lord,"
she murmured, while his perceptive eyes watched the emotion that
the sound of his name had aroused.

"Allegra *mia*," his voice was deeply melodious and compelling,
"I am not the ogre that they say. I am only a very lonely man, a
wanderer on this earth who has no home, no lasting home, but I
have sorrows to forget." He sighed. "Could you spare pity for
one who is lonely—could you give me a little of the precious kindness that I see in your eyes? . . ." His hand held hers again. A
tightening of his fingers and a tiny knowing smile answered the
tremor that she could not control. "It is fate that we have met. I
pray you, give me your friendship." His lips moved warmly
against her soft fingertips.

Adriana appeared in the balcony doorway. "There you are,
Allegra. Marina is asking for you, and for you too, milord."
Allegra woke painfully from the starry dream. She awkwardly
withdrew her hand from his.

Adriana gave Byron a childlike smile, a little admiring,
acknowledging his handsomeness. With a teasing flash of his
eyes, he bowed over the old lady's hand. "The men of Italy are to
be envied for the beauty of their women."

"And you are a naughty boy—just as I have heard!" she
chuckled, and his deep laugh joined hers.

He turned to Allegra. "*Contessa*, it has been a pleasure. Surely
the fates will let us meet again." He took their arms to lead them
back into the salon. Then, with a smile, he walked way, limping
slightly, and was soon engulfed by Marina Benzoni's clamoring
guests.

For the rest of the evening Allegra was not herself. She conversed
with people but was hardly aware of what she said. Her eyes were
searching for sight of his proud head, watching for the play of expression on his face. *How could this be?* she said over and over in-

side her confused mind. *This is the face of the man I love. How could this be?* A sudden thought of Barretto was like a finger of ice stabbing into her breast. Life was indeed cruel to let her glimpse the one she yearned for and then to make more than that impossible. It would be better had she never seen him, for now every nerve in her body longed for the touch of his hand.

Adriana was growing tired. "Let us go home, Allegra," she said. "I have seen enough faces for one night and my bones are thinking of bed."

With a tremble of reluctance, she agreed. Her heart felt like lead. At the door, while she turned for one last look back into the crowded salon, his voice again spoke to her.

"My lady, I must thank you for your kindness. You have given me a moment of that special kind of joy that is distilled of sorrow . . . bitter and yet more than sweet." He bent over her hand with practiced courtesy. She felt him press a small folded paper into her palm, and her hand closed tightly over it. He looked for an instant deeply into her eyes, and his lips soundlessly formed the word, "Trust."

In the cool night air she drew long breaths to steady herself. She was afraid she would faint. As they moved toward the Ca' d'Argenti in the smooth rhythm of the gondola, she held her fingers clenched around her precious token. She was afire to know what he had written to her. The world was glittering with beauty and expectancy—and terrifying consequences.

"Are you all right, Allegra? Allegra?" Adriana's voice penetrated to her mind. "You don't look at all well."

She gathered her thoughts. "I'm fine . . . just a little tired."

"Poor child," she smiled, "it was stuffy at Benzoni's. She always has too much heat. What a scandalous woman she is—all that blond hair—it can't be natural, but I wish I knew how she keeps her face so smooth. Maybe it's the fat on her body. You know, she goes out to her appointments in her gondola with a bag of hot polenta in her bosom, to keep her warm and to nibble on while she goes from one feast to the next. . . ."

Allegra nodded her head in agreement from time to time, while her heart urged the gondola home. The note burned in her hand.

Finally, they reached the Ca', and Adriana went to bed. Gina went to fetch a hot drink for Allegra, because she had seen that her mistress was upset and nervous. Quickly Allegra unfolded the little paper and read the words:

My gondola will wait by the side entrance of the Ca' d'Argenti at 2 o'clock this morning. My man Tita is discreet. He will take you to me, only a short distance away. You need not fear discovery.
    I beg you to consider my need and be kind. Trust.

Byron

Her mind was in turmoil. How could she not answer his plea? It was impossible to think straight. But this is Byron, part of her argued—not just any man, but a seducer of women. *He needs me,* she answered, *and I would be lacking in compassion to refuse to help him.* The memory of his sorrowful eyes and gentle voice impelled her to her decision. She had to see that beautiful face again, to feel his touch. She had to go to him.

Gina took an agonizingly long time putting away her clothes. The ormolu clock beside her bed was ticking off the minutes swiftly. If she were late, would the gondolier wait? At last Gina blew out the candles and went to her own rest.

Allegra sprang from bed and raced to dress. She quickly chose a delicate blue silk morning dress with lace at the throat and hem. Her long dusky hair was tied back, its heavy waves confined by blue ribbon. She looked into the big ornate mirror in her dressing room and saw a very young and eager girl, her dark eyes huge and a vivid spot of pink on each cheek.

She drew a heavy hooded cloak around her and crept down the back stairs, through the kitchens. Only the old watchdog Bruno, who belonged to the kitchen staff, raised his head from his mat by the damped fire. Satisfied, he went back to snoring. Allegra let herself out the servants' entrance and stood uncertainly on the narrow water steps, not knowing which way to turn.

The firm thud of the door behind her sounded like a terrible deafening accusation. Guilt and dread fought with the painful urgency to be with Byron again and feel the wonder of his magnetic presence.

Then a flash of light struck on the golden notched prow of a black gondola, which was easing from the shadows as silently as a phantom dream. The tall gondolier came close to the quay and extended his big hand. Allegra took it quickly, seating herself into the thick velvet cushions. She kept her face lowered, out of view of the world.

No word was spoken. The man poled his craft expertly into a side canal. They threaded the complex waterways and soon came past the ornate facade of the church of Santa Maria Zobenigo. Part of Allegra could not believe what she had just done . . . that she was actually moving through this quiet spring night to an assignation with a man. All of her precious attitudes and thoughts should have been making this impossible, but her heart was shouting louder than her fears. *I'll just go this once to offer him my friendship,* she insisted to herself, *that is all.*

Once again the large hand was extended to her and she put her feet onto damp water stairs. A dark figure beckoned from the shadows and Allegra ran across the silent small *campo* toward her fate. . .

CHAPTER SIX

THE HEAT FROM HIS HAND flowed through her, as he led her up a short flight of stairs and opened the door to the cozy rooms of a small apartment. He was silent as he gently pushed the hood back from her face. His fingers drew a line of blissful sensation along her cheek. This place, his touch . . . they were like remembrances to her.

He unfastened the clasp of her cloak and let it fall away from her shoulders, while his eyes searched hers with such intensity that she began to tremble. For the first time since she had made her choice to come to him, she realized this was real, and not a dream.

The look in his eyes was a burning intimate caress, and she was powerless in the grip of this new delight. *He is my true love!* her heart cried out with each uneven beat. *His is no stranger, this beloved being, this amazing and marvelous man whose face is that of a glorious angel.*

Tears welled in his eyes, making them shine with what she knew must be joy, and her eyes responded with their own tears. With a groaning breath he drew her against his strong body. The fine linen of his shirt was soft to the touch of her cheek. Now her trembling was uncontrollable, and he moved one hand soothingly along her shoulders and held her closer to him.

"Poor child," his smooth deep voice vibrated through her like an irresistible force. "Come. This is my special hideaway. At the Palazzo Mocenigo I am usually plagued at all hours by people and servants. And privacy is very precious to me."

Without releasing her from his sure, enfolding arm, he moved with her into the room. Dimly she saw that the walls were papered in a rich red pattern. There was a small crackling fire and a low carved table with wine and glasses and a dish of English biscuits. He brought her to a soft couch covered with a woven Oriental spread, and then turned to pour the wine. The deepening silence in the room began to erode her courage.

Allegra hugged into herself, her arms tense against her sides. He held out a glass to her and she took it with a shaking hand. Tiny bubbles swam in the amber liquid. In a swift motion he dropped to the floor and turned to sit close against her knees, leaning one elbow on the cushions. He touched his glass to hers.

"To the most sweet and lovely lady of Venice—a gift of God's kindness to a man adrift in an acid sea of pain and frustration. Come, shy Allegra, you must drink to what you are. I think you have been too long pressed into a mold of dreariness and despair, and you do not yet know what wonderful loveliness is yours." His beguiling voice thrilled along her nerves. She found it difficult to look into the finely chiseled face so near to her.

He drained his glass and set it aside, then watched her intently. She managed a swallow of wine under his searching eyes. The tingle of the wine's penetrating fire sent a relaxing warmth into her breast. He reached to take the glass from her, capturing her small cold hands in the heat of his own.

"Poor little bird, your fingers are icy. Surely you are not afraid of me, Allegra *mia*. . . ." He bent his head to kiss each imprisoned palm. Allegra looked down at his tightly curled auburn hair with its glint of gray, and her heart melted into a pool of love so intense that she could scarcely breathe. When he raised his head again he gazed deeply at her, so that a tangible force flowed between them. His eyes seemed to her to be full of light, like open windows to some mysterious and wonderful place, far from the world outside. They were like water glistening over gray brook stones, deep and clear. Magic eyes of the prince of her dreams.

With her hands warming in his, she sighed in complete trust, and his face broke into a heart-catching smile. "Now," he said softly, "that is better. Tell me about yourself, my little love. I want to hear everything, and then I shall bore you with the tale of my misspent years."

Haltingly, and prodded by his questions, her short life was spread out for his understanding. She left out nothing, not even her hopeless prayers to Santa Chiara. When she came to the story of her betrothal to Barretto, he cursed softly under his breath in his own language. Then, to her own surprise, she poured out her fear of Barretto and the painful tale of her wedding night, and his terrifying use of her.

Looking up through tears, she saw his face twist in sympathy and felt him sweep her into his arms tightly against his breast. "My God, my God," he whispered, "what irony the fates play upon the helpless." He stroked her hair and lightly kissed her eyelids before he drew her away. "So, now you have a child, poor little devil—and that old monument to Italian male stupidity for a husband, and you think, Allegra *mia*, that all love and all sex is bound to have a canker of pain in it." He raised one of her hands to his lips and kissed its palm lingeringly.

She sat enthralled by his touch, his words and his beauty. *How quickly and completely everything can change,* she thought, *because one person exists in my life who did not exist before.*

He drew himself up onto the couch and ran a light fingertip over the outline of her lips. "Your lips are very warm and soft, *cara mia.* I can teach them things about love and loving. It is so much sweeter when there has first been sorrow." He leaned close to her, his lips moving over hers with a butterfly touch, teasing and promising. Then he let her go and smiled into her wide needy eyes. "I will teach you only if you wish it, dear little Allegra. But you should not go on with your life with never an experience of what real love can be. It is for you to decide whether you will give me the gift of yourself and heal my own wounded spirit with your joy."

She was completely enchanted by him, not really thinking about what he was proposing to her, until a kind of unwilling common sense whispered through her excitement, *You can't simply fall into his arms. . . .*

With an effort, she gathered together her shaken emotions enough to draw back from his embrace and find her voice. "Please tell me about yourself, milord," she said in an uneven whisper. "Am I to be the only one who speaks in trust and truth? I came to you because you asked me to consider your need . . . and I thought that need was more of the spirit than . . . . ." She met his luminous penetrating eyes bravely.

The smile that had started on his lips was washed away by an expression of such fierce pain that she drew in her breath at the impact of it. He dropped her hands and turned his face away. "You don't know what you are asking, *madonna*. If I give you truth, you may flee from me in disgust," he muttered. "How can anyone understand my heart if I do not? Only one woman has ever known me well, and she . . . ." He looked away, slipping again to the floor beside her, where he laid his head on her knees. She put her hand quietly on those springing, vital curls.

Like a child he sighed, "Poor Byron . . . poor B," and then sat up quickly with a sudden shift of mood. "You must call me Byron. I will have none of this milord."

He looked at the ceiling with an impish grin. "So, where shall I begin? George Gordon Byron was born one cold January day in London, from a mother who had been unwise in trusting the words of an adventurer and a charmer, my father. She bore me alone and in relative poverty, my father having gone through her small fortune. My childhood was bleak, mostly in Scotland, my mother's homeland. But one day, when I was still a little lad, however precocious, my wicked old grand-uncle, Lord Byron of Newstead in England, died of his sins—and suddenly I was George Gordon, *Lord* Byron, the sixth of the title. But poor young Lord B. was not happy, because this was not an ordinary English fairy tale." The puckish lilt left his voice, and he looked tormented again. He looked away from her as he started to describe the uncontrollable emotions that drew him to women.

"It has never been fully satisfying to love a woman. It is different with the friendship of men—Hobhouse, the friend of my schooldays, is an example. He loves me despite myself, as I love him. Friends are the salt that makes life palatable." He swept on, telling her of his youth . . . his long travels in Europe and the Ottoman empire.

"There are too many things not suitable to your sweet ears," he said with a laugh. "I will tell you instead about how I became a poet. I kept a kind of poetic traveling account as I went from place to place . . . I called it *Childe Harold's Pilgrimage*. Almost as a joke I gave the manuscript to my cousin to see if he could get it published. My mother had died just as I returned home. I was too filled with pain and guilt at her death to care what happened for a while. But a capricious universe had plans for me. The thing was published, and one day I woke up to find myself famous.''

Allegra found it difficult to follow his story of a life so different from her own. She couldn't understand his vehemence about London society. A bittersweet theme ran through his memories whenever he mentioned his half sister, Augusta. "She is gentle, like you,'' he said on a note of love. "I never really knew her until I corresponded with her in my college days, and then grew close after I became the literary lion of society. She is married to a fool who does nothing but think of horses and gambling and breed children on her. I've helped her out financially since I have been able to do so.''

He held his head in his hands and was silent, his back taut and his body strained. Then he burst out, "She was the only one who ever knew me. She is like me; she has deep fire under her compliant ways . . . a fire only I have known. She could laugh away my troubles. With her the world was a place of possibilities and probable joy, and now she is forever cut away from me by that self-righteous cold Clytemnestra, the one above reproach, Lady Byron—my wife.''

He paced the room with uneven lame strides. The story of his life in London, the pursuit of women, rolled on. "They thundered after me . . . I had not the pleasure of a chase. They were like ripe fruit. Caro Lamb—she's an example. Made my life miserable, and her husband's, too!''

Seeing Allegra's white face, he stopped suddenly and rushed to sit beside her, to hold her. "Damn my stupid tongue. I always say too much. It's a fatal Byron trait. I'm not saying that all women . . . that you . . . . Don't you think I know a pure spirit when I see one? I know you came to me out of sweetness and concern.'' He raised her face, and his lips moved over hers in a gentle kiss . . . for her alone. She felt reassured.

He leaned back on the couch, holding her hand and playing tantalizingly with her fingers, while he went on with his story. Perhaps he didn't know how arousing his touch was, or maybe he did. Allegra struggled to take her attention from her hand and focus it on his deep voice and the continuation of his story. But her body seemed to have its own life apart from her will. Its sudden awakening made her flush with a heat that was unfamiliar to her. Fortunately Byron was deep in his confessions and was not watching her. Was this the little nun, the woman who could not bear her husband's touch and who looked with cool eyes at other men? She had worked so hard to prevent this very thing—this tidal wave of the heart.

Byron was speaking of his marriage. "I had to marry," he said bitterly. "I was as much of a sacrifice to society as you were, Allegra. It was necessary to produce an heir to the Byron name . . . and also to make me respectable. I was in a scrape, one that I cannot speak about without hurting one who is innocent of anything but kindness and unquestioning love.

"Good God, what games we play with life! Anyway, I chose what seemed to be a suitable woman. She was of impeccable reputation, not beautiful, but attractive. An only child, heiress to a fortune, educated and well read. I thought we might do well together. There was no love, you understand, it was a correct arrangement, or so I thought. We were married, and from the first she turned her eyes on me like some kind of ethical yardstick. I need a gentle hand, Allegra—one can rule me by laughing with me far better than by frowning.

"She irritated me with those steady blue eyes, as if she kept a list in her mind of my foolish actions. So, of course, I gave her more to add to the list. Everyone thought we were a perfect match, but Gus knew—that's Augusta, my sister.

"She tried to calm me down and to be a friend to Annabella, my wife. What a tangle we all had: the sale of Newstead, my ancestral home, would have got me out of debt, but it was delayed; the bailiffs were at the door; Annabella was pregnant and near her time; poor Gus was there trying to keep peace. I found some forgetfulness in the bottle. Then the child came—a girl we named Ada. I saw her only a few times. Her mother decided to take her away to her parents' home for a recuperation from the birth. When she left I fully expected to join her, after I had settled my pressing affairs.

"The next thing that happened was that a miserable cur of a solicitor called me in to say my wife wanted a legal separation. I pleaded with her to reconsider because of the child. Then she whispered into his ear that I was crazy and that I did other unspeakable things with Augusta as an accomplice. . . . After that, I was turned upon by the society that had fawned over me. The women who had wanted my favors shunned me. My good friend Cam Hobhouse and others stood by. Poor Gus, she suffered too. Finally it seemed best to leave England, for Augusta's sake and for my child's."

Byron's voice had grown rough, and now he covered his face as sobs convulsed him. Allegra felt helpless in the wake of his agonizing. She held his hand hard and waited for the storm to settle. She knew that he needed her.

"I must carry my secrets to the grave," he said in a strangled voice. "My wife had cause—I was angry with her and said things out of irritation that I regret, but she sits there now, a pillar of respectability, and spreads rumors. Her vengeance is more terrible than anything I ever did to her—even if she knew I preferred . . . ." He ceased speaking and started pacing the room again.

"My foot . . ." he said abruptly, stopping in front of her. "You can see I limp. I was born so. Does it make a difference? Are you disgusted with a lame man?"

Allegra shook her head. "I think you are beautiful," she said in utter truth.

"Mmm." He leaned down to look into her eyes more closely. She bore his gaze steadily. "Thank you, Allegra, I value that bit of innocent honesty. So now, here I am, the beast who was thrust out of British society. At least in Italy you don't have the prudery of whited sepulchers. I have not lost my creative talent. I shall live to some purpose before my life is over. They listen to me in London, even if they turn their backs. My poetry sells, and I have stirred up a hornet's nest with the first cantos of *Don Juan* . . . but you wouldn't understand about that. I'm not very proud of my life since I've come here. I've let myself go."

He turned his back to her. "I have a bastard child named Allegra—a name I love. Her mother was one of those brass bold

English girls who flung themselves after me. At least I am taking care of the child. I have her here in Venice with me. She's pretty and bright—a Byron, no doubt of it.

"Allegra, I think I have been a little insane since I left England." He came back and sat beside her, speaking on a deep note. "I am not by nature a truly decadent man. When I saw you tonight, all of the purity and goodness of woman was recalled to my mind, as is the hope of heaven to one who is damned. Your eyes seemed to heal my hot heart. Maybe fate has brought us together because we have so much to give to one another."

With a gentle hand he smoothed the dark curls away from her face, and his touch ignited the fire in her again. "So like Augusta," he murmured, "yet not the same. Your eyes have known a saintly sorrow. You have endured a man's legal rape of woman, but the rest of you is as untouched as a child—and you have had only a tiny glimpse of the madness of human behavior. When you see it more fully, what will you be?"

His hand caressed her cheek. "Such pure sweetness. As for Augusta, she has seen it all but refuses to look at what she has seen. In the midst of utter confusion she stands and laughs. Come, she seems to say, let us laugh and gather what little joys we may. Can you laugh, little Allegra, at all the pains and fears of life?"

She gazed into his eyes, hypnotized by his velvet voice. The rhythm of his slight accent made him even more fascinating to her, but she was becoming confused by all he had said. What did he mean? She was not sure. She knew one thing unquestioningly—she loved this amazing, complicated, beautiful being with all her heart.

"I want to give you happiness," she said earnestly to his brilliant and watching eyes. "I feel I can tell you everything and you will understand. You can trust me—" she hesitated over his name "—*mio* Byron." The name stayed on her tongue like magic wine and the taste of a world of adventure that she had never seen.

He smiled and kissed her hand. "It is close to dawn, *cara mia*. I must let you go. I want no harm to come to you, and old di Rienzi has a reputation that even I find despicable.'' He raised her to her feet, and she clung to his hands. He smiled again, ''Don't fear, *cara*, we shall meet again.'' He lifted her chin lightly to gaze into the dilated pupils of her large eyes. ''I want you to think carefully. You are a woman of great loveliness, and I wish to know that sweetness of yours—all of it.''

She shivered at the sudden male energy of his touch, as its fire flowed into her. His vibrating voice searched out the tenderness of her sensitive nerves, sending signals of pleasure to her body.

''I can never be only your friend,'' he continued, ''because in my heart I am already your lover. You must consider this before you see me again. I promise you that I can wipe away all the pain that the aging satyr has put upon you. I want to give you joy, Allegra . . . sweet Allegra.'' He bent to kiss her lips with a fragile touch. ''Tita will be waiting again at midnight. You must choose—will you give and take the exquisite gift that life offers, or not?''

He let her go and plucked up her cloak. Without a word he wrapped her in it and moved with her toward the stairs. She looked once more around the room, to imprint it on her memory. Tita was roused from a small room downstairs.

Byron handed her into the gondola. A slight smile edged his beautiful lips, and then Tita's surging push on the great oar sent her sliding into the night, away from him.

A very faint light was whispering in the eastern sky. She prayed that no one would be wakeful in the Ca'. Tita helped her out in silence and with a bow. The door swung open to her key, and Bruno's warning growl sank into a tail-wagging thumping.

She hurried up the narrow back stairs to the security of her rooms. The house was soundless in its sleep. She pulled off her cloak in haste and then noticed that a fire still glowed in the grate. Someone moved in the shadows, and she gasped.

''Don't be afraid, *madonna*,'' Gina's quiet voice said. Allegra was shivering beyond control, and Gina moved toward her with concern. ''Are you all right? I have stayed here to help you. I will not betray you.''

Tears suddenly flooded into Allegra's eyes and down her face.

With a murmur of sympathy Gina's arms enfolded her, and she wept against the comforting shoulder. She let herself be put to bed like a child, almost bursting with the need to speak to someone. "Please," she said, "I must make a heavy decision. I have no one else to talk to. . . ."

Gina sat on the edge of the bed and took Allegra's hand in a firm grasp, as the story flooded ecstatically from her lips. A flicker of a grimace moved over Gina's face at the name of Byron. "Have you heard of his reputation, my lady?"

"He has told me about himself. I know he has been foolish—he is a genius, his emotions are strong. . . ." She hesitated at Gina's strange expression. "He is a good man. He is gentle and perceptive. He is kind, he loves children and animals. He is a faithful friend . . . and I love him!"

Gina only nodded. "He is a great contrast to the *conte*, and I have heard he is kind to those in need. But what about his use of women? What of the scandal that sent him from England? . . . It is said that it involved his passion for his sister. . . ."

"He loves her dearly. She is his half sister, and he says that they are very much alike—they have an affinity of tastes and moods." Allegra wanted to explain everything so that Gina wouldn't think ill of him. "He feels at ease with her more than with others. She tried to help his wife, but there was jealousy. I don't know, Gina, except that he says his sister is now very religious and withdrawn from him, and this distresses him." She heard her busy flow of words and felt irritated that she should be trying to convince anyone of the rightness of her feelings. Neither of the women in the shadowy room spoke for a while.

After a long moment Allegra said, "Gina, if I do not take this love now, I will regret it all of my life. This man is the one whose face I have always seen in my dreams, even when I prayed to Santa Chiara. I'm not imagining this. I love him—I cannot help it."

Gina sighed. "I understand. You have had too much that was harsh, and you have hope for little else until the *conte* dies. You are so young, and milord is a very beautiful man. I know you will see him if I help you or not, so I will help. I want you to be happy, *cara*; I would not stand in the way. Yet I am very uneasy. . . .

Forgive me, but I feel that Lord Byron is not a steady man to hold to. He has too many deep and dark places in himself, fascinating and charming as he may be. There are women in Venice of many classes of society, whom he has pursued for a time . . . and just for a little time, *cara*.'' She didn't want to say those last words.

A shadow moved over Allegra's face. ''I know. But they could not give him what he needed. I believe he is capable of a true love; it is what he wants.''

Gina released her hand and stood up. ''You can count on me. My woman's heart understands, but I pray you, *cara*, think well. Even your Byron has told you to consider carefully. I find that when a man warns a woman, he has good reasons to do so.''

She busied herself putting away Allegra's dress and cloak and then left quickly. Allegra threw off the bedclothes. She went to her desk to get her inkpot, pen and diary, and sat down on the yellow-tiled hearth in the flickering light of the little fire. Her hand wrote furiously:

20 March
This is my diary, my own companion, who will not judge me nor whisper to others who would. For I must tell what is flooding into my soul this night . . . I have met him! The sun has found me in my small, dark cave. Him! Byron! Let me say his name again . . . Byron! O merciful heaven, he has come to take me from my gray world. I will never be alone again. Byron has found me!

I shall record every word and look and touch, for I fear I shall forget a small whisper of his lips and shall be the less for forgetting. . . .

SHE LAY IN HER WARM BED in a cocoon of joy. There was no need for thought. She smiled in the dark. There was no choice to be made after all; no considered decision. This was truly fate—what must be. She was totally sure. It had helped her to talk to Gina, but the fears were groundless. She saw again the light in his luminous eyes, and she slept, relaxed into contentment. Tonight

Tita would be waiting in the dark canal. The world was full of promise, and she would meet what was to come with an eager heart.

SHE MANAGED to get through the next day without betraying her excitement. She talked with Aunt Adriana, who teased her about having Lord Byron alone on a balcony at la Benzoni's last night. Allegra only smiled and grudgingly admitted, under Adriana's prodding, that milord was an attractive man.

"More than attractive, Allegra, he's an Adonis. I'm shocked at how unobservant you can be about men. . . ."

Gemma and Lipia came to tea, as shallow as ever, hinting that Allegra should have a formal ball, so that they could meet eligible men who might offer for them. They were annoying—their total world was still bound up in selfish desires.

"You are so fortunate, Allegra," Gemma said, not for the first time. "Why don't you take advantage of it all? Buy some really stylish gowns for yourself. Your Barretto is indulgent now that he has a son."

Allegra tried to ignore their chatter. What would they think if they knew she had refused Barretto, that he had threatened to kill her . . . and that she was about to give herself to the famous Lord Byron? At least Adriana would applaud her daring and appreciate her taste in men.

She wondered about herself. This was an Allegra who was strange even to herself. This passionate woman whose body went hot and cold at the thought of the coming night . . . this woman about to deceive the husband she had defied . . . was this the real Allegra? All her values were turned upside down, and she was not even afraid of the consequences.

She rejoiced when the pearl and orange glow of sunset spread over the sky and reflected onto the Grand Canal like a ribbon of pink fire. She dined with Adriana and was so absentminded that the old woman looked at her curiously.

"Are you well, my dear?" she said with a kindly pat on her hand. "You are very quiet tonight."

Allegra pleaded a headache and made an early escape to her rooms, where she paced restlessly. Adriana probably thought she was pregnant again. Just as well. It would help to explain her moodiness.

The evening was interminable. Finally she rested on her bed with a book on her lap, trying to focus on its pages, but Byron's face floated over the words. She saw him close, the fine texture of his skin, the shining glint of his hair, the heart-shaking molding of his lips moving toward hers.

Sometime she must have drifted to sleep, because she awoke to find Gina beside her bed, smiling at her. "You will want to bathe, *cara,* it is already eleven o'clock."

Gina helped her to dress in a simple pink lacy gown and brushed her hair into deep waves and soft curls. In the mirror she saw that she was beautiful. A glow of rose was on her cheeks, and her eyes were pools of mystery, their pupils wide and dark with excitement.

Gina smiled at her reflection. "He will find you irresistible, *madonna.*"

At last the small clock on her table chimed the hour of midnight. It was echoed by the campanile of San Marco's. Gina wrapped the dark cloak around her and then suddenly held her close.

"Be happy," she said in a choked voice and turned away.

Allegra stole through the sleeping house again and out the side door beyond the kitchen. Once more the golden prow of the gondola slid soundlessly from the shadows.

CHAPTER SEVEN

ALLEGRA SANK BACK into the scarlet cushions. The oiled black canvas shell had been raised over the passenger seats as a protection against the weather, and she thought about drawing the curtains around her.

Tita poled his dark craft in the narrow zigzagging canals behind the palaces that were neighbors of the Ca' d'Argenti. Allegra became aware that they were not going in the direction of the small apartment near Santa Maria Zobenigo.

They came out onto the Grand Canal near one of its great curves and moved silently up to the water stairs of the Palazzo Mocenigo. Everything was dark and quiet. Only a few lanterns showed blurred halos of yellow light from atop water poles. Tita helped her onto the steps without speaking a word and ushered her through the great door, which whispered conspiratorially on its hinges. He lighted a small lamp, handing it to a second man, who led her up a wide central staircase.

"Follow me, ma'am, if you please. I am Fletcher, milord's man." Allegra was grateful for his easy smile. There was no hint of judgment in his voice.

It was difficult to see anything in the dim light. Frayed tapestries and gold-framed portraits gleamed out of the darkness and faded into dusk again as they passed. They came to a door ajar, with light within.

Fletcher rapped softly and then left Allegra at the door. A voice answered, "Come." Byron was sitting at a large table desk. A shaded lamp cast a small bright circle over his scattered papers. He rose, and his face broke into a melting smile that made Allegra's legs quiver into weakness. He came to her in a rush, drawing her into his arms, as she closed her eyes to enter into the refuge of his embrace.

Her cheek rested against the smooth velvet of his loose jacket. He raised her face gently while a rain of soft kisses moved over her eyes, her forehead, the tip of her nose, her chin—until his lips found hers, covering them in a lingering, searching kiss. She pressed close to his vital warmth.

"Allegra *mia*," he said in a rough whisper, "am I to understand that you are here because your decision has been taken in my favor?"

Her eyes shone up at him with complete love and trust. "I could do nothing else," her small voice replied.

A shadow of concern, and then joy, passed over his face, and with a deep sigh he drew her close again. He held her against himself tenderly, as if she were fragile and cherished. She felt the rapid, heavy beat of his heart against her. She never wanted to be separate from him . . . her home was in his arms.

He drew away a little. "*Cara*, I have brought you here so that you will not be frightened. I do not want to press you, much as I long to find fulfillment with your sweet self and body. I thought to let you see where I work and sleep, so that your heart will know I share my most intimate life with you."

He turned her toward the table, which was covered with a disarray of writing materials. "Here is where I scribble my verses far into the night. I can write best when the world sleeps." He picked up a paper. "See, I have started a verse for you. . . ."

> I found a sweet and gentle bird,
> A nun from convent walls released.
> Aquiver in my hand she stirred
> My heart until the pain had ceased. . . .

He broke off, smiling at her puzzled face. "You do not understand? Maybe it's just as well."

"No, no," she said quickly, "I understand the English. But what is 'aquiver'? What is it in Italian?" she said, trying to speak in his language.

He put back his head in an appreciative laugh. "What ramshackle English!" Then, seeing her confusion, he chuckled again and put out his hand to caress her cheek. His fingers moved to her lips and pressed lightly, exploringly. A shiver of delight ran over her. "*That*, little Allegra, is 'aquiver.' I feel it in you when I touch you, and it is in me also. You are like a little trembling bird, my love, so sweet and innocent of what joys are possible. Even with your child and your experience of marriage, you are an innocent." He looked seriously into her eyes. "Maybe I am wrong to teach you those things. Maybe you would be happier not to know and not to yearn."

He turned back to his papers on the desk, shuffling them into some order. "This is my latest poetizing, my *Don Juan*. . . . I call it Donny Johnny. What a tool it is in my hands! How jolly it is on the surface, and how filled with prods and scratches beneath. . . ." He barked a short laugh. "How else can I speak to the truth of things and probe at the damned cant of my countrymen!"

Her eyes were wide and questioning. Should she not have come? *Perhaps it is a bad time for him to see me,* she thought. He was restless, as if only a part of his mind knew that she was there.

His face changed again and he turned to sweep her into his arms. "Poor little one," he said against the dark curls at her forehead. "Poor little bird! Here you have come to give me your great gift, and I am talking of things that have no meaning for you. Forgive me, my sweet. I told you that I am not an easy man to understand." He bent to kiss her gently and then more urgently, while certainty flooded back into her breast.

"With you I have no will except to draw from you the nectar of your sweetness. May God forgive me." He held her face between his warm hands and looked intently at her. "Allegra, are you sure? I have the curse to often spoil the goodness that comes to me. I do not wish the role of scoundrel."

She looked up into his eyes. They were brilliant and fascinating to her. "I am sure," she said from the depths of her heart. He uttered a low sound and pulled her tightly against him once more. They stood for a long time locked together. His warmth penetrated her body, as she reveled in the force of energy that flowed between them. They were standing alone on the whirling world, wrapped in an indescribable delight, where nothing existed but this moment.

Suddenly, a great flash of light pierced through the shutters of the room from outside the windows, and a crash of thunder echoed over the canal waters.

"By God—a storm!" he cried out with a child's pleasure. He went to fling the shutters wide, just as another flashing bolt of silver struck into the canal. She ran to the open window beside him and laughed, as the thunder rolled over the rooftops. She wanted to shout her happiness into the crackling air. It was a gift from God to be with Byron, with the storm crashing all around—to be safely with her dearest Byron.

"So, you are like me. You love the wildness!" He cupped her face in his hand, and while thunder came again he kissed her until she was weak from desire for him. Laughing, he picked her up and carried her to the back of the big room, where a carved bed and several chairs made an island of furniture.

He laid her on the soft goose-down comforter and then swiftly undressed. His body was compact and graceful. His shoulders were wide and smoothly muscled. He was beautiful, as she knew he would be—so different from Barretto's gnarled coarseness.

She watched him as he came to her and smiled when his hands drew her dress from her. For a dim moment she marveled at his expertise—he must have undressed many willing women. The thought fled from her mind, as he gently ran his hands over her body. She shivered again.

"I will not hurt you, *cara* . . . trust me," he whispered. But nervous tremors started inside her, and memories of Barretto tightened her body. He seemed to understand. Insistently and lovingly he soothed her. His lips tenderly explored her secret sensitive places, and she bathed her starved senses in the most delicious urgency.

At last she thought no more. She was caught up in an indescribable sensation, and she clung to him, feeling herself merge into him. Light and joy exploded in her, and outside the departing thunder growled across the distant lagoon. She had never imagined that there could be such a feeling in her body, and her heart beat with overflowing love and gratitude.

"Thank you, my beloved, thank you," she whispered, as he raised his head from her breast and looked deeply into her glow ing face. Suddenly his eyes filled with tears. Deep sobs shook his body, and he held her to him again. She was smiling with love. He was hers now. Somehow she would find a way to ease the terrible pain in her heart.

"Oh, God . . . God . . ." he muttered to himself. She could feel the deep tension in him still, and then finally he was asleep.

She lay quiet, holding his head against her, and sent up a prayer of gratitude to Santa Chiara. Now she comprehended . . . she knew the wonder of Héloise as she loved Abelard, and the bittersweet passion of Giulietta. For the first time she truly believed in that strange thing called love. It was hers now, to keep and to savor.

Rain was falling lightly outside the open window, and she heard a discreet tapping on the door. Byron roused himself to the sound and answered. Fletcher's voice announced the hour, and a knot of apprehension clutched at her breast. It was nearly morning.

"Do not fear, little one, Tita will get you safely home." Byron turned to kiss her. Their lips were still warm from sleep, and passion began to stir again. "Time is damnable," he said, "Now I want you again, but I must wait the long hours until night. Were you happy with me, *cara*? Will you now remember only the joy?"

She nodded. "You have given me the sweetest moment of my life."

"But now we must come back to a harsher reality." He rolled easily from the bed and started to dress. He appeared not to see her as she reached for her own scattered garments and hastily fastened her bodice and stockings. With a laugh he handed her one of his hairbrushes and led her to a standing mirror.

"Delightfully disheveled," he whispered. "I like to see you this way . . . a natural creature. But, for the sake of propriety . . . ." He stroked her dark curls with his fingers, as if he were making love to her in his mind. "I want you," he said.

She made order out of herself and picked up her cape from where it had fallen hours earlier. He pulled it around her shoulders and showered her with swift teasing little kisses. Then he took her lips with a flood of passion. "That is a promise for tomorrow."

They walked slowly from the room and down the quiet hall with their arms entwined and their steps in unison. "I must show you something." He pushed open a door. It was a sparsely furnished room with a small bed, which was guarded by an enormous Newfoundland dog, who rose wagging and welcoming. A child was asleep in the bed. Her auburn curls and dimpled chin were a tiny copy of Byron's. "The other Allegra," he said in a whisper. "Now I have two."

Allegra looked at the sleep-flushed small face, and then at Byron. Love was in his face as he watched her. She thought of the solemn little Renaldo and felt the familiar regret that she had nothing in her heart for him. But perhaps that would change. What could keep her from loving every child in the world now that her heart had been opened wide? She caught her breath quickly.

Byron's urging hand drew her through the dark house and down the stairs. There were rugs on the floor, but not many pieces of furniture. He was obviously not intending to stay in the Palazzo Mocenigo forever.

Tita was waiting, and Byron lifted her into the gondola with a parting kiss. "Until tomorrow, my treasure."

She floated home as in a dream. Her whole being felt weightless. She put out her hand on the cushioned seat, reaching for Byron's touch. Her fingers curled in his absent clasp, responding to his love.

The silvery rain slanted down into the water, and some sea gulls rose up from a floating tidbit with strident cries. It didn't matter to Allegra what happened in the rainy world. Everything was different now. The patient, painful, dutiful little nun was gone. In her place was a woman who would not count the cost of love. She touched her lips with her finger. They would never be the same. He was right. All the taste of Barretto was gone.

Gina was waiting, dozing by the fire. One look into Allegra's bemused eyes told her everything. With a sound of concern she helped her out of her clothes and into bed.

"I am happy, Gina. I am so happy!" She pulled the bedclothes closely around herself and was quickly asleep.

Gina turned away and finished folding Allegra's wrinkled cloak. Her dark eyes were clouded. She looked at the calm face of Santa Chiara in the wall shrine. A candle flickered next to it.

"Why did you bring such a man to her?" she whispered. "Surely he will break her heart. It would have been better to refuse her prayer!" The saint gazed back serenely, and Gina crossed herself with an almost angry gesture. "I do not understand," she said with a sigh. She left the room, and Allegra slept, while the dawn brightened and the bells of Santa Maria della Salute sang their resonant song into the freshening morning.

CHAPTER EIGHT

AFTER THAT NIGHT Allegra lived for the sight of Byron. During the day she felt intoxicated by the sensations of the previous night. She tried not to appear changed and forced herself into her usual routines, but Aunt Adriana's face was puzzled by Allegra's vague replies to her chatty conversations.

In the nursery, Renaldo's dreary face could not easily be coaxed to smiles. Most often he retreated against his nursemaid and played halfheartedly with his toys. *If he were Byron's child, how would I feel,* she thought painfully. But Barretto's face looked at her under the childish softness.

Memories of the dark-haired little girl in the Palazzo Mocenigo bothered her. What did that small being feel, tossed from parent to parent and now living such a strange life?

ELLETRA INVITED her to luncheon at Florian's. She was tempted almost beyond control to tell her everything. The red velvet-lined booths were ideal nooks for confidences, but fear restrained her. The fewer people who knew, the better.

She was tuned to the highest pitch of physical sensitivity. Ripples of delicious sensation flowed through her body whenever she thought of Byron, and a smile curved her lips.

Elletra teased her, "You look so glowing that if I didn't know better, I would say you had a lover." Allegra couldn't answer the statement but looked away from Elletra's clever eyes.

In her times of rest before the dinner hour she began to spin imaginary stories. Barretto would die—a natural death, of course—leaving her mistress of the Ca' d'Argenti. Byron would at last divorce his wife, and they would marry. She would heal his tortured heart. He would become even more famous as a writer. Together they would be patrons of many wonderful causes. The dreams spun off in all directions . . . they would travel to Greece and walk under the ancient olive groves and watch the sun set from the Acropolis. He would hold her and kiss her while the golden light spread all around them. And he would present her to others as his greatest love.

With one part of her mind she knew the dreams were just so much fantasy, but she did expect that their love would have some arrangement of permanence. She toyed with hopes that danced provocatively just out of reach. How could she know what Byron wanted or what he would do?

SHE COULD HARDLY WAIT for the midnight bells of the campanile, and the sight of the gondola waiting by the side canal. Most often they went to his hideaway rooms near Santa Maria Zobenigo. For the first few nights their lovemaking was so intense that not much communication on other levels took place.

He was to her the perfect lover, gentle and passionate. He brought her to heights of bliss that left her floating in time-lessness. When Dante described the levels of heaven he should have described this one, she thought, but it was beyond words; it was almost beyond bearing.

Afterward, while Byron slept, she raised herself on one elbow to look at his handsome face, aching with love and offering her whole being to his happiness. Sometimes he awoke to find her gaze on him, and he teased her about her earnest eyes.

"Do not hang over me, *cara*," he laughed. "It is like awakening to find the round moon shining through the window onto my face."

At other times, when their lovemaking had reached its climax, he turned from her, as he had done that first time, with tears running against the pillow, which he pressed to his face. Then, as if to compensate, he would become gay and teasing.

She was alert to the flow of deep tension that existed beneath his outer actions. Forces that she could not fathom pushed at him, and this was distressing, because he needed her understanding. Hadn't he told her, at first, that she alone could ease and heal him? She did not quite know how to begin a conversation about that, to remind him that she was prepared to help him.

On the fourth night Tita took her to the Palazzo Mocenigo, but only to pick up a waiting Byron, who stood in the shadows wrapped in a dark cape. He limped quickly down the water steps and jumped into the gondola, sweeping her into his arms. The boat surged along the Grand Canal and then took a shortcut through small canals toward the Lagoon.

Byron leaned to kiss her ear. "Look at the moon, *cara*. I could not stay in on a night like this."

Allegra looked out at the bright silver shine on the water, and then upward at the round white coin of the moon. Byron drew her closer. His beautiful profile was edged with moonlight. A smile was on his lips. How deeply she wanted him to be happy!

With a quick turn, Tita moved his boat out into the open waters of the Lagoon. Several ships were anchored there, their masts and folded sails dark against a deep indigo sky. The stars were drowned in the moonshine, and a path of glittering silver stretched toward the long flat outline of the Lido.

"We are going to picnic on the Lido," Byron laughed. "And you are going to meet some of my best friends. Do not fear, *cara mia,* they cannot speak—they are my horses."

Tita poled them swiftly toward the distant low expanse of land, beyond the island of San Giorgio with its domed church. It was like riding on the strong back of some great black swan. Allegra shyly voiced her simile, and Byron looked at her moon-flecked eyes with a tender smile.

"So, you are a poet also, my Allegra. Maybe I shall be outdone by my gentle lady. What more have you locked up in that lovely head, tell me?" He leaned closer as if expecting her to say more, but she could think of nothing but the line of his lips and the play of light on his face. She put up a trembling hand to caress his hair, and he caught it and kissed its palm with lingering pleasure.

"It is a moon for true love, a magic world," she ventured.

He was quiet and then said in an odd voice, "Magic it is, my lovely, but can you tell me what is true love?" His words had a hard edge. He settled back into his seat as if he expected no answer. For Allegra a cold bit of ice had grown suddenly around her heart, yet his warm hand held hers securely. It would not be wise to try to define true love to him, she realized.

She watched the moon's glitter racing along the tops of small waves, a flash of brilliance that lost itself in the dark almost immediately. Was love like this? Was love a brief shine of magic on a dark moving sea, absorbed into its depths without a trace? The glow of utter joy, which had enclosed her since she had met him, retreated into a more real world.

"Do not look so sad, *cara mia*, I think the moon is too big, and all this splash and gleam is almost too much for the heart to hold. Let me kiss you. That is reality." She sank into the amazing comfort of his touch. He was the master of delight, who could play upon her body and spirit and caress her into an aching yearning.

They were gliding past the small island of San Lazzaro. He smiled indulgently into her bemused eyes. "I study there with the Armenian fathers from time to time. I am learning their confounded, complicated, brilliant language. What a place of peace it is in that monastery! Even old Boney didn't have the heart to confiscate their property, as he did all the other religious establishments . . . or maybe it was because their alphabet is a regular Waterloo, and he feared defeat!"

He sighed and turned his head as Tita poled near to the dock, and they could see the outlines of the buildings of San Lazzaro. "These Armenian monks are fine fellows. Sometimes when I sit and talk of religion with them, I think that I would be better off taking vows and retreating from the world. How good it would be to spend my days cultivating the fruit trees and roses, following a routine of work and prayer!"

The delicious scent of spring flowers hung on the air near the island. It was green with trees and frosted with the silver of olive leaves. Stone balustrades edged its sea stairs. Pots of bright flowers bloomed along its walls, and a sound of bells floated on the night air. "That is where I should go," he said. "If I lived there I should do honest work and should live longer . . . because, little Allegra, I have a premonition that if I do not, I shall die young."

Allegra had been watching his moon-shadowed face. She desperately wanted to say words of comfort to him, but she feared sounding naive. She wanted to say something that was steady and wise, but all she could feel was an aching love for him. "I think it will not matter whether you die young or old . . . the beauty you have to give will make its mark. It can never be erased, and it is good—I know it is good!"

He turned fully toward her, his listening face still in shadow. He lifted her hand to his lips, and his voice was a shaken whisper. "Allegra . . . Allegra! How can I live up to your picture of me? I am not a good man. I am wise only when I want to be, and the devil in me too often counsels foolishness. Yes, I am a fool, for who can be a greater fool than to do what he ought not. . . ."

"I don't think you are as bad as you would have me believe," she answered softly.

He chuckled. "So, you think that you have found me out. There is much you do not know, little one. Thank God you do not have the blood of the Byrons to contend with." He leaned closer. "Do you think you can manage me, little nun—because I need managing." Sighing, he said, "I weary of the pursuit. I need a woman to hold me close, to laugh with me when I am a fool, to comfort me when life hurts and to complete me so that I will be at peace."

He drew back from her and flung his head against the scarlet cushions. "Good God, this moonlight makes me burn with some inner fire along my nerves! How do I get free of this web of being? My head is bursting from too much power . . . the moon is pouring it out and I cannot contain it!" He dropped from the low seat to his knees, laying his head into her lap. "Put your sweet hand on my hot head. It will cool the pain."

Shaking from the force of his outburst, she put her hands on his thick curls. "Christ!" he groaned, "your touch is a blessing." Her love flowed to him through her hands.

Tita brought them to a small landing at the midpoint of the long dark line of the Lido, that island of sand, grass and scrub growth. Allegra could make out a few simple houses and buildings nearby.

Byron jumped from the boat and pulled her to her feet, lifting her out onto the quay. "You have cured me, my angel! Tita, we will return in a while." The silent giant nodded, already wrapping his cloak around himself to curl to sleep in the black cradle of his gondola.

"Come!" Byron's voice was charged with energy, as he took her hand and guided her along a path in the tall grass. They moved past the silent houses and toward a larger building. A muscular brown watchdog rumbled a growl and then dissolved into happy wagging. "This is old Piero." Byron ruffled the bronze coat and rubbed the flapping ears. Allegra received a sniff of approval and a wet kiss.

Piero escorted them in the direction of the building. It was thick-walled and whitewashed. An unmistakable breath of warm horse odor wafted from its partly open door.

Byron drew her inside and reached for a lantern to light it. There were six horse stalls along one wall, with stacks of hay piled in the corners. The inquiring heads of four horses turned to them and whinnied as Byron approached. He introduced each to Allegra by name in a formal manner. She had not been near horses since her convent days, but she patted the great warm heads and tried to respond in the spirit of the introductions. She repeated each name and executed a little bow.

Byron laughed delightedly, and she joined him. She was trying to be the woman he needed—the one who could laugh with him. Together they fed the expectant faces with carrots from his pockets. He had brought a sweet tidbit for Piero, too.

It was cozy in the stable, and Allegra's tension relaxed its uncomfortable hold on her. Byron enfolded her in a tight embrace, which quickly flared into warm passion.

"You're a devil of a temptation, Allegra." He picked her up and carried her to a pile of soft fragrant hay. With a laugh he was beside her, pulling her into his arms.

His lovemaking filled her with eager hunger, and she followed her urgency. All thought left her but the overpowering joy of his body joined to hers. She floated in a moment of eternity with him.

When they had spent their last bit of ecstasy she drifted slowly back to awareness. He was looking at her, and his eyes were smiling. "What a situation for a *contessa*," he chuckled. She laughed with him, proud of the soft light sound of her voice. She was determined to give him laughter if that was his need. She traced the full curve of his fine lips with a delicate fingertip while he kissed it.

"Your cheeks are all pink like peonies—what a lovely woman you are!" He smiled while her blush deepened. Such a rush of feeling moved in her heart that it poured out into tears. He leaned to kiss her. "Have I healed you, my love?" His eyes were serious. "I think I find no more bad memories. Your body is no longer afraid and gives you pleasure, is this not so?"

"So much . . . ." Her voice broke a little with its weight of love.

"I am glad." He leaped to his feet holding out his hand to draw her up. They happily brushed hay from themselves and adjusted their clothes. The horses nudged their hands in farewell, while Byron blew out the old lantern to return it to its hook. Piero escorted them back down the path.

Tita was there, waiting like a huge shadow and holding a parcel in his hands. Byron collected the covered basket from him and led Allegra down another path into the scrub grasses. They came to a little hollow place where wild roses were growing in a tangled circle along its edges, looking like white star clusters in the bright moonlight. Byron knelt down and opened the basket.

A flask of wine and two glasses appeared, and then a box of English soda biscuits—his favorites. There was a lacy napkin full of sugared almonds and a folded paper of wedges of cheese.

"Our picnic," he said in a mock theatrical voice. "You cannot accuse me of being a boring lover." He spread his hands to indicate his offering.

She sat down in the hollow. The deep grass shut out everything but the sky above them. The moonlight was a palpable thing. She felt that she should be able to gather up handfuls of it.

"Here, *cara*." He handed her a glass and poured the wine. "What shall we have . . . one part moon silver and two parts of wine?" He lifted his glass to hers. "To life—such as it is," he said, draining his wine. Allegra sipped at hers.

He fed her with bites of cheese and pieces of biscuit and rewarded her with a pink-covered almond. Then he reached over and plucked an open white rose and a bud. His hand lifted her chin while he laid the rose petals against her lips, and his warm mouth pressed the cool sweetness of the rose against hers in a delicious, perfumed kiss.

Afterward, while his hands still cradled her face and the rose petals had dropped into her lap, he said, "What a brave child you are . . . you are not afraid of love, even after all of your suffering. Women amaze me. They are born for joy and are given pain as a consequence. . . ."

With a swift peck of a kiss he drew away and gathered up the remains of their picnic into the basket. His mind had gone to other things, she could tell. Allegra put the rose petals and the bud carefully into her bosom, hiding them under the lace ruffles of her gown. Perhaps he would laugh at her for saving them, perhaps not, but she hid them anyway.

The moon was moving low in the sky as they walked back toward the gondola. Deep black shadows spread out from buildings and trees. White mist was drifting in patches over the Lagoon, and the moonshine had lost its glitter. A light brisk breeze bent the grass and blew ripples against the quay.

Tita lifted her into the boat, and Byron settled himself beside her, still silent in his thoughts. The water was rougher on the return. Sea currents ran with the breeze, and Tita had to swing his full weight against the oar. Pockets of mist blew around them in dense wet clouds, leaving drops of moisture on their hair and cloaks.

Byron drew out a large linen handkerchief from an inner pocket. "Here, *cara*. Tie this over your curls. I think I must help Tita." He jumped up onto the rowing platform. They shared the stroke of the oar, relieving each other. She put his handkerchief into her bosom with the roses and pulled her cloak around her head. She would not return it to him. It would be her treasure.

She watched him with Tita. He seemed exhilarated by the weather, and he held up his face into the misty wind, smiling. His melancholy had left him, and he looked young and full of life.

A dim light was edging the horizon when they moved past the quays of San Marco. Tita swung the boat into a side canal to avoid the swift water flowing in white-capped wavelets down the Grand Canal. The buildings offered protection, and soon they were at the water steps beside the Ca' d'Argenti. Byron lifted her lightly onto the landing, kissing her. "Hurry, *cara*," he whispered, "the dawn is running fast to catch us. Until to-night . . . ."

SHE RAN TOWARD THE DOOR and up the back stairs to her rooms. Gina turned from the window. "Thank God, *madonna*, you are here!" Allegra saw the tired face, and her heart was suddenly guilty. Gina was drawing off the wet cloak. "Where have you been? You are wet, and here is straw on your skirt. I pray no one else was wakeful."

"I have been to the Lido, Gina. The moon was so bright, and we had a picnic in the grass, among the white roses. The straw is from his stable, where he keeps his riding horses. Coming back the wind blew up, and the mist. It took us longer to return."

Gina grunted with dissatisfaction at the accounting. She stripped Allegra's clothes away and bathed her in warm water from a pitcher. "Your hair," she said severely, "it smells of the horses." She pulled Allegra's head down toward the basin and washed vigorously, then toweled it almost dry. "That is better. I will wash these clothes myself, so that there will be no notice of the odor among the servants."

She hurried Allegra into bed and then relented of her anger. "The Lido, I suppose it was beautiful in all that moonlight—but wasn't it a foolish thing to go there, my lady? Suppose something had happened, or that you had been seen?"

"But it was so lovely. Oh, Gina, you understand, every moment with him is precious." Suddenly she sat up. "Where is the rose, and the handkerchief?"

"Here, by your bed." Gina's face was smiling, but pity lay

underneath. "My lady, you are like a young girl. You must calm yourself. You must remember that milord is not all of your life, only a part of it. You have found love, and I am glad for it. You deserve your joy, but you must be careful . . . you must not be rash. If I have seen you coming and going, others may have also."

Allegra lay back on the pillows. "Gina, nothing seems quite real. I am so happy . . . but I can still feel pain inside me. My life is all turned aound, and I don't seem to care." She caught Gina's disapproving eyes. "Yes, I know. I promise. You are right, I must think and act wisely . . . but now I must sleep, and so must you."

Gina nodded and left the room with the bundle of clothes. Excitement and weariness fought in Allegra's mind and body. She reached out for his handkerchief and snuggled it under her cheek. Her mind began to relive the night, and she fell asleep hearing the deep vibrant tones of his voice and remembering the rose petals on her lips as he kissed her.

CHAPTER NINE

SHE WOKE AT NOON and spent time at her desk, remembering and writing in her diary. She carefully pressed the rosebud into the pages. The handkerchief was hidden inside her bodice next to her heart. Without conscious thought she raised her hand to feel it there. Gina said little, but her eyes were charged with watchfulness.

Zeno's small figure was again moving about the Ca'. He had recovered from his illness enough to resume his duties. Gina was determined to keep track of him. His sudden appearance in a room set Allegra's nerves on edge. She would have to be more careful. She didn't trust herself to appear innocent. . . . In spite of her worry, there were moments when she wanted to run through the vast corridors calling out her love for Byron.

Adriana and Gemma came for tea, chattering and full of inconsequential thoughts. The subject of a grand ball came up again.

"How can any man approach father for one of us, unless he has become interested first?" Gemma said dolefully. "We must be seen in a setting that is suitable for us. Now that father is better off financially, he does not think about us—he is always making investments and drinking with his broken-down old friends—" She broke off with a guilty gasp. "I didn't mean Barretto . . . he is very attractive. I love those strong, hard men." She gave a shiver of appreciation. "And he has such fine manners."

"I will talk to father," Allegra said.

Adriana was eager to talk about fashions and the latest gossip. Allegra's mind flowed away into expectation of the coming night, until Byron's name drew her sharp attention. What had they said?

Gemma answered the unspoken question. "Father's gondolier says that Milord Byron has cleared all the low women out of the Mocenigo, because he is putting his attention on ladies of a higher class. . . ." The words tumbled out. "Did you know that he was

pursuing Bianca Massini's best friend, Angelina, until he fell int
the canal climbing up to her balcony?" There was quick gigglir
as she went on, "Bianca says Angelina wanted him to divorce h
wife and marry her, but he refused. She's miserable, poor thing
and her father is furious."

"Angelina deserves what she gets if she is foolish enough to g
caught in such a net," Adriana said.

"Not only that," Gemma continued, "he refuses to be
cavaliere servente for anyone. Cousin Elletra says he is the mo
exciting man to come to Venice since Paganini. Now if you coul
get your Barretto to consent to a ball, Allegra, we could invi
him and see for ourselves what the gossip is all about."

The conversation reverted to Paris fashions, and Allegra s
with her heart beating uncomfortably. Was it true? She had trie
not to pay attention to the stories that came her way. Surely I
was not such a philanderer. In her mind she saw his cle
eyes—they were honest eyes. She could not be so mistaken abo
his character. Hadn't he confessed to her that he had been sel
indulgent?

"Mischief feeds on self-pity," he had said to her. "I need
woman to hold me steady—but until someone does, I will get int
scrapes." His tales of escapades only caused a deeper love an
compassion to rise in her, which he sensed.

"Don't pity me," he said sharply. "If there is one thing I ha
it is pity—unless I do it myself. Why aren't you like my wife, wh
would read me a moral lecture, or like Augusta, who would sa
'Oh dear, oh dear . . . poor naughty B.!' and never do anythir
more?"

But there were so many soft spots of kindness in him, which I
attempted to cover by eccentric behavior. He had already give
her money to help with the Redentore. He didn't want his nam
attached to the gift and made light of her caring for homele
children. "Victims of the war between man and woman," he ha
said with an edge of sarcasm.

THAT NIGHT, at their secret place near Santa Maria Zobenigo, I
gave her a small, finely-worked wooden box with a gold and crin

son design embossed on its leather lid . . . the Byron family crest.
Inside she found a folded piece of paper resting on the velvet lin-
ing.

He had written another poem for her. As she tried to read it she
felt uneasy because she could not be sure of its meaning. It spoke
of weeping and joy and goodbyes. But he had written it for *her*,
and so she accepted it with love.

"Crede Byron," she read quietly, as her finger traced the lines
of the motto beneath the crest.

"Trust Byron." His voice was heavy. "How to trust Byron,
when he cannot trust himself?"

She examined the handsome shield with its mythical horses
rampant and said firmly, "Crede Byron . . . *I* trust Byron . . . I
believe in Byron."

To her distress he turned on her, his eyes looking at her from
beneath lowered brows. "My God, Allegra! Where have you been
all of your life? You trust too much, you little fool!"

Color flew into her startled face. Again his expression changed,
and he quickly wrapped her in his arms. "God forgive me, what
am I doing to you? You were made to be loved and protected . . .
and no one will do it for you. Poor sweet Allegra!"

Then they made love. When body spoke to body there were no
words to shatter the understanding between them. Afterward he
held her close to him.

"I am so happy," she whispered, her face against his warm
shoulder.

"Hmm." She felt him kiss her hair.

Unbidden, the conversation with Gemma pricked at her. Her
anxiety not to lose him drove her to test his commitment. "Barretto will be home soon. We will have to work something out,
because I will not be as free as now. Barretto may be more
reasonable toward me . . . he might even accept a *cavaliére
servente*. . . ." Her voice trailed away.

The arms that had held her pushed her away, and he sat up
abruptly from their soft nest on the couch. His lips tightened in a
mirthless smile. "I fancy old di Rienzi would not be a pleasant

wearer of the horns." He tapped a chiding fingertip on the end of her nose. "I have no desire to find a dagger in my ribs."

He rose and began to dress, humming a carnival tune under his breath. Tears stung in her eyes, but she was learning a hard wisdom. She must be silent about her hopes. He must make the decisions.

She turned her face to the wall next to her, which was covered in a velvet paper. A piece of it had separated from a seam and was loose. On impulse she tore a small bit away and put it next to the box with the Byron crest, then dressed in silence, fearing what mood he might be in.

When she looked up, he was smiling and pouring two small glasses of wine. "A toast," he said with solemnity, "to the di Rienzi horns!" He drained his glass and threw back his head in a boyish laugh. She watched him, not drinking. Was this her answer? She could not ask. His quicksilver temperament defied understanding.

"It is late, my dear." He picked up her cloak and saw the scrap of wallpaper. "What the devil is this? Are you about to tear down my little *casa*?"

She felt foolish. "A keepsake," she said to his teasing smile.

"So, you wish to remember our place of love. What a sentimental child you are. So am I." His eyes had become tender. He took the fragment to his writing table and picked up a sheet of writing paper.

"Come." He drew her to him and handed her a pen. "You must inscribe it." His arm was around her, and he was lightly kissing the curls by her ear.

She wrote quickly, the trembling of her hand causing a drop of ink to slide onto the paper: "From the place of my joy."

As she replaced the pen he drew her close. "I am glad it is a place of joy for you, my love," he murmured. "I would want you to remember only joy with me." His kiss was reassuring in its tenderness.

He folded the paper around the torn scrap and placed it into the box with the poem. "Never lose the box, Allegra. It bears the Byron crest, and part of me will always be in it."

THE CA' WAS SILENT when she returned, but she sensed Zeno's presence and took extra care to reach her rooms without making a sound. She had been holding the little box closely in her hands, and now she placed it on her bed, lifting the lid. She opened the new poem again and puzzled over the words:

> Close in the shadows of whispered goodbyes
> Are yesterdays filled with my tears and my sighs,
> And kisses remembered, when I am with you;
> Are you she or another! Would my heart knew.
> Joy is thy name—the taste I would keep,
> But bitter fruit lingers and still I must weep.

Why did he write of love and bitterness together, as if he could not separate them—and what did he mean, "Are you she or another"? By now there should be no confusion in his mind about her. The words lodged in her thoughts, repeating themselves. If her English were more fluent, she would understand. Perhaps it was just his poetic way of writing. . . .

She put the pressed rosebud and the handkerchief inside the box next to the poem. She had told Gina not to stay up for her, but now she missed that quiet, sympathetic presence.

Somehow she had dreamed that once love came, everything would be clear and comforting—without problems, filled with happiness. She loved Byron so much, but she shared such a little part of his real being.

As she prayed before the pure and gentle eyes of Santa Chiara, which gazed out of the small shrine, she felt pangs of embarrassment, meeting those eyes after her hours of intimate love with Byron. "Why did you send him to me if I should not love him?" she whispered and then rose wearily from her knees. She slept that night with the Byron box tucked under the edge of her pillow.

GINA ENCOURAGED HER to return to her work at the Redentore. She was determined that Allegra should keep touch with the realities of life and not lose herself so totally in Byron's strange world.

The influenza was almost gone from Venice, and there was no reason for Allegra to cut herself off from the one activity that seemed to nourish her. Gina had grave doubts about the future of the obsessive passion. She was prepared to face the *conte* herself, if he objected to Allegra's working again.

Allegra agreed to the proposal. "I have run out of things to talk with Adriana about," she smiled. "She is certain that I have something wrong with me. Now she will have to hear about my Latin students, poor thing."

She lost no time in walking to the Redentore, stopping at the church of Santa Maria Zobenigo on the way, to light a candle and to pray for Byron. The church was so close to their hidden room that maybe the power of her prayers would reach him.

It was good to have the times of distraction from her constant thoughts of him. Signora Nicolo was away from the orphanage, traveling to Vienna with some of her girls who were making a concert tour, and Allegra was relieved not to have to stand scrutiny under those penetrating, understanding eyes.

She tried not to admit to herself that something was wrong with the perfect love she shared with Byron, but when she was with him she sensed something that she couldn't put into words. One day she fell asleep on her knees in the cold little church of the Zobenigo, on the way home from the Redentore. Gina found her and walked with her back to the Ca'. She wept then, in a kind of deep futility, and Gina's eyes were shadowed with worry.

IT HAD BEEN NINE NIGHTS since their first time of lovemaking. They had always met at midnight or later. Allegra knew that he usually went to social events earlier to which she could not come. On the tenth night she met him as usual, and he was in one of his strange moods. Dressed in a formal way, he had obviously been a guest at some *conversazione*. The pungent fragrance of women's perfume and fine snuff clung to his clothes.

"You are a fool to love me," he said teasingly, but his eyes were more serious. She did not know how to answer him. The confusion and love on her face made him relent. "Do you know that your eyes conceal nothing of your thoughts?" He swept her against him with a rain of kisses, until she smiled again. "What a child you are, *cara*, so easy to be kissed to happiness."

He tossed extra cushions onto the couch to make it more comfortable, and they relaxed in front of the warm grate of glowing coals, her head against his shoulder. Their kisses were gentle and sweet without the urgency of passion. She told herself that men of genius were never easy. If life with him was going to be part heaven and part hell, she would accept it, because heaven was worth it.

He was tender and lightly teasing. There was another gift for her—a dainty gold filigree necklace, studded with pink coral beads, with a tiny gold locket suspended from it.

"I saw it as I rushed by a shop on my way to an appointment with the British Consul, and it caught my eye. I went back and woke up the proprietor from his late afternoon nap and bought it. It reminded me of you, sweet Allegra."

So—he thought of her as he moved about on the business of his life that she could not share! She occupied more than a few brief hours of his life, then. She looked up at his tumbling auburn curls and wanted a strand for the locket.

At first he laughed and refused. "Why is it that women always want locks of hair? In London, when I was the new literary rage, the women who begged me for it would have left me bald ten times over." With a rueful smile he let her cut a small curl and fit it into the locket.

"Now I have something of you to keep close." She kissed him happily, but he would not let her go for a long silent moment. She felt a tremor in his body and smiled at his display of emotion.

They did not make love as they sat before the fire. Her hand pressed her new treasure against her breast, and she nestled against him in quiet joy. When he finally spoke she was surprised to find that his thoughts were far away from their love.

"I am not an old man yet . . . I cannot scribble poetry forever. Maybe I should go back to England and take my stand in the political scene. The world is changing, Allegra; the poor need their champions as new inventions disrupt the old ways of life."

He kissed her ear absently. "Maybe I should go to the United States. Think of the opportunities in that new land!"

She listened, not making the mistake of suggesting that she go with him. That would come, in its good time.

It was growing late again, and he roused himself from his silent musing. "It's near morning, my sweetheart. I will always remember these nights." He kissed her as he had on their first night together, his lips moving sweetly over her face until they found their perfect mates and joined in a gentle, deep and long kiss. She saw tears gleam in his eyes.

"You were made to love and comfort a man, Allegra . . . and you have brought me such goodness. I doubted that it really existed. That goodness will always heal and protect you. Pray for me . . . I will forever need your prayers."

He went with her to the waiting gondola and kissed her once more, as he lifted her into the velvet cushioned seat. "*Addio,* little Allegra," he whispered and turned away with a wave of his hand.

Her heart was content as she moved through the serene night. The soft surging of the boat, the lapping sound of water on stone, the scrabbling scuttle of the crabs that lived under the edges of stone foundations . . . all were sounds of happiness. She loved everything—her beautiful city and all its sleeping people. When the bells of Santa Maria della Salute rang the hour she prayed for all, and for her beloved.

CHAPTER TEN

SHE SLEPT LATE into the day. Gina roused her with word that Luciano was waiting downstairs with a message from Barretto. She dressed quickly and saw him in the library. Her mind was filled to overflowing with the presence of Byron, and she had no apprehension about seeing Luciano. Love enclosed her like a castle with high walls, past which no other man could intrude.

She saw that Luciano had grown more assured, more prosperous looking, if that were possible, since their earlier encounter. His dark brown clothes were beautifully cut, his gestures those of a man of quality. He paid her just the right deference with a shade of male admiration. She could not fault his manners; they were impeccable, but she still mistrusted him. She thought of Byron, who also favored dark elegant colors of dress, and she sighed unconsciously.

His sharp attention missed nothing. He straightened from his bow over her hand. "You sigh, my lady. It is too long a time for Conte Barretto to leave you in this quiet place. But I come with good news . . . he will return within a week. His business has gone well. The vineyards thrive along the Loire and in the Veneto."

Allegra mustered a smile as Luciano continued to speak. "He is eager to see the small Renaldo, and I am to take back news of the child when I join him in Milano, two days from now. Of course I shall tell him that the mother gives the most loving care to the boy."

"We can go to see Renaldo now, if you wish," she said, wanting to move out of the situation of being alone with him. His eyes made her nervous, as if they saw too much into her. Beneath his smooth words was something else.

They walked upstairs to the nursery, and she stood aside while Luciano played with Renaldo. She was puzzled by the change that came over him when he picked up the infant from his silver cradle. He brought a smile to the tiny face with his dangling watch fob, and like a fond uncle he made faces and played with the child.

Allegra found it difficult to observe her baby, who was usually so withdrawn and unresponsive. How could other people find him lovable? Was it possible for a woman to be so repulsed by the energy of a man that she would always feel that same energy in the child . . . as if it had been directly transmitted into the womb? Barretto's iron-gray eyes looked at her from the baby face, and she shivered in the grip of her unmotherly feelings.

"You are good with children," she said to Luciano, envying him in that moment, "and you have helped at the Redentore. I saw you there."

He gave a strained smile that covered his surprise at her words. "Yes, I like children. They should at least have a time of happiness before they learn what harsh disappointments life has waiting for them." He ruffled the dark brown wisps of Renaldo's baby hair. "You might say I go to the Redentore because I have an affinity for bastards, since I am one myself." His voice was dryly ironic. "Now, this young Signor Renaldo . . . he appears to be in most fortunate circumstances, but even his inheritance and his title and his protective parents cannot stand between him and what unhappiness will come to him in life—" He broke off. "Forgive me, *madonna,* I should not give my cynical views to you. We will believe that Renaldo will grow up with his father's strength and the sweetness of his mother."

He set the child down among his toys and was rewarded by loud howls of protest, hushed by the nursemaid. "I can see he is healthy and full of life. His father will be glad."

She walked in silence from the nursery with Luciano beside her. Who was this man—surely not just the brash, newly fashionable person who stalked women for his amusement? He knew pain and could be touched in his heart.

She was reluctantly grateful to him. He had helped to untie a bit of the knot in her breast, which separated her from her child. She was ashamed of her own blindness—all this time praying eagerly for love for herself, while she was unwilling to give love to her baby or forgiveness to his father. She could not blame

Renaldo for having eyes like Barretto . . . they were not Barretto's eyes, but his own. The guilt that had been kept at bay was restless to be cleansed, and she was surprised by its intensity.

Luciano's words broke through her thoughts. "You seem so sad, *madonna*. Yet when I saw you first today, I thought that you were like a glowing damask rose, which had begun to open to the sun."

Allegra instinctively pulled back from him. There was too much warmth in his voice. He reached to take her hand and held it in a firm clasp. "I have always found that virtuous women suffer greatly in life. Perhaps they deserve to. After all, what is a virtuous woman, really?" His eyes battered at her as if seeking an entry though her protective wall. "Are you suffering, *madonna*? Shall I say this to your husband, or shall I say that all is well at his house?"

His kiss lingered on her hand, leaving her with a light sting of fear. "*Addio, contessa*. I trust that all *is* well, hmm?"

She watched him as he strode toward the entrance doors. What was he hinting at . . . or was he just probing in order to disturb her? A strange and unnerving man. Thank God he was gone, she breathed to herself, and settled her tension by conjuring up visions of Byron in her arms.

AT MIDNIGHT she slipped down the servants' staircase like a small hurried ghost, but no gondola slid out of the darkness to meet her. She strained to see into the deserted small canal as her heart began to panic.

Quiet footfalls came toward her along the narrow walkway that skirted the back of the Ca'. She shrank into the shadows and then saw that it was only Byron's manservant, Fletcher. She smiled in relief at his familiar figure.

He came to her with an awkward bow and put an envelope into her hand. "Milord says that he is unable to meet you, my lady. He has had visitors . . . unexpected . . . from England." He turned and walked away, leaving her openmouthed with disbelief. Then, trembling with a sudden awful foreboding, she went quickly back into the Ca'.

She ran up the stairs and along the hall to her rooms where she tore open the envelope. In the flickering firelight she read:

Cara Mia,

How can I say what must be said and not cause pain? I have discovered that the swift sharp knife is often the most healing. You know what I am and what I have been, and my heart, I regret, was a hard pillow for your gentle head.

I would be honest with you, sweet Allegra. It was your great resemblance to that other one so dear to me that drew me, but there is terrible danger in love for such a reason.

I must tell you truthfully that I have found love with one who has no resemblance to any other in my crowded mind. She is like a blooming tree whose generous fruit will heal my sores of pain.

Forgive me, Allegra, with all your sweet soul, and go back to your rightful life as though I had not been. Life would be most cruel to you should the world know of our time together.

Pray for the peace of one whose soul battles the powers of darkness. Your heart will mend, my dear. Hearts have infinite capacity for such renewal.

Addio, Byron

She sat for a long time staring at the paper in her hands. She was like stone. She sensed Gina's presence nearby speaking her name, and the letter slipped from her fingers to the floor. Gina knew what it said even before she picked it up and read its scrawled lines.

A deep moan of pity escaped from her lips, as she put her arms around Allegra. There was no response in the rigid body. She began to speak soothingly, urging her to move. "Come, *cara*, how cold your hands are . . . let me help you to bed. You must sleep . . . then things will be more understandable." Gina blamed herself. Tears of self-recrimination and alarm flowed down her face.

In Allegra's mind there were no thoughts, no words. Her eyes were open but blind to sight. She allowed herself to be undressed. Numbly she drank the laudanum Gina proffered and finally, with Gina watching by the bed, she slept.

WHEN GINA KNOCKED and entered the next morning Allegra was already dressed and seated at her writing desk. Her eyes were bright and swollen with weeping. "I made a terrible mistake. It is all my fault . . . I demanded too much of him." Byron's letter lay beside a clean sheet on the desk. Allegra held her pen poised to write. "I shall just explain it to him, then he will understand. . . ."

"*Madonna,* I do not think it wise," Gina cautioned.

"But we are lovers. You don't just stop being lovers. He couldn't . . . he told me things . . . he can't have forgotten everything." Her voice was not normal, the tone like a little girl's.

"Please, *cara,* men are different from women. Let him go. . . ."

"How can I? That is like telling the sun to leave the earth. We belong together. Promise me you will get this letter delivered to his hands, Gina, promise me."

Her expression drew a reluctant answer from Gina's lips. "*Si, madonna,* I promise." She stood nearby as the pen moved erratically over the page. The words were pleading ones that made Gina angry, but Allegra paid no attention to anything but the compulsion to write them.

. . . I did not mean to ask you to change your life, only let me be near you. I will not bother you, only be there when you want me. I love you and I know I can give you comfort, because you said so. Surely you have not suddenly stopped all feeling for me. . . .

Toward the end the words were as angry as she could muster:

What can that woman do for you that I cannot? I would give up anything for you. Will she do the same? Oh, my Byron, give me a chance to show you my love. It has been such a short time and I was afraid. I will do anything you want. . . .

Gina silently took the envelope from her when it was sealed and left the room. She debated destroying it. Why should such a fine lady bare her wounds to a man like this English milord?

She walked quickly to the Palazzo Mocenigo and gave the letter into the hands of the servant at the door. Her distaste was visible, and the servant did not engage her in even a passing conversation. "Give this to your master," she said and turned away.

By nightfall there had been no response from the Mocenigo. Allegra paced the perimeter of her rooms a hundred times, waiting, fully expecting an answer from him. Gina couldn't bear to watch her and cursed the soul of the Englishman. Laudanum was necessary again that evening as midnight approached.

Allegra feigned sleep so that Gina would leave her. Then she threw a cape around her shoulders and thrust her feet into satin slippers. She wanted to believe that he had not sent an answering message because he planned to send Tita that night with the gondola and bring her to him. She moved through the dark hallways on the familiar path to joy, but at the side door she was stopped. Gina stood blocking the exit.

"He is not out there, *madonna*. Nothing is there. You must go back to bed," she said quietly.

"But he *must* be!" she stammered and dissolved into tears.

"No, *cara*. You have let yourself love a man who cannot truly love a woman. You were too good for him, believe me. Now, we must be very quiet, or Zeno will hear us and our troubles will only be worse." She guided Allegra's uneven steps back upstairs, praying for strength of heart to see her dear *contessa* safely through her agony.

Allegra stayed in her bed through the next day, saying very little and refusing all food. Two thoughts took turns in her churning mind: the first was that he had a good reason for not answering her letter . . . perhaps he was very ill; the second was that all reason for living had been taken from her and she would rather die than live without Byron.

Maybe I have gone mad, she told herself. *I have imagined all this and Byron is still waiting for me to come to him.*

Then Gina would appear next to her with a gentle word, and she would have to believe that it was all true. Toward the end of the day she managed to pull herself together enough to realize that her situation could not go unnoticed in the Ca' d'Argenti.

"Tell Aunt Adriana that I am ill and wish to be alone."

"I have already done so," she smiled. "The household has been informed that you have influenza—not a bad case—and they will stay away for fear of contracting it themselves. But, my dear lady, you cannot be this way for many more days. Perhaps a visit from your cousin would be helpful."

"No, I don't want others around me. I am remembering my times with Byron. They make me happy again. Leave me alone with my little scraps of happiness, Gina."

In her own room in the servants' wing Gina was in utter distress. For the rest of the week she observed Allegra's growing withdrawal and lethargy. She had to do something.

Finally she resolved on action. She presented herself at the door of the Palazzo Mocenigo once again and demanded to speak to milord. Fletcher tried to stop her, but she pushed past him and into the room where Byron sat working on his manuscripts.

He looked up and with swift perceptiveness knew why she was there. A look of pain swept over his face. "Do not say anything, dear lady," his voice trembled. "Do you think I have not said it all to myself already?"

Gina was not prepared for the man she now saw. His face seemed vulnerable and suffering. She steeled herself from feelings of sympathy. She did not want to find him appealing.

"She was a child," he said directly, "and I have hurt her beyond mending."

"Milord, she is ill from grief. . . ."

"You love her, I see, but love is no protection in this harsh world. My God, we run blind on our fates!"

In spite of herself she was becoming beguiled by his beautiful face and evident pain. He sighed heavily and went on: "I would only hurt her more if I saw her again. Please believe me, it was an astonishing resemblance to one I love that drew me at first, and then she was so hungry, so needful of love. I knew her circumstances. She could not plan a life with me. And I must be honest . . . I love her, but not as much as a man should love a woman. I, too, was hungry, and she is very sweet. But now . . . ."

His eyes filled with tears, and he looked at her with no effort at concealment. "I have found true love. This time I think that I love this woman more than myself. I pray God it is so." He brushed the tears away. Gina stared, forgetting her indignation.

He held out a pleading hand. "Tell me, you who have an evident loving heart. What would you do in my place? Would you choose to hurt an innocent heart even more—not because you wished to hurt, but because it could not be helped—or would you try to make the wound clean and sharp so that it can heal in time? I am not a stranger to suffering, both in giving and receiving." His voice ended in a sad whisper.

Gina knew she was beaten, not by this man with his strange honesty, but by the web of life itself. Who was right and who was wrong? The love of hearts did not work on outward reason.

"Forgive me, milord." She could see how the magic of his presence had been irresistible to Allegra. "I have done what perhaps was not my business, except that I cannot bear such terrible grief."

He nodded, and she finished what she had to say. "I will hope, as you hope, that it will heal with time. Should I tell her that I have seen you? She did not send me."

"Tell her what you feel will erase her feeling for me. I will not mind what you say. It probably will be true." He rose and limped toward her. To her surprise he took her hand and kissed it gently. "You are a friend, and friends of a true kind are rare. The little one is fortunate in you. Take care of her and pray that a good love will come to her. God knows, she deserves it. I wish I were the man she thought I was. . . ."

He returned to his work. Gina looked at him from the doorway. What more could be said to this man whose head was resting in his hands with such soul-weariness?

SHE LET HERSELF into the rear door of the Ca', to find that Conte di Rienzi had come home and was demanding his wife's attendance with him at a dinner at the Palazzo Strozzi. She debated what to tell the white-faced *contessa*, who was, of necessity, pulling herself together.

"Bankers and their wives," Allegra said flatly. "Barretto wants me by his side like a pet dog to show off for these people."

"I shall tell him you are too ill to come."

"He was already in my rooms and found me dressed and well. I have no choice but to go with him." She smiled wanly, "Santa Chiara is not being much help to me these days, is she?"

"Don't speak like that, *madonna*. It will take time, but life will again be beautiful for you." She decided to say nothing about her interview with Byron, as she deftly assisted Allegra with her gown and pearl necklace.

"What does a virtuous woman look like, I wonder," Allegra said into the mirror. "Luciano suspects something, I know. It will be a problem now that he and Barretto have come back. Tell me, Gina, why should I continue to live?" She moved to the door and left Gina to worry until her return.

To ALLEGRA'S JAUNDICED SIGHT the festivities at the elegant palazzo of the Strozzi family were designed to torture her further. At supper the gossip of the ladies rippled in waves over her, while the heavy laughter of the men reminded her of the one beautiful laugh that she longed to hear again.

Over demitasses of rich Turkish coffee, when the men had retired into the library for their cognac, the ladies enjoyed the delightful scandals in the best Venetian houses. Allegra agonized over the moments that she was forced to sit with a pleasant expression on her face.

She was jolted to attention by the words of one elderly *contessa*. ". . . and she calls out to him in a loud voice, '*mio* Byron!' In public! What a brash little thing she is!"

Another voice continued. "And milord follows her around like a fish on a line."

Allegra's cup rattled against its saucer as she set it down. "Who?" she managed to say in a small voice.

"Teresa Guiccioli, of course. . . . Where have you been, Allegra? The drawing rooms have been full of it this past week. The little minx has stolen the heart of the heartless Byron. What poetic justice!"

The women laughed, and their attention shifted to the question of whether Paganini's mistress was or was not pregnant, leaving Allegra aghast. Teresa! So now she knew.

The chatter flowed around her amid the clink of cups, as the thought of Teresa Guiccioli sparked vivid pictures in her mind: Little Teresa Gamba, a younger classmate of the convent of Santa Chiara, bright and charming. She remembered her small full figure and honey-gold hair and great expressive eyes . . . little Teresa! She would be only about eighteen. She was never shy. She demanded what she wanted, and now her clear high voice was calling out the precious name of Byron for the world to hear. It was horrid to imagine the two of them together.

She couldn't make herself believe that this girl was the one who could fill the ache and need of his heart. If she could only ask more questions of these gossipy women. . . . How had they met? Was Byron writing poetry to her? One question burned her with its urgency. . . . Where did they meet to make love? He couldn't, she wept inwardly, not after he loved me so completely.

When the gentlemen reappeared and the evening drew to a close, Allegra's mind was a turmoil of images. In the gondola Barretto scolded her for making no effort to be polite.

"Is there something I should know, my dear?" he said acidly. "Do you wish to talk about what is troubling you?" When she said nothing he turned her face roughly toward him. "You are not living up to your obligations. The very least I demand is a proper companion in public. You have displeased me, Allegra, very much."

As they entered the Ca' he embraced her without warmth and whispered into her ear, "I shall be away for a few days in Padua. Never forget that you belong to this house and to me, *contessa*. Good night." He left her standing in the foyer and returned to his gondola.

She climbed the grand staircase slowly. In the *galleria* the di Rienzi portraits looked at her through dead eyes. She felt as dead herself.

Gina met her at the door to her rooms, quickly understanding that something had happened during the evening to make things worse.

"Teresa," Allegra said in a monotone, "it's Teresa Guiccioli."

"Si." Gina helped her with her clothes and prepared a draft of laudanum. She was not surprised at the name. Her friend, Fanny Silvestrini, was the young Contessa Guiccioli's personal maid and had recently been hinting that her mistress had a famous lover.

"Why didn't she go back home to Ravenna? Why did she come to Venice? It all would have been different if she had gone," Allegra murmured as she let herself be put to bed. She drank the draft quickly and turned her head away from Gina.

"Maybe so," Gina answered halfheartedly. She knew men, and she knew that Milord Byron would have taken another woman . . . Contessa Guiccioli or someone else, it didn't matter very much with men of his passionate temperament. Her eyes lifted to the wall shrine. *What can I do to help my mistress now, when the world is crumbling around her innocent head? She has suffered enough from this man—surely she deserves some peace for her heart.*

She snuffed out the candles in the room and left.

THROUGH THE HOURS OF THE NIGHT Allegra made a decision. Now that the mysterious woman had a name—a name she knew very well—it was useless to hope. She could see how Byron might have been charmed by Teresa. She was very winning and clever with her tongue, fluent in several languages and the classics—one of the more intellectual girls at Santa Chiara.

Allegra felt her own inadequacy to compete against such attributes. She was not a match for his genius . . . she appealed to him only because of his sister Augusta. *He was honest about that from the start. He is not to blame for growing tired of me.*

BY THE TIME GINA KNOCKED again at her door, she had woven a plausible garment of reasons to explain her loss of Byron. She came to the irrational conclusion that great men cannot be tied to a single woman's love.

Gina listened and grunted skeptically. "Great men are no different from common men, *cara*. But if that comforts you, then I am happy. I thank the Blessed Mother that you have found a way to live with your disappointment. You are a far better soul than I can hope to be. I still have the capacity for anger."

"I will never forget him," Allegra said, as she carefully put the Byron box far back into a drawer of her desk, "but I have no more strength for torment. I will write him one more letter, wishing him joy in his life."

She couldn't admit that she was following a strong urge to have something she had touched come into his hands. At least for that moment he would think of her. "Then I want to dress and go to the Redentore. Signora Nicolo is home from her trip and is probably wondering what has happened to her little nun." She managed a small laugh.

Gina took the letter to the post office. She had no heart for personally delivering such a message.

AUNT ADRIANA INSISTED on having tea with Allegra in the walled garden of the Ca'. The mid-April air carried the fresh scents of spring, and red geraniums in profusion overflowed their ancient ceramic pots. Allegra was feeling better. Sending the letter to Byron was like giving him permission to go his own way. It took some of the sting from his rejection. And being with the children of the Redentore—having to force her mind to the task of Latin tutoring—brought her a little peace from questions which still swarmed her mind.

Unfortunately, Adriana was interested in the newest affair of the great poet. She had just been with Contessa Benzoni and was dying to tell Allegra all the news.

"Marina takes all the credit for introducing them," she said knowingly. "It was at her *conversazione* two weeks ago. . . . I think it was just before you took sick. Anyway, there he was, and there she was . . . and by the end of the evening they had arranged their first rendezvous."

Gina brought out the tea table and set it up next to Adriana. She had already heard the story of the meeting at Benzoni's. Teresa Guiccioli's maid, Fanny, was free to talk about it, since the whole of Venice seemed to know anyway. She watched Allegra's face and was pleased to see it remaining steady.

"Old Guicciolo doesn't know what to make of it all, Marina tells me. Here is his little wife, three months' pregnant with their first child, and demanding to take a *cavaliere servente*. He isn't happy, to say the least. But he took the situation into his own hands and hauled her off to Ravenna this morning. That should settle her down a bit, I should say."

Allegra involuntarily shivered. She tried to let the story slide away from her, as if it were any other bit of casual gossip.

"Well, what do you think?" Adriana prodded. "You aren't still feeling ill, are you? Dear me, I hope last evening's dinner party wasn't too much."

"No, Adriana, I'm feeling much better, thanks. I'm just sorry to hear about Teresa." It was the truth. If Teresa was torn from the man she loved and taken away by her angry husband, she must be suffering. For that she felt sympathy. "What about the . . . the Englishman?" she asked.

"Who knows? He's such a mystery. But Marina says he is in some anguish. You can't really tell with a poet, can you?"

THERE WAS HOPE. In the weeks that followed, when she walked out into the small *campos* on her way to the Redentore, her eyes searched the crowds for the sight of the dark curled head, the uneven step, the face that she loved. She imagined that they would meet suddenly amid the busy activities of the city, and it would be an instant of blissful homecoming.

At night she wished she had the daring to go to him. Her diary lay unused, and Byron's poems to her were read and reread for hints that he had made a commitment to her.

Meanwhile, she came and went in her daily activities. Barretto made no attempts to come to her bed, for which she was grateful. Adriana was once more at her house on the mainland; Allegra's father and Gemma and Lipia called infrequently. On the surface, Allegra's life returned to normal. Even Gina was lulled into believing that time was at last laying a soothing hand over the grief.

ON THE FIRST OF JUNE the news was all over Venice: Lord Byron had gathered his entourage into his great Napoleonic traveling coach and had set off for Ravenna to be with Teresa Guiccioli.

"That is not the only news," Allegra said to Gina that night. "I am pregnant."

CHAPTER ELEVEN

"IF GOD HAD HAD A CHOICE of calamities and punishments to visit upon me, He could not have chosen a better one," Allegra said dully, "one that could reach out and touch everyone I love. Barretto can only kill me, but what of the baby—Byron's baby. What will Barretto do in his anger? Disgrace my father and ruin my sisters . . . Adriana would never recover from his rage, nor you, Gina." She was recalling with horror the story that Elletra told her about the castrated lover of Barretto's mistress. Why hadn't she considered the possibility that she would become pregnant, before she made the reckless decision to love Byron?

Gina took the latest development with strength. "We shall find a way, *madonna*. You are not the first to have this problem. But there is time to think of the wisest action to take." She chose her next words carefully: "There are women skilled in herbs . . . you are not far advanced. I can find someone . . . ."

"No!" Allegra whirled to face her. Gina drew back, startled. "I want this child, Gina!" The eyes that looked at her from Allegra's face were black pools of emotion suddenly. The voice speaking from the blanched face rang with inflexibility. "God has granted me one sweet irony in all of this. Byron may have withdrawn himself from me, but he left his seed in my womb—a living essence of himself. It is mine to keep. It is all I have of him. I will not let it be taken from me!

"I have thought it out, Gina," she went on with weary determination. "Byron would want the child himself—I cannot tell him. He must never know." She placed her hands dramatically over her belly. "Now, all of my love is centered here. This child has made me strong . . . I am changed. With poor little Renaldo it was different, because of his father in him, but Byron is in this child and there is nothing I would not do to keep it!"

"But you just said that you fear the *conte*'s vengeance, *cara*. What other choice do we have? In time he will discover . . . ."

"I will have to go away. We have time to decide where I must go. I will find some way to disappear from this place and not hurt others in doing it. Never speak of the herb woman again!"

SHE ALTERNATELY THANKED GOD for her pregnancy and despaired of ever finding peace again. She wrote in her diary: "How can I have this child without Barretto's knowledge? How can I escape from his spies and where could I possibly go that he could not find me?"

As summer wore on, her life assumed a regularity that protected her secret. Days at the Redentore and tea with Adriana or Gemma . . . rare dinner parties where she was escorted by Barretto. Gina was adept at fixing her gowns to create an illusion of slenderness, and by the grace of God she did not get a great belly like some women. But it was more difficult to conceal her condition, in spite of the high Empire waistlines in style.

Each morning she woke to a terrible fear of discovery. If Barretto even suspected . . . there would be a convenient accident, and Conte di Rienzi would mourn the demise of yet another wife.

Gina proposed many schemes of evasion, which they mulled over endlessly in the evenings. At last there seemed only one reasonable path of action. She must go to Odile Berier, her French childhood nurse, who lived in retirement in Marseilles.

The widowed old woman had a strong protective instinct and loved Allegra deeply. The baby could be born there, and Allegra would be safe.

They drafted a letter that said just enough about Allegra's plight, but not enough to tell the entire truth. Gina posted it herself. A reply might take a month or more, well into September, and they had to trust that Odile would receive their letter and offer sanctuary. It was arranged for her to send her reply to Elletra's maid, who would give it to Gina. No suspicion must fall on that faithful friend.

In late August, Barretto summoned Allegra to his study. He hadn't requested a private interview with her for months, since last December when he had made his terrible threats to her.

"What should I do, Gina? He must have found out," she said after Zeno gave her the message.

"And maybe not, *cara*. You are too easily threatened by him. Act as if you have nothing to fear."

"Pack a few of my things while I am with him. We may have to leave quickly. . . ." Her face was white.

Gina took her in her arms. "He does not know, he does not know . . . here, let me pinch your cheeks to bring the color back."

BARRETTO'S STUDY WAS PANELED in rich mahogany with a coffered ceiling. Miniatures of the di Rienzi merchant ships showed impressively on the shelves of a Louis XIV étagère. His collection of Bedouin rifles hung against one wall. They were sheathed in silver, and each was as tall as a man.

Barretto met her with a broad smile on his deeply lined face. He took her by the shoulders and held her at arm's length to look at her.

"You are indeed a lovely woman, Allegra, and I have something very important to speak to you about."

Allegra's mouth went dry as he scrutinized her. Was he playing with her, just waiting for her to betray herself and then to strike?

"I have decided that we should give a grand ball," he said as he released her. "I want the best people of Venice to meet my son. It has been too long since they have given proper consideration to the house of di Rienzi, and now that I have an heir, I want them all to pay their respects," he ended with a satisfied laugh.

"A . . . a . . . ball?" she said in disbelief.

"Yes, and a magnificent one. I want them to see the di Rienzi cradle filled with the lifeblood of my line . . . we shall receive them in splendor. I want them to see my *contessa* and know that where there is one son there will be more!" He looked at her with a possessive gleam that she had not seen for many months.

He pulled her face toward him for a kiss. "I have spent too

much time away from you, *madonna*," he breathed. She dared not move for fear he would press his body to hers and discover her secret.

He let her go and walked toward his Moroccan desk, where he opened a drawer and drew out a slim jewel box. Smiling, he put it into her hands. "You may be satisfied with pearls, but I wish to see you wearing these for our celebration."

Allegra's shaking fingers released the clasp, and the lid of the inlaid rosewood box sprang open. Inside, arranged on its silken cushion was a dazzling necklace of violet-colored stones . . . like a magical jeweled spider's web at dawn, with violet dewdrops of precious stones clinging to rows of graceful golden loops. In the center, suspended from the intricate strands, hung a large pear-shaped stone, which glowed warmly in the candlelight.

"Oriental sapphires from India. Put them on."

Allegra's first thought was a guarded one. Barretto never gave her anything without a price. As he stood behind her to fasten the exquisite necklace around her throat, he answered her speculation.

"One more son, Allegra, that is all you must do for me," he whispered. "It has been too long, and I have been patient to a fault. But I will not press you, my dear. We shall find the proper moment, hmm? Perhaps after I have returned from my next trip. Perhaps after the ball . . . we shall make another son for our great House of Silver."

She touched the cool web of stones at her throat, remembering the last time he came to her bed. "When will the ball take place?" she ventured.

"In three weeks' time. While I am gone Luciano will take care of the preparations. You have no concerns with it at all. You must simply attend on my arm and be beautiful. I will be back in time to oversee the final touches. All Venice will envy us," he smiled. "Some influential men from the emperor's court will be there as well. I want them to see how a great house becomes greater with age. Now, leave me, Allegra, I have work to do." He turned his back on her, as she quickly found her way to the door.

Upstairs Gina was waiting anxiously for her. "What is it, *cara*, what did he say?" she urged, as Allegra threw herself facedown upon the bed and started to laugh hysterically.

"A ball . . . he's giving a ball!" She shook with laughter until Gina had to join in.

"That's all?" she managed to ask.

"He gave me jewels and told me to be beautiful for his friends at the ball. . . ." She brought herself back to equilibrium and sat up. "But, Gina, that's not everything. He is asking for another son. I can't wait much longer. Thank God he will be gone for a while. We must make plans for my escape. There isn't time to wait for a reply from Odile. Who knows, the letter might not have reached her. I'm willing to take the chance that she is still in Marseilles and won't turn me away when I arrive there."

Gina waited for her to finish. "When is the ball?"

"Three weeks. I'm almost sure Barretto will go off again on business afterward . . . he's always traveling. As soon as the ball is over and he has left Venice, I will go. You must arrange things!"

"Trust me, *madonna*, I will have everything ready for the day."

THE BALL WAS A WEEK AWAY, and strangers were everywhere in the Ca', workmen and extra maids and cooks. Barges pulled up to the water stairs to deliver materials for the decoration of the ballroom and the salon.

Allegra's senses were heightened by her dangerous situation. Gina had already made two trips to the mainland at Mestre to find a coach that would go as far as Milano. It was her plan that Allegra would make the first part of her journey in a hired coach, not a public one. From Milano westward she would be safer, and she could easily arrange to purchase a seat on one of the large public post chaises.

Gina was discreetly gathering as much money as possible, without drawing attention to herself, in the jewelers' shops in the Jewish quarter of the city. A ring here, a brooch there—nothing too extravagant for a woman of her class to be selling. She felt a terrible apprehension about Allegra's flight and prayed more urgently than she had ever done in her life.

Aunt Adriana was beside herself with expectations for the ball. Gemma and Lipia could talk of nothing else, until the very sight of them at tea was tedious. One late afternoon, after joining them for tea cakes, Allegra returned to her rooms to find Luciano sitting at her desk.

"May I help you, *signore*?" she said in a tight, irritated voice.

He turned around with an ingratiating smile on his lips. "Ah *contessa*, I was just leaving you a note to tell you I have delivered your new ball gown. It is in the box on your bed. Conte di Rienzi wanted to surprise you with something very special from Vienna." He rose and kissed her hand.

Allegra noticed that the drawer was slightly open, an observation that Luciano was quick to detect. "I was without paper for my little message to you, and so I knew you would not mind if I found something of yours to write upon." His eyes never wavered in their gaze at her.

"Thank you, *signore*, but I am tired now and wish to be alone. Good day."

He slowly moved toward the door, while she stood motionless waiting for him to be gone. In an instant she had pulled open the drawer. Her diary and the Byron box were far in the rear, behind a high stack of papers and a satin sachet. They did not seem to have been disturbed. How stupid of her to leave her precious and incriminating things there! Luciano knew very well that she was at tea. He could easily have spoken to her in the garden terrace. Why had he found it necessary to come to her rooms? He knew something or would not look at her like that—he would not have dared trespass so blatantly.

Every nerve in her body cried out for her to leave the Ca'. Now . . . tonight, and not wait for the ball. It was agony to pretend another day longer that her life was normal.

She stared at the large box that lay on her bed. With a sigh of resignation she pulled away the wrapping and appraised the ball gown inside. She knew that the fine parchment-colored laces and burgundy silk were exquisite, but she hadn't any heart left to appreciate them. Instead, she thought first of the way her swelling body would be betrayed if she wore this dress.

She held it against herself and ran to the tall mirror.

"It will fit you, *madonna*," Gina said from the doorway. "Don't worry."

"But the waist isn't high enough to conceal and the bodice is cut too low. Barretto will see how large my breasts have become. . . ."

"With more lace and a subtle gather or two under the bodice no one will notice a thing, I promise. . . ."

"Luciano was here," she interrupted. "I think he knows."

Gina was silent. "We must wait one more week, *cara*. The *conte* is once more in the Ca', and you cannot leave yet. The coach is ready to take you away from here, when I give the moment. You must behave as if nothing disturbs you . . . for your own safety, I beg you."

TORCHLIGHT BLAZED from iron brackets in the outer walls of the Ca', cutting through the humid mist of the September night. The massive doors were opened wide, and garlands of white roses made a fragrant pathway from the water steps to the reception hall. As the ball guests presented their invitations at the threshold, droplets of mist clung to their cloaks, making ghostly auras around them until they entered the warmth of the interior.

Aunt Adriana was watching happily from her vigil at the upstairs balustrade overlooking the scene. "All those black gondolas and sober guests! You'd think we still had the old sumptuary laws! What has happened to Venetians, Allegra? I remember balls at the Ca' d'Argenti when everybody was in costume, and the gowns were so splendid with gold cloth and *diamante* that it took your breath away. . . ."

"That was a long time ago," Allegra answered. "What do you think of my gown? Barretto had it designed for the evening." She wanted to test Gina's alterations on Adriana, before coming under Barretto's scrutiny. She turned a full circle to let the fine lines of the burgundy-red skirt fall into place.

"It is so covered up . . . where are your breasts? That is what I mean; there is no zest anymore. My nephew seems to want to keep you a secret. But I must say, you look very beautiful anyway . . . shall we say ethereal . . . in spite of the gown. And those jewels are fit for a sultan's wife! Barretto is so clever in his purchases," she said with a gentle pat on Allegra's cheek.

Allegra had to smile. Adriana's own black taffeta gown would surely raise an eyebrow or two tonight. What on earth did she do to her corset to lift her old white flesh so high?

"Very beautiful indeed, Contessa Allegra." Luciano's tall gaunt figure appeared next to them, giving her a start. His eyes were insolent as they slowly moved upward to her face. "I am to escort you to the *conte*'s study, where he awaits you."

Allegra took his arm, silently noting that he smelled of fine cologne and that his black-and-gold brocaded coat was as well cut and fitted as any Venetian aristocrat's. He had come a long way in his brief association with Barretto. She tried to hold herself in dignity as she walked next to him along the *galleria*. Music and laughter rippled through the Ca' from the rooms below.

Barretto met her at the door to his study. He was the very picture of self-assured splendor, with heavy diamond and onyx rings on his fingers and a diamond chain draped across his silver moiré vest. His coat was watered silk—pearl gray, lined in crimson. Luciano bowed and left them.

"Very good, my dear," he said approvingly, "let me see you." He held her hand and turned her around before him. "Exactly the effect I had in mind. The sapphires are the final touch to make you look like a queen." He kissed her hand with hard cool lips and looking meaningfully into her eyes with a pleased smile on his face. "It was not a mistake to marry you, *contessa*, in spite of your flaws. You merely had to learn that rebellion leads nowhere. After my next business trip I am retiring into the life of a man of leisure. It means I will be home to tend to my affairs here. We will be together more, and we will have long periods of time to become reacquainted." He looked to be sure she understood his intention.

"Where is Renaldo?" she said to break the mood.

"Dressed to receive his guests in the grand foyer. It is time for us to join him there." He carefully placed her white-gloved hand on his arm, giving it a possessive squeeze as they walked out to make their entrance.

She wished with all that was in her that she did not have to go through Barretto's society ritual tonight, that she and her precious child of love were safely on the road to Marseilles. She looked down at the wine-red color of her skirt and saw again the red flocked wallpaper from the secret room . . . the red velvet cushions of Byron's gondola. Why had Barretto chosen that particular color for her gown? It mocked her.

"You tremble, my dear. I trust the excitement will not be too great for you." His grip tightened. She took a breath to steady herself, shaking off the potent memories of her love.

The odor of fine perfumes rose up to meet them, as they walked slowly down the grand staircase. Gardenias, lavender and roses mixed into a heady bouquet, which rushed into Allegra's senses with their own haunting messages . . . the smell of gardenias in Elletra's balcony pots . . . the lavender of the wedding bed . . . the white roses from that moonlit night on the Lido . . . .

In the ballroom a small orchestra was playing a vivid tune from one of Galuppi's popular comic operas. The music made the atmosphere in the Ca' seem light and gay. It was so strange to hear music in the House of Silver. . . . For so long there had not even been the sound of a voice singing.

The great treasure room of the first di Rienzi was filled with sound. Servants staggered under their trays of champagne, Barretto's finest vintage from his estates in France. Diamonds and lace fans fluttered in the hands of the women, but the silver of the treasures outshone them all. It was as Barretto had planned it. This would be a night that his guests would remember.

As Barretto and Allegra made their entrance, polite and extravagant greetings immediately surrounded them, from people Allegra knew only slightly, if at all. Curious glances probed at her, eyes speculating, as was usual for Venetians.

She let her cheek be kissed by the smiling insincere lips of the subtly painted women of society. The opulence of their gowns spoke of vanity and competition. She and Barretto could not proceed into the room for a long while, as their guests paid effusive lavish compliments.

Gemma and Lipia looked at Allegra excitedly, from eyes that were large and dark from belladonna—no doubt administered without their father's knowledge. Allegra was embarrassed to see their desperately hopeful glances, searching for eligible young Austrian officers from the emperor's elite regiments. They had their hoped-for ball at last. Allegra had to admit that the flash of uniforms did add to the air of festivity. She turned her own eyes away uncomfortably, under the hotly admiring stares of the proud erect young soldiers.

At last Allegra took a goblet of champagne for herself and moved with Barretto to a small dais to the side of the ballroom, where several maids in freshly starched aprons were positioned next to the imposing di Rienzi silver cradle. A flurry of activity resulted in the appearance of little Renaldo, excitedly wriggling and splendidly dressed in cloth-of-silver, ready for Barretto's arms. He signaled for the music to stop and held his son high above him to be seen.

"The new strength of the house of di Rienzi!" he announced proudly. "Renaldo Barretto Ugo, I introduce to you the noble families of Venice and the representatives of His Imperial Highness."

Renaldo seemed frightened by the noise and applause and started to cry, to Barretto's irritation. He gave him back to the care of the maids, bestowing first a fatherly kiss on each cheek. Allegra overheard a woman's voice commenting in a stage whisper that the *conte* did not make such a fuss over the birth of his bastards. When she turned to see who spoke, several amused faces averted their eyes quickly.

Barretto raised his glass. "Music! I wish this to be a night of feasting and enjoyment!" The orchestra struck up a bright tune and the din of voices immediately rose to equal loudness. Barretto stood by the cradle to receive congratulations and warned Allegra with his eyes that she must be there as well. It was a task she found distasteful. She felt like Barretto's jeweled mare in his breeding stable, on public display.

The larger orchestra in the ballroom beyond had begun to play a waltz. She let her gaze wander to the high arched entrance where liveried footmen stood in new blue satin uniforms. The great chandelier was ablaze with candles in the center of the room. Garlands of bright glass flowers glittered along its many shining arms. High above, cherubs played among fleecy clouds on the brilliantly painted ceiling, and rich, red, brocaded panels on the walls glowed with faceted crystal wall sconces. Everywhere huge vases overflowed with blooming roses, and great swags of flowers and greenery hung in riots of color. The effect was dazzling. She knew that Barretto had planned everything to be the most beautiful . . . the most breathtaking . . . the most pretentious. It had all been accomplished by the artistic hands of the set decorators from La Fenice opera house.

One of the footmen whispered a message into Barretto's ear and called him away. "I will send you a suitable companion for these few minutes," he promised, kissing her hand for the benefit of the watching eyes.

She excused herself from the guests in the salon and moved into the ballroom, where the lilting music was flowing rhythmically. People were pairing off to dance to the alluring music. *Just like the picture on my first diary,* she thought, envying in that moment the couples who looked so happy in each other's arms. Byron let it be known that he did not dance; but what if he did not have his lame foot . . . how would it be, to be held tightly in his vital embrace, moving with him as the room whirled about them and she could see only the face of her beloved?

The ballroom was warm with the emanations of many bodies and the golden flickers of candle flame. Her tight nerves were easing, and her lips softened from their controlled expression. She let her eyes wander, savoring the exciting textures and colors of the evening. There had never been a grand ball in her father's house.

The French doors along the terrace were draped with sky-blue velvet, and heavily framed paintings hung in the few unadorned spaces of the ballroom's walls. Barretto was proud of his Bellinis and Tintorettos. He loved to tell about cheating Napoleon's agents out of the masterpieces. When the French first invaded, priceless paintings were being ripped from their frames in Venetian churches and taken to France in the saddlebags of patriotic soldiers.

The emperor's agents had come to the Ca' d'Argenti to offer a poor price for Barretto's old masters. Wily Barretto had laughed. "They are only clever fakes," he told them. "Surely such honorable and learned agents should hesitate to present these pretty imitations to the Louvre." He had soothed the duped agents on their way with a case of excellent claret.

A man's voice startled her from her thoughts. "You have earned your jewels, *contessa*," Luciano said. "The *conte* has given me permission to escort you to the dance floor, since he is occupied with some business matters in the study. Someone needs a loan, perhaps," he laughed.

Allegra hesitated, then placed her gloved hand lightly on his arm and let herself be guided into the area of the dancing. Of all people, she didn't want to dance with Luciano. She kept her eyes from his, but she felt his intent gaze almost like a touch on her skin, and unwilling color rose into her face.

He took her into his arms, drawing her smoothly into the enveloping motion of the waltz. She sensed with irritation the interested attention of many guests. She would far rather have danced with her father. Why had Barretto sent his bold lackey!

"I have been watching you—" his voice had a self-confident purr "—and I congratulate you." Without waiting for a reply, he pulled her into a breathless series of turns, holding her close to him. "You have courage, *madonna*—I admire that. It hasn't been easy for you with the old stallion. Even Veronica Bardolini suffers from his demands." His arrogance shocked her to silence for a moment.

"I think my husband would find your conversation impertinent," she said, attempting to move away from him, but she was no match for his strong hands. She looked up to find a teasing fire in his eyes.

"*Contessa*, I am a man who dares. I know that you will not mention our conversation, is it not so? The *conte* would only think you encouraged me, and we would both be dead," he laughed deep in his throat.

Allegra had to agree. A reluctant smile quirked the corners of her lips. *Just a little while more,* she thought, *and I will not be under Barretto's control.* "*Signore*, I don't wish to speak of personal matters. I shall finish this dance with you and then excuse myself."

"Of course."

They danced in silence, as Allegra grew more aware of the heat of his body near hers. When the music stopped, he did not release her but took her hand, leading her toward a flower-draped alcove. "One more thing, my virtuous *contessa*, before I leave you . . . tell me, how is it that the *conte* says he wishes to sire another child upon you, yet he has no knowledge of the one you carry now?" He kissed her hand elegantly and left her standing aghast among the bowers of roses.

The music was playing again. She turned slowly toward the ballroom, almost stumbling from the weakness in her legs.

She knew she couldn't break and run to her rooms, as her instincts demanded. Instead she found Adriana at the edge of the dance floor, talking with her elderly suitor, and thrust herself into their company. Luciano smiled in her direction as if he had enjoyed the game. She turned her back on him, struggling to regain her composure. How long would it be before he informed Barretto?

"We were just remembering, my dear, how it was before Napoleon put an end to the old Venice," Adriana said with a flirtatious wave of her fan. "You young girls can't imagine how it was when our Carnival lasted most of the year, and everyone went around masked. Why, you didn't know if you were kissing the doge or the dustman! It was delightful!"

Adriana's gentleman, Bernardo Giulini, took a long drink from his goblet of champagne. "Since the French burned the Golden Book, there will never again be a proper list of the great families of Venice. We have seen the last of our doges, God knows. I have refused to take the title of *conte*," he said to Allegra when Adriana's attention wandered, "just because the Austrians insist. There were never Venetian *contes* before the Austrians came, and I see no good reason for *contes* to exist now." He then smiled sheepishly at Allegra. "I understand about your husband, my dear. His family is an old one, of course, and the title is a help to his business with Vienna."

"Hush, Bernardo," Adriana said with her finger to her lips. "You are not too old to rot in prison for speaking out of turn."

"Well, then, dance with me, my lady, before I become too angry to enjoy myself." With a bow he begged leave from Allegra.

She studied the faces around her. Luciano was dancing with a young woman. Maybe he was just guessing, trying to find a weak spot to bring her down to his level. But why had he said those exact words? He must know. He must have felt the hardness of her belly when he pulled her close in the waltz. She put her hands over her baby and knew that she was not noticeably large. It was only a guess, then. She would be wise not to react to him.

For the next hour she was part of many circles of guests, and numbers of unmemorable men took their obligatory turn dancing with her. Barretto had still not joined his guests. Conte Lamberti put a fatherly arm around her waist and kissed her.

"A delightful evening, Allegra. I would be honored to escort you to the garden for something to take the edge off all the excellent wine I have drunk."

The walled terrace had been transformed into a Chinese temple garden with delicate paper lanterns hanging from the corners of a large latticework pergola. Inside, banquet tables beckoned with their crystal trays of delicacies . . . fantastic ice sculptures of peacocks . . . sorbets made from the juice of exotic fruits . . . sliced meats of every description arranged as if for a painting. Small intimate round tables awaited the diners.

Luciano was already preparing a dish for himself when Allegra and her father arrived. She decided to meet his clever guessing with nonchalance, as difficult as that was, and she steeled herself to speak to him.

"My husband says that you are responsible for the arrangements this evening, and I wish to express my thanks," she said, looking straight into his eyes.

He returned her gaze. "It was my pleasure, *contessa*. And I would like to apologize for any discomfort I may have caused you this evening. . . ."

"I'm sure the discomfort was yours, *signore*, for overstepping your place." Her heart was beating fast. She felt as if everything depended on keeping a steady cool tone to her words.

Conte Lamberti cleared his throat. "Well, I'm going to take my fill from this garden of delight. Come, my child, show me to a table where I can rest my tired feet. I haven't danced like this in years. . . ."

As Allegra and her father walked away she saw Luciano spear a sugared wild strawberry into his mouth. *No doubt,* she thought, *he is busy calculating.* . . . At the same time, she was determined that he would have no more reason for his suspicions. Just in case, she would stay close to Barretto for the rest of the evening and play her role well.

Barretto emerged from his downstairs study with a worn, slack-jawed expression on his face. He looked, from a distance, like a very old man. With him were three robust Austrian men, laughing heartily as if satisfied with the just completed business. He was no longer a young man, in spite of his vigor, she observed. *He could die at any time and leave me free . . . I would not have to leave him at all. But free for what? Luciano? Or the soldiers who follow me with their keen eyes?*

She took his arm, and they danced their first waltz together. Light applause followed them, and bravos from the guests who watched them.

"I have never felt younger," Barretto slurred. His breath was redolent of sour wine. "Pride keeps a man young." He spun her into a dizzying circuit of the dance floor. She knew he had been drinking more than was his custom, and she held his hand tightly, for fear he would misstep and bring them both crashing to the floor.

She stayed at his side until the last guests departed, and the musicians were packing their instruments. He wanted to receive every last compliment, extract from his evening the last measure of satisfaction. Luciano waited until the end to make his goodbyes.

"I have learned much this evening," he said to Barretto, "about how an old and esteemed house retains its standing among the great houses of Venice."

Barretto appreciated Luciano's observation and slapped him convivially on the back. "It requires first a man of power, then the money to stay ahead of the bloodsuckers outside my door, and last, a woman of proper pedigree to breed strong sons."

"And sons you shall have," Luciano smiled at Allegra, "I am sure of it."

Barretto looked at her, too, and started to laugh. "It is only a matter of time, and there will be more babies in my house!"

"Could anyone doubt it?" he said smoothly, taking Allegra's hand for a courtesy kiss. "*Addio, contessa . . . conte. . . .*"

BARRETTO TURNED TO HER with drooping eyes. "Help me to my bed, Allegra, I seem to be having trouble with my legs." He leaned against her, as she put her arm around his waist to give support.

"Are you ill, my lord?"

"Not ill, just tired." He straightened a little to give the appearance of strength. One of the footmen came to assist Barretto up the stairs, when he stumbled and almost fell.

"I shall rest a while and then come to you," he whispered to her, as he let the footman support him.

"Perhaps it would be better for you to sleep," she spoke, as he slowly mounted the steps. He turned sharply with a look of weary petulance, silently ordering her to prepare for him.

SHE HAD TOLD GINA not to stay up to attend her after the ball, but now she regretted it. She needed to talk, to try to figure out how much danger there was to her after tonight. If only she knew Luciano's motives. He seemed to enjoy toying with her. How much was just a game, and how much real danger to her . . . ?

She locked her door carefully and pushed the Byzantine chest against it. She really didn't know what she would do if Barretto demanded entrance. She wanted to keep some shred of peace between them, until she could flee the Ca'. He mustn't have reason for dissatisfaction with her. But he mustn't suspect. It was a puzzle without an answer.

Some time later as she lay unsleeping in her bed, a hand fumbled with the latch at her door. It turned it several times and then stopped. Footsteps moved away after a moment of silence. She spent the rest of the few hours until dawn imagining what it would be like to be at last in Marseilles with Odile . . . with another name. She tried to see the face of her unborn child and saw only the beguiling face of Byron.

CHAPTER TWELVE

"WHERE IS THE *CONTE*, GINA?" Allegra demanded anxiously, as she opened the door to her in the morning.

"In his rooms, *madonna*. The servants tell me he was not well last night after the ball and has asked that breakfast be brought to his bed. It is not like him. . . ."

"Then it was not he who came to my door. . . ." She shivered with the thought that it could have been Luciano's hand on her latch, and not Barretto's. "Gina, everything is suddenly worse for me. I'm certain Luciano knows now. I *must* leave this place immediately. If I stay another day he will have told Barretto. . . ."

"I don't think so, *cara*," Gina said quickly, as she poured coffee into the small Turkish cup. "The *conte* is determined to leave for Vienna in a few hours and will not hear opposition to his plan. Luciano will not be at the Ca' before that, because he is meeting one of your husband's ships, which arrived this morning from Morocco. He will have no chance to deliver his evil message," she ended, smiling through her feelings of anger for the men who had caused so much grief to her mistress.

"Then I leave tomorrow before dawn. Barretto will be far enough away. You must tell the coach to be ready!"

"Before tea hour I will have arranged it, *madonna*, do not fear."

The entire Ca' slept late, giving Allegra and Gina time to pack without the worry that Adriana or someone else would summon them. Allegra sent a carefully worded note to Barretto, expressing concern for his health and wishing him a fruitful trip to Vienna. "Just like a good wife," she said, as she gave the little envelope to Gina's hands.

She looked at everything for the last time . . . the beauty of her yellow sitting room . . . the view from her windows of the grand palaces along the canal. Would she miss Venice, she wondered. She could not imagine what Marseilles would be like, but she knew it was a busy port city. She wrote Odile's address on a piece of paper and put it into a jewel pouch, along with some loose gemstones, which could easily be sold if necessary. The money Gina had collected went into a small soft purse.

Gina returned in late afternoon, bearing a tea tray and news that the coachman at Mestre would be there at dawn. Allegra had no appetite for food. She checked and rechecked her meager belongings: she would carry a small common-looking basket, which held foodstuffs and a change of clothes. Hidden at the bottom would be the Byron box and her current diary, the jewels and the money.

None of the preparations seemed real—more like the rehearsals for her convent plays. "You must pay attention, *cara*," Gina was saying. "I put your mother's pearls into the pouch with the stones. I would feel better if you carried the valuable things on your body."

"Now I am the one who has to say 'don't worry.' As soon as I am safely inside the coach with the curtain drawn, I will have nothing to do but rest and thank Santa Chiara."

Gina frowned at Allegra's new bravado. "There is no true safety until you are in your nurse's loving arms, *madonna,* remember that." To herself she said, . . . *and until the conte has died and has no more venom left.* . . .

That night Allegra made her last visit to her child, feeling no wrench at parting. He was Barretto's, not hers. He would not miss her.

She slept a little with the basket next to her on the bed. Her potent talismans of love gave her courage. When Gina tapped gently on her door long before dawn light she was ready. There were few words spoken as they moved stealthily along the corridors and down the back stairs. Allegra wore a loosely hanging dress, which Gina had bought—the simple woven garment of a country-woman. Her dark travel cloak covered her, the hood pulled close over her head.

They walked quickly along the narrow passage behind the Ca', and through the silent cool night until they reached the gondola pool near the Piazza San Marco. Gina negotiated with a drowsing gondolier to take them across to the mainland at Mestre. Once there, Gina held her hand until the last, when she had a whispered conversation with the coach driver and helped Allegra inside. "God be with you, *cara mia,*" she said through her tears.

Allegra reached from the window to touch Gina's hand one last time. "Don't worry about me, I'll be safe. . . ." She had to look away so that Gina would not remember her weeping.

The coachman lurched the clumsy wheels into motion. He was a surly man, and he drove his poor horses hard. Inside, the horsehair and springs in the seats were worn and protruding. The compartment smelled of stale body odor and garlic. Allegra closed her eyes and tried to find a comfortable position, but the swaying motion of the coach brought nausea.

After a long time of fighting down her sickness, she asked the driver to stop at the nearest town. She must find an inn for a little respite. The child was pressing heavily in her, causing the first real pain she had felt with this pregnancy. She feared that something was wrong. She leaned out of the window a second time to ask the man to stop. He was reluctant until he saw her pale face.

They stopped at a village where the innkeeper's wife helped her. "Will your family be waiting for you in Ravenna?" she asked in concern.

Allegra drew an astonished breath. Ravenna! They were not supposed to be going south. Just then the driver knocked on the door wanting to leave. Was it an innocent misunderstanding on his part? He did not look like an intelligent man.

To avoid an argument for which she hadn't the strength, she made a quick decision: Byron was in Ravenna now. She would go to him. She would ask his help to get to France. He need not discover she was pregnant . . . and if he did, she would say it was Barretto's child. The innkeeper's wife gave her a draft of a hot herbal mixture, which eased the nausea.

She returned to the coach, trying to rally her strength. "When we get to Ravenna," she said to the driver in her best voice of authority, "take me to the Palazzo Guiccioli." The man's face showed a flash of what might have been surprise, but he agreed. He whipped up the horses, and soon she was in the grip of the swaying rhythm of the post chaise.

She would have to face Teresa. The thought made her twist in embarrassment. Even as a younger girl at the convent, Teresa had had a presence. She remembered that Teresa was kind, even if headstrong and full of her own status. She might even be sympathetic to her story that she was running away from Barretto.

They had been driving many hours since dawn. Allegra finally fell asleep, exhausted. She awoke to find the coach door being opened by a man of unsavory looks—not her driver. He held out his hand, and she got out, clutching her basket.

There was no palazzo, no city, only an isolated farmhouse at the edge of a pine forest. It was early evening. Before she could open her mouth to ask where she was, she was hustled roughly into the building. There was a fire in the low-ceilinged room. The man said nothing but left her immediately. She heard a key turn.

Time passed in silence and paralyzing anticipation of what might await her. She huddled by the fire. Her confused mind found it hard to take in the situation. One thing was clear, someone had planned her abduction. She wasn't just the victim of the coachman's sudden decision to spirit her away.

Barretto could not have found out so soon. He was on his way to Vienna, but he might have lied to the household about his plans in order to follow her. She hugged her hands over the precious life in her. She understood now the powerful mother instinct to love and protect.

The lock clicked again, and Luciano strode into the room. *"Buona sera, contessa,"* he bowed with a cold smile.

She sat mute, staring her defiance at him. How stupid she was to imagine Luciano did not tell Barretto! "Is my husband with you?"

"My dear lady, what an idea!" he said, with a tilt of his head in amusement. "Conte di Rienzi is no doubt entertaining a beautiful woman in a Trieste drawing room at this very moment. No, I have come here on my own account. He knows nothing of your precipitate flight from the Ca'."

As the impact of his words filtered into her tired mind, her fear of Luciano grew. "I demand to know why I am being held here," she said, standing erect before him.

He came close and took her cold hands. After a lingering kiss upon each of them, he looked up with a glistening smile. "I am no novice to life's little distresses, and it was a simple matter to decipher your condition. What surprises me is that no one else in the household of the *conte* figured it out—only Luciano Antonino. You see, I can understand an outcast, and you surely need someone who understands you. . . . Is that not so, *contessa* . . . Allegra?" He forced her hands to encircle his body and pressed himself against her while her flesh shivered away from him. His face came down hard over hers in a searching, invasive kiss.

"If you only knew how much I have dreamed about you, desired you. . . ."

She wrenched herself free from his hold and screamed. She screamed until she had no more breath and slumped to the floor. Luciano waited for her to open her eyes. He spread a blanket over her and sat in a chair nearby, waiting.

"I have a proposition to make to you. When you are feeling better, you will see how reasonable it is. I am on my way to Tunis, where I have friends. I intend to start a business there with the money your husband will give me for ransom."

She looked at him in disbelief, pulling the blanket tightly around her body. "He will not pay."

"But he will," he laughed. "He will want the pleasure of killing you his own way." He watched her in silence for a while. "There is an alternative. You can come with me to Tunis as my loving companion." He cocked his head again. "Do not pretend that there is no fire in you, little false nun. Babies are not made at the prayer stool! If you cannot see the advantage of coming with me willingly, there are slave markets there, where lovely white-skinned women bring good prices. Pregnancy is an asset . . . two for the price of one." His smooth satin voice had the tone of a gentleman of great courtesy, but she heard his words like the terrors in a nightmare.

She could not fathom the quality of his emotions. Then his face suddenly lost its elegant gloss, and his eyes softened. "Come here, little one, let me care for you."

He called for the man in the next room to bring hot water and a towel and then bathed her blanched and furrowed face with tender hands.

"I have no intention of leaving you in some slave market. I have not put myself in this dangerous position with the *conte* just so that I can lose you again. Don't you know how much I love you? I know how you have suffered at his hands. Love me a little, Allegra." He folded her into his arms. She was unable to resist his physical control. "I will care for your bastard as my own, you will see. . . ."

A terrible repulsion grew as she felt his hot mouth on hers and his exploring hands moving over her breasts and down to her thighs. With a desperate effort she pushed him away and vomited.

Luciano raised his hand and struck her face with a powerful blow. "Go to the devil, you bitch!" he spat at her and left the room with angry strides, locking the door again.

Allegra pulled herself nearer to the fire. She drank from a pitcher of cold water and then splashed some over her face. Luciano's intimate touch was still on her skin, far more painful than the sting where he had hit her.

She put more bundles of pine twigs into the flames, then made a tour of the room looking for a way out. A door was in the back wall. She tried the latch. Unexpectedly, it opened, and beyond was a stone corridor and another door. She crept down the hall and put her eye to the large keyhole. This door led outside; she saw dim shapes of the outside angles of the house. But the door was locked.

Faint starlight filtered in from a high open niche, but it was too high to reach and too small to go through. Her mind was busy with possibilities. A memory shot into her thoughts—from the convent days, when there had been a *festa* in the village nearby, and sounds of music had come drifting over the walls to tantalize the imagination of the girls. They had picked the lock on the door in the wall. She remembered standing close to the girl, while she pressed a piece of wire into the lock. In Allegra's mind she could see the motion of the girl's hand and hear the click as the bolt turned. The girls had gone out to the *festa* that long-ago night, but her own timid conscience had held her back. The girls had laughed at her as usual.

She sped back to the large room. Her basket was next to the fireplace. She quickly removed the jewelry pouch and rolled it into a scarf, which she bound around her waist beneath the band of her underskirt. The money purse was stuffed into her bosom. What could she do to protect the Byron box? She couldn't leave it behind. The answer came instantly: she tore a piece of cloth from a ragged table cover on the table in the corner and made a kind of sling to bind the box to her arm.

After a frantic searching of the room she found a piece of wire twisted around a basket handle. The old wire resisted her fingers, but finally she was able to work a length of it free from the handle. She stayed still for a moment, listening. There was no sound of people in the house. Pray God they were sleeping!

With the sling over her arm and her skirts lifted for speed, she ran from the room and into the corridor. She was clumsy with the wire, almost losing hope that she could succeed. Then there was a slight movement in response to her probings . . . a series of clicks and the handle moved freely.

Cautiously, she pushed at the door and looked out. There was no sign of life. Across the fields the woods beckoned, if she could just make it to their protection. The air was cold and reviving. She felt a surge of strength in her body.

As carefully as possible she took a deep breath and ran into the fields, cringing as her feet made snapping sounds on the dry stubble of grain. No one followed. There was no light in the house. The woods were very close now, and at last she was in the shelter of the trees.

She spent the rest of the night moving frantically through the brambles and underbrush among the thick stands of stone pines. Sometimes she came onto a little forest path and went more swiftly, but she was constantly aware of the danger, and she stayed mostly in the brambly growth.

Her hands and legs were scratched and bleeding. She forced herself forward in the direction that she hoped was Ravenna, keeping the sea and coastline on her left. If she could get to Byron and Teresa . . . she did not think much beyond that. Now Teresa was taking on the image of a blond guardian angel.

The forest noises made her tense with fear each time a branch cracked or something small scuttled across her path. Then she heard the undeniable sounds of human presence. It was growing light, and she rolled under a thicket of vines and pulled them over herself, waiting. Her child kicked inside her. Her eyes were hot and dry, beyond tears.

Men on horseback were near, riding back and forth. She heard Luciano's voice barking orders, and then the sounds faded into the distance. After a long time she found the courage to move again. She was wet and filthy and stiff, aching in every bone.

She had gone only a short distance when the sound of galloping returned. She dropped to the ground and held her breath, but it was no use this time. She felt rough hands drag her to her feet.

"Here!" the man shouted. Another man rode up. There was a quick dialogue between them. They were not satisfied with the money Luciano was paying them for this job.

Then Luciano arrived, and there was angry accusation among them while the one man held Allegra. She could not struggle for fear of harming her baby. The men were demanding more money for finding her. Luciano refused, and the second man struck out at him. Luciano stumbled and went down, hitting his head against a fallen tree stump. He lay still. The man turned him over.

"He's alive. Now what?"

"No use staying around to get anything from him. Let's take her to the ships." The two men agreed to take her to Rimini to sell her to the slave trader there. Allegra listened to them with a sense of complete unreality.

They searched Luciano and relieved him of money and a gold ring. He showed signs of reviving, and they tied him to a tree.

With several sharp blows, they made sure he would not return to wakefulness too soon.

Allegra watched the brutal treatment with her head swimming. She slumped against one of her captors, who used the moment to discover her money purse. Her mind retreated from the touch of his hands against her bosom. He was more ¸nterested in the money.

"And what is in the box?" he demanded.

"Only keepsakes," she whispered. He took it from her and saw with disgust that it was only papers and letters. Allegra lost her last shred of composure. "It's mine!" she shrieked, "mine!" Her cries were so hysterical that the man handed back the box. She stood holding it to her breast silently.

"Better let her keep it, otherwise she'll shout the whole world down on us."

She drew breath for another scream and was quickly stopped with a gag. "A prickly one she is," one said with a shrug. Allegra prayed that they would let her alone and not find the jewels concealed around her waist.

The leader caught Luciano's horse and climbed into the saddle, while the other man hoisted Allegra up to him, box and all. "The woman's pregnant," he snorted. "Maybe we should try to make a deal with the old *conte* for her, after all."

"I don't trust him." The other swung into his saddle with the third horse on lead. "He's dangerous. He could kill us before he pays us. I'd rather deal with Besim . . . we know him, and this little one wouldn't be bad looking if she were in better shape. Just the thing his pasha'd like for a tidbit."

The other laughed. "Yes, you'll fetch us a good price!" He gave Allegra a squeeze. She hardly heard him. She was in a nightmare daze and could do nothing more. She managed to get the precious box tied onto her arm again. She was aware from time to time that the men rested. They gave her water and covered her with a blanket. She was growing ill, and a shivering fever clouded her mind further until she was in a state of numbness.

They rode by hidden paths along the coast, avoiding contact

with people. At last they were in sight of a city on a wide beach. It was nearing dusk. Some ships were at anchor off the beach—fishing boats and a larger one with long smooth lines.

They approached carefully, riding slowly. They paused to replace the gag in Allegra's mouth. "No use to risk your howls," one growled. "Don't fuss, you can keep your box." She clutched it to her, her eyes wide.

Finally they stopped in front of a large old building on a dark street close to the waterfront. Allegra went limp, as she was carried inside. A big-boned woman rose heavily to meet them.

"It's about time—Besim's nervous. Where's Luciano?"

"He couldn't come . . . told us to work it out."

"Humph." The woman turned to a door behind her. "He's got two fine Englishwomen—blond and white as milk—and a Spanish terror. She's a beauty, if she doesn't bite your hand off." She pushed the door open. "He's in here."

The man holding Allegra stood her up and propelled her forward. The door closed, and she wavered on her feet. A tall man rose from a straight chair. His skin was a dark burnished bronze, and his features were sharp and hard. Very dark eyes were set at a strange slant under his fine brows. It was a perceptive face, but uncompromising. He motioned to the man, who took the gag from Allegra's mouth.

"This one screams the roof down if you touch her box. Nothing of value in it—some personal things of hers."

"Hmm." The tall man moved toward her. "Is this true, *signora*?" He looked into her painful eyes. "Well, I shall not take it from you." His Italian had a guttural accent. He touched her face lightly, turning it for inspection.

"I am Abou Besim. I shall take you and three other lovely ladies to Tunis, for the choice of the pashas. If you please them, your life will be one of luxury, *madonna,* far greater than in this cold land." He drew the chair toward her. "Rest," he said gently.

In an odd way she felt comforted. An indefinable quality in the man made her feel that he was kind.

The bargaining began—a lot of it—which Allegra could not follow. She was detached from it in her mind. The fever only heightened her sense of remoteness. At last the men concluded their business. Money changed hands. The scene before her wavered in and out of focus. She shivered and fell forward in a faint.

Her next clear sight was of Abou Besim holding her head and urging her to drink something that had a pungent flavor. She was in bed in a bunklike place, and her skin was drenched in sweat.

"Good," he said quietly when she swallowed. Alarm showed in her eyes, and he smiled. "You are on my ship, *madonna* . . . and your box is there." He pointed to a shelf. "You have been sick, and we have had a delaying storm. Maybe tonight we sail." She looked up at him. "You are so silent, little one, is it that you cannot speak? I do not even know your name."

She realized suddenly that she was in a nightrobe, and her face went scarlet. A smile touched the sensitive lips of Abou Besim. "Women's bodies are not a mystery to me. You were in need. Now," he took her hand, "please tell me what you wish me to know."

Allegra looked into his deep brown eyes, where she saw again the mark of kindness. "You deal in slaves?"

"Yes, but I have not always done so."

"I have heard that this happens, but I did not believe that men . . . ."

"Your voice and manner, *madonna* . . . these are of a woman of quality. You must tell me how you have come to this situation."

What did it matter, she was his slave. At least she could speak to this impersonal but listening face. Her story came out haltingly. She gave no names, but she was honest about her marriage and about her love affair.

"The box contains all my memories of him," she said on a sigh, "and here is the rest." Her hands covered her child.

He was silent for a time. "This lover, surely he would help with the child."

"I will not tell him. He has gone to a new life and must be happy. I am glad I could not reach him in Ravenna."

"You have no anger toward him—no hate?"

She shook her head. "None."

"And the punishing husband, what do you feel toward him?"

"I pray for him."

He stared at her in curiosity. "What of the man Luciano? Is he worthy of prayers?"

"There are none who are unworthy of prayers."

"By Allah!" He sat pondering. "So you wish to get to Marseilles, to your old nurse to bear your child. . . . What if I should tell you that, as a man, I am not proud of the actions of my life." He turned a ring over on one of his long fingers, then looked up swiftly. "Would you pray for me also, *madonna*? Allah hears your prayers, I am sure."

"I will pray for you," she said gently.

"Even as I take you to a life of slavery?"

She nodded.

"In my faith it is made possible that we can have, at any time, four wives. The Prophet knew the nature of men." His voice was sardonic. "Yet the Prophet told us to honor women . . . and I have not. But, I swear to you, I do not put them into the slave markets. I see that they are in positions of comfort. Some are not unwilling. The two English, from homes of poverty, have come willingly, seeking comfort in a rich man's harem." Allegra said nothing. "Your story, *madonna*, has made me think of the suffering of women given unwillingly to men. I will not forget."

He stood and paced in the small cabin. "I believe that there is a true fire that grows between a man and a woman. When that is felt there is love and faithfulness, and forgiveness . . . ." He swung away with his back to her. "Allah forgive me! There was such a woman for me once, and I did not understand!"

He sat beside her again. "I will take you to Brindisi. I will put you on the ship of Luigi Bartello. He is an old man. He takes a cargo of hashish into Genoa and then to Marseilles." He caught the look on her face. "Yes, the world of men is full of death and evil. But Luigi is not a bad old man. In his own way he can be trusted. He will take you to the port. From there you can find your own way."

Allegra's eyes filled with tears. "You are letting me go?"

"By Allah the Compassionate. Do not weep." He bent to touch her cheek with his lips. "Live for the child, *madonna,* and pray for me. Perhaps this prayer will be remembered, when I must show my life to the angel of Death."

She tried to thank him, but she had no adequate words, and he waved away her attempts. Then she remembered the pearls and the jewels.

"Yes, they are with your box."

"Will you take them? You will have to account for the absence of a woman."

"I can find another woman. . . ." He stopped his line of thought because of the expression in her eyes. "I see. It is better the stones than a woman—agreed." He picked up the little pouch and emptied it on the bed. Several brilliant stones tumbled out with the pearls.

Allegra saw with a start that they were not her mother's pearls, but Barretto's. Gina must have put them there by mistake. She saw a swift image of her beautiful pearls on Veronica Bardolini's perfumed breast and sighed. At least they would not be going to the jewelry bazaars of the Barbary Coast.

Abou Besim fingered the pearls. "These will do for me. The rest you must keep. Who knows what situation your old nurse may have."

He left her alone then, and she sank into semiconsciousness, feeling the heat of fever ebbing and flowing through her body. The ship was moving, but she had no more fear. She believed the dark serious man, who promised her she could have her baby in Marseilles. From time to time during the next few days Abou sat with her quietly and held her hand. Sometimes he spoke to himself in his own tongue, thinking she was asleep.

Her body felt stronger by the time he escorted her from his ship and up the boarding plank of a broken-down cargo boat, which belonged to the old man named Luigi. She had Byron's box with her and was content.

To ensure her safety, Abou chose a time to bring her aboard

when Luigi's crew was ashore. He smiled. "Do not think ill of all men, but do not trust them, either," he said in farewell, lifting her hand for a light kiss.

Luigi was a gap-toothed, slightly smelly man with one eye, which looked a little to the side. He deferred to Abou and nodded vigorously to Abou's instructions. Luigi was not the kind of man she could possibly feel afraid of. She smiled at his disheveled appearance and turned to go to the cabin, which Luigi had indicated.

Abou Besim's voice hailed her at the last moment, and she returned to the railing to hear his words.

"Pray for me!" he said through cupped hands.

LUIGI'S WEATHER-BEATEN OLD VESSEL dropped anchor near the entrance to Genoa harbor, a safe distance away from the docks and custom-houses. His crew worked fast to unload their shrouded boxes of cargo onto the broad deck of a barge, which had pulled snugly against the ship in the night.

It was more than a week since Allegra had become part of Luigi's entourage. She had stayed in the tiny cabin, and now she watched from the single porthole as the contraband cargo was transferred to the barge. There was a feeling of urgency in the actions of both crews.

Luigi pulled anchor at dusk and slipped out of the harbor. When they were well under way, he brought in a stew of rice and fish and presented her with a basket of pomegranates.

"My Genovese friends see to my tastes," he grinned. "You should not concern yourself with anything but eating and sleeping. The babe needs a healthy mama." He patted her cheek like an old grandfather. Despite his blackened teeth and foul breath, he was good-hearted. He had given Allegra a key, so that she could lock the door from the inside.

"We have some crew members who are new, and I don't know their habits yet," he explained and then left her alone. Allegra was sure that Abou Besim had paid him well to look after her.

It was several days more before they reached Marseilles. Allegra was restless from confinement in the crowded little cabin, but the sea had eased her in every other respect. The baby was kicking hard now, reminding her of how much she had to live for. She imagined that it would have Byron's beautiful face and musical voice. As she lay on the hard narrow bunk, she put her hands lovingly over her swelling abdomen.

"I'm taking you to a place where you will be safe. Now all we have to do is find Odile." She opened her locket and gently touched the spiral of chestnut-colored hair, which was proof to her of Byron's existence.

At dawn she awoke to the noise of the heavy anchor chain rumbling over the side of the ship. Luigi knocked at her door and told her that a dinghy would be ready to take her to shore within the hour.

She wrapped the box inside a rough cotton cloth, which she found in the small sea chest at the foot of the bunk, and tied it around her waist in the manner of a peasant woman. She had sponged some of the dirt from her cloak, so that it had a modicum of respectability. The damp sea air made her hair stand out like a dark halo of springy curls around her face. There was little trace of the Contessa di Rienzi.

"If I am not Contessa di Rienzi, who shall I be . . . who shall we be, my precious one?" she whispered, feeling a sudden surge of excitement and freedom. She could be anyone she wished.

A flash of inspiration told her her new name: she would be Francesca Gordoni, a widow—she would have to invent a husband, who had died and left her without property. That would be simple. She laughed softly at the name. Francesca was one of the many names given to her at birth, and so it was not entirely an invention. Gordoni, Byron's surname with an Italian ending, made her feel close to him, even if he never learned what had become of her. It gave legitimacy of a sort to their child of love.

As she waited for Luigi's call, she sat on the edge of the sea chest in a state of expectancy. How many women were ever given a chance to start their lives again . . . to change the parts of themselves that they felt couldn't be changed? Francesca Gordoni was a clean page, and she believed in her strength to write upon it without fear. She wished Gina could see her now, as she was about to find the safety they had both worried so much about.

LUIGI SAT NEXT TO ALLEGRA as the two oarsmen rowed the dinghy toward shore. Even from a distance Marseilles looked drab and dirty.

"This is a sailor's town," he said almost apologetically. "Are you certain that you have a home here?"

As they neared the landing dock, she saw a confusion of ships, fishing boats, boxes and huge nets. Men crawled over them all like ants, hauling and shouting.

Luigi's eyes narrowed with suspicion. "You didn't come here to—ah—work . . . ?"

She took a moment to understand what he was asking. "No!" she laughed. "I have family in Marseilles, and I assure you that if I find work it will be honorable employment."

"Thank the Holy Mother . . . you are too young and sweet to be thrown to the likes of the scum on the wharfs. Forgive me, but Abou Besim told me nothing about you. He deals in all kinds, you know. . . ."

He bounded from the boat like a young man and took Allegra's hand to help her to the dock. She refused his offer to escort her to the home of her relatives. At that moment she could not extend her trust to anyone, not even this old man.

"I have the address," she said. "It is not far from here."

He shook his head. "If you insist, but a woman must have money in a place like this," he said in a rough emotional voice. "Just in case you can't find the ones you are looking for. Here . . . ." He pressed a small leather pouch of coins into her hand and started to walk away.

She called after him, "Thank you, Luigi!" and he lifted his arm in a farewell gesture as he stepped back into the boat.

The smell of fish was strong around her, as she walked the length of the wide wooden dock. She ignored the calls of men and aimed her steps toward the main streets of the city. It felt strange to be on land again. At first the ground beneath her feet seemed to rise and fall, making it difficult to walk a straight line.

She kept a tight grip on the scrap of paper with Odile's address. Most of the streets were barely wide enough for a small carriage to pass through. Odile had said that her house was on a hilly street that ran down to the harbor.

Allegra entered a dark passageway, which meandered between two rows of gray stone buildings. The lane intersected another, leading her deeper into the teeming, evil-smelling labyrinths of the city. The sunlight hardly penetrated to the cobbled pavements where she walked. Shrill screams and laughter ricocheted off the walls of the houses, and sailors in jaunty black hats and white uniforms reached their hands toward her as she passed.

She gave a wide berth to the women who slouched in doorways, calling after the men. Allegra saw no one who looked even remotely civil or kindly. She tried other streets, thinking that one of them might be Odile's. Soon she was running, feeling desperate to find someone who didn't look menacing . . . someone who would help her. How foolish to refuse Luigi's offer! Maybe she could find him again.

By now she was so turned around and lost that she had no idea which winding foul lane would bring her back to the harbor. Some of them led below the level of the street, disappearing into darkness beneath the city. She began to fear for her life. People were jostling her, as she stood immobile in the midst of the crowds.

She didn't dare speak French. Her accent was Parisian, and the nuns at Santa Chiara had made sure that her French was refined. She might be robbed if anyone suspected her of being highborn.

Finally the streets she walked became cleaner, less crowded, the smells less dreadful. She was on a rise and could see down toward the bay and tall-masted ships. From a distance they looked beautiful. Around her in this street were small shops selling marine equipment, but she was still lost and nearly exhausted.

In despair she approached a woman who was selling vegetables from a cart. She showed her the scrap of paper and didn't speak.

"Keep walking," the woman said in slurred words. "At the top of that hill . . . ."

Allegra looked up the steep lane and wondered if she had the strength to climb it. The woman could have been wrong. She kept her eyes down at her feet to avoid stumbling over the rounded cobblestones. One hand moved instinctively to cover the child within her. Near the crest of the hill her legs were throbbing with pain.

There were no numbers on the doors. She had to find one. Becoming more frantic by the moment, she stopped a small boy and in a shaky voice asked for the house of Madame Berier. He pointed a stubby finger to a nearby doorway.

Allegra hesitated at the azure blue door. What if Odile didn't live here any longer? It had been almost a year since she had received a letter from her, not since the birth of little Renaldo.

The narrow house seemed silent and deserted, its windows shuttered. There was no nameplate on the door. She gathered her strength and pulled the bell chain, then waited, straining to hear something from within. But there was too much noise in the street. She pulled the chain a second time.

A woman's voice called out in French, "Who is there?"

Allegra's knees went suddenly weak. "Odile!"

The door moved partially open, and a short heavy woman with white hair and weathered skin stood at the threshold. "Odile . . . it's Allegra!" she cried, rushing to embrace the old woman, who stiffened with surprise and then gathered Allegra into her arms.

"*Mon Dieu* . . . it can't be!" She held Allegra out at arm's length to look at her. "What has happened?" Her bright blue eyes brimmed with kindness and tears. She looked virtuous and capable, just as Allegra had remembered her.

She drew Allegra quickly inside to a warm open kitchen, where a fire burned in the large hearth. Odile's face drew itself into a mass of frowning wrinkles. "Who has done this to you? No—don't talk. *Mon Dieu, mon Dieu*—you are the last person in all the world I expected at my doorstep." She removed the dirty cloak and put a soft shawl around Allegra's shoulders. Allegra was enclosed in a warm motherly aura and felt her tight nerves start to relax.

A relieved smile moved over Odile's round honest face. It was then that she noticed Allegra's condition, and a whistle blew lightly through her pursed lips. "My precious girl, I think I understand. You will be safe here, I promise you. No one will find you if that is your wish."

Allegra took one of Odile's dark hands and kissed it. "My husband would punish me if he knew. I think he might even kill me."

"When will the baby come?"

"At the end of December."

"So, you are seven months along. You are alone and hundreds of miles away from Venice. I doubt that an angel lifted you from your bedroom at the Ca' d'Argenti and carried you gently to my house. But surely the good Lord watched over you in your travels. See, I bolt the door now. You are safe with me, *ma petite.*" She drew a strong metal hasp across the latch and put a large kettle of water over the fire to boil.

Allegra sighed deeply, a sigh she had been keeping for just this moment. Odile set to work brewing a hot drink, which brought with its herbal fragrance a flood of childhood memories. Allegra used to love being close to her nursemaid, cuddled within the billows of apron skirts. Odile always smelled of grasses and earth. She never cared about politics or Napoleon or the wars.

She made a comfortable couch for Allegra with pillows and blankets and puttered about, shaking her head at the state of her torn clothes and wet shoes. She had not received the letter Gina had sent from Venice.

As soon as Allegra was asleep, Odile's mind began to race. The more she thought about it, the angrier she became. *What man would do this to her? I was afraid this would happen. Conte Lamberti never understood the needs of his little girls. It was a crime to marry that dear child to the old goat di Rienzi.*

She noticed the cloth bundle tied at Allegra's waist and eased the uncomfortable knots loose. The box came into her hands, and the gold embossed name, Byron, stood out clearly against the dark leather. Her practical intelligence knew at once what it meant. She would never ask Allegra for the name of her lover, but she would forever consider this man Byron an enemy.

"My poor baby!" she murmured, carefully laying the elegant little box next to Allegra on the couch.

Allegra slept deeply in the cozy kitchen with the soothing touch of Odile's hand on her forehead. Sometime after dark she awoke with a start of confusion.

"La, la, *mon enfant* . . . I am here," Odile's soft voice said.

Allegra sat up quickly. "My box . . . where . . . ."

"It is next to you. Now go back to sleep."

She slept and awoke and slept again over many hours, gradually relaxing the defensive tightness that her body had carried for all the long months. Odile was still with her when she came out of her heavy sleep the following morning. Her clothes were in a neat folded pile near the hearth, and she was wearing one of Odile's voluminous white nightgowns with knitted bedsocks on her feet. The sweet odor of clean clothes was a delight to her senses.

Odile smiled. "I have been busy while you slept. There is a loft above the next floor, where I have made a fresh bed for you." She pointed to the ceiling above her room. "Do you see a trapdoor?" Allegra shook her head and Odile laughed. "You never minded sleeping in odd corners and crannies when you were small, I recall. You will feel safer out of sight of visitors."

The loft was well concealed. If a person did not know what to look for, the entrance to it would be invisible. The walls and ceiling of Odile's bedroom were decorated with finely beveled strips of wood laid into a pattern of squares and diamonds.

"My René was a genius with his woodworking," Odile said proudly. "Now come downstairs to the kitchen, and I will show you more of his clever work." She chuckled to herself as Allegra followed her down the narrow steep steps. "This house has more secrets than the little loft room. Look here."

She pressed her hand against the back of the tall open cupboard near the hearth. A section of wood moved to her touch and slid sideways, revealing an open space behind. "There is a mechanism of weights and pulleys, which carries supplies up the shaft from here to the loft. It is also good for communicating between the rooms. My dear husband had many friends who were what you would call political outlaws when Napoleon was in power. There were plenty of people here who blamed Napoleon for the bad times in Marseilles. René's friends needed a hiding place in case they got into big trouble with their political activities, and so he set to work. The day never came when we had to use the loft or the secret shaft behind the cupboard. Napoleon was defeated and trade returned—that was all my husband's friends cared about.

Leave the politics to the politicians, we always said." She sighed
with a reflective smile. "But that's past history. Come back to my
bedroom, and I will show you how the loft opens."

They climbed the little staircase again, Odile's hand lovingly
holding Allegra's. "It is by God's grace that this room is here now
for your need. I must go and light a candle of thanksgiving later."

From beside the bedroom hearth she picked up a metal rod and
lifted it to the ceiling, hooking its bent end into a hole in one of
the dowels. Allegra watched the opening of the loft with fascination. A large hinged section of the paneled ceiling dropped slowly
and silently at Odile's gentle pull, until it hung down far enough
for the small ladder inside to be caught and eased down to the
floor along its oiled tracks.

They climbed into the little room. Inside, the loft ceiling was
slanted, and a bed was snugly set into a corner formed by an angle
in the pitch of the roof. It was a comfortable room, and since
winter had been mild, the warm air that rose from the lower
rooms was enough. Odile grinned and guided Allegra to a dormer
window, where a bench concealed the outlet to the secret kitchen
shaft.

"I'll send up some bread and cheese and some apples." Odile
disappeared back down the ladder, smiling. Within minutes a
food-laden platform rose up the shaft and stopped in the square
opening beneath the bench. She called up, "If there is trouble I
will send you a signal from here. Watch the curtain at the window. I can make it move by pulling a cord from down here. René
thought of it to warn his political friends if Napoleon ever came
to visit," she laughed. "If the curtain moves, that is my warning
to you. Not a sound until I move it again, understand?"

Allegra shouted down into the shaft, "It's perfect! I feel as safe
as a lamb in a fold."

"No need to raise your voice, my lamb, I can hear everything
clearly." Allegra could imagine the broadly smiling face in the
kitchen below. "Now listen, my love; if we are to have food for
our mouths, I must leave the house and go to work. René left
me—bless his soul—with nothing more than this small house and
a few sous. Most mornings I take meat pies to the docks and sell

them to the men there. They tell me I am the best cook in Marseilles! I will lock the door from outside and return at midday, so do not fear. Let us hope nobody saw you come here. That's the way I want it, until I think of a story to explain you to my neighbors."

Allegra heard sounds of kitchen preparations and then Odile's voice again. "Get some rest, Allegra, while I go down to the harbor and keep my eyes open."

She spent the day in her thoughts. If only she knew how far Barretto's nets extended, she could embark on her new life with a clearer mind. She decided that it was best to stay concealed until after the first of the year. If by then no one had come to Odile asking after the lost Contessa di Rienzi, they never would. And by the first of the year the baby would be born. It would be 1820, but it seemed an eternity away.

She explored the small house. There were two rooms at street level, the kitchen and a sitting room alcove; only Odile's room on the second level, and then the loft. She felt safer in her little place beneath the eaves of the roof and spent the rest of the day there. Her dormer window opened to the street side of the house. The blue shutters were closed, but light came in through several broken slats. Allegra prepared herself for a long stay in the loft.

They took their evening meal together in the kitchen, and Odile reported that a Venetian ship had anchored the night before and set sail again with the tide at mid-afternoon.

"They could have put some men ashore before they left, but I can only wait until they start asking questions in town. My friends will tell me if strangers are looking for me . . . or for an Italian woman who has wandered away from her home."

She looked defiant. "I almost welcome them. They have not had to deal with a good Frenchwoman. It will be a pleasure to send them off on a wild-goose chase." Her eyes glistened in anticipation. "Still—I don't like the situation of your husband's spies here in town, and I may have to divert them from your trail by talking to them. I might even bring them here so that they can see with their own eyes that I live alone."

The image of Zeno searching for her in order to gain Barretto's

favor made Allegra shudder. She didn't want to think about Luciano at all; his cleverness and anger made him even more
dangerous.

Odile tilted her large head for a moment of thought. "It is time
you retired to your loft, my pet—not just for sleeping, but for a
good period of time. There must not be a trace of your presence
here."

That night a burning pain shot into Allegra's lower back, waking her from sleep. The spasm released its hold after a few
minutes, leaving a shadow of an ache. She awoke in the morning
having forgotten about it. The baby was moving as usual, and
Allegra came into the habit of resting one hand over her precious
love child while she did other things.

With Odile gone during the days, Allegra wrote in her diary,
filling in the events since the April night when Byron sent her his
letter of farewell. The anguish of her heart had not found its way
onto the pages during those black times. But the words would
have to be written someday, so that children and grandchildren
could know what had really happened. Maybe even Renaldo
would forgive her when he grew to be a man. She prayed that the
diary would come into the hands of her descendants.

But half of her story was missing . . . the diary that told about
the first year with Barretto. She wished she had thought to bring
it. Now who would ever find it, hidden away in the attic closet in
the underskirts of an old gown?

Tucked into the pages of this diary was the fragment of the first
poem that Byron had given to her. Her eyes ran over the words
again.

> I found a sweet and gentle bird,
> A nun from convent walls released.
> Aquiver in my hand she stirred
> My heart until the pain had ceased . . .

Had she been able to ease his heart's pain? Or did the poem only
speak of his momentary need of her . . . until the pain had ceased.

She could have fled from his beguiling energies that night if she had been able to understand the true meaning of his words. *No,* she caught herself, *that is a lie. I couldn't have left him one moment earlier. I treasure every breath we shared, every touch. I regret nothing.* The baby moved strongly inside her, as if in agreement. She could feel its sharp little elbows and knees pressing against her firm belly. *Only another month, my dear little love, and I will be able to hold you and kiss you and tell you about your father whom I loved with all my heart.*

Odile brought books for her to read in French, and she pressed her mind to concentrate on understanding the writings of Rousseau. She was sure that Odile had never read them, but it was more for helping Allegra to master the language than anything else.

She loved the small house, which had been built with love; the pieces of furniture in it were handsome and solid, as she imagined René himself had been. Odile had been so happy to marry him, after spending most of her life in the service of others, in other people's houses. When Odile left the Palazzo Lamberti, Allegra and her sisters were just entering the convent. They were beyond the need for a nurse, and Odile married soon after that.

Allegra had no idea that Odile had been left with so little. She didn't want her sudden visit to be a burden. Somehow she would have to find a way to sell a piece of her jewelry without causing attention.

She mentioned it one afternoon when the old woman returned from the docks with her handcart. Odile wouldn't hear of it. "You are my guest, and I will not allow you to sell even a single piece of lace from your camisole! If you mention this again, I shall be wounded and insulted!" She feigned indignation the way she used to when Allegra would try to give her a gift, years ago. Odile had a good-humored pride, but it was not to be pressed upon.

"Then teach me to cook," Allegra said. "I can make food for your sailors."

"You?"

"My name is Francesca Gordoni now, and I am capable of using my two hands to be useful. I cannot sit here like a cat on a cushion all day."

"Francesca . . ." she stumbled over the name with a dubious face.

"Gordoni. Allegra di Rienzi is no more. The sooner we both think of me as this new person the safer we shall be. If Barretto's agents ask for me, you can say with truth that you have not seen me."

Odile looked hard at Allegra's determined face. "I promise you, my dear child, that no one shall hear my lips betray you. If you want to be this Francesca or the Queen of Spain or anybody else, that is who you are." The two women embraced with a flow of love and trust.

Odile's eyes crinkled into a humorous smile. "Perhaps I can be a long lost cousin of yours, but one of us will have to change to make that seem believable—just a bit," she said, patting her large girth and primping her wiry gray hair. She was quickly serious again. "Just tell me what you want me to know, and no more. It is better that I never hear the entire story. It will only make me upset, and that would be dangerous for both of us. I still cannot believe that you are the same shy little girl I used to cradle in my arms to keep from being frightened by thunder."

"I'm not. I have grown up since you last saw me. I had to learn some things about life."

Odile wrapped her in her ample arms. "So much wisdom for twenty years, my little precious. I am proud of you!"

"I'm going to survive, Odile, that I know."

THE FIRST LETTER FROM GINA arrived, addressed to Odile. It had been forwarded by Elletra's maid, who could be trusted to tell her secret to no one, not even Elletra. The tone of the letter was light, in part, but Gina's fear showed through her words.

"You can imagine," she wrote, "what is the condition of the *conte!*"

He came back from Vienna as soon as Zeno reported your disappearance. Zeno fears for his miserable life. I have been questioned, but I managed to pretend great shock and disbelief. I even suggested that you might have been kidnapped, in order to turn his attention away from your refuge with Odile. The *conte* has offered a fat reward to anyone who finds you, and he threatens to have Zeno's worthless head if he slackens his search for you. Take precautions, *cara*, do not feel safe yet. Even though Zeno is a fool, he is also desperate.

The *conte* may have agents I am unaware of. Luciano has just returned from Rome. He says he was set upon by robbers on the road and beaten. He watches me and I cannot trust him, either. He has joined the search for you.

I think your husband believes you have run away. Your father has taken your sisters with him to Milano for the season, most likely to escape the *conte*'s anger. Nowadays it is best to be invisible.

Do not worry about Renaldo. He is healthy. I will let you know when it will be safe for you to write me, but not soon. Take nothing for granted. The *conte* will not stop until he is satisfied. I pray for you each day.

Gina

"And I have my agents as well," Odile said scornfully, after Allegra gave her the letter. "There's not a man at the docks who would not do me a favor."

Allegra's entire world became the loft. She saw Odile only in the early morning and at the end of the day, after the men at the docks had bought her stock of meat pies. There was still no sign of Zeno or anyone else looking for her, and Allegra was starting to believe that no one ever would find her.

But there had been Gina's warning. It was now four weeks since she came to Marseilles, a full two months since she fled from the Ca' d'Argenti. She disciplined her restlessness to wait a while longer in her small room.

She spent her time embroidering a collar for Odile, a gift for Christmas; and she made some baby clothes from materials that the thrifty old woman had saved over the years. Her self-imposed French lessons were progressing well, and she was now reading a history of Charlemagne to pass the time.

It was the middle of November. The baby in her womb was big now and active. Allegra had come to think of the outside life beyond these walls as almost a dream.

There hadn't been another letter from Gina, and it was easy to believe that there was no Venice, no Barretto—nothing but this place. Then one day Odile returned from her work with an anxious face. Some Italians just outside the city were stopping the drivers of the public coaches along the main roads to ask questions and examine the passengers. They claimed to have authority to do so.

"They asked about a young woman who disappeared from her home in Venice and may have amnesia. The husband offers a huge reward. It is what we have been expecting, *ma petite*; we must be very careful now! Tell me again, did anyone notice you when you arrived at my house the first day?"

Allegra remembered the day. "Just some sailors, who would have noticed anything in skirts. I asked a woman for directions. That was at the bottom of your street. And there was the boy, just outside, who told me which was your door . . . ."

Odile's eyes sharpened. "What woman? Can you describe her?"

"She had a vegetable cart. She limped, I think, and slurred her words. . . ."

"Old Marianne," she said with a sigh of relief. "Thank God! She drinks too much red wine. She probably forgot you the next minute. But what about the boy? It could have been little Antoine, the scamp. . . ."

"He was only about six or seven."

"I can handle him. His father was a friend of my husband. And no one else saw you come here, are you sure?"

THERE WAS NOTHING TO DO but wait. While Odile was at the harbor the next day time dragged, until Allegra's nerves were almost to the breaking point. The old fear was back with a vengeance. Early in the afternoon she was halfheartedly picking at the food on her tray, when she glanced toward the window. Her eyes focused through the openings left by the broken slats of the shutters.

Something was happening in the street directly below. What was that little boy doing, pointing to the house? It was the same child she had talked to when she first came here. A nondescript man was with him, looking at the house with interest.

As she watched them, another of the searing pains she had felt on her first night in the loft burned through her back and down into her legs. She cried out and dropped to her knees, hugging her baby and rocking back and forth, until the fiery spasm relented.

The episode left her shaking and weak. She laid herself on the bed and pulled the coverlet over her. Something was wrong—she could feel it. The baby wasn't supposed to come for another month. With little Renaldo the first pains hadn't been so sharp.

A second wave tightened like a band around her. Her mind was clearing now. She would have to be ready for whatever was to come. She didn't expect Odile for hours yet.

She removed her dress and changed into a loose nightgown, gathering all the towels and pillows around her on the bed. With pillows at her back and under her knees she tried to relax against the contractions. She wasn't afraid. How different this was from that day a year ago, in the ghastly bed of the di Rienzi merchant prince, as she struggled to bring his sad little namesake into the world. She felt clean this time—undefiled.

The pains came at uneven intervals, and she was starting to perspire from every pore. She knew that an eight-month baby had a good chance of surviving, even after all this one had gone through. Never for a moment did she doubt that Byron's child would be born alive.

The hours wore on, as she worked to bring her child to birth.

She prayed to every saint she knew for help. Odile was long in coming home—far later than usual. Finally there were sounds of footsteps in the rooms below, and Allegra drew breath to call out. She cut off her words with a gasp, when she saw the curtain moving back and forth at the window. The signal! Someone was in the house with Odile.

She heard men's voices. Heavy footsteps moved around the house, and the voices came nearer until they were in the bedroom below. Odile was speaking loudly. . . .

". . . It breaks my heart to hear she is missing. Let's hope it is a temporary amnesia. . . . You must forgive my tears, gentlemen, but I loved my little Allegra . . . a sweet child. But, look on the bright side—she's likely back home again as we stand and talk about her!"

The men mumbled and followed her downstairs again. Her voice carried clearly from the kitchen up the shaft. "I won't let you leave without some good hot coffee to warm your insides. . . ." The voices became more cheerful.

Allegra stifled a cry as a new and much harder contraction started. She held the pillow tightly over her face. Almost immediately the next pain came, and moments after, the next. A burst of laughter sounded in the kitchen. Odile was taking too long. She must be having trouble getting rid of them. Tears of effort flowed down Allegra's face. Why did the baby decide to come today?

Odile's sharp voice penetrated up through the shaft. "My René always said if a wife runs away, let her go. It's better than forcing her to stay and ending up with poison in your bouillabaisse!" More laughter.

One of the men said, "If it wasn't for the gold, we'd be back in Venice in bed with our own wives."

"Then why don't you tell the old *conte* you found Allegra—dead and buried somewhere—and collect your coins? You could make a good story of it. Then go home and stay in bed for a week with your woman!"

Allegra knew it was almost time. But what if the child's first cries were heard? She used her failing strength to move to the window seat and shut the little door to the shaft. With both hands she pulled a folded coverlet from the seat and stuffed it against the secret door, then she slowly eased her body back upon the low bed. At the same time the water suddenly burst, drenching her.

She packed more towels under her legs. "Push with me, my darling," she whispered. She dimly heard more noises from the kitchen—the clatter of chairs being moved. At last, when all thought and sounds became a blur, and nothing else existed but herself and her child, four long downward thrusts brought an end to the labor.

The baby, wet and entwined in its pulsating thick cord, lay between her legs. She strained forward to see the tiny silent creature, her daughter. The cord would have to be cut, but how? She hadn't thought of that. A knife lay on the table across the room just out of reach. She strained to stand up, but the afterbirth was starting to come out, and she sat down again on the edge of the bed.

The baby was lying too still. Her face was bluish, and she had not started to cry. There was no choice to be made, no caring about the danger from downstairs. She picked up her baby and vigorously slapped her back until she heard the wonderful clear gasping cries of her child. She was alive . . . and she had auburn hair, like Byron's! Allegra pressed the little bit of squalling life to herself and wept and laughed. "Thank God . . . thank God!"

The trapdoor to the loft dropped down as Odile's voice called up, "That's the last we'll see of them . . . *Sacre* . . . !" she exclaimed when she saw Allegra. "Of all the times to have your baby . . . !"

She rushed to the table and fetched the knife. In one swift motion she cut the cord cleanly. She cleared away the afterbirth and ran to the kitchen for a basin of warm water. In a few minutes the baby was bathed and wrapped in a soft linen blanket.

"I want to take her to my breast, Odile."

"Of course you do, *ma chère*." She deftly changed the bedding while Allegra held her precious child. "Now rest. I'll bring up some broth and then I'll tell you all about those Venetian buffoons!''

"No one will ever take you from me," Allegra said to the eagerly sucking infant at her breast. There was no hesitation in her mind about choosing a name. She was to be called Allegra—the name that Byron loved . . . Allegra Gordoni.

"She may be called Allegra, but she is not going to become a mirror image of her mother," Odile said thoughtfully, as she offered a bowl of steaming fish broth. "She will be a handful—willful and stubborn—I can see it in her face already . . . and it's not from her mother that she gets those qualities," she smiled a little ruefully.

Allegra looked at the tiny contented face and could not see what Odile was describing. "She seems so peaceful."

"I sometimes think I was given the gift of sight, but then I can be wrong. Are you certain that you won't tell the father about her birth?" It was as close as she had come to asking about this man Byron. She was familiar with the gossip about him: he was a charmer and a notorious womanizer. It made her angry every time she thought about it. He didn't deserve the love of a fine girl like Allegra.

"I'm certain. But I want her christened. Can you help me to find a priest who will do it? I will have to tell a little lie, but after everything else, God shouldn't care about one more."

She tried to make her voice sound offhand, but it did worry her very much that she was compounding her sins at every turn. She was determined that little Allegra never be thought of as a bastard in the eyes of the world. She would learn about her true father someday, perhaps, but for now it was best that she be the daughter of a man named Gordoni, who died before she was born.

Odile sat beside the bed and held Allegra's hand. "Father Aristide is my good friend, and he will do what I ask. Those two men who came here . . . I gave them something to think about. Somebody—I think it was that naughty child you talked to—told them that a foreign woman visited me. They said that they would be paid a fat purse to find you. After a while I got them to be more friendly. I gave them free meat pies from my cart. They were full of gossip about your disappearance. People will believe anything! There have been reports that you ran away to be a nun . . . that you have become the mistress of that mad violinist, Paganini . . . a dozen ridiculous tales. I brought them to the house so that they could see I had nothing to conceal. I only regret that I was not with you during your ordeal. My poor angel, it must have been so difficult to be alone and afraid. . . .''

"I didn't feel alone."

"And you still do not want him to know . . . ?"

"Not yet. Maybe someday he will learn that he has a fine daughter, but not yet. And you were right—she will probably be willful and full of energy, just like her father."

"Oh, my dear! It's not really Paganini!" Odile said in pretended horror.

"No! What an awful thought!"

They both laughed until the baby awoke and looked up with Byron's eyes. "Paganini's baby would never be as beautiful," Allegra smiled.

Odile's heart twisted.

THE CHRISTENING TOOK PLACE in Odile's kitchen, with the elderly priest giving God's blessing upon the baby. He had objected to performing the ceremony outside the church, but Odile convinced him that the mother would imperil her health if she ventured forth into the chilly November weather.

If he suspected the truth, he never revealed it by his expression. Allegra had a brief strong urge to make a confession to him, but the impulse was quickly subdued.

Odile walked with him to the door afterward. "I trust you, father," she whispered. "This young woman is truly in danger, but not from illness. She is being hounded by an evil man, who would kill her if he knew her whereabouts."

The old priest nodded. He had heard many things in his years of service in Marseilles, and he was used to making allowances for situations. Odile pressed a few coins into his hand.

"Do not register this birth in the book yet. If Francesca Gordoni were discovered, it would be on both our souls."

He nodded again and turned to make the sign of the cross in the doorway. "Life is more important than the name on a line of paper. Tell your young lady not to fear. I shall pray to the Lord to bless you both—and the infant."

At that moment a thin cry came from inside the house. It was quickly joined by a far louder infant cry from the house next door. Odile smiled. God was taking care of everything today. The sound of Madame Fénélon's lusty twins would be such a good noise to cover up the tiny wails of Allegra's child.

She crossed herself and closed the door after her.

CHAPTER FOURTEEN

CHRISTMAS CAME AND WENT, and Twelfth Night. Marseilles had been deluged with rain for many weeks—a bleak beginning for the year 1820.

Odile brought small gifts to Allegra and the child—whom they called Allegrina—little Allegra—gifts of clothing, which Odile's clever fingers had fashioned in the late hours of the nights. Allegra offered her one of the tiny treasures that Abou had allowed her to keep . . . an unset ruby, not large, but very clear and deeply red. Odile refused to accept it.

"What would people think of me with such a thing? Imagine the attention I would get. The trail would lead directly back to you."

"Then keep it for one day in the future, after I am gone from here, and then find a way to sell it to some rich traveler. I want you to have it, Odile. It is all I can do to repay your love."

Odile made a doubting sound in her throat. "I will hold it for you, Allegra, and if you ever need the money it can bring, it will be here for you. My love is given freely and desires no gift in return."

As the dreary days blended into one another, no more news of Barretto's search came to Odile's ears. Gina managed to have another letter forwarded via Elletra's maid. She never mentioned Byron or Teresa Guiccioli. . . .

I realized soon after you left that you had taken the wrong pearls. Your mother's necklace is safe with me. Do not worry that it will end up on the neck of some unworthy woman. I will guard it until Renaldo is older—if I am allowed to stay on at the Ca'—and then I will give the pearls to him and pray that he will give them to his wife one day.

If there were any way that I could get them to you without danger, I would. The *conte* has aged greatly in the past months . . . his anger eats at him. It is not yet safe for you, *cara*. Even though Zeno tells me that the search in Marseilles is finished and is being directed to Milano and Florence, he may be lying . . . just waiting for me to contact you. Luciano comes and goes. I do not know what he is up to.

I wish I could put you at peace, but I cannot. I pray every day for your soul and the soul of your new baby. . . .

Gina

MARCH

THE BABY WAS GROWING WELL and quickly, and Allegra refused to stay confined in the loft after Gina's second letter. But Odile's instincts advised caution. Allegra was longing to be free to leave the house and walk with her baby to the public parks, but it disturbed Odile to see her becoming too fearless, as if by calling herself Francesca Gordoni she could become another person and erase the realities of her past.

"Why not?" she argued, when the first spring warmth was clearing the winter skies. "Allegrina cannot grow up like this, never seeing the light of day." Her eyes flared with energy. "Why can't we make up a likely story about me? . . . I could be a widowed relative of a family you once knew when you were a nursemaid in Venice. . . ."

"No, not Venice," Odile said quickly. "I also worked for a time in Aosta. You could be from there. Nobody should think you are from Venice."

Allegra smiled. "Then you agree."

"Only a little. It is against my better judgment, but I think we can find a way to bring Madame Gordoni and her daughter to town. You cannot simply walk out of my house one day and say good-morning to my neighbors . . . they are too suspicious. You must first arrive in Marseilles in a normal way, like any other traveler." Her face took on a shrewd look. "If that is what you want, I think I have enough friends on the docks to make it work . . . but I don't like it."

Allegra lay with her infant close to her that night. A feeling of anticipation kept sleep away, and her thoughts kept returning to Byron. Where was he at this moment? She could feel the heat of his body against hers and smell the special fragrance of his skin. Was he still with Teresa, or had he left her? Was he looking for his lost Allegra, so that he could hold her to his breast and weep for her forgiveness?

She put her fingers around the gold locket and stopped her breathless mental pictures. *Have I so little grasp of life,* she thought to herself. *If he has left Teresa, it is for the arms of a new woman who can excite him. Not only did I make him uncomfortable, but I bored him with my love. . . . How I have changed,* she smiled. *No wonder I bored him. I was a naive child who was blind to his real needs. He didn't want a dead weight of love hanging around his neck.*

It was in the late night hours in the hidden loft that her emotions could be most easily stirred by memories. All of her knowledge of love between man and woman had been taught by Byron in the hours of darkness . . . she would always have a problem with the nights.

In a few days "Francesca Gordoni" would be born, and her life would begin in earnest on the passenger docks of Marseilles. That new woman would not be trusting and weak and inexperienced; she had learned a lifetime of lessons in the past year. It was enough that Allegra had her memories and the greatest gift that could be left to her. She ran her finger along the strong curve of her baby's lips and stroked the auburn curls. Perhaps she already had the best of Byron in this fresh new life by her side . . . little Allegrina.

Her natural joy in life was wakening again. She could stand at her dormer window and see in the distance the sun sparkle on the sea—hear the shouts of children playing . . . the far-off sound of a concertina—all bringing a surging sense of life into her heart.

"Hearts mend," Byron had written. Hers was healing over the deep cuts that love had made. She would always love him, but the tenderness of the scars was easing. There was less pain and more happiness when she thought of him.

THE PREPARATIONS for Francesca's so-called arrival were like a plan of battle for an invasion. Odile thought of everything—she studied the lists of ships that were due in port until she found just the right one . . . a packet from Genoa, which carried passengers and cargo and made a regular short run between the two cities. Little fuss was made about its comings and goings, no more than if it were a public coach arriving from the highways.

She chose the day with care so that there would be no Venetian ships in the harbor. She and Allegra would load the cart with empty trunks and slip down to the waterfront long before dawn.

Even if anyone had seen Allegra's first arrival at Odile's door, it would be unlikely that she would be recognized now. Months of good care and plentiful food had made changes. Her fragile figure was fuller and more womanly, and her face bloomed with health.

Allegra wore a simple black travel dress, skillfully remade from an old one of Odile's, for a young widow. Odile helped her with her hair, making it into a style of a middle-class woman. It framed her face with dark waves beneath which her eyes looked luminous and beautiful.

"A far cry from the waif that I found at my doorstep," Odile laughed.

It was four o'clock in the morning when they left the house. Allegrina was swaddled and sleeping in a basket in the cart. "There will be five very large and threatening-looking dock-workers who are ready to swear that you got off the packet from Genoa today. Only a fool would dare question their eyesight."

Near the harbor they were met by Odile's five rough men, who were in reality old friends of hers from many years back. They surrounded the little party and put the baggage into a dinghy. One man, named Claude, lifted Allegra and her child as if they were feather pillows and deposited them into the boat.

Odile stayed behind on the quay with her cart, ready to greet them when they returned. She watched Claude row the boat part-way out into the harbor and then make a wide arc next to the Genoa packet, before returning to the landing. Odile let out a loud shout of greeting.

As Allegra stepped ashore again she was swept into a great embrace and heard her name repeated again and again . . . "Francesca! Francesca, my dear!"

Few heads turned at the commonplace event of a traveler arriving to the welcome of friends and family. Other men and women were also arriving from the packet at the same time. Odile talked loudly, expressing her delight that Francesca and the baby would be living with her now, and her dockmen friends joined in with heavy-voiced greetings. It was a fine performance. By the time they had all accompanied the loaded cart back up the hill to Odile's house, there was no doubt that a young woman from Aosta had arrived with her baby for a long visit.

After the men had enjoyed their mugs of strong coffee and eaten their cheese and bread, they took turns with good-hearted embraces of the newcomer and promised help if ever she should need it.

"It is valuable to have friends like that," Odile said after they left. "They have a sense of honor that is strong. If they give a promise to you it is a good one. Besides, all men have a soft heart for widows," she smiled. "For a while yet you will have to wear mourning black, but by summer we can say a year has passed since your husband passed on. . . ."

Allegra threw her arms around Odile's large warm body. "You have made me so happy! You won't regret it! Now I can help you with your work, and you needn't ever worry about making enough money for all of us. I will cook with you and go to the harbor with you. We can do twice as much business!"

Allegra's enthusiasm wasn't immediately shared. Odile still had serious regrets about bringing her out into the world so soon. Years of living had made her cautious, and she knew enough about men to understand that vengeance often bides its time. She crossed herself hastily. "In good time, *ma chère*, in good time."

The next day Allegra insisted on taking Allegrina with her to Father Aristide's small parish church, where she felt drawn to offer a prayer of thanks for her safety. She wished that she could enter her name and her child's on the church rolls. Something very deep in her mourned her estrangement from the sacraments. She wanted to be part of the beauty, the assurances, the forgiveness—but she could not unless she let herself enter the confessional.

She longed for forgiveness. She had no intention of committing further sins. There would be no more adultery—how could there be? The figure of the Holy Mother stood in a carved niche beneath a slender stained-glass window. The morning sun pierced the fragments of glass, bathing the graceful statue in color. Allegra stood before it with a prayer that one day she would feel cleansed in the depths of her soul. She turned Allegrina's face to the statue to receive blessing. The face of the Holy Mother had a slight smile, and Allegra felt a communication of hearts—from woman to woman. A peaceful energy settled over her emotions.

She walked quickly from the gray stone church at the top of the hill to find Odile. It was a crisp morning. This time the jostling crowds and sailors seemed part of the music of life, not ugly and dreary. Even the smells of humanity and its garbage were not so terrible.

She found Odile at the waterfront with her cart and caught her in an embrace, almost losing hold of the baby.

"So you have had a good morning," Odile said, sizing up Allegra's mood. "Well, so have I. I have sold everything down to the wood slats of the cart. Spring fever makes men hungry," she laughed.

Two of the dockworkers were just finishing their pastry snack and greeted Allegra by her new name. They were as polite as their rough vocabulary would allow and laughed easily, taking time to play with the baby. In that moment she wished Gina could see her, surrounded by this new family, and know that she was at last safe.

For a few weeks after that Odile kept Allegra busy in the kitchen baking meat pies and pastries. Allegra discovered that she had a true talent for cooking, and she delighted in making her hands create useful and attractive things. She had never before been allowed in kitchens, at the Palazzo Lamberti or the Ca' d'Argenti. With Allegrina in a cradle by the hearth and Odile singing at her work, there was love and contentment in the little house on Rue Gaston.

Odile invented short errands for her and encouraged her to take the baby for walks in the little park at the top of the hill near the church. She wanted to keep her away from the harbor. There was still a chance that someone would be looking for her. Odile's intuition was strong on this point, and Allegra did not treat it lightly.

JUNE

ALLEGRA HAD RECEIVED several more communications from Gina, each letter carrying a warning that Barretto had not lessened his determination to find her and bring her back. But it had been nine months now . . . and no sign of Barretto's agents in Marseilles since the one visit to Odile's house last winter.

It seemed to Allegra that the long time of anxiety had taken a heavy toll on Odile. She walked a little more slowly now and tried to deny that her health was poor.

Allegra finally exerted her will over Odile's and insisted on sharing the work at the docks. Whatever the risks, she could not allow Odile to work herself to death when there was a perfectly good solution to the problem—and she managed to have the last word in the argument: "I refuse to play the part of a pampered lady, dabbling in the kitchen and walking in the parks while you make yourself ill working to support us."

THE SUMMER HEAT hung over the city, but on the docks a light breeze stirred Allegra's dark curls, now escaping from the white lace French cap, which Odile had insisted that she wear. She was pushing the flat-topped wooden cart. René had built it so that its well-oiled wheels trundled easily over the stone paving and wood planks of the quays.

The baby, well wrapped, lay sleeping in the curve of the cart's wide handle, where some reed matting made a roomy cradle. Her little pink face with its top of dark red curls was framed in more lace.

Allegra smiled at the tight tiny fists and the dark lashes. The little one slept hard. She gave all her energy to sleep, with the same emotional vitality of her father. *My Allegra will not walk softly in life,* she thought, *but she will be curious and eager and charming.* Already the baby lips could form into a beguiling smile, and the eyes had changed color to a fascinating gray brown, like those well-remembered ones, which still smiled at her in dreams.

She shook off her reverie and gave attention to her work. The pies and cakes, which she was spreading on the top of the cart, gave off a tantalizing odor. Customers from among the workers would flock around her, as soon as she removed the white cloth cover.

After weeks of begging Odile for the chance to come to the dock with the cart, Allegra had her chance, but now she was not as sure of herself as she wanted to be. She was tense and felt unprotected. The thought of Barretto intruded uncomfortably into her mind. She imagined she felt his iron-cold anger thrust toward her and realized that he would never give up the pursuit.

She had almost decided to return up the hill to the safety of the house, when several men approached with money in their hands expecting to be sold meat pies. She put a protective hand over the coin purse secured at her belt and took a deep breath.

How strange everything now seemed! What was she doing in this place? Her heart felt tight again, and the heaviness in her breast, which had lingered since Byron's final letter to her, was like a cold finger pressing against her.

She gave herself a shake to clear her mind. *Odile expects me to be the strong, fearless woman I told her I was. . . .*

After she had gone through the motions of serving the first group of men, the mood of apprehension began to lift. Several large ships were in harbor, among the smaller packets and launches. One stood out because of its clear lines and high masts. A few men were hanging by ropes over its sleek sides, scraping at its prow by the waterline; others were scrubbing its beautiful figurehead with brushes, and still others were repainting the long jutting bowsprit.

Allegra gazed at the vigorous vital ship. It looked so taut and eager to move. There was no doubt that it could fly over the sea, spreading the water easily, unhindered. There was a sense of excitement in its long lines. The proud figurehead gleamed with colors. It was unlike most of the carved figures that she had seen on the ships in the harbor. It was common enough to have a carved woman, but this one had a body that grew out of the wood of the prow, and her head was raised away from the rest of the wood. A bright blue liberty cap covered her streaming golden hair. Across her breast was draped a flag, as though pressed to her body by a playful wind . . . brilliant with red and white stripes. The part that was molded over her shoulder showed a circle of gold stars on a blue ground. Allegra recognized the flag of the United States of America, that young and growing republic, which had fought its way to freedom from Britain not long ago.

The woman at the bow bobbed in the swell of the harbor tide, and light from the water glinted on the gleaming gold face. At first Allegra thought it was a trick of morning light, but then she saw that the golden face was smiling. It was a triumphant, challenging, daring smile. Whoever carved those red laughing lips had infused the very essence of adventure into them.

Allegra's eyes followed the long line of the ship until she saw in raised golden letters a name, *Laughing Liberty,* then beneath in small letters, *Boston.* How exciting to be the master of such a ship, she thought. It was a real being, with a life of its own, full of energy like the New World from which it came.

A voice at her elbow made her jump. "I see you're admiring my beautiful lady, ma'am." The voice spoke in Byron's tongue. She looked up into the face of a tall man, who was smiling at her out of the keenest and clearest blue eyes she had ever seen. "Do you speak English? My French is too poor to use when I am hungry," he smiled.

"Yes," she said, as soon as she pulled herself together from the shock of hearing that language again after so many months. The man had a slight accent, different from Byron's, which she found hard to follow.

"I was drawn by the fragrance of your hotcakes, ma'am. I am Captain John Appleby of the *Laughing Liberty,* at your service." He gave a bow. He was disconcerting . . . so big. His long finely chiseled face was so ruddy and his long nose so imposing, while his eyes glinted at her with hidden laughter. He was the perfect captain to sail such a ship.

"Forgive me," she had to smile. "It is the English. I am not of great proficiency." She took a piece of thin paper, which was ready for the baked goods, and began to wrap his pies, while he watched her out of those very blue eyes.

"It was rude of me," he said in French. "I can speak your language well enough to get by." His accent was that of a cultured man.

"Thank you," Allegra smiled again. "I regret my English is difficult."

"But you are not French," he said with conviction. "I would guess Italian, from your voice and because of your eyes, am I right?"

Allegra's fears flooded back. Why was he questioning her? Yet his fine sensitive lips had no look of cruelty or deception. His was a strong and trustworthy face.

"I am from Italy," she answered in a small voice. "From Venice." As soon as the words were out, she was horrified that she had not said Aosta.

"Hmm." He had the most perceiving eyes. It was as if he were able to notice more details than people usually did. His gaze was not impolite, but its intensity made Allegra breathe faster. She had not felt such a reaction to any man since she had first looked into Byron's penetrating eyes. Her nerves relaxed a little. . . . There was a kind and trustworthy quality in the captain's face.

She broke from his gaze and hastily offered the package to him. He extracted a purse from a pocket of his dark blue coat. She saw that the material was fine and was cut expertly to the measure of his broad shoulders. His long legs were covered in equally well-tailored trousers, and his boots shone with high polish. She fixed her eyes on the gold fob and chain of his waistcoat, while he counted out change for the pies. His soft linen neck cloth was gleaming white, as she looked up at him. The bright sun brought out golden lights in his wavy brown hair. His eyes crinkled into a boyish smile as he took the package, sniffing at it appreciatively.

From under one arm he drew a cocked hat, discreetly trimmed in gold braid with a small insignia on one side. He set the hat squarely on his thick hair, and his expression sobered. The boyish look dissolved into that of the dignified and courteous captain. Allegra expected him to move away, but he lingered, looking down at the tiny Allegrina.

"Your child, ma'am?"

Allegra nodded. He put a gentle finger to the little curled hand. "Like a baby starfish," he smiled. Allegrina responded and closed her fingers around his. His face was intent as he looked at the tugging small fist. "What small beginnings we have! Sometimes I cannot believe that some men were ever babies. Think of old Boney out there on Elba . . . or portly George of England . . . or for that matter, Caroline of Brunswick." He laughed. The pictures he made were hard to resist, and Allegra laughed too.

He grew serious again. "At the risk of impertinence, ma'am, why do you work like this, and with the little one? Is your husband unable to work?" She saw real concern in the startlingly blue eyes bent to hers.

"I am a widow, sir, and I must have a livelihood."

His face lightened, even while he voiced his regrets. "My men and I will eat many pies and cakes," he assured her. "We are in harbor for repairs. There was heavy weather off Malta. We shall be here several weeks at least, before we sail for home." He stood silently looking out at the *Laughing Liberty*. "She is a beauty, is she not?"

Allegra felt his pride in the great ship. "The most beautiful I have ever seen," she said and was rewarded by a smile so delightful that her breath caught again.

John Appleby's face relaxed into its usual strong lines. "May I inquire your name, ma'am, so that I may recommend your wares to my men?"

"My name is Francesca Gordoni." Her voice was small and uncertain. Somehow, in perfect courtesy, this man had thrust himself into her awareness. She was not sure what she wanted to feel. His strong presence reminded her that she was a woman, and that was upsetting. She stood with her eyes down, looking at her baby's sleeping face.

"A lovely name . . . Francesca," she heard his deep voice linger on the name. "Very fitting for so lovely a lady. Good day, ma'am," he said in English and suddenly was striding with long steps away from her and toward the mooring of the *Laughing Liberty*.

She pushed the cart slowly, and many of Odile's regular customers stopped to buy. The men were courteous in their own rough way. They had a protective attitude toward her and the baby. She heard them talking about the *Laughing Liberty* among themselves.

They admired both the ship and its captain. It was not the first time his voyages had brought him to Marseilles, and he was known. She listened with interest. The ship had several times been around the Cape of Good Hope and had traded with China and India, as well as Turkey and Egypt. Captain Appleby was one of a group of independent captains from the United States, who had grown rich from trade and whose ship was a small empire in itself.

"I wouldn't mind shipping on with him," one of the younger men said through a mouthful of meat pie. "He won't stand for any nonsense, but his men say he's fair and just. Won't tolerate having slaves on his ship. He refused a big offer from a friend of the Duke of Wellington, because the man insisted on bringing a slave he'd bought in Morocco."

"He's stiff in the lip on that subject," a new man said in labored French. "I'm on his ship. He runs things with a firm hand, all right. There's not much to complain about, except maybe the constant cleaning. I've never sailed on such a clean one."

Their conversation moved on to other things. They bought more and more, until Allegra's supply was gone and Allegrina was fretful. One man, an old friend of Odile, insisted on pushing the cart up the long hill.

Odile was delighted with Allegra's first day's success and had already baked a huge supply for the next day. She noticed the new restlessness in Allegra but would wait until she spoke of what was bothering her.

When Allegra unwrapped the baby, she found a few coins tucked into the blanket and blinked away sudden tears. The men in their simple way were very kind.

The brilliant blue eyes of Captain Appleby stuck in her mind. Later in the day she described him to Odile, who listened with a knowing smile. "I have heard of the ship, child. I've not seen the captain, but he is a legend among the men. They say that he is a wealthy man in his home city, but that the sea calls him. He is married to his ship . . . that's what they say."

The next day, crewmen from the *Laughing Liberty* swarmed ashore and bought up the lion's share of Odile's pies. Allegra tried not to look for the tall captain. Then he appeared, striding along the quay just when her supply had run out. He pulled a disappointed face.

She was starting her apologies when the bustling, starched figure of Odile appeared, full of smiles. "I have come to help you with the cart." She flirted a smiling eye at the captain.

"My men have eaten the pies and left none for me," he complained good-naturedly. "Are you the maker of these delicious things, ma'am?"

Odile capitulated to his potent masculine appeal. "If you care to come with us to the top of that hill, sir, I've a hot batch ready baked for tomorrow, which I might be willing to share with a hungry man."

Allegra felt a sudden discomfort. Why was Odile encouraging him? She was irritated with herself and with Odile, but a familiar feeling of unbidden excitement began to tingle along her nerves.

"Let me push the cart." Captain Appleby's strong hands took the handle from her. Allegra snatched the baby up into her arms.

"I'll go on ahead, Odile. She needs feeding, and I'm tired."

She sounded petulant, even to herself. As she sped up the hill with Allegrina starting to wail in her arms, she decided what to do to shake off this disconcerting feeling.

She retreated to the loft room with the baby's food. Presently she heard the captain's deep tones and Odile's laugh. The smell of hot coffee came tantalizingly to her nose.

"Francesca," Odile called up the stairs, "come and have some coffee; it will revive you."

"Thank you, but I would rather rest," Allegra replied. She wished that René had devised a system of mirrors in his dumb-waiter shaft, so that she could see what was happening in the kitchen below. From the sounds of amiable chatting, the captain must be sitting at ease by the table eating Odile's meat pies. The worst of it was that she couldn't quite hear what they were saying!

Finally the captain left after full-voiced compliments on the cooking. "You don't know what it means, ma'am, after being at sea for a month, to have fresh food and good cooking. We stopped in Turkey and Egypt, but I've no stomach for their spices."

Allegra frowned deeply when she heard Odile giving him an open hearty invitation to dine with them. She knew Odile meant well, but she wanted no situation with the handsome captain. Even though her marriage as not one of the heart, still she was a married woman. Now that Byron was lost to her, her conscience was troubled enough to last a lifetime.

There could be no more men in her life. She puzzled again over the meaning of marriage. Surely the blind obedience and use of her body, which Barretto expected, was not true marriage. Where was love—that missing part of her marriage? It was with Byron. He, too, had used her, but with her consent. He had always been honest with her. It was she who confused reality with hope and dream.

She could still hear the bleak misery in his haunting voice. "I have a way of choosing on the high point of passion . . . and then when I wake up to more sanity, I have hurt where I did not intend." He had turned to look at her with his brilliant gaze, beneath dark brows. "What do you see to admire in such a man, Allegra?"

She winced, remembering how she had rushed to speak of her love to him . . . from the depth of her uncomplicated heart. It was beginning to seem so long ago.

Why had she suddenly remembered all of this, she questioned herself, as she stood waiting for Odile's inevitable visit to her room, and the loving accusations. *Because,* she answered honestly, *I must not let Byron fade before the bright presence of John Appleby. I don't want to forget.*

She sighed and looked at the face of her sleeping child, wondering again if she should let Byron know about her. Should she deny Allegrina her own father? What a legacy it would be to know a father of such genius!

ODILE SCOLDED HER for not entertaining the captain. "He is a fine man. He is the kind I would trust . . . and so charming. La! He makes me wish I was young again! And what a delicious accent—forthright and honest, like his own country!"

Allegra made no reply. That night when she went to bed the animated face of John Appleby came without effort into her mind. She saw again the fine line of his lips. They were the kind of lips that would make a woman wonder what their kiss would be like.

CHAPTER FIFTEEN

JULY

ALLEGRA AND ODILE alternated days at the dockside with the cart. Allegra insisted. Odile should be at home more, now that it was midsummer and so hot.

On Odile's days at the harbor, there was always a message for Allegra: "Captain Appleby asked after you and Allegrina."

Allegra found her working days to be a blend of happiness and anxiety. John Appleby was there each morning to buy cakes and talk. He tried to draw her into conversation about herself, and when that failed he told her exciting and amusing stories of his own adventures. There was a crackling energy, which flowed out of his tall body. She feared the lift of heart that came to her when she saw his graceful vigorous figure striding toward her.

Her growing confusion impelled her to spend more hours on her knees in the small church. Someone had made a little shrine to Santa Chiara—they called her Sainte Claire. At first she avoided it and went instead to pray to other saints. She could not bear to bring her failures to the clear eyes of Santa Chiara.

When she finally had to do something about her inner distress, she made a dedication to Santa Chiara, promising that she would never again let herself come under the spell of a man and enter into an adulterous relationship. "That is my promise," she whispered.

She paused on her way out to light candles for Renaldo and Barretto. "I give honor and prayers to my husband and son, but I will never return to them."

The cloud of indecision removed itself from her after that, and she felt able to look with cool kindness into the energetic and probing eyes of Captain John Appleby. She wished that his ship would be repaired.

She often asked in a quiet little voice when he would be sailing for home. Whenever she did, an odd quirk of a smile would flicker over his attractive firm mouth, and he would say, "Soon enough . . . I still have business here."

She knew that he was buying porcelain from the famous factories outside the city, which made tableware and art objects. He told her that he had been commissioned by his friend, Acton Lewes, to bring him a complete set of porcelain dinnerware to Boston.

"He is a younger son of the Duke of Penryn. He came to the United States to work for a friend of his father on an estate in Massachusetts." He laughed at her puzzled face when he spoke the odd name. "That is the name of one of our states. It is a word of the American Indians, who were the original inhabitants.

"Anyway, Acton is learning how to manage land, and his father has given him an old estate for his patrimony. Acton became my friend when he decided to pursue some special studies in chemistry at Harvard College, where I was also a student. He is especially interested in fine art objects, their manufacture and the glazes used. He should have been an artist-craftsman, but now he's the owner of Penriding, an estate gone to seed, but worthwhile. He has dropped his title and has become an American citizen." The captain smiled. "He is to be married in the fall, and this is to be a gift to his wife."

Allegra murmured suitable words of interest. Why was he telling her so much about his life and his friends? Every time he started one of his narratives, she felt as if he were extending a beautiful silvery net, which sought to capture her imagination and draw her closer to him.

"Have you seen any of the Marseilles porcelains?" he was asking.

She shook her head. "I am too occupied, sir."

"Hmm," he observed. "Don't you ever wish to marry again, ma'am? You are a lovely lady, one whom a man would be very proud to love and care for."

A thrill rushed through her at the tone in his voice. What a sweet and good thing it was to be gently courted by this man! What would he think if he knew the truth about his virtuous widow? But she did not want to give him hope . . . she wouldn't allow that to happen. Still, she wondered how it would be to come under the love and protection of such a man of honor.

She silenced her clamoring sense and said in a quiet voice, "I do not intend to remarry. My marriage was arranged . . . and . . . it did not give me a taste for continuing in that state. Now that I am widowed and have my child, I wish for my own life of freedom."

"Hmm," he repeated. "I have never been a believer in arranged marriages, but most of society seems to think otherwise." As was his habit, he pulled his hat from under his arm, set it jauntily on his head, and with a glittering glance from his fine eyes and a slight bow, he strode away.

Allegra gazed after him in puzzlement. Maybe she had only imagined he was courting her. Maybe he was just being polite, and it was his stomach that brought him to buy her pies and to drop by for coffee on Odile's days home. She felt an unreasonable irritation and frowned fiercely at the remaining stock of food on her cart.

Odile's friends, who always tempered their swearing tongues and salty manners in her presence, soon bought up the rest of her day's stock. Their usual pleasantries and puns got only a brief response from her, and they eyed each other over her head with commiserating smiles: the little one was out of sorts.

She went home in a bad humor and was snappish with Odile, who asked her if she was sickening for something and gave her a spoonful of her herbal tonic.

THE NEXT TIME she went to the harbor, Captain Appleby was absent. Odile had not reported seeing him the day before. She calmed herself with prayer at Father Aristide's little church and told herself to stop looking for John Appleby's striding form.

A few days later Allegra stood with her cart on the quays, not far from John Appleby's ship. She saw the captain draw up to the dock in a fine open carriage. He was with another gentleman and two ladies. He gallantly assisted the ladies to alight and seemed to linger over the hand of one of them longer than Allegra thought necessary, from her vantage point.

The men and ladies, in their height-of-fashion dresses, were rowed out to the *Laughing Liberty*. Allegra heard only echoes of voices and laughter. Meanwhile she was busy selling, but whenever possible she kept an unobtrusive watch over the ship. After some time she saw the captain emerge on deck with the flirtatious lady. He escorted her with his hand under her elbow and was obviously showing her the fine points of the *Laughing Liberty*.

They stood close together, while his hand pointed up to the graceful masts. Allegra was too far away to see clearly, but she knew with grinding irritation that the woman's eyes were looking up invitingly into the captain's handsome face.

When she could stand it no longer, she quickly sold the last of her pies and trundled the cart back up the hill. At home she snatched Allegrina out of Odile's arms and held her fiercely close. Odile knew that behind Allegra's recent moodiness lay the person of John Appleby.

Byron's eyes looked up at Allegra from Allegrina's self-possessed little face. She was a tiny child, dainty and willful, even at eight months. Allegra's love for Byron flowed painfully into her heart, where it clashed with the image of the blue-eyed sea captain. She sat down by the small table in the kitchen, unaware that Odile's eyes were shrewdly observant.

"It's so hot!" Allegra threw back the lace-edged fichu from around her throat.

Odile smiled broadly. "Then you will not refuse my special sherbet, with strawberries, which I have made for the evening meal."

"Sherbet?" Allegra was startled. "You went all the way to the ice house in this heat and did all the work turning the freezing pail?"

Odile nodded, looking pleased. "I have added a measure of thick sweet cream and just a touch of bitter almond to the berries. *Formidable!*" She kissed her fingers in salute to the ineffable flavor of the waiting sherbet. "And now," she turned toward the kitchen, "I have for you a sweet lemon drink cooled with ice."

Allegra savored the tart coolness, and her irritation with herself and the captain eased. "You are so kind to me, Odile—and I have upset your life."

"Nonsense, my dear girl, it is good to be useful once more." She took the restless baby from Allegra's arms. "I will feed this impatient one and put her to sleep. You must rest, *chérie*, so that you can help me to entertain the charming Captain Appleby for supper tonight."

Allegra gasped. "I should have known!"

"I knew he wanted to be invited to dine," Odile smiled innocently, "and so I asked him." Her look quickly became serious. "He is a good man, *petite,* he is one to be trusted, and that cannot be said for many men. Treat him kindly as our guest. Now go and rest."

It was no use arguing. Allegra went, secretly fuming, to the loft. She deliberately made no special toilette for the captain's arrival. She put on a dress of violet cotton, which Odile had made for her. It was a color widows often wore once the formal mourning period was over, and it was plain and cool.

On impulse, she took out the gold-and-coral necklace from the Byron box and put it around her neck. Her hand touched the locket at her throat. The curl of Byron's hair still carried a vibration that she could feel. It would be her talisman against her treacherous body and the energies of Captain John Appleby.

He had already arrived when she came downstairs into the cozy lower room. He sat at ease in the broad window seat with a glass of golden sherry. When she entered he rose and bowed over her hand. She felt the warm touch of his lips move softly on her fingers, and she swiftly withdrew from his touch.

Odile bustled in from the kitchen with a flowered blue tureen and placed it on the table, set with her best linen and plate. The captain sniffed approvingly at the pungent mouth-watering aroma, which steamed out of the tureen.

"How fortunate can a man be?" he asked the hot smiling face of Odile. "To be with two such lovely ladies and to dine on what I know will be the gift of an incomparable cook." He thrust his hand into one of the big pockets of his long coat and drew out two small packages wrapped in white paper.

"I have not come empty-handed." He extended one package to Odile and the other to Allegra. Odile, laughing, pulled open the paper to find a tiny box containing a porcelain thimble, decorated with gold and flowers. Allegra smiled at Odile's pleasure.

"What is in yours, *petite*?" the old woman prodded.

Slowly Allegra unwrapped the narrow package. Inside was a miniature figurine, its flowing robes painted warm brown and belted with a cord. A white veil hung daintily over the small sweet face of a woman. On her breast hung a fine golden cross.

Allegra's breath stopped momentarily. Surely it was Santa Chiara! She looked into the waiting eyes of Captain Appleby, not knowing what to say.

"I hope you like it, ma'am. It reminded me of you. There were other pretty things, but I kept coming back to this, as if it should belong to you."

With an effort she controlled the strange feeling of awe, which shivered at the back of her mind. Why had he chosen this? It was doubtful that he was a Roman Catholic. She had not mentioned Santa Chiara to him before. Was the saint sending her a message?

She thanked him in genuine pleasure, and his heart-turning smile made her blink to avoid betraying her response to him. "I am glad I have pleased you," he said. "I sometimes think I don't know how to win your friendship."

Other meanings hung beneath his words, making Allegra draw in uncomfortably. *Santa Chiara is reminding me of my promise to her,* she thought.

They ate Odile's especially delicious meal with much talk between the captain and the inquisitive old lady. She led him into describing his home life in the United States. He had wonderful tales to tell of the great port of Boston and his home there. He sounded like a man of culture, but his attitude was so different from the men Allegra had known. He told about the native Americans—the Indians—in his state and was so good at descriptions that he swept Allegra's thoughts into a completely different mood. With him she saw the great forests of the new land sweeping westward to unexplored territory, and the busy port city, whose energetic citizens had set in motion the first step for freedom from Britain.

"We are free men," he said with pride. "We rule with just

laws, and one day, God willing, we will make an end of slavery
and indentured service. I believe that no human being should be
the slave of another . . . no matter what tradition or men's foolish
laws decree." He looked at Allegra as he ended his speech.

She loved hearing his vibrant voice speaking about human
rights. Ever since her experience with Abou Besim, she had been
troubled by thoughts of a world of terror outside her sheltered
life. She let down her walls and entered the conversation.

The captain enjoyed Odile's strawberry ice extravagantly, and
ate several large servings. Despite Odile's objections he helped to
clear the table, then reached for a long-stemmed pipe in his outer
coat pocket. "I got it in Holland. May I smoke, ladies?" He settled
down on the wide window seat with the look of a completely
satisfied man.

Allegra wondered how she could decently slip away to her
room. His easy presence sent out far too pleasant signals into her
nerves.

Odile reappeared in the sitting room with a basket over her
arm. "My friend, Madame Lefèbvre, has been ill," she said to
their guest. "I want to take her some of the sherbet. It is not far,
and Francesca will entertain you until I return."

"No," Allegra said quickly. "You must be tired, let me go."
She tried in vain to take the basket, but Odile's eyes shot darts of
determination at her, and she was out the door with a swoop of
energy.

John Appleby chuckled. "That lady knows what she wants to
do. What a fine woman she is!"

Allegra sat down sedately in one of the well-polished chairs by
the table. In a small voice she began to ask questions about the city
of Boston—anything to keep the undercurrent of emotion at bay,
which had started rising in moments of silence between them.

He answered her questions briefly. He was no longer bent on
entertaining with stories. She looked up to find an expression in
his eyes that halted her next question on her lips.

Suddenly he rose from the window seat, and with a swift few
steps he was on one knee beside her chair. He gathered her tightly
clasped nervous hands into his large protective ones.

"Francesca . . . I beg you, listen to me."

His closeness, the warmth from his body, made her light-headed. Her eyes were drawn to his, and she could not look away.

"I would have preferred to court you longer, Francesca—but necessity must speak now. I leave for Boston in a week. . . ." He drew a faltering breath. "I love you. . . . I have never married, because I have never found a woman I wished to share my life with. I have lived a satisfying life, but now I want a home and children. I want to take care of you. I want to adopt your little one as my own. I will give you a good life, my beloved." His voice dropped to a deeper tone. "You can trust me, Francesca, I am a faithful man."

She stiffened at his words. . . . Was there a faithful man? He felt her response, and his hands tightened over hers. He bent his head to them, and she felt his gentle kisses. His head with its shining thick hair—so close to her now—was wonderfully vital and comforting. His eyes were raised to hers, and she could not avoid them. In their brilliant blue depths was honesty. He would be a faithful man.

Shaken almost beyond thought, she realized that his voice was speaking of hope and love. "I know that you have been badly hurt, my darling, but I will make you forget."

A painful echo of a similar promise wrenched at her heart.

"I will not press you. You can tell me only what you wish about the past." He drew her hands to his breast. "My life will never be complete again, if you are not with me. I have watched your sweetness, and love has filled me from the first day you raised your lovely, distressed eyes to mine. I beg you to be my wife!"

His strong face was so near. How easy it would be to lean forward for his kiss. A flash of deep anguish flooded her mind. If it had only been different . . . if there were not so many other voices clamoring in her crowded memory: Barretto's harsh one, little Renaldo's plaintive cry, and those beguiling, fascinating tones that had awakened her to love and would always sound in her dreams . . . Byron.

Tears welled in her eyes. With a murmur of love, John tried to draw her close, but she pulled her hands from his and pushed herself away from him. A look of loss flashed over his face.

She leaned back in her chair, covering her eyes with her hands. She felt him draw away and rise to his feet. The removal of his closeness was like a withdrawal of comfort and safety . . . a desolate feeling, but he mustn't know. Santa Chiara had accepted her promise—she could not take the gift of this man's love.

The silence deepened, and finally she looked up. He was gazing down at her with such a look of pity, kindness and love that she longed to be in his arms. He held out a steady hand and helped her to her feet. She tried to speak, but he shook his head with a rueful smile.

"Do not distress yourself, Francesca. I understand. I had thought that there was a response to me in your eyes, these past days. I still do not think I was entirely wrong." He sighed. "Please think carefully in this next week. The *Laughing Liberty* sails in seven days. I will not trouble you again, but I will wait for a message. I want you to know that no matter what you decide, I am your servant, my sweet lady, my dearest Francesca. You can place your complete trust in me. . . . If you are ever in need, I will be there."

He lifted her hand to his lips, then picked up his hat, stuffed his pipe into his pocket, and with a slight salute marched toward the door. As his hand was on the latch he said, "Please tell Madame Berier that I have seldom enjoyed a meal as much." From across the room his eyes held hers.

"I'm sorry," she whispered.

He nodded curtly, a mixture of strength and frustration that made him look older and severe. Then he was gone.

Allegra sank down into her chair. The odor of his tobacco lingered in the air. Some of his vitality still moved in the room. She felt cold and lifeless, unable to move or to weep. *What is it that I am supposed to do,* she agonized. *I'm trying to understand, but I can't. . . .*

It was no better when Odile came home. She bustled in with her empty basket and an inquiring hopeful glance toward Allegra. Her face suddenly fell when she saw the listless eyes.

"Good heavens," she said under her breath and sat down at

the table. "You have sent him away. But why? I had hoped . . . ."

"How could you hope, Odile? Hope for what? I am a married woman."

"Zut!" she spat. "That was no marriage. Is rape marriage? Not one of the holy saints could say that Barretto di Rienzi fulfilled the true actions of a husband. "Pshaw! That life is over—and you have been ill-used, but now I see a chance for you to have a real man, because I would wager my life that he is to be trusted . . . and what a man he is!"

Tears finally spilled from Allegra's eyes, and she brushed them away.

"Crying is no use," Odile said harshly. "You were always too gentle. When you came here, I was amazed and delighted that at last you had the courage to take something from life for yourself. At least you ran from that old satyr, di Rienzi. I could not believe my eyes when I read in your sister Gemma's letter that you had agreed to marry him." She looked a little contrite at Allegra's pale face. "No, no, I do not blame you, you were tied into a knot of necessity."

She stopped, and the lines of her face grew softer. "The man who was your lover, *chérie,* I think to win you he was not an ordinary man. Am I right?"

Allegra nodded, mute before this unexpected inquisition.

"So," Odile continued, "I have guessed some possible identity and deduced something from the face of Allegrina. If he is the one I think, I don't doubt that you felt it was worth it." She smiled sadly. "You have known the worst and possibly some of the best."

She fell silent, pulling thoughtfully on a lock of curly gray hair at her temple. She knew what she was doing, but she had to find the right words. "You were able to leave the little Renaldo. . . ." She waved away Allegra's protest. "It was best for him to stay to inherit his duty and his title. I know that. But all of that is over. . . ."

She swept her arm out in a wide arc. "You must look at what you have now, little one. I am an old woman. I had planned in time to move in with two companions from my childhood, Marie and Emma Christophe, on their farm near Arles. There I would be able to work a little and die peacefully. We would be three elderly women, who understand each other very well.

"What have I been able to do for you, Allegra? I have given you refuge for a short moment in your life when you needed it. You cannot spend all your youth wheeling a cart for hungry sailors. God surely did not have that in mind for you. You should have a man . . . one to cherish you and to help with the baby, and to give you a family. You have changed your name—now you must *become* Francesca. John Appleby will make you happy, and you can do the same for him. You would be far away in the New World . . . a fresh start where no one could know."

"God would know," Allegra whispered.

"Of course God would know!" Odile gave a bark of a laugh. "Use your head, child. I know that you love the Blessed Sainte Claire. She was a woman who loved very deeply. Do you think she would condemn you for loving the one man God sent to teach you about love itself? Now, has not the good God sent you the perfect man for your needs? That does not feel like God's anger, now, does it?"

Her words seemed to pound at Allegra. "Please, Odile— please. I have already committed adultery. I cannot add bigamy to my sins!"

"Sins!" she snorted. "Who says what are sins! Is it some puny man of a bishop? What can he know about the painful life of a woman trapped by man's laws? Have I not seen you from the time you were a tiny child . . . do I not know your sweetness and kindness? Take your sins to the Blessed Mother, instead . . . she will understand."

"I am so confused. I only know that I have promised Santa Chiara. I could not be a wife to John Appleby, except in name, and that would not be fair to him."

"Humph," she snorted again. "I think he loves you, child, and would accept you on any terms. Furthermore, I think you come close to feeling love for him."

Allegra stood up. She couldn't stand more of Odile's persuasions. "I must tend the baby."

She fed Allegrina wordlessly, while Odile kept a loud silence in which her thoughts were all too clear. At last Allegra escaped to her bed, taking John's tiny statue with her.

Complicated emotions flowed like deep waves through her tired mind. Her heart beat painfully. Byron's face looked at her, beautiful and sad. She could feel his kisses still, but it was as if he called to her across time . . . from far away. She unlocked the drawer where she kept the Byron box and went through the motions of removing the necklace. Almost automatically, her fingers opened the small gold locket. The dark curl of his hair sprang vigorously to her touch, clinging against her fingers. She struggled to hold back a sob as she patted the curl back into its tiny nest and snapped the locket closed.

Her hands strayed over the soft leather top of the box, where the crest was so carefully tooled in gold, red and blue: Crede Byron. Bittersweet thoughts raced around her memories. She opened the lid and put the necklace away in its velvet bag. A tightly folded paper lay next to it. She already knew by heart what was written there, in that note of his, slipped into her hand the night of their first meeting at Contessa Benzoni's. But she had to look at it again. The paper crackled open, and there was his swift commanding script. . . . "Trust Byron."

She stared at the last words. Her throat ached with the need to weep. Quickly she locked the box away in the drawer. "Trust!" she whispered, "trust. . . ." How eagerly she had trusted him!

"Was I such a fool?" she asked the misty old mirror, which reflected her dismal face. She searched in her heart for anger, but found only love. "He could not help it, and I could not help it," she said on a sigh.

Are you any wiser now, her reflection demanded. *Are you ready to trust again?*

She turned away to undress, busy with the question. Her own father could not be trusted to care about her happiness, if it threatened his security. Barretto could only be trusted to be harsh and cruel. She could trust that he would do harm to her and the baby, if he found her. Even Luciano had said that he loved her, but he was ready to treat her like a prize of war.

And Byron. "Poor B!" She could hear him say it. He was honest in his own way, but he never considered that the wild swings of his own unhappy heart might be untrustworthy. If he had known about Allegrina, he surely would have been kind. It was just that he considered his needs to be the most necessary of all.

Finally, John Appleby's voice spoke through the other images in her mind: "I am a man you can trust," he said, and her heart believed him. It was not the bedazzled trust she had given to Byron, but a clearer sight, earned by experience.

What use was it now to be no longer the naive romantic? She had no right to claim the strength and trust that John Appleby offered her.

There was no Gina here to wrap her in sympathy. Odile was a practical Frenchwoman, and Allegra would have to be strong, but she did not mind. In some way she would care for Allegrina herself, without the help of any man.

She looked at her sleeping child, and her love flowed round the intense little being, so like her father. She sighed and went to bed, picking up the porcelain miniature of Santa Chiara as she passed the table. The thought of John Appleby's face made her utterly desolate.

CHAPTER SIXTEEN

FOR THREE DAYS Allegra refused to go to the docks. "I am waiting until he has gone," she told an exasperated Odile. The old woman chose not to force the issue.

Every day Allegra looked down into the harbor and saw the *Laughing Liberty* moving with the tides, stretching at its anchor. The captain was still waiting. Odile trudged home with the empty cart, saying nothing, and Allegra was too proud to question if he had asked for her.

She spent more time than usual in church. While Allegrina slept in her basket at the feet of Santa Chiara, or crawled around on the cool stone floor, Allegra prayed. She prayed for her own peace and for strength to wipe away the persistent thought of the man who expected her to send him a message of hope. Either the saint was busy elsewhere with other more worthy supplicants, or she simply could not help.

Allegra found some ease in lighting candles and praying for Renaldo, Barretto, Gina, Byron, Teresa and all of the others. For John she only whispered, "Give him joy."

ON THE MORNING OF THE FOURTH DAY Odile greeted her with a cup of hot coffee and the words, "You can take the cart today. I am tired, *petite* . . . and the captain has put to sea."

Odile watched Allegra's white face and then drew her to the doorstep. "Look." A brisk breeze moved whitecaps on dancing waves in the harbor, but the *Laughing Liberty* no longer bobbed her bright prow to the water's rhythm. Without a word Allegra went inside and tied a scarf over her head.

"Leave the baby," Odile said, not unkindly, "I will care for her."

She took the cart at a brisk pace down the hill. There was a numb ache, a cold heaviness in her breast. Several of the dockworkers were already waiting for the cart, and they asked for her health . . . they had missed her these days. Was the little one all right? Their rough kindness warmed her, and she smiled and spoke with them, while another part of her mind pretended that she could still look up and see the carved wooden woman of the *Laughing Liberty*—wrapped in her windblown painted flag and smiling her strange painted smile.

He had gone. His voice was still clear in her mind. *I will wait for a message* . . . but he hadn't waited. She felt empty. *So much for trustworthiness,* she said bitterly to herself.

She knew she was being unfair. After all, she was the one who had hidden away. She would have sent no message at the end of the week. Had she expected him to come begging for her? No; John Appleby was also proud—he would not beg again.

The day moved on toward noon, and trade grew slack. The men were either enjoying a siesta or working slowly in the hot sun. She had just three pies left unsold, and she decided to leave. The rest she would give to the poor children, who hung around the quays, and would put in her own money so that Odile would not know. She was anxious to be gone from the lonely dock.

The shadow of a man fell across the cart. One last customer. She turned to serve him and gasped. Luciano stood smiling ironically at her. There was no mistaking him, despite the full beard, black and neatly clipped.

Luciano was dressed with his usual quiet elegance. He swept her a mocking bow. *"Buon giorno, contessa.* So we meet again." His eyes were hard and hot beneath the heavy dark lashes.

"You are mistaken, *monsieur,*" she said desperately in French.

"I do not mistake you, Allegra! It has cost me a lot to remember you." His voice grated on the words. "To think I would find you acting as a vendor with a wooden cart . . . God! How the untouchable little nun has fallen! Surely you sell more than these common little pastas. Tell me," his voice dripped venom, "what is your price?"

Allegra was shaking, her new security cracked and falling under his anger. His face was contorted in a strange look of pain, but his eyes were frightening.

"Have you nothing to say, *contessa*?" he asked in the same un-nerving quiet voice.

She pulled herself together, and her head went up. "Nothing! I am not anyone that you know. Please go away."

"Ha! Would you like to hear, poor foolish little one, that Barretto di Rienzi has sworn to find you? He will make you pay for dragging his pride in the dirt. You will wish that you had never been born. He will break you, *contessa*, in his own way, until you can answer only 'yes' to his every demand. He will enjoy the sport! By the way, what has become of your little whelp?"

She was looking away from him, trying not to hear, thinking of some way to escape. She set the cart in motion, but he fell into stride beside her. Where could she go? Not to Odile's . . . .

A detaining hand on her arm stopped her. "There is an alternative, Madonna Allegra. I need not reveal your existence to the *conte*, as I once told you when we were in a certain farmhouse near Ravenna . . . but the price is yourself. You will come with me to Rome as my woman. I have friends who will guard you when I am absent in the employ of your husband . . . for I, too, am a jealous man. Your life will be entirely mine, and you will only care for my comfort. What an excellent revenge on old di Rienzi . . . his money will support us!"

Husky intimacy filled his voice. It was terrifyingly familiar. "If you behave yourself, Allegra, I will teach you pleasures that you could not imagine. You will live in great comfort—not among whores and sailors. . . ." He bent toward her, and one hand quickly drew her closer, while the other raised her face to his.

His touch shattered her trance of fear. She saw his red lips under the jet-black beard, and her mouth opened in a scream, which was instantly strangled by his hand. She struggled and tried to cry out. Luciano cursed and kept his hand over her mouth. "Be quiet!" he hissed. "I'll tell the world that I am from the *conte*. . . ."

A large work-hardened hand suddenly swung him away from her as if he were a piece of flotsam. "Is this man annoying you, *madame*?" It was Pierre Dalquoit, one of Odile's good friends.

Other angry faces loomed behind Pierre. Luciano tried to pull away, but strong hands grabbed and held him.

"He threatened me!" Allegra could hear the tremor in her voice. "I don't want anything to do with him!"

"That is enough for me." Pierre looked around at the men. "Shall we take care of the situation for our little lady?" Deep murmured assent followed his question, and Luciano started to speak.

"You will regret this. I am a gentleman . . . this woman is a runaway adultress. . . ." His voice gurgled to a stop behind a heavy fist, and he slumped into the arms of the surrounding men.

Allegra was near collapse. Her legs felt spongy and strange. "Don't faint," Pierre said, observing her blanched face. He singled out two of the men. "Claude, André, take her back to the house."

She let herself be helped by supportive hands. "What will you do with him?" she had to ask, as a kind of pity stirred in her for Luciano, with his fine silk coat now muddy from the wet quay, and his elegantly cared-for head only inches away from the rough sabots of the dockmen.

"This man intends harm to you," Pierre stated, nudging at Luciano's body. She nodded. The men cursed softly. "Then, little lady, leave it to us. He will not bother you again. It is no longer your concern."

"You will not kill him?"

Pierre looked around at the men, whose faces broke into wolfish grins. "Of course not . . . only a little discipline to make him think more carefully, and then perhaps he would like a trip to Morocco, eh, my friends?"

"Old Ben Hassan's tub sails in an hour. He always needs extra hands," one said, a foot prodding at Luciano. "He won't remember a thing!"

Allegra started to speak, but Pierre waved her to silence. The two men beside her almost lifted her off her feet and started up Odile's steep street. A third came behind with the cart.

Odile met them at the door like a worried mother. "What has happened, *chérie*? My God, you are white as flour!"

The men left after awkward but kindly encouraging words. Odile folded Allegra into her arms. "What is it, my sweet child? . . . What has happened?"

Allegra had no desire to weep. Her courage was up. Luciano and Barretto would not win. She told the story in an even voice.

Odile was not so calm. "But he must have servants with him . . . other agents of your husband . . . you must get away! We will pack tonight. Tomorrow you must leave! But to where?" She paced her small parlor. "If only the captain had not gone! He would be safety for you." Her hands were shaking, and Allegra's conscience hurt for all the trouble she had brought into poor Odile's peaceful life. Odile went on, "You should have sent for him . . . the man loves you. He would give his life . . . heaven help you . . . he was a gift of God, and you refused it."

With a futile gesture she sat down heavily in her big chair. "We will not talk about that anymore. What is done cannot be changed. I must think."

Odile held her curly gray head in her hands, while Allegra's thoughts wound themselves unhappily around the picture of Captain John Appleby skimming along the high seas, with the *Laughing Liberty* throwing back foam and spray against his face. She could see the bright drops sparkle on his thick brown hair and firm lips.

"There is a convent in the hills above Nîmes." Odile's words brought Allegra back to reality. "I know some of the nuns. We were schoolgirls together. I will give you a letter to them. The mother superior is a kind woman. They will surely take you and Allegrina into care for a time. Then I will contact my two dear old friends in Arles—you can work on their farm. You will like them, *petite*. Then we will pray that this man cannot trace you. There should be another change of names—French ones this time. I can be frank with my friends. Your French accent is improving. That will help." She rose energetically. "We will pack."

Allegra went to bed that night with a sense of despair and failure. *Maybe I should enter the convent,* she thought in her loneliness. *It would have been best if I had stayed at Santa Chiara long ago. . . .*

Sounds from the downstairs rooms woke her before dawn. She dressed quickly, leaving the baby asleep. Empty cups were on the kitchen table.

"Pierre and Claude were here," Odile greeted her. "They tell me that the Italian is on his way to Morocco—to the slave markets." She smiled at Allegra's look of distress. "If you ask me, it's no more than just. He would have sent you there. I have a feeling that his prosperity is not just from his job with di Rienzi. He may have had business with the African coast. The American gunboats didn't cure the slave problem when they stopped the Barbary pirates."

She set out a big breakfast. "You must eat well. I have sworn all the men to silence. No one has seen a thing, and no one remembers anything."

Allegra reached for the busy hand and kissed it.

"How I wish it was different, *petite*, but you will see, things will work out. I have made a very special prayer to Sainte-Marthe. . . . She is one who came ashore on this coast with the Blessed Saint Joseph of Arimathea, fleeing from the Romans. I have faith in her. But—I waste time. . . ."

Odile brought out a piece of paper with a map sketched on it. They were both studying the route to the convent, when the sound of swiftly running feet and a rapping at the door interrupted Odile's explanations.

A boy stood in the doorway. He was about twelve years old, dressed in neat britches and a black vest over a snowy clean shirt. In one hand was a bouquet of flowers.

"Good morning, ma'am!" he said in a voice wobbly with adolescence. His plain face spread into a smile, and he bowed boyishly. "Is it Madame Berier and Madame Gordoni?"

The two heads nodded. He assumed a serious pose. "Then," he announced, "I am Nathaniel Thompson from the ship *Laughing Liberty*. May I present the compliments of Captain Appleby." He was obviously trying to remember the exact message. His French was carefully spoken. "He says that he will call on you within the hour, unless I give him your word not to come." He let out a small sigh of relief, and his eyes fixed themselves in fascination on the dish of sweet rolls on the table. Then he remembered his job. He extended the flowers toward Allegra. "These are for you, ma'am."

Odile moved to offer him the plate of rolls. "Enjoy this, Nathaniel. We will have your return message in a moment. Here, sit by the table."

Allegra took the bouquet and tried to stay calm. *It couldn't be!* her incredulous mind insisted. All the feeling of John's supportive presence flowed around her. She was like a dying plant, which had just been watered.

Odile's firm tug at her arm drew her into the kitchen. "Sainte-Marthe has heard me!" Her eyes looked amazed. "I told her that I would pay for an orphan to go to the convent if she would bring the captain back!" Her large arms circled Allegra in a strong embrace. "You must see, *chérie*, that you have been given a very special gift of happiness. He will care for you and the child. It is all that I could have wished!"

There was a sound from the threshold, and Pierre Dalquoit stood there with a sober face.

"What is it, my friend?"

"There are others looking," he said, "at least two more Italians."

Odile turned to Nathaniel, who was stuffing the last of the hot roll into his mouth. "This is the message. Tell your captain to come immediately." She looked back at Allegra. "That's all, isn't it?" Allegra could only nod. "Then run, child, and bring Captain Appleby!"

His eyes grew serious, and he tried to bow again. *"Zut!"* Odile cried. "Be off, boy!" He flashed out the door.

Pierre smiled and then frowned again. "They are looking for the Italian. His servants are asking questions. No one will say a thing . . . but you should leave, *madame*, and soon," he said to Allegra.

Odile interrupted him. "I suppose I can tell you. Captain Appleby has returned just in time. He will take charge now. He has asked our Francesca to marry him. She will go to the United States of America for a new life."

Pierre exploded a laugh. "So! I told the men that the captain had an honorable purpose. You will be happy, sweet lady. I'll go back and tell the others. We'll see you off." He winked. "That's a beauty of a ship. . . ." He hurried away again.

"Odile . . . Odile!" Allegra stammered. "What have you done?"

"I have only done what is right," she said calmly. "You can't look me in the eye and tell me that you don't want to go with him!"

"But my promise . . . I told you . . . Odile!"

"I only know that the saints have brought him back. Marry him, *ma chère*, it will be your first real marriage to a real man. Now I can settle into my old age without worry. You will be happy. I trust John Appleby. Now, hurry, he will be here any minute."

A light brisk knock sounded on the door frame. They turned to see John Appleby smiling at them. Allegra's heart leaped into an alarmingly wild rhythm. She knew then that no matter what happened, she would go with him. She could not lose him again.

CHAPTER SEVENTEEN

It took John only a moment to understand. He strode through Odile's doorway and picked Allegra up into his arms for a kiss that promised her his love.

There was hardly time for one last look at the comfortable room that had sheltered her, before they were hurrying down the familiar steep street toward the harbor. John strode along, cradling the surprised Allegrina in his arms. Behind them, in a ragtag procession, seamen carried Allegra's few possessions, and Odile was laughing and weeping, holding a basket of her baked goods.

"You see, you see," she said close to Allegra's ear, "he is a protector!"

There was no time for careful thought or doubts. She was being swept along by a tide of loving people. At the dock, Pierre and his friends waited with bouquets of flowers for her. She could not imagine where they got them on such short notice.

The trim white captain's boat waited at the quay, and a second boat was being loaded with the baby's cradle and Allegra's things. She had a sudden picture of the Byron box being left behind in all the rush to leave. She turned to Odile.

"Everything is here, *petite,* including your so-precious box." *Curse the box,* Odile said under her breath, *it would be better at the bottom of the bay.* Aloud she said, "Now, let us get into the boat before it leaves without you."

Allegra stopped before the rough men whom she had come to know so well. Smiles creased their sun-darkened faces, as one by one they kissed her hand with French flourish. "You must not worry, *madame,*" Pierre said quietly out of John's hearing, "all will be well for you now." He winked.

She wished that everything were as simple as that. She looked at John Appleby's tall busy figure, and her heart lifted despite the problems that were waiting still in the back of her mind.

Odile came with them onto the ship. They were taken to a pleasant cabin with sunlight angling brightly into small square windows. The bunk was covered with fine heavy silk and curtained in matching fabric. John entered briefly to deliver Allegrina and the cradle, then tactfully withdrew.

Allegra and Odile fussed over the baby, not able to look at each other. Suddenly the old woman pulled her close.

"Be happy, my little one."

"You will visit us one day . . . I insist."

"God willing," Odile smiled, "but you must write to me— often. I will send on Gina's letters." She looked fiercely into Allegra's eyes. "This is the best way! Someday old di Rienzi will die, and then you will no longer have such a conscience. But . . . if love makes a marriage, then you will be truly wed to John Appleby." She sighed. "What joy to be sailing away with such a man! . . ."

Back on deck they joined John and several officers. Allegra received curious but friendly looks during John's introductions. The first mate, Mr. Nichols, and his men were hardy and self-sufficient in their appearance.

"Where is the Reverend Jarret?" John asked.

"He is coming with his lady," Mr. Nichols smiled.

John was formal in his address, but Allegra sensed his delight in the new situation, hidden beneath an exterior correctness. "He is a Protestant minister from Boston," he said to her. "He and his wife have been traveling to the Holy Land. They are not young, but they are determined. Now I take them home."

He put a warm hand on Odile's shoulder. "It was to pick up the Jarrets that I made the short run across to Leghorn . . . and to give the *Liberty* a chance to try her seaworthiness after the repairs. I pray my departure caused no problems." He smiled and looked past them. "Ah, there you are, sir, ma'am."

Allegra turned to find two elderly faces beaming cheerfully at her. John made the introductions and gave her a happy smile. "He will perform the ceremony for us. And Mrs. Jarret will be company for you, my darling," he ended on a loving tone. Allegra immediately liked the honest eyes of both of them.

"Good!" Odile said. "Now I must leave you. The wind is coming up, and you have to catch the tide." She laughed at John, "I haven't lived by the ships without knowing a little of the sea."

John took the plump little figure into his arms for a tight embrace. She gave him a smacking kiss on the cheek. "La! I wish I was young again."

"I will care for her," he said quietly.

Allegra received her kiss without words. Odile was handed down the sea ladder, and Pierre waited in a dinghy to row her ashore.

"PUT TO SEA, MR. NICHOLS." John's voice had a ring of satisfaction. The first mate shouted an order, and the sound of the anchor chain was loud and brisk. Sailors swarmed into the rigging, and the sails drew in the sweet wind. Allegra felt the ship come alive as it slipped from the harbor, tacked into the wind several times and moved swiftly out to sea.

John stood with her at the forward rail, his hand securely wrapped around hers, until he was called away by Mr. Nichols. John kissed her hand and looked into her eyes. "I won't be long, dearest. Have no fear that you will ever be alone again."

Allegra's mind was in happy confusion, watching the hills of Marseilles move away from them, with every moment taking her farther and farther from danger.

Mrs. Jarret found her and led her cheerfully back to the cabin. She had already busied herself feeding and changing Allegrina, who slept in her gently swaying cradle in time with the thrusting rhythm of the ship.

"My dear, we are so happy for John." She spoke French with a strong English accent. "All the way from Leghorn he sang your praises. Now I see why. It's so good to see him take a wife at last." She laughed with a comfortable sound. "Please call me Patience. After all, we are old friends of John's, and we will be together for three months on this ship of his."

She talked on, not seeming to care if Allegra answered or not. "You must look at what he has arranged for you." She opened a sliding panel to reveal a narrow closet with several pretty dresses and a warm cloak of light brown wool trimmed with fur on its hood . . . and an oiled foul-weather cape, which Patience pointed out especially. "We'll all have need of this piece of clothing, for the rough seas. It's a bit late in the year to be starting an Atlantic crossing. We'll be well into winter weather the last few weeks." She smiled confidentially, "Everything will fit you. Your good friend the Frenchwoman gave John the measurements."

One of the dresses was blue green, like the inside of a sea wave, edged at throat and wrists with beautiful heavy lace. "Your wedding dress." A misty smile was in the faded blue eyes. "And may you be as happy as I have been with my dear Adam."

She went to a sea chest, which was bound in polished brass, and opened it wide. Inside were shoes and rain boots, slippers and underclothing. Dainty embroidered petticoats and nightgowns were folded amid scattered blossoms of lavender. "These are from the nuns of Sant' Ippolita, near Leghorn . . . Livorno to you, of course. How the British made Leghorn out of Livorno, I shall never know." She chatted happily on about John's sending her on a special visit to the convent to buy these things for Allegra. "He loves you very much, my dear."

Allegra made appropriate responses, but her thoughts were torn between delight in John's kindness, pique that he had undoubtedly expected her to say yes to him—with Odile's conniving—and deep guilt that she would accept his love and help and not give fully in return.

Patience saw her look of weariness. "I've been selfish, talking so much. Rest now. Very soon we will be well out to sea, and John asked Adam to marry you at sunset." She kissed Allegra gently. "You must be fresh and beautiful for your husband."

With a long sigh Allegra sank down upon the soft mattress of her bunk, but sleep was far from her mind. She heard the muffled sounds of men on the deck above her, the quick orders, the reassuring "talking" of the ship itself, as it adjusted to the flow of the sea.

If only my soul were as clear as my baby's, she thought, watching Allegrina sleep so soundly in her swaying cradle. Was there really a Venice somewhere, with Barretto and their child in it?

Could she ever wipe away the memory of her past, merely by sailing away from it? Perhaps someday she could convince herself that Byron was only a poetic invention of hers. She sighed again. Tonight was to be her wedding night, but she couldn't . . . wouldn't . . . .

And then what would John do? He was no passive man to be put off with vague excuses. He had honored her with his love, and now she would hurt him when she should have given him joy. Her heart was heavy, and her eyes ached with hot tears, but she finally drifted into a state when no more thoughts disturbed her.

SHE WOKE TO THE LIGHT TOUCH of Patience Jarret's hand on her shoulder. "The sun will be setting in an hour. It's time to dress, my dear." She studied Allegra's swollen eyes. "I'll bring you some drops of eyebright. It does wonders. Now, don't worry about a thing . . . I'll feed the baby in our cabin, and young Nathaniel will stay with her later tonight." She scooped Allegrina from the cradle and went away with efficient steps.

For a frantic moment Allegra thought of sending a message to John. . . . "I cannot marry you, and you must not ask me why. Just take me as a passenger to your free world. . . ." But she stopped herself. "I cannot lose you," she whispered. She could feel the strength and comfort of him, like a home fire toward which her spirit yearned.

She slowly put on the sea-blue dress. Patience was right, it did fit. There was a small mirror on the cupboard door. She smiled at her reflection, and at how becoming the dress was . . . how soft her hair looked with the rose velvet ribbon from John's chest of gifts. A small clear-faced clock ticked on the wall. The hour was almost up. A nervous lump tied itself into her stomach. Suddenly her hands were cold, and her knees shook. What was she doing, standing at the mirror admiring herself and waiting to be married. . . .

Patience knocked lightly at the door and stood beaming at her, dressed in what must have been her best frock. "You look lovely!" she said admiringly.

Beyond her tiny figure the face of Mr. Nichols appeared. He

was immaculately turned out in a close-fitting coat of superfine with brass buttons. "I am to escort you to the captain's cabin, ma'am."

"Then I'll run on." Patience reached up to give Allegra a motherly kiss. She was light on her feet despite her age. Allegra and Mr. Nichols both smiled, as they watched her swiftly departing figure.

It was then that she noticed the bouquet of small white roses in Mr. Nichols's hand. They were tied with silvery ribbons. "From the captain, ma'am."

Her hand reached to the roses, and a pang of distress caught her heart. For a moment she smelled the sweetness of another rose and felt the feather touch of moonlight on her face—and a perfumed kiss on her lips. The withered rose in the Byron box still held a whisper of its fragrance. Why had John Appleby chosen white roses?

"Are you ready, ma'am?" Mr. Nichols was watching her curiously. She pulled a smile to her lips and went with him.

In John's cabin, deep golden light poured into the room from the small windows. She stood beside him and faced the Reverend Mr. Jarret. John's hand was strong on her. She made responses as directed, but her mind seemed to have come to a stop. She felt only the warmth of him next to her, and when he kissed her she reached her face to him.

After the brief ceremony, they walked out on deck to find a wedding cake and all the ship's men gathered to raise their mugs of spirits and shout good wishes. The sky blazed with a blanket of orange and gold, while gulls flew white patterns in the freshening wind.

John kept his strong arm around Allegra and greeted his men with appropriate jokes and laughter. Then in a voice that all could hear he called out, "Set a course for home, Mr. Nichols!" while whistles, shouts and the ship's bell answered him.

At supper that night there were toasts by Adam Jarret and the first mate. Allegra could feel the intensity of John's eyes on her, and she was hot and cold by turns. The touch of his hand made shivers race along her nerves. Her distress grew with every tender touch and word. He was so happy, so sure . . . and very soon she would have to quench that fire of joy.

The Jarrets finally left, and Mr. Nichols quietly wished them well and went about his duties. Nathaniel cleared away the table, and then they were alone.

John drew her into his arms. His lips were gentle but exploring. She could feel his passion held in check. He would be a considerate lover, but she couldn't allow it. She willed herself to respond only slightly to his kisses.

John pulled back and looked down into her shadowed eyes. "What is it, Francesca? Are you afraid of me? You know I love you . . . I could never hurt you." The love in his deep eyes brought tears to her own. With a murmur of concern he gently cradled her head against his breast. She could not stop the tears.

He carried her to his big bunk and held her gently to him. "What is it, my darling? I must know."

She accepted his handkerchief and wiped at the tears. "Forgive me," she whispered, "I cannot give myself tonight. Maybe not for a long time." She looked up to see a pained and thoughtful expression wipe away the glow of happiness that had been so clear a moment earlier.

"Can you tell me why?" His voice was low.

"I told you that my first marriage was arranged. My husband was much older. My wedding night . . . was a rape. I vowed not to marry again after his death . . . then you came . . . I told you that I could not make you as happy as you deserve. Forgive me!"

His eyes watched her steadily. "Go on."

"I feel a terrible sense of . . . repugnance to the act of sex. It is not distaste of you, please understand. . . . Odile told me that I should be safe with you—that eventually I would be . . . normal. I pray it will be so. But it is not fair to you. I should not have let my need and my heart do this to you. I never wanted to hurt you." She buried her hot eyes in the clean coolness of his linen handkerchief.

He was silent a long time, then she felt his urging hand lift her face.

"Listen to me." His voice was tense with emotion. "I love you, my darling. I will try to understand. It is enough that you are here with me. If you will allow me to hold you, to kiss you without demanding more, I will be grateful. There is nothing to forgive, beloved. It is my privilege to serve and protect you . . . that is my promise. When you feel that you can give more, then tell me. I will wait without complaint at the doors of paradise, as long as you are with me."

She looked into the depths of his beautiful keen eyes and what she saw shook her with amazement. Here was truth. His soul spoke to her of love from their clear blue light. She reached up to kiss him softly. "I am grateful, John, so grateful! Be patient with me. I want you to be happy, more than you can know."

"Do you love me, Francesca?"

"Yes," she answered without hesitation.

He straightened his shoulders. "Your cabin is next to mine. Go and put on your nightrobe and return here. You will sleep on my bed tonight. I'll bunk on the floor. Don't fret—I've slept on many harder places. I'll let it be known tomorrow that you will sleep in your quarters because of the child. I will visit you at night and then return here. No one will be the wiser."

"Thank you," she said in a whisper.

"I'll have none of that. We are joined by the power of love and God, and it is for us to find our way to the greatest expression of that power. I have waited all my life for you, and I will happily wait a little longer." He drew her into a long and gentle embrace.

FOR ALLEGRA, crossing the Atlantic Ocean was like another birth. Space and time expanded, changing her perception of life itself. There was the endless sea, the great ship, the sun and storms—a whole new world.

And John was a new world also; his loving patience, his humor and his strength were so different from any man she had ever known. There was a vital freedom in him—like his ship, fearless and steady. The rules of his life were made by him and not by any society. It took her several weeks to begin to understand the depth of this man she had married so hastily.

John—dear, honest, kind John—was true to his word. He often held her close, making no attempt at passion, and yet she could feel the yearning in him and the burn of desire in his eyes when he watched her. She felt a deep unease of conscience, but her good Santa Chiara gave no answers to her prayers. Allegra pondered and worried. How could she—the imperfect and foolish Allegra have found a man of such quality?

The voyage was long and wearying, and the weather soon changed to high rolling waves and gale winds, but there were happy moments. The baby thrived on the clean sea air, and the sailors played with her like a fragile doll. The Jarrets were dear and kind. They loved to talk about their lives and travels, and it pained Allegra to have to be evasive when they asked innocent questions about her past.

Patience Jarret was determined to teach her some good New England English, so that her life as an American would start easily. The lessons were long and Patience was an unrelenting taskmaster, but Allegra learned to speak John's language, much to his amusement. No matter how she tried, her accent was hopelessly Italian and always brought a smile to his lips.

In the last month of the voyage, the milk of the cow on board dried up to a trickle, but Allegrina was able to eat the seamen's dish they called scouse, made of bread, bits of fish, onions and potatoes. It became the mainstay of everyone, as the food supplies dwindled. Water was replenished by storms, and Allegra came to love the sea.

OCTOBER

THEN, ONE EVENING AFTER SUPPER, as she and John were standing on deck and he was explaining the stars to her, she noticed a faint flickering beam close to the horizon. A murmur was growing among the crew on watch, and John leaned close to her with a special lift to his voice. "It's the Boston Light," he said, "the first thing a sailor sees that tells him he's home."

He held her close, and they watched for a long time, as the light grew nearer and brighter in the blowing winter sky.

The men were laughing and shouting as they worked aloft in the great riggings. "They can smell home," John said with pride, raising his nose into the breeze, "and so can I." He gave a signal to the first mate, and one of the cannons barked out an explosive sound. The men cheered. "We fire at intervals to call for a pilot. By morning he will be here to take us past the islands and into Boston Harbor."

That night the men of the *Laughing Liberty* were given an extra ration of grog.

Allegra forced her mind to believe that nothing, even a new land and strange people, could threaten her as long as John stood beside her. She let herself be carried through the formalities of introduction to the harbor master, the officers of the customhouse, the merchants who came to inspect their newly arrived cargo.

At the end of the long morning, when she was finally standing on firm ground and looking at this place called Boston, John turned from her to observe a woman, who was alighting from a carriage at the quay.

"It's Hannah," he said briefly and went to greet her.

Allegra held the baby tightly to her and watched John walk away. A sudden moment of panic started in her breast. *No!* she wanted to scream, *don't leave me, John!* Her head felt light, and then everything blurred until she was swaying dizzily.

A strong arm came quickly around her waist to stop her fall. Voices swam in and out of her awareness. "Poor little thing," one said. "And the babe . . . let me take her."

John's strong clear voice demanded her attention: "Francesca! Look at me—look at me!" When she opened her eyes she was in his arms, safe. A worried looking, middle-aged woman was next to him, stroking at Allegra's forehead with a handkerchief, and they were riding in a very fine black carriage.

"I shan't ask what beastly things the poor child has had to endure on your ship," the woman chided him in an affectionate tone. "To take a baby on such a journey, as well . . . ." She sniffed as she scrutinized Allegrina's flushed and weathered little face.

"All for the best, Hannah, I promise you," John grinned. He

had Allegra's hand held fast in his own and bent to kiss it with gentle lips. "My dearest, let me present my sister, Hannah Appleby."

Allegra managed a smile and started to say something but was interrupted. "John knows how I detest surprises, but I forgive him this time. Just when I was finding Boston a lonely place for myself, I am given a new family. This makes me very happy, my dear sister."

John let out his breath in an explosive burst. "Thank God! And bless you, Hannah, for welcoming Francesca and the child. I wasn't certain ... .."

"Nonsense! When have I been less than welcoming?" she asked archly. "Only when I disapproved of your taste in women, and that is certainly not the case here, is it?" She laughed heartily and drew John and Allegra into her mood. Even Allegrina started to laugh.

John's house was near the Commons, much larger than he had described it to Allegra, but with a cozy charm unlike anything in Venice or Marseilles. It was painted white and sat squarely upon its parcel of land near the banks of the river that flowed through the city.

The furnishings were simple, the best of the craft that flourished in this new land. There were beautiful things from England in the house, as well, and from elsewhere in the world. John's father had been a captain, too, and the house reflected his travels in far-flung places.

Allegra found herself the mistress of this place, and with the help of John's old housekeeper-cook and Hannah, she felt her way cautiously into the rhythm of her new life.

The first night was difficult. Their bedroom was dominated by a large four-poster bed, which looked so perfect for a marriage bed. John said nothing as he prepared for sleep, but Allegra stood next to the bed in her heavy winter nightgown, wondering what to do. She didn't want to send John away from her; his nearness was too vital to her happiness. But how could she ask him to sleep in the same bed with her and not allow him his rights as a husband?

John looked over at her, as he turned down the wick of the lamp next to the bed. "Let me tuck you in, Francesca. You look so fragile and cold standing there—like a little girl," he laughed gently.

"But . . ." her voice wavered.

"Do I have to call for Hannah to put you to bed properly?" he scolded.

The picture of the stiff-spined woman, marching across the street from her own house to act as nursemaid to Allegra, broke the spell of tension in her, and she smiled at John. "No," she said. "But I must ask you something."

"What, my love?"

"Would you stay with me, at least for tonight?"

"A husband usually sleeps with his wife in America. But I will stay to my own side of the bed until invited, do not worry. Haven't I promised my love to you, come what may?" He drew back the covers on her side and bent to kiss her very sweetly.

As she lay beside him, unable to sleep for several hours of the night, she wondered at the ways of fate. Was there no way out of her tangle of memories and obligations? If she compounded her sins and took John's love to herself with the passion she was starting to feel, would she be able to live with herself? She almost wished that she had no soul at all, no conscience to torment her, no past to pull at her.

THE ENERGY AND SPIRIT of the New World were so different from the tired society of Venice. No Napoleon had set foot here to draw the heart from people. They had fought off Britain and were proud and thriving. Allegra quickly sensed the American pride. She resolved to speak English only, and not lapse into French, which she discovered was the second language of many of the New England gentry. She would do this for John; she would become an American for him and for her child. This new land was safety for all of them.

Hannah was like the embodiment of the strong core of the young nation. Starchy, and a confirmed spinster, her blunt and perceptive comments on life helped Allegra to adjust. Some of John's friends had been cool at first; they seemed to be waiting until they knew more about Allegra, testing her for credentials of acceptability. For those friends John had little patience.

But others were just naturally kind and open, especially his friend Acton Lewes and the pretty and cheerful woman he was about to marry, Ellen Jeffers. The couple gave several comfortable dinner parties for Allegra and John, and John was proud to see that Allegra's sweetness and charm drew people to her, once they set aside any initial prejudice about a foreign woman. There were very few Italians in the New World, which was another factor of safety against Allegra's fear of discovery.

Hannah had her own small home nearby, but she spent much of her time at John's house with Allegra. One day, as they were chatting about children and how fast the baby was responding to English words, two ladies alighted from a carriage and knocked at the door.

Allegra could see them through the narrow glass windows beside the front door. The younger woman was all blond shining curls and blue eyes. Her pink dress was a heavenly concoction of ruffles and lace.

"Ah!" Hannah grumbled. "The de Peysters are back from England. That is Melissa—and Harriett, her mother. Wealthy snobs, as you will soon see. The father is an attorney. Melissa had her heart set on capturing John. For a while I was worried."

She rose and shook her starched white ruffled collar into place with a grin of satisfaction. "They have heard about you, my dear. Oh, what pleasure it gives me to show them John's sweet bride . . . may God forgive me," she smiled as she started toward the door. "Let nothing they say upset you, Francesca; they're not worth it."

Hannah greeted them at the door and invited them to stay to tea. The two women's eyed assessed Allegra without warmth. Their attitude spoke quite clearly: *You never know what ridiculous entanglements a good-looking man can get into abroad.*

Light laughter rippled over Melissa's barbed words. "John and I have known each other forever . . . Francesca, was it? What a winning little name! We had a silly quarrel before he left on his last trip, but I never dreamed I had hurt him so much. . . ."

Allegra kept a calm face, but her emotions were boiling.

John came into the house near the end of the interminable tea, and Melissa rushed to embrace him. "How naughty you were to get married behind my back," she cooed, holding his hand.

He treated her indulgently, like a child. He made polite responses and went to his study, pleading business.

When the de Peysters finally left, Hannah said, "You did well. I'd say it was a rout, at least for now. Just keep John satisfied, Francesca, and you need not worry. Melissa will try to make trouble—depend on it." With a pat of her hand Hannah turned to her needlework, leaving Allegra with the echo of her words twisting sharply in her heart.

That night John was restless. He paced about the bedroom and then sat down heavily on the edge of the bed. "Did you know that I was born in this bed?" His eyes had a bright glitter. "I'd like a child born here, my darling. Do you feel that one day you would be willing . . .?" There was an edge of urgency in his voice. "I'm a man, Francesca, and I don't know how long I can go on this way, sleeping next to you, smelling the sweetness of your body—" He broke off and began to pace again.

"I think I—it must be soon," she spoke from the depths of her distress.

He swung toward her, his face alight with excitement. "A promise?"

"Yes." The picture of Melissa's devouring blue eyes looking into his swamped all else from her mind. ". . . Very soon. Not tonight, but soon."

CHAPTER EIGHTEEN

TWO DAYS LATER ALLEGRA RECEIVED a hand-delivered invitation to dinner at the home of the de Peysters. She invented an excuse to refuse. She knew that she could not bear to see John and Melissa together while John might be susceptible. And it was all her fault for not giving herself to him completely when she should have.

Another fear rattled around in her mind now. What if John were planning another voyage with the *Laughing Liberty*? Had she sent him away from her by her indecision? He hadn't told her, but she knew he spent his mornings at the harbor with other shipowners and merchants, and she wouldn't have blamed him for taking a cargo on consignment and sailing away. That was his real life, not this day-to-day living as half a man with a wife who made him wait for what was his by right.

The fear was almost more than she could stand, and there was only one person to whom she could show her distress—Father Liam. Allegra had found his small Catholic church one day in her walks. Since then she had hovered around the edges of the young priest's parish, usually leaving Mass before Communion, never confessing.

Father Liam seemed welcoming in those occasional moments when she happened past his church and stayed to talk about life. He was wise enough to let her guide the friendship. Allegra knew very well that he understood her need for guidance, and she knew that her concern about her marriage was apparent to his perceptive eyes.

Once he asked her outright if she loved her husband, seeking an entry point for a deeper conversation. Her answer had been swift: "Yes!" If he suspected something irregular about her marriage, he said nothing to alarm her.

She talked to him about many lighter things and then returned to her major concern: was marriage without love a true one in the eyes of God? What did he think about arranged marriages in Europe? Was a promise made under duress still binding? She became embarrassed to bother him further and had not seen him for several weeks.

Today Allegra found him outside the church, on his way to the home of a parishioner. John was heavily on her mind and she had to talk, but she couldn't. She talked instead about Santa Chiara. "She is most special to me," she said to Father Liam, as they strolled together. "I used to have a little shrine with a beautiful picture of her, but . . . but I lost it."

Father Liam stopped. "If you'll wait here, I'll be right back." He walked quickly back toward the rectory. When he returned he was smiling to himself and carrying a small wood plaque with a painting of the saint. "I want you to have it. I believe it is even Italian, so it must be meant for you."

Allegra took it from him and knew that the moment had come to say what was really on her mind. "Father," she started, "in my girlhood I prayed to her for love in marriage. I suffered . . . and now I have found love, but . . . ." Her face was contorted, and she couldn't finish.

He put a hand on her arm. "Love brought by the saint herself cannot be anything but good." He hurried on in his words to prevent her from blurting out something they might both regret. "Oftentimes, my dear little friend, I have prayed to God like this: 'Dear God, if You want me to know something, then I'll do what I can. But what I don't know, I will judge that You have kept from me because You understand what should be done far better than I could . . . and You don't want me meddling.' "

He looked steadily into her eyes. "John Appleby is a good man and fortunate in his marriage to you. Now, let us talk of something else, the weather, perhaps," and he set a good pace back down the street.

Her heart felt it had received a kind of absolution. When she reached home, she set the picture of Santa Chiara on a small table in the upstairs sitting room. She showed it to John when he came home and confessed her girlish prayers for love. "And now she has given me the love that I prayed for." His arm came around her, and she looked into his eyes with unguarded feeling.

That night she gave herself to him. She drew him to her in their big bed, and neither one said a word. His lovemaking was masterful and gentle. She wanted the touch of his vital self close to her, but to her horror—even as she was filled with shaking excitement—her body refused to share the beauty of John's love. He made every effort to please her, to be sensitive to her needs, to give her time to respond . . . but still no pleasure came to her.

She tried not to let him know what had happened, but she sensed by the tension of his body as he withdrew from her that he did know. She had failed him after all his months of loving patience.

A sudden vision of the pink and gold of Melissa de Peyster, palpitating eagerly for John, ready to meet his slightest desire, swept her with despair, and she was weeping. John reached to cradle her against his breast.

Why was this coldness in her when she loved his firm body with such pleasure? She turned to kiss John's smooth naked shoulder, which was wet with her tears. More than anything, she loved to feel him close to her. There was a clean goodness in him that was reflected in his taut, balanced muscles, his skin that had its own warm fragrance, the intense energy that flowed out of his whole being.

She could only compare him to what she had known. He was far more of a man than Byron; John was the kind of lover women dreamed of and seldom found. She had given herself to Byron as fully as she could, but that was then, in another time. Now there were these terrible barriers in the way of the much deeper surrender that should be her gift to John.

He kissed her lightly, but his face did not show fulfillment. "It will take time, my love, my poor little bird," he said softly. The endearment held the echo of another voice and she shivered. She was not yet absolved.

THE NEXT MORNING, after John had gone to the harbor, she opened the Byron box and sat quietly holding the locket. She wondered where he was, and Teresa. How was little Renaldo growing up, and what would he be told about his mother who deserted him? Of Barretto she refused to think. No news had come from Gina, but it took a long time for mail to reach Boston.

She shut the box away again. She had heard the latest talk about Byron from people who had returned from England. His poetry was more popular all the time, it seemed, and he was being called a genius. The gossip about him had not died out—he was still the scandalous expatriate living in sin with his Italian *contessa*, and it all seemed very far away. Not just in distance and time, but far away from any reality.

JOHN MADE SWEET AND GENTLE LOVE to her a few more times after that first night, but then he stopped. "There will be a time when you want me, my darling." His serious expression made her weep inside. "I want you to tell me when."

But he continued to be her good and loving companion, and when she realized soon after that she was pregnant, he was delighted. He brought her little gifts and watched over her. How different from Barretto's iron watchfulness! John would love the child, boy or girl, but she wanted to give him a boy. A boy to carry on his name might make up for the lack in her.

Often at night, hearing his deep quiet breathing beside her, she yearned to touch him, to caress his wonderful body into passion, but she was afraid now. Suppose something irreversible had happened to her, and she would never change? What if she tried again and the coldness came? She couldn't fail again with John. The strength in his eyes, the graceful energy of his stride, the fine line of his lips—all aroused her. To touch his hand sent warm waves of delight into her nerves and down her body. How much more time would he give to her before she would have to try again?

Dear, sensible Hannah Appleby kept her from too much repetitious pondering. Hannah was a woman of action, never one to let a day slip by without something accomplished. Winter was settling quietly over the New England countryside, and Hannah went to great lengths to describe "Christmassing."

"John's a traditional man, Francesca. It's time I taught you the family recipes and all the little special things he loves, don't you agree?''

Their first Christmas together would be a joyful one, Allegra promised herself. John had surprised her with an early Christmas present, a fine baby carriage, black and luxurious enough for royalty. "Allegrina can use it for now, but it will be just right for our new babe," he had smiled, while Hannah had looked on with practical eyes.

He turned an amused face to his sister. "Don't lecture me on thrift, Hannah. I've never been a father before."

"That wasn't what I was about to say, John Appleby. You'll be fortunate if you see much of your dear wife from now on until Christmas."

His eyebrows shot up. "Oh?"

"Don't you see, with this great wheeled contraption she'll be free as a bird to take the little one on every sort of frivolous errand!" She winked at Allegra. "And I think it's excellent."

Christmas was two weeks away, and Allegra took advantage of Hannah's prophecy, spending more and more time shopping for special imported delicacies from London, decorations for the house and something that was the most difficult of all: a gift for John that expressed the depth of her love.

Usually Hannah went cheerfully along with her on these excursions, but one day she refused, pleading aching joints and an attack of *la grippe*. Allegra set out anyway with Allegrina and the new carriage. Its well-oiled wheels moved easily through the powdery snow that was just beginning to fall on the paths of Boston Commons.

The child, wrapped in a fleecy wool coat and knitted cap, sat cozily like a small princess among the blankets. She was now a year old, with dark laughing eyes, and she practiced her few words in a chirping voice, which brought smiles from passersby.

"We're going to see John," Allegra said to her daughter, "and then we'll see if he'll come home with us for tea."

As she neared the customhouse she saw him, but something was wrong; a woman was greeting him. It was Melissa, with her china-blue eyes turned up to him adoringly. His hand came under her elbow, and his head bent to hers with a smile.

A knot of annoyance filled her chest, and she turned the carriage abruptly and hurried away from the customhouse. "*Una gatta sporca,* the dirty cat!" she muttered to herself in Italian. She had had her fill of Melissa and all the worries over losing John to her!

In one moment of total clarity and determination, she promised herself that tonight would be the night when John would discover just how much passion she could give to him. She would have no more thoughts of being unable—she was a woman with fire in her, and that fire could never be snuffed out. Her face was hot with the excitement of her decision, and she felt almost euphoric.

She walked with light steps into the center of the city, where a shop that sold fine crystal and china had set aside a special item for her. She had wanted to have more time to search for just the right gift for John, but after what she had just seen she was certain that this was it: a tiny crystal heart, pure and clear. It was hardly a practical gift for a man, but it was the heart she wished him to have—her own, unclouded by the past. It was faceted to reflect light in many-colored darts. It would be her secret message to him, which he would keep hidden in a pocket; he had only to touch it to be assured of her love.

A nearby tea shop provided a warm refuge for Allegra and the baby. An icy wind was blowing off the harbor. It was difficult to believe that she had been in this clean and bustling city for more than two months. The past was retreating, and she would will it to retreat faster. Beloved John—she would give him his son and all the joy he could imagine.

With that thought planted firmly in her mind, she started for home. She began to notice and to enjoy the candles, which were being lighted in the windows around her. She had stayed out much longer than she had intended, and it was growing dark. The odors of cooking drifted along, pierced by the sharp cold of the snowflakes.

She hastened her pace. John would certainly be home by the

fire in their parlor. How good and kind and deeply exciting he was! Her heart began to beat with anticipation.

Just then Allegrina gave a peevish cry and threw a small toy out of the carriage. Allegra bent to pick it up, but another hand reached for it first. She straightened up with thanks on her lips and looked directly into the dark, speculative eyes of Luciano Antonino.

He put the toy back into the carriage and nonchalantly fell into step with her. A helpless horror deprived her of speech, like a shivering bird entranced before a snake. The long-expected evil had come at last and now was walking beside her. Her thoughts were in turmoil. Pictures of Barretto, John, Allegrina, flew into her mind. She was numb and silent, waiting to know what Luciano intended to do.

He looked much older than when she had last seen him six months ago. There were haggard lines in his face and a hint of gray in his hair, yet he still had the fine clothes and the self-sufficient strut so characteristic of him.

She felt her life begin to crumble even as she walked. "You didn't make it easy for me, Allegra," he began, looking straight ahead. "It's amazing how you seem to have protection around you. . . . Last time your protectors very nearly made an end of me. Did you intend that?"

Dumbly, she shook her head.

"Hmm, I thought not." He turned to give her an ironic glance. "But I'm not one to be put off . . . and time means nothing to a man in love. So . . . this is the child," he said. "Was she worth it, Allegra?"

She let him talk while her mind raced. She turned her steps back toward the center of town, like a mother animal drawing an intruder far away from her nest. John was home waiting for her, waiting for his wife to come in from her long walk.

After a while she became convinced that Luciano was acting on his own account, for some reason she could not understand. . . . It had nothing to do with Barretto. Was it to avenge her flight from him so long ago? His eyes gave no indication of his state of mind, and that was in itself frightening. She didn't know how to fend him off. He was acting cordial on the surface, the way he had done when he came around her in Venice.

In a rash moment she decided on a path of action that would either be the ruin of her or would rid her of him forever. She was weary of deception and fear.

She stopped and faced him. "*Signore,* I beg you to come to my home for a cup of tea before you leave again. There is something I want to show you."

It was his turn to be disarmed, and he went with her the short distance to her home. All the way she prayed desperately to Santa Chiara for help.

John was sitting in front of a crackling fire. Allegrina, released from the carriage, toddled to him and was given a fatherly kiss. He rose and embraced Allegra, saying that she should take more care to keep herself warm, especially with a baby on the way. He extended his large honest hand to Luciano, as Allegra introduced him as a friend of her family from Italy.

"We met by chance just now." She marveled at how normal her voice sounded.

"I am happy to greet you, sir," John said. "Francesca hardly ever sees anyone from Italy. I've hoped to return with her for a visit someday when the children are old enough."

Luciano looked boldly at Allegra, "Yes, we all miss our Francesca, too." His voice held a touch of irony.

John looked puzzled but said nothing more. Allegra watched her husband's trusting face and knew that she would rather die than shatter his love for her. She was a fool to bring Luciano here; she saw that now, but it was too late.

She brought them hot tea and cakes with trembling hands. *Dear God,* she prayed silently, *I'll do anything you ask, but please help me now!*

Allegrina was being charming, enjoying the company—a miniature of Byron, obviously not the child of John Appleby. Allegra tried to make light conversation about their home and their hopes for the new baby. She couldn't fathom what Luciano planned to do next. His Italian manners were impeccable.

Sitting at ease by the cozy fire, he complimented her on the attractivness of her home. "I can tell Francesca's friends how comfortable a place Boston is," he said to John in a pleasant tone, "although the way of building is so different from in Italy. You see, captain, this is my first visit to the United States. I am only a wide-eyed tourist, and I can see that it is a place of challenge to a man of spirit."

Luciano turned to Allegra with a smile that did not reach his eyes. "I am sure that you will want to hear the news of Venice . . . hmm . . . what would interest you?"

Fear closed Allegra's throat.

"Let me see," he drawled, "I believe you were friendly with the Lamberti girls. You remember the eldest one, who married the old Conte di Rienzi?" He turned to John to explain the names while nauseating tension held Allegra silent. "It was a big scandal in Venice. You must have left about the same time it happened, Francesca. The old *conte* was obsessed with having a son, and he married for the third time this Lamberti daughter, whose old aristocratic family had fallen on bad times. Her father sold her for a brood mare in exchange for debts paid . . . the poor thing. She gave the *conte* a son and then ran away. No one has ever found her, even though the *conte* paid well for the search." He gave a short laugh. "Old Conte di Rienzi, alas, has no more interest in finding his lost *contessa,* now, anyway. He died suddenly, a little more than six months ago . . . his heart, you see." His eyes probed Allegra's while he said in a cordial voice, "Where have you been since Venice? Tell me, how did you meet the captain?"

Allegra's head whirled with faintness. Barretto was dead! She clutched the arms of her chair, fighting down her emotion. Barretto had been dead, then, when Luciano came to Marseilles. She heard John's quiet voice explaining that they had met in Marseilles, where Francesca lived with her old nurse.

"I'm afraid that I was impetuous," John was saying. "It was a whirlwind courtship, because I had to return home and I knew I could not go without Francesca." He gave her a loving smile with a spark of anxiety behind it. He could see that she was upset.

She pulled herself together while her mind was shouting, *Bar-*

retto was dead before I married John. . . . There was no sin! . . .
She stopped herself. He could be lying to her.

She told Luciano in a small voice, "My old nurse wished to retire to live with friends and, just at that time, my dear John sailed his beautiful ship into the harbor. It was an answer to prayer. I am very happy."

"No more than I," John said in his rich voice.

Luciano grew silent and stared into the fire while Allegra found courage to ask, "What happened to my friends, the Lambertis, and to the *conte*'s child?"

Luciano withdrew his eyes from contemplation of the fire. "Ah, *si*, the child inherited the title. Since the *conte* had no male relations alive, the Lambertis took the boy. I believe they all live in the Ca' d'Argenti. They will care for the boy until he is of age. The remaining sisters are not married yet, I believe. It's a step up for the Lambertis."

He began to ramble on about Venice and then said, "Remember the Redentore orphanage, Francesca? What you never knew was that one of the little girls there was a bastard of mine. I got her an education there . . . and now she's married to a young man who plays in the Vienna Symphony. Not bad for a bastard father and his daughter."

Then suddenly he was speaking about Byron. . . . "He's never returned to Venice. There were some rumors that he was part of the Contessa di Rienzi's problems. I hear he's still caught tight by the Contessa Guiccioli in Ravenna. She knows how to handle him and her old husband, too. She demands and they back down," he chuckled, watching Allegra with curiously piercing eyes.

Allegra began to sense that he was telling the truth about Barretto.

"But your husband won't care about any more Venetian gossip," he continued. "I have an appointment with a friend now, and tomorrow I go to New York and then home to Italy. I've just spent some weeks in Morocco. . . . Now, that's a place I won't yearn to visit again, although I did make some money there." Finally he rose to leave, with courteous farewells to John.

Allegra told John she would see their visitor to the door.

"Maybe you have messages for friends in Venice," Luciano said. His lips had a sardonic twist and his eyes met Allegra's with a spark of anger.

She went outside into the snowy cold with him. Her breathing was difficult. She was prepared to beg for mercy, to do anything that would protect her husband and her child. She didn't care about herself—she didn't matter anymore.

He had an odd expression on his face as he started to speak. "You are happy, it seems," he said in a rough voice.

"Yes, I am very happy," she began, with all the force of will she could put into words. "There is nothing in the world that can separate me from my family here." She stood regarding him with the courage of a fighter. "Did you know that Barretto was dead when you came to Marseilles?"

He shook his head. "He died after I left Venice, and I did not get the news until after my pleasant sojourn in Morocco."

She sighed deeply, and he raised her face with an urging hand, looking into her eyes. He suddenly smiled. "The little girl will be a beautiful woman like her mother. Bastards have a difficult life. I have no intention of making your next child one, also. You see, Allegra, you misjudged me. Even an ambitious bastard has some good in him. You want to know why I came? I couldn't let you go from my memory until I had told you something: long ago in the Ca' d'Argenti I made a clumsy approach to you, and you chose to find me offensive and beneath you. I could have helped you then, but . . . . If you had seen me with clear eyes, you would have known I had real feelings toward you. I hated you for disregarding me, and I wanted the pleasure of seeing you after you had been hurt by life as life had hurt me. But I did care for you, and your suffering did not bring me the joy I expected. My heart is complicated. It hates and loves at the same time. Perhaps my debt is paid by my own pains. You are fortunate to have so much love around you."

He bowed slowly and took Allegra's shaking hand to his lips. "I will not bother you again. *Addio,* Mrs. Appleby."

Allegra watched Luciano move away down the darkening street. His lonely figure, walking jauntily among the snowflakes, aroused her pity. She would light a candle for him in Father Liam's church.

All she could think of now was that the danger was over, and Barretto was dead. She turned back to her own door. Inside was all the love and warmth she had ever asked for, but she must make sure of it. . . .

Over dinner John made little reference to Luciano, except to say that he seemed to be a capable fellow who could make his fortune easily. He watched her loving eyes with a spark of impatience that excited her and told her what she must do.

Later, on their big bed, she rolled over close to him and felt him grow tense at her touch.

"Don't play with me, Francesca," he said in a suddenly harsh voice. "I'm in no mood to be the gentleman, after watching that manipulating Italian stare at you."

She raised herself to lean over him and began to kiss his lips. A delicious heat was moving through her . . . she was no longer cool. She had never wanted anything as much as John's full love. She began to tremble, and John's arms pulled her down to him with a strength that made her gasp.

"Say it, Francesca!" She felt his hand heavy on her breast. His lips forced hers, and she laughed, turning to put her mouth against his ear.

"Take me, John, I want you," she whispered with passion, "I love you."

She heard his answer "—I love you forever—" before she lost all thought of word or time or place. This, at last, was the completed love she had dreamed and prayed for . . . the union not only of body but of spirit. The look of joy on John's face told her she need never fear Melissa nor any other woman again.

AFTERWORD

Eventually the mail brought a letter from Gina, forwarded by Odile, who was happy with her friends on the farm near Arles. Gina wrote that Barretto was dead. "You can now return to Venice if you wish," the letter said. "You can be Renaldo's guardian. Few will blame you for running from your husband. . . ."

Allegra wrote to Odile:

Tell Gina that I send my love and gratitude. I will not write to her, so that she will have no clue to where I am. You must say only that I will never forget her in my prayers. It is better that I am not remembered in Venice. That life is over for me, Odile. You were right, John is all that I could have asked for. It is a new life, for a new woman named Francesca Appleby.

ALLEGRA'S SON was born in late summer, to John's great pride. Allegrina was growing into a headstrong and beguiling child. Allegra sensed the struggle with the Byron blood in her. She saw the restless fire in the beautiful wide eyes and wondered . . . on what rocky paths of life would those driving energies take her? A flash of sadness moved in Allegra whenever her daughter's face reflected the Byron moods.

There was a bittersweet moment in 1824, when news came that Lord Byron had died, fighting for Greek independence from the Turks. Allegra remembered the times he had spoken to her about human freedom and how his words had come from true emotion. Somehow she knew that, finally, he had found his use as a man. Poor Teresa—no woman could fight against the deeper needs that lay in him. The newspaper she read had an artist's sketch of him against a stormy sky, his beautiful face set in determination. She put the picture and the story inside the Byron box.

And then she sat down with her pen and inkpot and wrote a
long letter addressed to her daughter Allegrina—and to those unborn girl children who would come after, carrying the Byron
blood. It was the lovingly told story of a Venetian *contessa's* passion for the eccentric, outrageous, fascinating English milord.
That, too, was put into the box, to be read someday when it could
be understood.

In another shorter letter were instructions to give the box and
its secret only to the women of the family line. Even John would
never learn of that one secret part of her life.

One last time she touched the mementos, lingering over each
with a special kind of feeling—not pain—and then she wrapped
the box and sealed it, with its cover letter on top.

Perhaps someday, she thought, when old passions are faded,
the story of the lost *contessa* will come back to the di Rienzis of
Venice. Some other hands than hers would carry it.

She placed the wrapped box, as in the old days in Venice, far
back in her desk drawer. How different it was now—no fear of
discovery shivered along her nerves.

Allegra smiled, recalling the difficult moments in that first year
in Boston, when John had asked more specifically about her life
in Italy.

"I don't intend to pry, my sweetheart," he said, his intent eyes
steady on hers. "I only need to know if there is danger around
you still. I knew there was in Marseilles. Odile told me as much."
He noticed Allegra's quick little frown. "She loves you—and so
do I. When I returned from Leghorn with the Jarrets, I had fully
intended to kidnap you, if you would not go willingly." He laughed
at her expression. "Don't you think I am capable of piracy?" She
nodded and he leaned to kiss her. "Then, my darling, please tell
me enough to set my nerves at ease. I could see how much that
Italian fellow upset you. . . ."

Allegra, her hands held gently in his, gave him an edited version
of her life. She gave no names. Allegrina was still to be thought of
as the child of her Italian husband. She had been driven to run
away by his ill-treatment. He was searching, she said, for his
child. He was desperate for a son and would have taken any child

away from her. He had died just before she married John . . . but she had not known it.

"So," John spoke quietly, "you married me, anyway." He drew her close. "You can't know how happy that makes me." She pulled away to look at him in surprise.

"My dearest, don't you understand? You loved me then . . . you didn't want to let me go." He held her shoulders and gave a little shake, "Now, tell me the rest."

"I was afraid, because one of his men had seen me on the docks. I didn't want to burden you with my problem, so I was going to go to a convent Odile knew of. I thought you had sailed away . . . that you were impatient. You can't imagine how terrible it was to look down at the harbor and see the *Laughing Liberty* gone!"

"And when did you find out that your elderly husband had died?"

"Luciano told me the day he came to Boston."

"Ah, that explains many things. I wish I had known. My poor dearest. Let there be trust between us now." He had asked no more, and if he knew of the existence of the Byron box he said nothing. For that she was grateful.

SHE LOOKED UP from her desk to the picture of Santa Chiara. The kind and loving eyes smiled at her, and a new wisdom came into Allegra's heart.

"Love is the power to absolve," she whispered. "I must accept what has been my life and distill love from it. That is what you wanted me to know, isn't it? Your special saintly gift wasn't to answer my prayers for people or things . . . but to teach me love."

She heard the sound of the big oak front door opening, and then John's quick vigorous step on the stairs. She turned eagerly waiting for his smile.

BOOK II
THE LAST ALLEGRA

CHAPTER ONE

BOSTON

ALLEGRA BRENT SAT ALONE in the rear of the black limousine. A hundred yards away the funeral director was discreetly fulfilling his prepaid tasks. *Nonna* was gone now. *Nonna*, the Italian grandmother, the proud and gentle Venetian war bride of 1918, who had brought up the orphaned child Allegra with tales of Italy.

Allegra was not a classic beauty, but her Italian blood showed in the luxuriant fall of sable hair, her great dark eyes and the melodic pitch of her voice.

And so now I am alone entirely, she thought, rolling up the car window against the light rain outside. Of course there was Grandmother Brent, but she was busy with her own life and a new husband. She had never bothered with the granddaughter who looked so foreign, so different from the fair New England Brents.

Well, I'm not unhappy, she smiled to herself. *If this is a beginning for* nonna *out there somewhere, then it is a beginning for me.* A familiar figure smiled in at her and motioned to her. She rolled the window down again. Clinton Meserve's wrinkled fatherly hand reached to take one of her own and held it.

"I loved her too, Allegra. But somehow I know she is where she has wanted to be for some time. You were the only thing that kept her here so long, and I promised her I would look after your legal affairs." He leaned inside to lay a manila envelope on the seat beside her. It was stamped with the name of his law firm.

"This is for you; she wrote it for you to read at her death. I have no idea what it is about. You know how she was—always a hint of mystery." He looked into her eyes for a warm moment and squeezed her hand again. "I have confidence in you, my girl. Come to lunch next week; we can go into the financial details then. And don't worry about that end of it. The house should bring a fair price, but you won't have to do anything about it for some time anyway. I'll call you Monday. By the way, is Larry going to be looking in on you? I expected to see him here today."

"Larry's anxious to console me, but I'm all right. Thanks, Clinton . . . ." The rain started falling harder.

"Monday then, Allegra. And don't worry, dear."

She looked at his concerned face and wished in an odd way that she could console him, too. As the driver turned the car through the gates of the cemetery, Allegra looked down at the envelope. Her fingers slipped apart the metal clasp. There was a cream-colored envelope inside. She wouldn't read it now; she knew where she wanted to be to receive her final message from *nonna*.

With her head back and eyes closed, she fought the fatigue of the past three days and held one picture in her mind—the old green frame house with its broad veranda and fragrant vines . . . the lavender crape myrtle tree, which shaded the sitting room. It was bare now, waiting for spring. The car slowed and stopped, and the door was held open for her.

Heavier drops of rain were bursting and splattering from the eaves above the porch, and she quickly passed through the wet curtain into the protection of the porch and turned the latch with her key. The old lion's-head door knocker rattled with the motion. It had been her first friend after the death of her parents, when she had come here to live as a lonely small child. "The lion of Venice," *nonna* had said then. For years the gentle lion on the door was privy to her innermost thoughts.

Before she could shed her damp coat the telephone rang. She didn't want to talk with Larry; the letter was waiting to be opened. With a heavy sigh she reached for the telephone.

"Really, I'm fine. I just need to get some rest. . . . No, don't come over, Larry. I'll call you in the morning."

She hung up the phone slowly. She would have to do something about Larry soon. She hadn't given him any reason to be so possessive of her, and it was growing uncomfortable, as if he assumed they had more of a relationship than they did. She didn't need his hovering humorless presence, even if he called it love. That was why she had told him not to come to the funeral. She lifted the receiver again and laid it down on the table next to the phone.

The house was quiet, yet it was a friendly silence, as if *nonna* stood smiling somewhere just outside the range of normal sight. Allegra picked up Clinton's envelope and went to sit down in her grandmother's favorite chair beside the fireplace. On impulse she reached out and set a match to the small tinder fire set there. The rain was drizzling quietly along the eaves, whispering down the library window. For a moment desolation flooded over her. It was the last fire *nonna* would ever set, her mind wept. She raised her hand to push away tears and took the small envelope from the protection of the larger one.

"To my beloved granddaughter." Peace flowed around her again, and the flames spoke softly as she put her finger under the edge of the fine linen envelope and gently pulled it open. She drew out several closely written sheets, and with them came a breath of *nonna*'s perfume.

My dearest child. I hope you have not been weeping, for, my little love, I am happy. The blessed saints have held out their arms to me across the threshold of new life, and I have found love that was lost for many weary years. If it had not been for you, dear child, the years after your grandfather died would have been sad ones. Now I bless you from that happy place where my soul lives, and I exercise the right of the women of your family to tell you a secret concerning your blood, your family, your inheritance. It would have been your mother's place to tell you, through whose line this treasure has come.

Allegra turned over the page with a shiver of excitement at a secret that could only wait for death. "You must go to the desk in the library." Allegra looked across the room at the big carved oak desk, which had always belonged to her family. "Pull out the top right-hand drawer," the letter went on, "and feel under it."

There is a key taped to the bottom. It opens the large bottom drawer, which I would not let you open when you were small. Unlock it and take out the box you find there. The things inside it belonged to the first Allegra in our family, your great-great-great-grandmother, and to the man who was your great-great-great-grandfather. I will let you discover for yourself the story of these two people whose moment of love changed lives and set others in motion. I will only say that in these mementos you have perhaps your most valuable legacy. If known to history, these letters would bring great excitement and much money. You must decide, child, whether to keep them secret, as have the other women of the family . . . or to give them to the world.

Allegra read on, fascinated.

Why have I not told you this before? Perhaps it was that brooding look in your eyes, the changing moods, my child, when you were growing into womanhood . . . that made me hesitate. You will soon understand how I watched you sit for hours curled up in the corner of the window seat, absorbed into another world, your romantic young mind reveling in the words of Byron's poems. Did you ever wonder why we had such a fine collection of his poetry, or why that fascinating voice spoke out of the books directly into your heart? Sometimes I was afraid of the blood that was yours, my darling, even though thinned by the strains of other lines. Yet I know it is potent still. It is in your eyes, child, and in your love of beauty and in your questing mind. No matter what comes around you, Allegra *mia*, you can never be ordinary. The contents of the box will tell you why.

One more thing. You know that there were other Allegras in the family line, but you do not know about the first Allegra. The name of your great-great-great-grandmother was Allegra di Rienzi. She was a Venetian *contessa.* There are still di Rienzis in Venice. When I was a girl I saw them come and go to their palazzo on the Grand Canal. You have few relatives here, child, but you have a family in Venice, even though distant.

Now, dear Allegra, discover the secret of Allegra di Rienzi, and may this knowledge bring you to a deeper understanding of the ways of love and life. My love is enduring. Remember.

Nonna

Allegra set down the last page in the pool of lamplight on the table. Almost fearfully she looked at the squat old desk, like a guardian presence, hiding its strange secret.

She remembered playing with that desk as a child and rattling angrily that great bottom drawer, trying to pull it open. It was as if something had beckoned her to that drawer and its contents. She remembered, too, the teenage hours immersed in Byron. Her eyes went to the familiar line of books on the shelf by the window—the journals, poetry and biographies of Byron. The covers were dim from many handlings. Why Byron? And what had *nonna* meant by "that brooding look . . . the changing moods"?

She sat staring until a small log crashed with sparks in the fireplace, blazing up for a bright instant. She had to find out what *nonna* meant. With a peculiar feeling of reluctance and urgency she walked slowly to the desk and pulled out the top drawer.

Yes, the key was there, old and dark—taped securely to the underside. She tore at the tape with trembling fingers and knelt to put the key into the lock of the lower drawer. The key wouldn't turn at first, but then she felt the lock give way against her insistent pressure. She grasped the two brass handles and pulled. The drawer groaned along its grooves.

Inside was one thing: a shallow box, about eight inches long and six inches wide. It had once been brave with gold and crimson and intricate scrolls of handwork on its worn leather top. She lifted it out gingerly and carried it to the lamplit table next to *nonna*'s letter. Her fingers touched the dim designs and stopped at the center medallion. Within it was a shield with a crest. She bent close to see the faded gold words around the rim. "Crede Byron," they read.

Her mind flew back to those dreaming days on the old window

seat, when she had followed the path of Byron's life in imagination. Crede Byron—Trust Byron. It was his family motto, and now it rested here under her fingertips. Her nerves shivered; an energy flowed from the unopened box. What was such a thing doing in the drawer of a New England sea captain's desk?

Almost afraid to move, she looked at the box. "It may be your most precious inheritance," *nonna* had said. Whatever this secret was, would it be better left unknown? If she opened the box she was sure her life would not be as it had been—ever again.

"Don't be such a coward," she chided herself aloud, gathering courage to do it. The lid was tightly fastened, and no lock was visible. By intuition her fingers explored the surface to find a hidden place of pressure in the center of the scrollwork design on the side. The lid flew open, and she drew in her breath sharply. There was the tang of an old perfume, a whisper of forgotten fragrance.

Inside the worn velvet interior, a small book, elaborately bound in faded red velvet, caught her eye. Its top cover had an inset miniature painting—the facade of a Venetian palace, the rippling canal water lapping at its foundations; and upon its water stairs a man and woman were alighting from a gondola. The book was held together by a silver clasp, whose small ornate key still lingered in the lock. The little painted scene was warm with mellow sunlight.

Tears stung in Allegra's eyes, as if the picture pulled at a long forgotten memory in her. Her hand moved to touch a smaller box, which lay beside the book. It was of inlaid wood, like those that come today from Sorrento, but this one had felt the press of many fingers, and one or two of its tiny fitted pieces were missing. The box had a wistfulness about it, almost as if a sad little face were looking up at her.

She was so engrossed in her thoughts that at first she didn't see the envelope that lay beside the book. She picked it up. "Read this before you proceed," it said in *nonna*'s hand. Allegra drew out more finely written pages. "Allegra *mia*," this letter began, "you are now about to trace a very strange story. No doubt you will have already noted the Byron crest on the larger box. George Gordon, Lord Byron, was your great-great-great-grandfather."

The words swam before her eyes. Incredible words and yet with the ring of truth. She sank down into her chair and read on, utterly absorbed.

In this box is the proof. The small book is the diary of Allegra di Rienzi, a sweet young Venetian woman who was the victim of a loveless, arranged marriage to the aging Conte Barretto di Rienzi—the head of a powerful family then. He had worn out two other wives in his desperate search for a son, and poor Allegra, after giving him his heir, could only look forward to a life of restriction, unpleasant sex and painful dullness. You must understand that she was an innocent, ripe for true romance to come into her hopeless life.

The diary of the consuming passion she found was left for the women of the family to discover, each in her turn. But let her speak for herself about the days of love and pain, which pressed her into new and unexpected paths.

And remember, Allegra—love wisely, and do not give your heart where it will not be truly valued.

Always my love,
Nonna

One last page remained to be read. *Nonna* had enclosed a genealogy, which traced the lines of descent from the first Allegra.

Allegra reached for the diary; she held it lightly in the palm of her hand, its velvet caressing her skin. She hesitated to turn the key in the tiny lock and release the emotions she knew were waiting. It opened with a light crackling sound, and more of the elusive fragrance came with it.

Inside, the handwriting was dim but legible. It had something of the elegance of *nonna*'s, but was less disciplined. Allegra held it to the light to read more clearly. It was in Italian, of course. How glad she was that *nonna* had insisted she learn to read and speak that beautiful language.

The fly leaf bore the date "3 December 1818." She turned the

FAMILY LINES OF ALLEGRA DI RIENZI

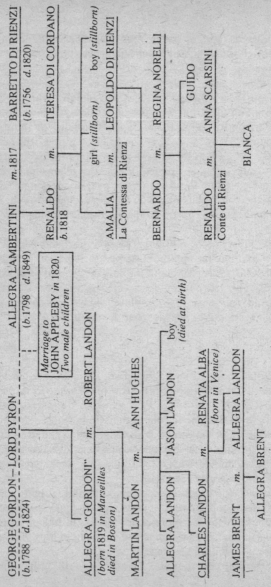

(Allegra dear. I have been in correspondence with the Italian office of records. This is as much as I know about the di Rienzi branch of the family. There may be some changes by the time you read this. The American line of descent is accurate.)

yellowed pages carefully. There were brief notations of teas, suppers and fittings with the dressmaker. Some mention of a portrait, Barretto, Gemma . . . . Allegra's eyes skimmed over the pages, feeling herself pulled into the consciousness of this other Allegra.

She stopped at one page and read it through. It was dated 19 March 1819.

. . . Barretto is in France for a month, negotiating a shipment of wines from the southern provinces. I am alone with little Renaldo and Aunt Adriana. Adriana is a good soul, kind and talkative. I'm afraid I'm not very exciting company for her. She's feeling shut away here and has convinced me it would be good for both of us to attend the salon of Contessa Benzoni tomorrow night. Adriana tells me that the *contessa*'s *conversazioni* are attracting the most interesting people in Venice—artists, writers, clever men. I've met her a time or two. A flamboyant woman with a big heart, an aging face and blond curls that cannot be real. Dear Adriana wants to fill her ears with gossip and she is especially hoping that the scandalous English poet, Milord Byron, will be there. At least it will be good to leave the Ca' for a few hours and see how the rest of the world entertains itself.

Allegra could almost feel the sigh of dullness and frustration from the writing on the little page. "No one needs me very much," the diary went on.

I often think now that it would be best if I went back to the convent. My little son is well cared for and—may the Blessed Mother forgive me—I cannot love him as I should . . . he is so like Barretto, even before he is six months old.

I know I am called "nun" by many. They say it is because I dress simply, but it is the urge of my heart that they are seeing. Tomorrow night I will wear my soft violet dress, no jewelry—and only a white rose from the garden on the roof. The last thing I wish is to call attention to myself in public.

Barretto would hear of it and then what would become of me? I think my heart is too weary for such an eventuality.

The entry on the next page was headed, "20 March—evening with Contessa Benzoni." The pen pressed darker lines onto the paper, and the writing seemed rushed and breathless. A shiver of excitement flowed out of the page to the present-day Allegra. She closed her eyes for a moment, almost fearing to know more, then she read on. One word stood out more boldly than all the others: "Byron." In ecstatic sentences the young *contessa* described her first meeting with the man who would change her life.

Allegra Brent was with her in her mind as she walked out onto that balcony to escape the crowded drawing room, as she heard the voice of the enchanter speak in a whisper near her ear, as she turned to face those arresting eyes so full of light on the dark spring night and became possessed by them, and as she felt the electrifying touch of his lips on her hand.

This was the lover to whom Allegra di Rienzi had prayed to her Santa Chiara. How hateful was Barretto's name on her lips as she told this stranger from the shadows who she was, and how frightening to hear the stranger's name in return! Byron!

"Spare some of your sweet pity for me," his deep persuasive voice had urged, as he spoke of his loneliness and sorrows. The blood rushed through her body like thunder. "Why have I met him now that it is too late!" she wrote in desperate words beneath his name.

Allegra Brent felt the heat in her own face and the fast uneven rhythm of her own heart, as she called back to life the scene on that faraway night in Venice: the painful secret farewell at the door of the salon, his furtive note pressed into her palm at the last moment before he turned away from her, her reckless decision to meet him, come what may. The words carried the distant sound of fate with them, and the eyes that were reading them now could sense disaster entwined hopelessly with delight.

She read how his dark gondola had waited silently each night in the shadows beside the Ca' d'Argenti to take her to him. Allegra di Rienzi loved him to the fullness of her newly awakened heart, yet she could not entirely understand all the complications in his tortured spirit. She tried; he was like a dark prince—amazing and wonderful—who had stopped in his dazzling ride through life to love her. He flooded her with pleasure and took her young body to paradise, confusing her vulnerable heart.

Then came the strangeness and the walls he built between them. He gave her a box, which bore his family crest, and he gave her a poem, which seemed to hint of goodbye.

> Have I not parted from you and left whispered good-
>   byes?
> Was it but yesterday my tears and my sighs,
> Or a thousand years ago we kissed—Who are you?
> Are you she, or another—Would my heart knew.
> Allegra! I taste thy sweet name. My tongue the joy would
>   keep,
> For bitter fruit lingers and still I must weep.

Allegra Brent felt a knot of anguish starting in her chest, when she found the tiny folded letter of farewell from Byron. It was honest in the way Byron was honest—painful and loving and final.

Cara Mia,
How can I say what must be said and not cause pain? I have discovered that the swift sharp knife is often more healing than otherwise. You know what I am and what I have been, and my heart, I regret, was a hard pillow for your gentle head. I would be honest with you, sweet Allegra. It was your great resemblance to that other so dear to me that drew me, but there is terrible danger in love for such a reason.

I must tell you truthfully that I have found one who has no resemblance to any other in my crowded mind. She is like a blooming tree whose generous fruit will heal my sores of pain.

Forgive me, Allegra, with all your sweet soul, and go back to your rightful life as though I had not been. Life would be most cruel to you should the world know of our time together.

Pray for the peace of one whose soul battles the powers of darkness. Your heart will mend, my dear. Hearts have infinite capacity for such renewal.

Addio,
Byron

It seemed unbelievable that Allegra Brent was reading these words, too agonizingly personal for anyone else's eyes but Allegra di Rienzi's.

The faded words had lost none of the emotion over the years. The writing in the diary went on with jerky spasms, as the pen moved in a shaking hand. There were blots of ink on the pages after this where Allegra had pressed too hard; and tearstains.

It was infinitely sad to read of Allegra di Rienzi's pregnancy and her fear of Barretto's fury, should he discover it. She was driven to save the child of her passion, and her dangerous flight from Venice to Marseilles said very little about the adventures she must have encountered.

The diary was interrupted until after she reached the safety of her old nursemaid, Odile Berier, who lived very humbly in the French port city. There was some joy with the birth of Byron's daughter, but fear of Barretto's agents was still strong in Allegra's mind. By then she had changed her name and taken on the identity of a respectable Italian widow, selling baked goods to the workers at the docks.

Months passed, and the diary entries gradually became lighter in tone, as if Allegra di Rienzi were at last thinking of a future for herself and her child. There was suddenly mention of John Appleby, a fine and dashing American sea captain, and his beautiful ship, the *Laughing Liberty*. Allegra wrote about the distant city of Boston and what it must be like. But she feared allowing John Appleby to pay court to her. Even with her new identity, she still had the past hovering threateningly around her.

Then, in the summer of 1820, one day of desperate choices found her fleeing from discovery by one of Barretto's spies, and running to John Appleby to accept his offer of marriage. Allegra Brent looked over at the genealogy and found his name. She then returned her attention to the diary and followed her ancestress from Marseilles to the New World; to Boston where the love child of Byron would live in peace—part of a happy family with the other children of John and Allegra Appleby. Allegra Brent studied the pages to find regret in Allegra Appleby's heart, and found none.

There was not another mention of Byron until 1824. The news of his death was contained in a brittle old Boston newspaper clipping, amost too old to handle. It bore a dramatic artist's sketch of him, cloak windblown against a turbulent sky. Allegra Brent could feel how the other Allegra's eyes searched the printed words, dwelling on the description of Byron's heroic death defending the Greeks against the Turkish domination. She must have felt a hint of pride to see how the world honored his genius. Would it have pleased his restless spirit to know about the curly-headed, vital child of his, who lived in the new free nation of the United States, the modern Allegra wondered?

The diary stopped then in 1824. There was a piece of fine linen paper folded into the back of the little book. On it, Allegra Appleby had written her request that the Byron box and its contents be handed down through the female line of the family—to the eldest daughters, or in the event that there were no females in a generation, it would go to the eldest daughter-in-law. The Byron secret.

"To know is to understand—to understand is to forgive," had been written very carefully and clearly just above the signature of Allegra Francesca Lamberti di Rienzi Appleby.

The voice of the first Allegra fell silent upon the yellowed pages. The modern Allegra was silent, too, trying to absorb the impact of what she had just read. No longer was she just Allegra Brent; she was a child of Byron's blood, and she also had the blood of old Venetian aristocracy.

The world was suddenly wider, exciting, beckoning. She looked at the diary again. On the inside back cover were recorded the birth of John Appleby's two sons and the death of John himself, but the date was too faded to read.

A shared feeling of loss flooded Allegra Brent's heart for a mo-

ment. Then she closed the diary and looked at the tiny picture of
Venice on its cover. There were still di Rienzis in Venice, *nonna*
had said. Had they ever discovered what had happened to their
contessa?

Surely they would want to know. It would only be history now,
but fascinating history. One more piece of paper remained at the
bottom of the Byron box, a loose, neatly written letter in Allegra
di Rienzi's script. It was the never-mailed last letter to him, dated
shortly before his death.

She lifted out the small inlaid box and opened it now. Inside
was a formal calling card, Byron's; on the reverse side was his
sprawling handwriting begging her to meet his gondola later that
night. Allegra Brent's fingers tingled with the urgency of his
words. Who could have refused his plea? Would she herself have
been able to resist the pulling force of a man like Byron? She smiled
a little to herself and put the card back into the box. Next to it was
a folded paper packet, which protected a fine linen handkerchief,
its whiteness aged to parchment tone; within the folds of the
handkerchief was a dainty necklace of gold chain and Italian pink
coral beads, ending in a locket, which was set with chip diamonds
and tiny baroque pearls.

Her fingers went instinctively along the edge of the locket to
open it. Nestled against the curved interior was a crisp curl of
dark auburn hair. She bent close to the dim writing on the outside
paper, which wrapped it, and read Allegra's note:

The necklace he gave me the night we went to the Mocenigo.
His handkerchief he gave me to tie up my hair in the wind on
the Lido. A curl of his hair I begged from him when we were
the last time together.

Allegra touched the curl with her fingertips. It clung to her, still
responsive with life. She shivered. How she wished she could have
seen him! They would have been friends; she could have
understood him. She analyzed her own thoughts: was this
the secret of his magic? Had he made every woman feel that she

alone was the one to solace and understand him? No, it had to be deeper.

She closed the locket carefully and took up another folded paper. In this was the faded brown ghost of a rose, and in his compelling writing, a poem to go with it. A last little packet protected a torn piece of what looked like wallpaper, a scroll pattern. *From the place of my joy,* the note said simply.

Allegra blinked back tears again. The pitiful remnants of happiness and pain wrung her heart. She replaced them all in the box. When she touched the handkerchief, she impulsively raised it to her lips and kissed it lightly, as she knew the other Allegra had done many many times. Then she gently closed the lids of both boxes and let out her breath on a long sigh.

The fire had burned out to whispering coals. She sat back and looked around the room. All was as it had been before, but all was changed. She knew now without doubt that she could not stay on as she was. She would have to take steps. Make new paths—go to Italy. Yes, go to Italy!

The secret belonged to the di Rienzis as well as to herself. She knew what a valuable thing she had in her possession, and what a sensation it would create in the literary world, but her mind refused to think of releasing this bittersweet story to public knowledge.

She rose slowly and picked up the box, listening to the chime of raindrops still falling outside. Upstairs she placed the box upon her nightstand and went to bed. She fell into a heavy sleep to dream of gondolas, roses and a deep musical voice speaking words she could not quite hear. And in the background she could see *nonna* smiling and nodding her head with satisfaction.

CHAPTER TWO

"ALLEGRA! ARE YOU IN THERE?"

Dull banging from somewhere outside of sleep confused her for a moment, and she took the anxious voice back into her dream. Then the doorbell buzzed on the back porch. "Allegra, it's me! Are you all right?"

She didn't open her eyes.

"Can you come to the door?"

"I'm not up yet. What time is it?"

"Ten o'clock. You didn't call me, and I wanted to make sure you weren't depressed. I took the day off so we could be together."

She lay still for a moment, not wanting to let go of the dream. A fresh breeze was blowing through her soul.

She buttoned her pink quilted robe and let Larry in. He tried to put his arms around her. "I waited for your call . . ." he said a bit defensively, feeling a slight reproach in her small body. "Maybe I should just go and let you catch some more rest."

"Maybe so," she heard herself saying. The aura of Byron was strong around her, and Larry was intruding. He looked searchingly into her eyes to confirm her brief words.

"I'm sorry. . . ." She didn't know what else to say. She could hear her voice sounding distant.

He stood back, a flush of color rising in his face. "Well, I guess I can find something to do with the day. The home office is sending me back to Chicago for a week. I thought you'd have a hard time without someone you could lean on."

Allegra didn't answer. Her mind was analyzing, looking at him for the first time, really, wondering what Larry Palmer was doing in her life at all.

"Allegra . . . . I said I'm going away for a few days."

"Yes, I know. That's fine," she answered.

Larry's voice was flat. "I don't know what's happening between us, but I think we should talk about it when I come back." His face was calm, but the cords of his neck were strained. He left without losing his composure.

Allegra was relieved to hear the car back out of the driveway. She was sorry about everything. She hadn't handled the situation very well at all. She should have been more honest with him from the beginning. But until last night she had just never known how completely wrong he was for her. It was a lame excuse, but it was the truth. Larry had become a pleasant enough habit that she had never had reason to try to break.

SEVERAL DAYS passed, partly in dreams of Byron and the first Allegra, partly in reviewing her own twenty-five years of life—and her resolve strengthened. A luncheon with Clinton Meserve brought up the problem of money and selling the house.

Clinton was not sure it was wise. "You've never had to think financially. The house won't make you wealthy, but it is a fair amount for a young woman to have to handle." He wanted to introduce her to his stockbroker, maybe get her into some high yield bonds and provide a small income.

"But I'm not retiring, Clinton," she laughed over coffee. "I have a job at the university and I can always support myself." She leaned toward him across the table and said, "I'm going to go to Italy. . . ." Then she waited for him to object.

There were dangers waiting for a woman alone who didn't know the ropes, he said. "At least let me give you the name of a good travel agent. He can get you into a reputable tour group."

Allegra accepted the slip of paper with a name on it. What good would it do to tell him that she didn't even know if she would return? "But first things first," she said, as he helped her into her taxi. "I have to sell the house." She went directly to the newspaper office and placed an appealingly worded ad under Houses For Sale. *Nonna*'s letter had clearly given her permission to set a new course.

A week went by, and Larry returned from Chicago. He called

to make an appointment to see her. He sounded serious and businesslike. It was not a meeting she wished to have, and she regretted letting things come to this pitiful kind of ending.

She understood now what had made her hold back all those times when he had pressed her to say she loved him. She was waiting for something of a very different kind to come into her life, but she had known it only instinctively then.

THEIR FINAL TALK took place in the cheerful sitting room. Allegra tried to be offhand and let him guide the conversation. She didn't want to say any more than was absolutely necessary.

"Why are you going?" he asked finally.

"It's something I've dreamed of doing."

"But why now, when I have plans . . . ?"

Allegra spoke quickly, to say the difficult words as fast as possible. "Because everything has changed, and I don't want to be serious about any relationship."

"You've never said you didn't like me. We had good times. I'm not going to let you go so easily. You just want to run away because of your grandmother's death. When you come to your senses, you'll realize what I have to offer you." He turned his face from her, after it was clear she was not going to respond. "I'd better go then," he said.

"I'm sorry," she said lamely. It seemed to be the only thing she said to him anymore.

"You should be," he snapped and wheeled around to leave.

She shut the door behind him and stood against it. She blamed herself for not understanding him sooner. She hated being cruel. But she was reasonably sure she had done no permanent damage to Larry's ego.

WEEKS PASSED. Allegra searched Byron's poetry to find any hint of Allegra di Rienzi, but could not. There was only the one poem, which rested in the Byron box upstairs, and the world knew nothing of it.

The house was sold now, and her passport was ready. Lately

she had worn the gold locket with its precious curl. She wondered if she was counting too much on this adventure to Italy, whose outcome could hardly be predicted. But the force of the very private stirrings in her heart set caution aside.

Larry had written her a letter. It was an analysis of her emotional problems, and it ended with a generous offer to give her another chance. She crumpled it in her hands and sighed with relief that that part of her life was truly over. Now she hadn't even the smallest nagging tie to this place.

It was mid-July, the peak of the tourist season, and she was lucky to get a direct flight to Milano. She packed carefully, including clothes for every season. How could she know how long Venice would hold her? The last thing she did was to gently place the carved Byron box within the folds of her lingerie and draw the inner strap tightly down upon it in the suitcase.

Clinton, the dear old soul, had called her several times the past few days to reassure her that everything would be looked after. He would take care of the storage of her furniture and close the house in preparation for the new owners. Dr. Allen, dean of the university art department, had asked her to return in the fall to be his secretary again, if she planned on continuing graduate work. She told him she wouldn't know for several weeks at least, and he was kind enough to say he would wait until September first before hiring somebody new.

The taxi honked for her, and a tug of affection for the only home she had ever known brought an instant of regret. The bronze lion stared at her through green eyes which had watched her comings and goings for most of her life. "I'll say hello to Venice for you, old friend," she said, giving the cool snout one last pat.

BY THE TIME HER PLANE TOUCHED DOWN at the Milano airport, she was feeling strangely light-headed. That was the moment when reality crowded in around her, and she sensed fully for the first time what a radical thing she was doing and how alone she was. The business of deplaning, claiming luggage and going through customs carried her along and prevented the newborn anxiety from growing out of control.

She had to concentrate her thoughts on survival—how to find a bus or taxi that could take her to the train station. She felt comforted by the ebb and flow of Italian words and was sure *nonna* was just out of sight, smiling.

A fatherly taxi driver appeared at curbside to offer his services, and she settled back, relieved, into the cab for a fast ride into the city. The great railway terminal was bustling, and porters were running the length of the station pushing their big carts of luggage. Everybody seemed to be in a hurry, but her driver stayed with her to make sure she boarded the correct train for Venice. It was a gesture of kindness, which she accepted with gratitude.

The Venice train was on the second track from the platform, panting on its rails, and within minutes its American passenger was settled comfortably inside for the last lap of her journey. She could stop feeling anxious about her luggage, since it now rested safely above her head on the storage shelf.

She watched the landscape unfold as the sun slanted westward. Names flashed past on road signs. Busy Fiats and Ferraris spun along modern highways, seemingly unaware that they were driving over the footsteps of history.

She wondered what it must have been like to travel with Byron in his great coach, a copy of Napoleon's. It had been equipped with all the comforts of travel to be found then. Compartments for food, his movable desk . . . she smiled to think of his retinue, as described in his journals. In it were Fletcher, his long-suffering valet, other complaining servants, and his traveling menagerie of dogs, cats, a crow, a monkey and an indignant goose, purchased for Christmas dinner but still alive, due to the soft heart of the English milord who could not bear to order it slain.

She was so entranced by the scenery, she was hardly aware of the bright brown watching eyes of the family who shared her compartment—a mother and a small boy, who wriggled uncomfortably inside his well-pressed linen suit. Finally a gentle voice broke through to her mind. It was speaking in careful English.

"Excuse me, *signorina,* may we share our sweets with you?"

Allegra turned to see the woman's smiling face.

"*Cannoli,*" the little boy ventured. It was like saying they were ambrosia. A pastry box was held out to her and a napkin.

Allegra focused her wandering thoughts and smiled back. "Oh, how very kind," she replied in Italian.

Surprise moved over the faces. "But you are not American?"

"Yes. But my grandmother taught me Italian." She took one of the rolled pastries from the box, its red cherry nestling amid cheese and cream.

"You travel to Venice, *signorina,*" the woman inquired between dainty bites, "but where will you stay?"

"The Tre Rose. It was arranged by my travel agent back home."

"A very nice hotel, but, *signorina,* this is summer, and the tourists are many. It might be difficult to feel at home in our city, when you stay in a hotel filled with travelers. So much coming and going—and you almost an Italian yourself. You do not wish to be just another tourist."

"We have a room that we sometimes rent to visitors," the boy said earnestly.

"Those whom we approve," his mother smiled. "I am Eleana Bugelli, and this is my son, Giorgio."

"My name is Allegra Brent. And thank you—I would love to rent your room, if you will have me."

"The rent is reasonable," Signora Bugelli explained. "Less than a hotel, and breakfast and other meals can be with us, if you desire. You can telephone from there to cancel your hotel."

"We have a bathroom with a running hot shower," Giorgio piped up pridefully, as though he described a special and marvelous fact.

The conversation grew more animated. Allegra told them about her home and the death of her grandmother, saying that she was fulfilling a desire to come to Venice because it was her *nonna*'s native city. She asked a few tentative questions. Was there a di Rienzi family still in Venice?

"Mio Dio!" Signora Bugelli exploded. "Is there a di Rienzi family? Who does not know the Ca' d'Argenti? Di Rienzis have lived there since the days of the glory of the doges."

"The House of Silver?"

"*Si*. In the old days a di Rienzi made a fortune trading through the Middle East. He always demanded to be paid in silver, so the legend says. He would not take goods in trade. He had his troubles, because all the robbers knew about his loads of silver coins, and he had to travel with many men. It was he who built the Ca' d'Argenti . . . Principe Renaldo di Rienzi, a nobleman of the doge's court and a prince of the church. Today, the di Rienzi men do not use their title, although the old woman is still la *contessa*. The present Renaldo di Rienzi, the same as his ancestor, is a man of business. He is famous as a designer *commerciale*."

Allegra's mind went back to *nonna*'s genealogy and the name of Renaldo. "I may have to call upon the family. I have a friend who knows them and has asked that I do so." She watched the two faces focus on her.

"I wish you luck!" Signora Bugelli laughed. "They are difficult, not easily intruded upon, you understand? I will point out the Ca' as we pass."

In her kind way she was saying that the di Rienzis were far beyond ordinary people. Allegra did not press further, but she could feel her spirits falling. Would she have the temerity to present herself as a relative—and a bastard relative, at that, to the noble and aloof di Rienzis?

She changed the subject. "My interests are in art and literature. I am going to be a teacher when I finish my graduate studies," she informed them.

"Then Venice is a treasure house for you. That is good."

Allegra smiled. "Will you show me the houses of Lord Byron and Robert Browning?

"The Ca' Rezzonico of Browning may be visited," Giorgio said helpfully.

"*Si,*" his mother added. "It is the property of Venice. But the Palazzo Mocenigo of Byron, it is private."

Allegra's mood slid lower. She had been counting on seeing the Mocenigo—to wander through its rooms and recall the first Allegra.

"We will make your visit happy," Signora Bugelli was saying. Giorgi had been yawning politely. His mother shifted bundles and the basket to make room for him to lean back comfortably. They were soon napping, lulled by the rhythm of the train.

But Allegra was wakeful. She turned back to her vigil at the window, falling again into that strange state between past and present, which had been her intermittent mood since she had opened the secret box.

Several hours passed, and the conductor came down the aisle to collect tickets. The scenery was changing—less farmland—distant factory smokestacks sent plumes of vapor into the air. In the distance the late sun shone with sparkles on placid lagoon waters. The highway and the train route came together again. Beyond the horizon Venice began to rise up into view. The sunset light in the west intensified the ocher colors of buildings. The air shimmered with golden reflections. They were running swiftly across a long bridge over water, while auto traffic buzzed along the roadway beside the tracks.

The Bugellis began to gather up their belongings.

"Soon we are home," the *signora* smiled at her. "Welcome to Venice, and may your stay be happy."

CHAPTER THREE

THEY WERE SLIDING INTO a big station with long, open-roofed areas. Their belongings were piled high on a porter's cart, and they followed his swift pace toward the nearby canalside. The sunset color was deepening. It shone on the domes of a small church across the canal and sent flashes of pink and yellow darting from the wakes of motorboats, the *motoscafi*—and from splashing gondola oars. *Nonna* had spoken regretfully of stories she had heard about the *motoscafi* taking over her beloved Venice, and Allegra had to agree.

"*Ciao*, Giovanni!" the mother called to a wiry little man in a gondola.

"*Ciao*, Eleana," he hailed back. He skillfully disentangled his smooth sleek craft from a shoving, shouting press of gondolas and *gondolieri*, and finally pulled in close to the water stairs. The porter started to toss the luggage across to him. He caught each piece adroitly, while Allegra held her breath, fearing for the suitcase with the precious box. The luggage secured in the gondola, Allegra grasped the hand of the smiling Giovanni and swung herself into the narrow black boat. The Bugellis clambered aboard, and with a quick stroke of his long oar Giovanni shot them out into the canal.

"Go by the Grand Canal, Giovanni." Signora Bugelli smiled at Allegra. "Our American friend wants to see the places of literary interest. Giovanni Fancelli, our cousin: Signorina Brent." When she introduced the gondolier, he managed a bow from his little podium at the stern.

They moved out into the stream of traffic. Motorboats whisked noisily past them. The larger double-decked *vaporetti,* loaded with people like city buses, chugged along sedately.

The light grew more glowing in the twilight afternoon sky, as if the air took fire all around them and they moved within the sunset itself. Signora Bugelli saw the enchantment in Allegra's face. "The light of Venice," she said gently. "Turner's light. He painted truth."

Allegra could only nod. She was lost again in the dream. Byron too had glided along on this same waterway. He had felt the smooth stroke of the great oar. What must he have thought while he rode home to the Palazzo Mocenigo? Loneliness—a deep longing loneliness. She felt the echoes of it even now. It thrilled along the channels of her blood as though she linked memories with him.

Allegra was waked from her reverie by the gentle touch of Eleana Bugelli's hand.

"Look, Signorina Allegra," she said softly. "There! See where the mooring poles are painted in blue-and-white stripes. The palazzo with the small landing area in front of it. That is the Mocenigo."

Allegra's eyes widened to see the burnt sienna face of the old palace. Windows, like eyes asleep, with curtains drawn and shutters partly closed, overlooked the canal. The face looked solid with the dignity of its age.

They glided past, and Allegra turned her head to look again. She drew in her breath quickly; she was sure she had seen a face at one of the windows. She shivered in the warm air—her imagination was playing with her, and she made an effort to talk to Eleana Bugelli.

Dutifully, she looked when Robert Browning's home was pointed out. Other literary names were spun from the ends of fingers pointing from one old palace to another. It was not the same but she made appropriate exclamations of interest.

"Now, *amica mia*," Signora Bugelli pointed this time to a dark wooden bridge near a curve in the canal. "Look to your left just before you come to the bridge. See the building with the windows set in pointed arches all along the second story?"

Allegra nodded. She was swallowing a lump in her throat. She recognized that ocher-colored facade. It was the building in the painting on the cover of the diary.

"It is the Ca' d'Argenti. Home of the di Rienzi family," Eleana said solemnly. They slid past the di Rienzi landing stairs in silence.

Suddenly, Giovanni thrust his gondola into the narrow mouth of a side canal. The canal twisted and turned, and at each blind corner he sang out, "Hoy! Hoy!" his voice echoing from the damp old walls. A little shrine was built into a corner wall, its saint's figure decrepit with age. Strings of family laundry hung high above from window to window. They turned from the narrow dark passageway where the sunset could not follow and came out onto a dusk-bright canal again. Giovanni poled the gondola expertly through an open wrought-iron gate, whose scrollwork bottom was eaten away by centuries of water. The boat bumped gently against a dock under the building. Giorgio scrambled out onto the worn, stone landing, and Allegra and his mother followed. Giovanni began to lift the luggage onto the dock.

A man of about forty—dark, stocky and pleasant faced—ran down the stairs at the end of the dock and gathered Giorgio into his arms as the boy shrieked, "Papa! Look! We have an American lady to stay with us!"

Eleana Bugelli shushed Giorgio and exchanged a loving smile of greeting with the man. "My husband, Fiorenzo Bugelli; Signorina Brent," she said.

Fiorenzo came forward to take Allegra's hand with a courtly gesture natural to Italy. "Welcome to our home." His voice was deep and friendly. "Was your journey a good one? We are happy that you are to stay with us."

He picked up her bags and led the way up marble stairs worn by many generations of feet. At its top a door led into a comfortable living room. Eleana continued to open doors ahead of them. They went down a short hall, through the kitchen and down another hall. She stopped before one of the doors, throwing it wide.

Allegra looked into a pleasant room. As the light glowed up from a small lamp she saw heavy carved furniture, lovingly polished. A great, dignified wardrobe dominated the small room. The bed looked comfortable.

Fiorenzo set down the bags and opened the shutters of the window. Sounds of Venice and the sigh of water came softly into the room. Allegra gazed down at the canal a story below. In the growing dusk, people were walking across a humped bridge a short distance away. She drew back from the window, smiling.

"You like it?" Eleana asked.

"I love it! You are so kind—how can I thank you . . . ?"

Fiorenzo gave a deep warm laugh. "Be happy, little one, be happy. Let Eleana's good pasta put the roses in your cheeks."

Behind his shoulder Eleana's sweet face beamed approval. "*Mamma mia*—the time passes too swiftly—and there are hungry mouths waiting. I will see to dinner. Rest, my little friend, and then come to the kitchen. You can find your way? Fiorenzo will telephone your hotel." Allegra nodded, and they left her. She heard their voices laughing together as they went down the hall.

A quick knock came on her door. Giorgio stood before her. "I am to say, *signorina*, that the bathroom is the second door on the left."

"*Grazie,* thank you," Allegra smiled, and he scampered away. She explored the bathroom and came back to her room, unpacked a few things, hanging them in the cavernous wardrobe. The window drew her to it.

On the warm air drifted scents of dampness, of age, of human activity and vitality. If history had an odor, she thought, then this is it. She sat on the windowsill and breathed in the tantalizing aromas. Looking up past the square shapes of rooflines and chimneys, she saw the sky still tinged with dark blue in which stars were beginning to shimmer. It was like floating in space, sky and water holding the city in an enchanted and timeless beauty.

Another knock found Giorgio again at her door to announce dinner. The family was gathered around a large table in a room opening out from the warm kitchen. Dishes of pasta swimming with tempting sauces, slices of melon, a steaming bowl of fresh spinach, bread, crisp and crusty, were being served by Eleana.

Allegra sat down next to Giorgio, who gave her a shy welcoming grin. The comfortable family scene enveloped her, and she ate ravenously. After dinner she helped to clear the table and went back to her room. She had not felt such a contentment for a very long time. She prepared for bed and then went again to the window. She had a desire to dream back into the past. Beyond the bridge was not the Venice of today, but of that yesterday when Byron would be writing in the light of candles, his dark-curled head bent over pages filled with swift angular script.

She shook herself from the dangerous dreaming. What potency was in his personality, she wondered, that was able to reach back through long years in such strength? She made sure the precious box was safe, locked in her suitcase in the wardrobe. Then she slept.

When she awoke the next morning the sun was probing warmly into her room. Shouts, snatches of song and an occasional sharp buzz of a motorboat came through the window. Out there, in the shimmering bright air, the past was stirring. It was not dead, only sleeping, and from it was growing what was to be. She was not afraid but exhilarated. Yet a strangeness lay close to the surface of what seemed to be reality. She dressed swiftly, hoping she was not late. Her watch, unwound, had stopped at a little past midnight.

She found Eleana in the kitchen and sat down at the big table alone for a breakfast of crisp rolls, honey and coffee. Eleana held conversation with her through the wide doorway. There was part of a fresco on the ceiling of the dining area, which disappeared under the room wall. Eleana followed her eyes. "This is one of the old houses of Venice," she said. "It has been divided into several homes. In long ago, it was owned by a wealthy merchant. We live in the present, but the past nourishes us."

Even the wholesome Eleana spoke with the undertone of the dream within the dream, the enchantment. Who had lived in this place, now divided so strangely? What shadows walked through walls of flimsy modern plaster?

Eleana was still talking. "Fiorenzo has gone to work. Soon I must go to market. If you wish to begin to see our city you can come with me to the market, and then Giorgio will show you to Piazza San Marco. If you observe well, you should be able to return here easily for the noon meal."

Allegra glanced at the kitchen wall clock and set her watch. Nine A.M. She hurried to her room, opened her suitcase and removed the box. On impulse, she put on the locket. It seemed appropriate to wear it on this first day. Placing the box carefully in her large handbag, she went to the kitchen again. Eleana was waiting with the small, self-important Giorgio.

"I am a good guide, *signorina*," he announced. "I can tell you many things. Often I have listened to the guides in Piazza San Marco."

"I'm sure you will show me many interesting things, Giorgio." Allegra smiled at his intense brown eyes. Already the small boy had the consciousness of the male position of authority.

"Just take care you do not deafen the *signorina* with your talk, Giorgio." His mother looked both proud and amused. "He will leave you in the piazza to explore. You will not want him at your heels all the time."

Giorgio looked crestfallen. "I will enjoy every step with you," Allegra laughed.

They all set out along narrow walkways between the old buildings. Allegra tried to memorize a few landmarks—a wall shrine, an inset white stone name-marker. Soon she was hopelessly confused and sure that she could never find her way back to the Casa Bugelli. Giorgio ran ahead, threading his way among the increasingly heavy foot traffic. Kittens skittered into holes under the edges of the old buildings. Eleana set a brisk pace.

They came out upon a paved area on the edge of the Grand Canal. To the right, humping its length to the other side, was the Rialto Bridge. There was no time to stare. Eleana hurried on past the shops on the bridge and down the other side. A small *campo* opened out, filled with covered stands and loud with the hum of voices. It was the market area. Vegetables and fruit shone bright against the background of fresh green leaves. Farther on an unmistakable odor proclaimed the fish market at canalside. Allegra looked in fascination at eels and squid still astir from the sea and stared at the jewellike eyes of bigger and more majestic specimens of the family of fin and scale.

Eleana got down to business; bargaining was brisk. Allegra found it hard to follow the swift Venetian patois. Giorgio danced around collecting fish heads for his container of twisted newspaper.

"For Neroni," he laughed. "My cat. He grows old and finds it hard to come to the market himself anymore." Eleana tucked the odorous parcel into one of her capacious string bags.

"You need not stay here, my friend." Eleana obviously wanted no tagalong tourist. "Giorgio, take the *signorina* to San Marco." She waved them on their way with a smile.

Allegra felt a little lost; the tide of human bodies intent on their own business flowed past her. Voices bellowed; *gondolieri* sang out in wheedling voices from under bridges, "Gondola, gondola, lady. Much easier than to walk." They gave her bold glances from bright shrewd eyes.

"Pshaw!" Giorgio spat expressively. "Come, pay no attention to them."

He led her back across the Rialto Bridge and along another wider walkway. Shops opened out on each side, and tiny squares were full of idling English and American summer shoppers. To the disgust of Giorgio, Allegra lingered, drawn to one enticing window display after another. Glass of every imaginable shape and color glittered in the sunlight. Goblets as fragile as a dream and as deeply red as rubies, wine carafes aglow with specks of gold embedded deep into their glass. Fantastic bowls and animals whose shapes were the stuff of fairy tales were frozen into crystal. Strings of beads hung shining in such profusion that their colors melted together into streams of kaleidoscopic color.

"Come on, *signorina*," Giorgio complained. "Any day you can shop with the tourists. Now I will show you San Marco."

They came suddenly to the piazza. Standing under an archway, Allegra caught her breath with a gasp of pleasure. Then her nerves jumped as a sonorous vibration beat down from above her head. Giorgio laughed. "It is only the clock striking the hour," he shouted over the encompassing resonance.

She stepped out into the great square. The soft sound of

pigeons greeted her. Plump little iridescent bodies walked sedately everywhere. She stood quite still in the midst of the cooing birds and let her eyes rise with the great sweep of the campanile. It rushed skyward from the wide pavement in a surge of ocher and white and gold. Her eyes came down from the soaring pinnacle, and she turned to look at the pearl-toned domes of St. Mark's cathedral, whose intricate Byzantine bubbles, frosted with friezes of saints, glowed with mosaics. The four famous bronze horses pranced eternally foward over the cathedral porch.

Giorgio took over his business as guide. "It was built for the Apostle San Marco, whose body was brought here from Egypt by sailors of the Republic of Venice. To get him here, they had to hide his body in a barrel of pickled pork. But the saint didn't mind. He wanted to come to Venice because he knew our people would build him a beautiful home, and he would be the patron saint of the city forever."

Allegra caught amused glances from people nearby who were listening. "The campanile fell down sometime before I was born, but they picked it all up and built it again. Just like before."

The pickled pork and the crashing campanile effectively brought her back to reality. She looked around the huge piazza. Spreading out from the arched arcades, which surrounded three sides, were areas of tables and chairs. Waiters were moving about in preparation for the luncheon hours.

"Where is Café Florian?" she asked Giorgio.

"Across the piazza, there—where the orchestra is," he pointed. "But, *signorina,* do you not wish to see San Marco?" He looked unhappy.

She pulled her mind back from the past, which drew her so insistently. Florian's, the restaurant that had been there in Byron's day. Where he had dined with his friend, Tom Moore, late into the Venetian night. How much had it changed? She yielded to the tugging insistent boyish hand and turned again to the cathedral.

With part of her mind she heard Giorgio's rough little voice telling her about the travels of the magnificent bronze horses. She turned around and looked up at them, so full of life. The church itself seemed to be weary with its weight of years. Giorgio urged her toward the central entrance door, over a high stone threshold and into the vast space of the cathedral. Like a marble sea, the ancient inlaid floor rippled away toward the distant altar. Centuries of devoted feet and years of floodwaters had sunk the floor into waves of levels.

"The blessed San Marco sleeps here. While he is with us, Venice will live," Giorgio whispered.

She wondered what the other Allegra had felt in this place. Perhaps the woman had come, bearing within her body the child of love and fear, to pray for the last time in the church where she had worshiped in her childhood. Allegra could almost see her, kneeling quietly near the altar, her head covered with a shawl of lace, her fingers nervously grasping the beads of her rosary. Even then, her head would have moved, her eyes searching whenever a group of people entered the nave, hoping to see the proud dark head—the figure, graceful despite its halting limp. But not for him this house of devotion; his devotion was set on other things.

Allegra shook herself mentally. She rested her hand on Giorgio's sturdy shoulder. "Come, my excellent guide. Shall I treat you to a *gelato* at Florian's? Would you like that?"

"I'd love it!" His eyes sparkled.

They left the timeless world of San Marco. A pair of policemen with swinging Napoleonic capes patrolled under the arcades. The orchestras of the restaurants were tuning up for their luncheon musicales, just as the iron Saracen figures on the clock tower began to strike their rhythmic notes. Answering voices came from the resounding deep bells of churches near and far. It was eleven o'clock. Music was starting in the bandstand at Florian's. They sat at one of the little tables and ordered.

"*Nocciola*—that is the best of all flavors, *signorina*," he said, rolling his eyes and waving expressive hands in an attempt to describe it. Large stemmed glasses filled with hazelnut ice cream topped with whipped cream were set before them. Giorgio became absorbed in the delight of his *gelato*.

Allegra turned to look back under the arcade into the interior of Florian's, catching glimpses of crimson brocaded walls and private partitioned tables. Surely they had not changed since 1819, she thought.

Giorgio finished his last delicious drop, scraping intently to get it all. *"Squisito,"* he said through a mouthful and smiled like an angel.

"Now, my friend, your mother is probably wondering where you are, and I have to call on someone this afternoon. Will you tell her that I have found you a most excellent guide and that I am not sure at what hour I will return?"

"But, *signorina*, how will you find the way home?" He looked worried.

"Oh, I'll find it. I watched the way we came," she said with more confidence than she felt.

"You remember our cousin Giovanni?" Giorgio asked. Allegra nodded. "His gondola is often at the water steps of the Piazzetta over there. If you are lost, he will bring you to us."

"I'll remember."

Reluctantly, the small boy left her, turning to wave to her with the beckoning gesture of Italy. She waved back until he finally melted into the crowd under the arcades.

She stood gazing around the piazza as if seeing it all for the first time. She went again into the cathedral and lighted a long white taper for *nonna,* and then, leaving the candle flame burning steadily, she knelt in a small side chapel.

"Let me do the right thing as I carry this story back to the place of its beginnings," she prayed silently. "Dear God, let me understand the force that urges me to visit this family. Let me speak the right words." Her mind ceased to flow in words and focused its energy on hope—hope for what, she was not truly sure.

She left the cathedral. The box made a heavy presence in her handbag, bumping against her with every step like an insistent push. *It has to be done,* she thought, and turned resolutely to the quay.

A breezy voice spoke at her elbow.

"Ciao, Signorina Brent. Do you want a ride back to my cousin's place?" Giovanni, the gondolier of last evening, stood grinning at her. In bright daylight she saw he was not so old as she

had thought, only spare and wiry. His homely face waited for her.

"*Ciao,* Signor Fancelli. No, I'm not going home yet. I have to make a call at the Ca' d'Argenti. Could you take me there?"

Giovanni Fancelli widened his eyes and pursed his lips in comical surprise. "Of course, *signorina.* But the Ca' d'Argenti does not easily receive visitors."

"Well, I will take a chance. I have business to do there. I'd appreciate having you take me. How much will it cost?"

Giovanni made an expressive gesture with his hand. "I will take you with pleasure, *signorina.* But for such a lovely lady and a friend of my cousins, there can be no charge." He waved away Allegra's protest. "It is a short distance only."

He jumped like an agile monkey into his beautiful black craft and, holding it steady with one arm around a painted mooring pole, he held out his free hand to her. She settled into its red velvet seat in relief.

Giovanni chuckled. "The wind sends the water a little rough today." He swung the gondola out into the open water, curving its course with long strokes as they skimmed toward the entrance to the Grand Canal. A *motoscafo* churned past them, leaving them rocking in its wake.

Giovanni bit off a curse. "They ruin Venice. Do you know, *signorina,* we were once ten thousand *gondolieri.* Now we are only five hundred. We must band together and put all fares into the association, so that we all may live and so that the gondola shall not die." He looked back angrily at the motorboat. "Pshaw!" he spat. "I grow to hate the smell of gasoline."

Allegra looked at the busy traffic of the canal and the headlong *vaporetti,* and sighed. The gondola took its silent smooth way toward the church of Santa Maria della Salute. The strong surging motion was like flight on the back of some great black bird, she thought. "Surely something can be done," she said to the tight face above her. "Venice wouldn't be Venice without the *gondolieri.*"

His face relaxed into a weary smile. "Speak to any you know who care for Venice," he answered.

They went in silence down the wide canal, past the hotel terraces and the closed facades of ancient buildings. She was feeling anxious again as Giovanni drew in toward the blue and white mooring poles capped in gilded finials.

"There," he smiled. "Ca' d'Argenti. Shall I wait to see if you are accepted inside, *signorina*?" He pulled up to the private water steps, leaped out and again offered his hand. Allegra clutched the precious purse close to her. *Suppose after all this time, the box fell in to the Adriatic,* she thought wildly. *Maybe just as well,* another nervous thought answered. Giovanni waited for her, an odd perceptive expression in his eyes. "Are you all right, Signorina?"

"Yes." She grasped his hand and stepped onto the wet stone landing.

"I shall wait to see you in," Giovanni stated.

"Thanks," Allegra said absently. She was concentrating on the beautiful old carved door ahead of her, at the top of a flight of circular steps. She mounted them and raised the great knocker ring, which hung from a silver lion's mouth. Suddenly she remembered her friend of childhood still on duty far away. The thought of the two lion door knockers eased her. This one, too, though far larger and more imposing, looked benevolent. She let the ring fall against its metal plate.

She was startled to have the door open almost immediately; a manservant in blue livery looked out at her. *"Signorina?"* he inquired coolly.

Allegra took a deep breath and drew herself into a dignified pose, head up. She was *nonna*'s child . . . even more, Byron's child. Her voice was strong and clear. "I wish to speak to the Contessa di Rienzi."

"She does not receive visitors without appointment." The man moved to close the door.

Something stronger than herself urged Allegra forward. "It is important business," she said firmly. "I have only a short time in Venice."

The man drew back, hesitated, and Allegra stepped over the

threshold marveling at her own temerity. The entrance hall was large; a great staircase curved up from it to a landing, carpeted in beautiful colors. The floor under her feet was of marble in a blend of subtle browns and pinks, graceful designs swirling away from her eyes.

She drew breath to speak to the servant again, when her attention was taken by the face of a woman who had entered the hall leaning on another servant's arm. She was tiny, but her presence was potent. Parchment skin was stretched taut over delicate bones, and she was obviously very old. Bright brown eyes looked from beneath delicately curved brows. The hair was white with streaks of russet mingled in it, dressed high on the small head in a psyche knot secured with a jeweled pin.

Allegra saw only the blurred details of elegant fabric and jewels at the throat of a high-necked dress. It was the old woman's face that arrested her. It was a stranger's face, yet familiar. She stood gazing into the wise, bright, aged eyes of the matriarch of the di Rienzis.

CHAPTER FOUR

"I AM AMALIA DI RIENZI," the old woman said, after a long silence, during which she took stock of the young woman before her. Allegra's Italian almost left her, in the sudden realization that she would now have to begin the long account that would bind her to the di Rienzi name. She gripped the bag more tightly and prayed for words.

"My name is Allegra Brent. I am from the United States, and I have in my possession several papers—from the last century—that belong to the di Rienzi family."

The old face lessened its austerity, yet kept its taut alertness. She motioned the servants away. "And what kind of papers could they be, Miss Brent?"

"They are of a very personal nature," she replied, suddenly feeling how very peculiar she must seem.

"Then I think we should speak together about it, since you appear to be such a serious young lady and have come such a long way with your very personal papers. Give me your arm, and we shall find a comfortable place to sit."

Allegra helped Contessa di Rienzi into a drawing room off the entrance hall. It was draped in pale blue brocade and contained at least two dozen elegantly carved chairs and small couches all upholstered in shades of blue. Allegra had never seen such a room. The old woman pointed with her silver cane to a love seat near a pair of tall French doors. Beyond was a walled garden, lined with cascading geraniums along its borders.

The sharp brown eyes fixed upon Allegra's face. "Now—what is this about the family di Rienzi?"

Allegra summoned a breath and began: "I believe I am connected to you . . . distantly," she added in a small voice. There was no response. "I was born in the United States, but in my family, many generations ago, was a woman named Allegra di Rienzi."

The watchful face grew intense. "And when was this?"

Allegra struggled to recall dates. "I think she came to America in 1820, after she had left her husband and infant son in Venice."

Another silence. The old woman leaned forward on her cane and closed her eyes. "You know something about the history of my family. How much do you know?"

"Not very much, *signora*. I was recently told by my grandmother that some roots of my family are in Italy—in Venice." She opened the bag and drew out the box. "Let me show you."

The Contessa di Rienzi opened her eyes. "What is this, child? That box—it is quite old."

"It belonged to my great-great-great-grandmother, Allegra."

"Well, open it then. I presume that is why you have brought it to us. I may inhabit an old and tired body, but there is nothing wrong with my mind." She passed her thin fingers over the embossed lid.

Allegra's self-consciousness began to fade with the excitement she felt. "I must tell you something about myself first, about the tradition in my family that has kept this box and its contents a secret for five generations." She explained the recent events of her life and what she had read in *nonna*'s letters. The *contessa* looked past her as if abstracted, and returned again.

"Your grandmother must have been a wise woman. Now, do not delay further. Show me what you bring in your beautiful old box."

"I have a diary," she said. "Allegra di Rienzi's diary. It starts in 1819 before she first met Lord Byron." She placed it in Contessa di Rienzi's hands and intently watched the old woman examine the cover. She drew forth a lorgnette from a long gold chain around her neck and studied the painted miniature of the Ca' d'Argenti.

"It appears to be of the period. The clasp is quite old, as is the binding. Miss Brent, I will tell you this in all candor, there is indeed a portion of our family's past that is still veiled in mystery. And there was an Allegra—my father's mother—who disappeared and was never found. But, before I open this book and read, I tell you that I have, over the long years of my life, inter-viewed scholars and rascals who have contrived tales for my ears.'' She tapped the diary with the lorgnette. ''I am not naive, nor am I too ancient to detect insincerity. There is something in your manner that is clear and honest. I do not wish to be disap-pointed. Almost, I wish you had not put this book into my hands.

''My father was badly scarred by the abandonment by his mother. He did not marry until he was past middle age, I think because of his distrust of love. He grew up with an awful secret, and cruel playmates taunted him.

''As I came to womanhood, I was aware of father's deep hurt. In his youth, visitors from other parts of Italy would bring him in-formation about the whereabouts of his mother. She had been seen, some said, wandering in a state of amnesia; others swore she was dancing on stage in Milano under an assumed name. When I was old enough to be responsible I intercepted these stories and did not allow them to reopen the wounds.'' She sighed. Allegra began to feel she should not have intruded with her own story of love and pain and deception. ''So you see, child, I could wish you had not found us, and yet I do not for my heart tells me that this time it may be different.''

Trembling fingers worked the lock and opened the diary. Allegra followed in her own mind's eye the words of the inscrip-tion upon the first page: ''This diary belongs to Allegra di Rienzi, and no eyes but hers may read further.''

The *contessa* finished reading the faded caveat. ''It is difficult for me to see clearly. Please . . . .'' She gave the little book over to Allegra's hands. Her eyes were covered in a mist of tears.

Allegra turned to the page about Contessa Benzoni's *conversa-zione.*

March 20
This is my diary, my own companion, who will not judge me, nor whisper to others who would. For I must tell what is flooding into my soul this night . . . I have met him! The sun has found me in my small, dark cave. Him! Byron! Let me

say his name again—Byron! O merciful heaven, he has come to take me from my misery. I will never be alone again. Byron has found me!

I shall record every word and look and touch, for I fear I shall forget a small whisper of his lips and shall be the less for forgetting.

The reading stopped abruptly when the elderly man in livery who had first opened the great doors to Allegra entered the drawing room.

"Miss Brent will be my guest at tea. Please do not disturb us until then," the *contessa* said. He bowed slightly and withdrew.

"And now, little one, it is enough emotion for the moment. You do not need to read farther, but tell me in your own words the story of this unfortunate young woman. And first fetch me a pillow for my back. The servants never think to keep pillows convenient to me."

Allegra obeyed.

The story in the diary came forth slowly and carefully. When it was done, Allegra waited. The *contessa* looked down at her delicate hands. "I wish my father could have known," she said simply. "How cruel it was to leave a small boy without even a goodbye or a token of her love. It is difficult to understand, and yet I have compassion for her. Perhaps only another woman can know the depths of despair and loneliness that are possible in a loveless union. Have you ever loved, my child?"

Allegra flushed, thinking of the poor little affection she had given to Larry. "Not really," she said.

Amalia di Rienzi sat a bit straighter and smiled. "I have. Many years ago—in another century. I was just seventeen when I fell irreversibly in love with my cousin Leopoldo. It was springtime, and we were vacationing in our country house near La Mira. He was older and studying the law. It was a love match that lasted fifty years. And I still remember all of it. Do not take less than love. I am sure your grandmother would say this to you."

The di Rienzi spell was weaving around her. In this fine old woman Allegra could see the living link between the distant past and the present. She brought reality to the sad romantic lives from the diary. The tale could not be told lightly anymore. It had substance and meaning to people alive today. The Ca' d'Argenti still carried the vibrations of Allegra di Rienzi and her little neglected child of duty. Allegra Brent could almost see them now, from the eyes and memory of the aged *contessa*.

"You have more in that surprising box of yours, I see. Show me—and then we shall go upstairs."

The remnants of Allegra's love for Byron were unwrapped one at a time and given over to the gentle old hands. Allegra unfastened the necklace. The *contessa's* fingers opened it carefully, and she drew in her breath and touched the auburn curl of hair. "How very sad," she said softly, as she closed the locket and gave it back to Allegra.

After a time of silence she said, "Put it all away again. My poor grandmother deserves her privacy. And so . . . ." she looked up with a cryptic expression, which softened into a smile, "and so, another di Rienzi woman takes the secret to her heart. But there is one other person who must know—my grandson, Renaldo. He will be more critical in his judgment of your recital, yet I think there is enough of the warm spirit in his blood for him to come to accept. Tell me, do you like children?" The question was pointed.

"Some children," Allegra equivocated. "I have worked with older children, directing them in art projects at my city's museum."

"Good. I want you to meet a very special child, Renaldo's daughter, Bianca. I think you will like her. Give me your arm now. These pillows are too soft, and I cannot stand without help."

They walked slowly together back into the grand foyer. Allegra noticed the sculptured cherub that stood near the curved stairway with his finger to one very fat pink marble cheek. He supported a beeswax candle with his other childish hand. Blue-and-cream Aubusson rugs ascended the steps to the landing. An enormous Venetian glass chandelier hung down into the center of the curve, glistening with reflected light.

A modern chair elevator waited at the bottom step. It was

upholstered in velveteen, deeply cushioned. The old servant who had come in earlier shuffled toward them, a look of concern on his face. Apparently, it was his privilege to escort Contessa di Rienzi into the elegant little lift.

Allegra walked beside her up the steps. The ocher glow of afternoon spread antique tones over the walls. When they reached the top, the *contessa* spoke. "I take a brief rest before tea. Perhaps you would refresh yourself also. Maria will see to your comfort." The *contessa* squeezed Allegra's hand and said gently, "Do not be apprehensive. I am a believer in fate. How else can one endure? We accept the secrets of life and wait for the hour that brings them forth for understanding."

A dark young woman smiled at Allegra and indicated a doorway. Inside was a high-ceilinged bedroom. A canopy bed draped in sheer yellow fabric was freshly turned back, and a cat whose fur was almost as yellow lay in the utmost repose in the middle. Maria shooed it off and pulled open the daffodil curtains at the windows. "I will knock at half-past three." She withdrew with the cat at her heels.

Allegra went to the windows and looked down. In the Grand Canal the shouts of the *gondolieri* fought against the motors of the *vaporetti*, and shadows deepened on the side canals. Directly under her was the garden she had seen from the downstairs sitting room. An ancient wall separated it from the busy activities of the canal, and two weathered griffins guarded the quiet retreat from atop small pillars in the wall.

She watched the changing light move on the old stones and thought of Allegra di Rienzi. Then she smiled at herself. How far she had come, even in this one day. Eleana Bugelli would be thunderstruck to look up and see her plain little traveling companion gazing down from a window of the intimidating Ca' d'Argenti.

She kicked off her shoes and for a while relaxed in a comfortable chair with her eyes closed, enjoying the soothing sounds from the canal.

A male voice raised itself in muffled tones from the hallway outside the room, and footsteps passed her door and faded away. Another door opened and closed. The maid rapped gently and announced it was half-past three. Allegra walked to the mirror on the door of the heavy oak armoire and looked at herself. The dampness and heat had overcurled her hair, removing all appearance of careful grooming, and she was skeptical in general about her appearance.

Behind her in the mirrored image the waters glistened and threw darts of color onto her pale cotton dress, making a harlequin of her. She had to smile. She would not be allowed to be colorless here.

The man's voice sounded again in the hall, and she ran a comb quickly through her hair. A ripple of apprehension broke through her musings. It was almost four o'clock, and no one had come for her. She sat on the edge of the bed holding the bag on her lap, wondering what to do, and finally steeled herself to walk out into the empty hall.

In both directions were closed doors and not a soul in view, except for the dark, heavily framed portraits that lined the walls. Generations of di Rienzi eyes watched her from dour faces. One of them might be Barretto, the husband of Allegra. A rapid appraisal showed her that there was a di Rienzi face—high forehead, deep-set eyes, strong high nose, and a certain look about the mouth, a slight smirk, especially in the men. It was pride.

She contemplated returning to her room when the double doors at the end of the wing swung open. A tall man stood there. His face was partly in shadow but behind him was a bright magnificent room in which sat the Contessa di Rienzi. For an instant it was like a tableau, and Allegra stood fixed to the spot.

"Miss Brent?" the man asked with crisp authority.

Apprehension was now in full cry inside her. She had been naive to dream of belonging here. A flush rose over her face, and the bag grew heavy and conspicuous. Her cozy room with the Bugellis beckoned to her urgently.

The cool man at the doorway stepped forward to offer his arm. "Grandmother is expecting you," he said, as if from a great distance. She stole a quick look at his face. There was no doubting the ancestry. The slim dark gray business suit only slightly diminished the intensity of his presence. He was startlingly handsome. Allegra was shaken by the power coming from his deeply shadowed eyes.

Two servants were adjusting the satin pillows of the *contessa*'s ornate antique chair, which could more accurately be called a throne. She wore a long, pale blue lace dress with sleeves that ended in airy points at her fingertips, and a fine alexandrite ring glowed gray lavender on her tiny hand. She was waving away the servants when Allegra appeared in the room.

"Come here, my dear—next to me." A smaller but equally exquisite chair was indicated. Allegra turned back instinctively to the man whose arm she still touched. His unwavering dark eyes held hers for a moment longer, stabbing at her composure. Something in his look drew forth a memory, a feeling she had once known and had hidden deep within herself.

She sat down and put the bag on the floor beside her. A gold inlaid tea table was brought before the hostess for approval. The aromas of fresh tea cakes and steeping flowery herbs blended deliciously, and the *contessa* raised her eyebrows in a silent accounting.

"It will do," she said at last. "Miss Brent, I see you have already met my grandson, Renaldo. He is rarely pleasant, but you must forgive his clouded countenance."

"It is business, Vecchia," he said calmly, as if he had grown used to privileged gibes of the family autocrat. Allegra assumed that his use of *vecchia*—"old one"—was a family pet name for the formidable *contessa*. "I have much on my mind," Renaldo went on, "and I know it bores you to hear of it." He kissed her hand lightly and sat down across from her chair.

While the *contessa* poured tea from the silver pot, which bore the family crest on its rounded sides, Allegra was looking down at her own tightly clenched hands, trying to feel at ease. It was not a simple thing to do. She had no way of knowing how much Renaldo already knew about her, nor whether the grandmother was actually only an intriguing but senile relic from the last century. Allegra pushed the bulky bag farther back under her chair with one foot and decided to wait and see.

After an interminable time of pouring, stirring and sipping, the *contessa* spoke. "Well, Aldo, what did I tell you?" she grinned. "She is not the adventuress at all."

Allegra lowered her eyes against Renaldo's hard gaze.

"*Nonna mia*," he answered seriously, "I have no wish to make Miss Brent uncomfortable, but I feel you have been too eager to accept as truth whatever story finds its way to our doorstep."

Allegra looked up, her nerves drawn tight into a kind of defensive dignity. "Signor di Rienzi, for my part, I do not wish to cause dissension. Your grandmother was most kind to me this afternoon when I came here. I want nothing from anyone. But I thought it was important that I bring my story to your family, where I feel it properly belongs."

Renaldo drew a long tan cigarette from a silver case and held it unlighted. "Why did you not write to us of your amazing discovery? It seems a long way to come with no preparation and no apparent connections in Venice."

The old woman put her hand on the arm of Allegra's chair. "She is young and alone. Why should she not come to Venice? We are not all as methodical as you." She winked at Allegra. "Venice would never have flowered if the ancient ones had been so guarded."

Allegra responded to the warmth and began to feel more herself. "I did not write, *signore*, simply because I have always dreamed of coming to Venice, and if I had failed to find the correct di Rienzi family, I would have found enough to do on my own." She picked up her teacup and smiled at him. "And I really don't need connections to find my way to San Marco."

"Good . . . good," the old voice chuckled. "Now, tell us again about your little treasures. Aldo, don't smoke. It bothers my eyes."

Allegra drew forth the bag and retold the tale. Renaldo listened without comment until she finished. "How do we know they are not forgeries?" His voice was mocking.

"They aren't. This has been in my family for five generations."

"Have you documentation that what we see here is authentic?"

"How could I? I am the first one in my family to let them be revealed. I have no doubt of their authenticity." *Don't you feel the truth of them,* she thought. *Are you completely unmoved by the words?*

"You think like a lawyer," the *contessa* said sharply. "Where is your heart?"

"But, Vecchia, you are too accepting. I have heard of frauds—excellent ones—in the literary world. And this Miss Brent does not even pretend to have references."

Allegra flushed in the silence that followed. The words wounded her. "I shouldn't have come," she said as she hastily put the diary and papers back into the little box and reclosed the bag. She was prepared for skepticism, but her pride would not stand for an attack on her scruples. She rose to leave.

"Aldo!" the old woman hissed. "Apologize immediately. Miss Brent, stay, please."

Renaldo softened slightly. "I am sorry. I was too harsh."

Allegra hesitated. "I do not want anything from you. Perhaps I am not clever, but I have no need for cleverness, since there is nothing to conceal." She stood level with his eyes. A faint look of concession started around the strong curve of his lips.

"Grandmother is not careful enough with strangers, Miss Brent. She does not take precautions, and it is left to me to protect her." It was a sort of apology, which Allegra recognized and accepted.

Contessa di Rienzi was ignoring her grandson's words and scrutinizing Allegra. "So, you will stay. Good! Let us go to my rooms, child. My ears are still curious and young. Aldo, we shall take our supper alone tonight." She took hold of Allegra's arm, easing herself up from the chair and turning from him.

"Vecchia . . ." Renaldo said.

"Do not have that tone with me," she said quickly. "I am still head of the house of di Rienzi and my judgment shall suffice."

Allegra did not look back. She was being swept along by a strong tide of will, which flowed from the old woman by her side.

But nothing had been resolved, and she still felt uneasy. She wasn't even sure she wished to stay for dinner. A momentary thought of Eleana and Giorgio brought her up short.

"I don't know if I should stay on, *contessa*. I am already expected for supper."

"That is not serious, I'm sure."

"But, Signora Bugelli will be disappointed if I do not return. I really must . . . ."

"Don't you want to stay here, child?" she said, suddenly downcast.

"I would like to, but they will be waiting for me, I know."

"Then telephone them," the *contessa* said. "The telephone is behind that door."

Allegra was angry with herself for giving in—but there was a prickling warning within her that a retreat from the di Rienzi citadel right now would be the end. There would be no other chance.

CHAPTER FIVE

ELEANA ANSWERED THE PHONE. Noises of family and cat and radio music crowded in upon the brief conversation. They were disappointed but thrilled that their Allegra would be dining within the walls of the great Ca'. She promised to tell them every detail tonight when she returned.

The *contessa* was waiting close to the door of the telephone closet. "Good." In her face was a hint of self-satisfaction. "Now, let us go to my apartment. There is someone to tell me of her day's activities. I think you will be pleased to meet her. She will not challenge your right to be here."

As they walked slowly down the length of the second-floor *galleria*, the old woman made low sounds to herself, moving her lips in barely audible phrases, which did not invite participation. At another pair of carved heavy doors, she stopped. "Her name is Bianca."

The doors opened inward upon an airy candlelit room. The gentle old manservant came forward to meet the old lady with a wheeled chair, which could never be called simply a wheelchair. It was high backed and cushioned in blue silk. The carved arms ended in lions' paws with the crevices between the claws worn where her fingers had nestled for years. At the top was a gilded crest. The wheels were at least a foot in diameter and appeared to have once been part of a proper English pram.

The servant carefully arranged the *contessa* in the soft chair. A little needlepoint-covered platform snapped into place beneath her feet.

"That is much better," she sighed.

The old man's face was patient and loving. He laid a soft blue coverlet over her lap and wheeled her nearer to the French doors that overlooked the canal.

Allegra's eyes absorbed the scene. The bisque-toned walls were paneled and hung with long slender mirrors. Light, silently alive from the candles in their golden glass sconces, multiplied from the mirrors. Glass-doored cabinets sat in the corners, with their antique crystal and gold contents glowing in the candlelight. The warmth of the declining sun bathed the room in a drowsy calm. Arrangements of roses, as if from a nineteenth-century oil painting, were set in marble bowls on several dainty round gilded tables. To one side of the room in a curved alcove was a beautiful bed, deeply carved and florentined in antique gold. On the opposite wall was a full-length portrait of a handsome man in the uniform of an officer.

A long white curved sofa faced out upon the water, with its back to the room. The *contessa* beckoned Allegra to it. There, asleep and oblivious on the velvet cushions was a dark-haired little girl in flowered pinafore and long white stockings. One olive-toned rounded arm hung over the side. The old woman smiled with adoring eyes.

"Bianca," she whispered. It was a shame to intrude on such delicious slumber. "My baby, wake up. We have a special visitor."

The child's dark brown eyes opened without seeing and then grew brighter.

"This is my friend, Miss Brent. She has come all the way from America to meet you."

The soft plump face looked serious. She hopped from the sofa and curtsied quickly, coming to rest by the arm of her great-grandmother's chair. "She is going to be a friend, Bianca. Come, give me my kiss."

The child leaned over to deliver the kiss, without taking her eyes from Allegra. Beneath the dark curls an unsophisticated brain was busy. "Do you know my father?" she asked in a low little voice.

"I have met him." Allegra smiled at the earnestness.

"Do you know Contessa Falieri?" She caught her grandmother's eye.

"This is only my first day in Venice. I haven't met very many people yet. Mostly cathedrals, great bronze horses and friendly cats.''

Bianca emerged a bit from behind the wheeled chair. "Have you seen my cat, Augustina? She is yellow, and she sleeps on my bed with me."

"Augustina introduced herself to me this afternoon, but she forgot to tell me she belonged to you."

"*Nonna*, she looks like the lady in the picture, the one in the old hallway." Bianca was suddenly excited, but her grandmother cast a sharp look back at her and quickly spoke to Allegra.

"You have the classic Italian facial structure."

Bianca looked puzzled by the tense explanation, and she retreated behind the great chair again to watch Allegra.

"Good," the *contessa* said, as if she were shutting a door. "So, my dear, you have a love of art and museums. I think Bianca will be happy to show you our Venice. But she has only seen it from the outside, because her father is often occupied with business, and I am not able to climb the steps that are the curse of most museums. I have not been able to mount the steps of the Uffizi in Florence for thirty years. But you have the strength and the time . . . how fortunate." She looked into the distance with a little sound in her throat, a kind of musing.

"Bianca, I would love to explore with you whenever you like."

The child looked as delighted as her young reserve would allow. "I can use the gondola sometimes . . . *nonna*?"

"You must arrange this with your father. He would not be pleased if he and Contessa Falieri wished to use it and little Bianca had gone to a museum," she said teasingly.

The child screwed up her face into a naughty expression. Allegra tried to imagine this other Venetian *contessa*, but the picture she conjured was a trifle intimidating, and she quickly let it fade.

"*Cara*, go to the kitchen and tell cook that we are three for supper. I cannot be certain your father has remembered. He has so much on his mind these days. And tell her to find something very special for our new friend."

When Bianca had left the room the two women sat silent for a time.

"You are perceptive, I see," the old one said. "Our household is not a simple one. The di Rienzis have weathered many storms of fortune and passion, and every generation has had its difficulties. Sometimes I feel the Fates have forced me to live so many years, so that my eyes may see more of the pains of life than others. When I was born there was a pall hovering over me and over this house—the scandal and heartbreak of my grandmother's flight and my father's depressions. I nursed him during the last years of his life, when he was not in control of his mind or his body.

"My own marriage was, thank God, long and happy. We prayed for a large family, to put life into the melancholy Ca', but it was very difficult for me to have babies. My son, Bernardo, was born to me when I was thirty-three. I lived to see him killed during the Second World War. His dear wife died that year, giving birth to their second child, Guido. Their first son, Renaldo, the man of affairs you met at tea, was still a baby, two years old.

"Who was there to shepherd their growth? Only La Vecchia—the old one. I have been old much longer than I was young. There was no time for me to become tired, like the other old women I knew. I have worked all my life with the souls that came to me in need."

Allegra listened to the clear voice next to her. An appreciation for the fortitude of this tiny dignified person was growing in her. What battles there must have been in a century of dealing with human problems! What must she have seen, even in the historical sense!

"And then," she continued, "when I felt I could find a quiet corner for my own self . . . after Aldo married . . ." she sighed deeply, "again it was not to be. Bianca was still an infant when her mother contracted a fever and died. It was a severe winter six years ago, and Anna had stayed out one night while Aldo was in Rome on business. I understand she was with a man, a lover. When she came home in the morning she was ill and refused to

say where she had been. She continued to decline for two weeks.
And then she died. Aldo was beyond consolation. Grief and rage
struggled within his breast. And while he suffered his secret
doubts and torments, there was a baby to be cared for . . . and
those tyrants of the affairs of men kept me alive to do my duty to
my family.''

Allegra was beginning to feel uncomfortable with these painful
memories. She did not deserve to be privy to them, yet they
fascinated her. The *contessa* turned her gaze to the dark canals.

''What do you sense around Renaldo, my child?''

''Pride,'' Allegra answered, deciding upon candor. ''He appears to be a cool man, rather guarded. My grandmother would
say he was not a comfortable tenant of his own skin.''

''You are right—it is so. But my greater concern now is for
Bianca, who is an innocent. Think how this man of pride and
ruined love regards his child. The face is a reproach, for it
becomes each day more like its mother's—and suspicions cloud
his natural feelings. He is not sure he is the sire. It is a terrible
emotion to give to a dear infant. So you see, I must live on to
resolve this latest knot of fortune.''

Allegra ached with sympathy. She was becoming less and less
the outsider. The forthright manner of Amalia, La Vecchia,
demanded honesty in return.

''Fate responds to necessity. And until Renaldo emerges from
his emotional cynicism, it is necessary for me to stay in my prison
of minor infirmities. Bianca needs a woman's love.''

''But doesn't she have relatives who could care for her? I would
think . . . .''

''Yes, one would suppose the child would not want for affection within the branches of an old family—but there is only an aged
aunt of great coldness, a few mindless cousins and some hangers-
on. And there is that Falieri woman, who pretends affection for
Renaldo's sake. But these women are all waiting for me to die.''
She laughed a light little cackle. ''Guido comes around from time
to time to play the fond uncle. He brings Bianca baubles. But he is

light in his head. Cannot concentrate for ten minutes, and I wouldn't trust him with a lira.

"No—the only worthwhile one is Guido's brother Renaldo. And I am like a cook who has a great bubbling stew upon her stove. If I leave, it may boil over and be ruined. If I stay to tend the fire a while longer, we may have a very tasty dish. The di Rienzi stew," she snorted. "And you probably wish you had not come into the kitchen."

Allegra began to protest, and the old woman smiled. The tension of the long narration suddenly crumbled, and they began to laugh. A small cool old hand patted the younger one. "Perhaps you bring me the salt, Miss Allegra Brent of America."

Allegra was alarmed to see La Vecchia's head quickly drop to her chest. She appeared to be asleep. Within seconds an unmistakable snore grumbled and popped from the old lips. It was fully dark now except for the candles in the room and the distant lighted windows along the side canal. Allegra was alone, reflecting upon the remarkable day. She tried to avoid thinking too much about Renaldo. He was disturbing, difficult to analyze with detachment.

She saw then her own reflection in the window, and it suddenly did not seem so very strange for her to be there.

The doors opened from the hallway, and Bianca stood with a servant next to a linen-draped cart.

"Is my *nonna* asleep?" she asked, in a voice that wished to sound mature. "I have brought our supper."

"I am not sleeping; just resting," replied the old one. "And quite ready for your supper table."

Maria, the sweet-faced servant, prepared the three plates.

"In my rooms I eat as I wish," the *contessa* said, smiling. "I am not comfortable with a heavy meal before I sleep."

As they spoke Allegra saw Bianca stealing glances at her and at her great-grandmother, obviously trying hard not to be rude, yet terribly curious to understand the new situation that was developing around her.

"I think Aunt Lidia is getting old," she said suddenly. "She probably won't be able to take me to the Lido."

La Vecchia smiled. "What are you telling us, my pigeon? You think perhaps you would like to find another escort to the seashore?"

Bianca's face flushed slightly, and she avoided Allegra's eyes. "Yes. I would like to very much."

"Well," La Vecchia sighed in mock seriousness, "I shall have to think for a time." She let Bianca dangle for an agonizing moment, then said, "Perhaps Miss Brent could find some time soon to go to the Lido with you."

The old *contessa* rang a silver bell, which dangled from the beak of a silver griffin, and Maria brought dessert. Three caramel custards shivered smoothly in their dishes, each sitting in its burnt sienna pool of sweet sauce. A vibration of warmth gradually settled upon the little company at the table, and La Vechhia seemed pleased.

"I think you should stay with us, Miss Brent. This is going to be a very busy time for our family, especially with the preparations for the birthday ball. You see, I shall be one hundred years old in less than a month, and everybody is so terribly disorganized I think I will end up planning it all myself. I intend to have a grand party," she announced as if to lay to rest any thoughts to the contrary.

Before Allegra could reply, Renaldo entered the room. The heaviness of tension accompanied him.

"Good evening, *nonna*." She leaned toward him to receive his kiss. "Bianca—Miss Brent. I trust your meal was a pleasant one."

"Yes, papa. We had a very nice time."

"Well, then, I suppose you have had enough woman talk for one day, my girl, and it is time to go to bed. Maria is waiting to help you undress."

Bianca looked pained, but she left her place at the table. *Nonna* kissed her good-night and whispered, "You must remember to write a letter to Aunt Lidia tomorrow. It will help her to recover. Good night, my child."

"Good night, papa. Will I see you in the morning?"

"Unfortunately, no. I am going to Milano for a day or two, but Contessa Falieri will look in on you. She will take you tomorrow to her niece's birthday, so you should wear something very pretty. Wear the pink dress she gave you. I haven't seen you in it, and she spent a long time shopping for it."

Bianca embraced her father and left the room without a word. At the door she turned back. "Good night, Signorina Brent," she said quickly and was gone.

"What is this about Lidia?" he asked, eliminating Allegra from his gaze.

"Bianca felt that Lidia would be indisposed for several days, and she wants to go to the Lido beach. Perhaps Miss Brent will take the child."

"Bianca is too impatient," he said crisply. "She must learn to control her desires and not impose on others. I'm sure Miss Brent has business of greater importance elsewhere."

"I am asking her to say here with us, Renaldo. Bianca needs a companion. You do not see how lonely she is and how many little games she must play with herself to fill the emptiness."

Allegra drew a breath to protest the *contessa*'s announcement, but Renaldo spoke first, his voice suddenly smooth.

"That should not be a problem, *nonna*. If I must be away, then Lidia or the servants will tend her . . . or Vera Falieri."

"Aldo, you know it is more than that; there is a need for a person of energy and youth, who has some depth of character to offer Bianca. Those you named are either too busy or disinclined to give up their pretty pleasures to understand a child."

Renaldo suddenly addressed Allegra. "Miss Brent, in what way are you peculiarly qualified to care for Bianca?"

If she had not had her earlier encounter with this Conte di Rienzi, she might have been intimidated. But since tea she had grown strong in the feeling of destiny. *Nonna* had invoked her Fates, and perhaps Allegra, too, was being directed.

"*Signore,*" she said in a steady voice, "if you wish to confirm my character, I will write the Dean of the School of Fine Arts at my university, and the director of children's art in the museum of my city. I could not take a position with your family on such a brief acquaintance. It was not my intention. Your daughter is a delightful child, and very bright."

La Vecchia jumped close upon her words. "And I need this young lady to bring order from the chaos of my birthday party."

He drew forth another of his long cigarettes with a decided flair. "So, you are efficient as well. You have presented yourself in a good light with my grandmother. I suppose it could do no harm if you stayed a short while." A slight acquiescence moved in his eyes again.

Allegra fought to control a sharp reply. She had to consider the *contessa* more than her own insulted pride. "If I could be of help for a few days, I would be happy to," she said. "You are most gracious," she couldn't help adding and hoped he felt the irony in her tone.

He avoided her flashing eyes and looked down at the bulky handbag that contained her precious legacy. "Is this all your luggage?"

"My clothes are with the Bugelli family. I have taken a room in their home."

"I assume you plan to bring your things here tonight," he said.

"I don't think so, *signore*. The Bugellis have been very generous to me. I wouldn't repay them by leaving without an explanation. Already it is late. I should return now, or they will begin to worry."

La Vecchia had frowned at her grandson's questioning. "See that Luigi prepares my gondola for Miss Brent, Aldo. We do not wish to keep her later than her conscience allows."

"As you wish, *nonna*," he said, grinding the cigarette into an inlaid stone ashtray. He stalked from the room.

With Renaldo gone, the atmosphere lightened again. The old woman smiled, but fatigue showed in her eyes. "So it is done, Allegra. A woman alone as you are needs the protection of a good house. Do not mind his moods. I think he will accept everything shortly. He is complex, but you will learn to see beneath his brittle mask. It is the remembrance of his wife, and his deep uncertainty about trusting a woman. Some devil in him rises up to challenge and fight. You have done well today, very well, for you have dignity. Of course, he will not understand this. He would almost prefer you to be calculating. In his strange way, he knows better how to deal with that. Now go, my dear, the gondola will be ready—and I must have my sleep.'' She rang the griffin bell again. ''Come tomorrow and we will talk more.'' La Vecchia extended her hand and Allegra, in a sudden rush of feeling, embraced her.

''Thank you,'' she said.

''And you,'' the *contessa* replied gently.

Maria appeared in the doorway, directing Allegra to wait in the hall at the bottom of the great stairs. The doors to La Vecchia's apartments closed silently, leaving Allegra to walk once more along the hall beneath the gaze of the di Rienzi portraits.

Removed from the warm comfort of Amalia di Rienzi's candlelit chambers, she smiled to herself, remembering Clinton Meserve's warnings about traveling alone. Then a little jab of tension disturbed her nerves—even before she looked down to see Renaldo standing in the foyer, watching her.

She walked down the stairs toward him, and he pulled open the tall entrance door for her. It swung inward soundlessly and smoothly. Smooth and silent and unbending like its owner, Allegra thought with a twinge of irritation.

A gondola came out of a side canal and drew up to the water steps of the palazzo. With perfect unimpeachable courtesy, Renaldo handed her into the boat. ''Luigi will take you to your destination.''

She made her way to the rear seat of the gondola, noting as she did the richness of the upholstery, the shining polish of the brass dolphins on the side. Renaldo's head was illumined by the bright moon, which was washing the water with silvery light. In the semidarkness his face was mapped with intense shadows. He could have been one of his ancestors standing there, austere, fascinating.

"The *signorina* will give you directions, Luigi." His moonlit eyes shone down at Allegra. He spoke in English: "You must find it very strange, little Allegra from across the sea—this life of the di Rienzis. If you enter it you will not be the same again. Think well. *Addio.*"

He turned on his heel, mounted the wide stone stairs with a quick lithe motion, while Allegra sat speechless and still. The great door in the facade of the palazzo opened, showing a breathtaking view of gleaming warmth and color for a sudden moment, then closed, and all was dark and silent—except for the lap of the water against the steps and the long black curve of the gondola.

CHAPTER SIX

"*SCUSI, SIGNORINA*—where do you wish to go?"

The voice of Luigi brought Allegra up short. He put the great oar in motion and sent the gondola sliding out into the wide canal. Suddenly, Allegra realized she had no idea how to get to the Bugelli home via the canals. Haltingly, she explained the predicament to Luigi, as he idled the gondola on the moonlit ripples.

"*Madonna mia!* Perhaps we should return and seek knowledge by telephone," he suggested.

Allegra shook her head. She was determined not to return to Renaldo in such a foolish situation. It seemed very important that he not find her inefficient. Then she had an inspiration.

"Do you know Giovanni Fancelli?"

"*Si,*" Luigi nodded. "He usually moors his gondola in the pool behind San Marco. We can hope that he is still there. But are you sure you would not wish to undertake to telephone?"

"Please . . . let's look for him," she begged. They sped down the Grand Canal, darted into a dark side passage, threading like a swift needle beneath shadowed stone walls, and into the gondola pool, which Allegra had passed on foot earlier in the day. A dozen or more gondolas rocked at their moorings; some were covered for the night, but in others *gondolieri* sat gossiping, speaking in guttural patois. People were still out moving along the walkways at the water's edge.

"Ho, Giovanni!" Luigi sang out, his voice echoing from the enclosing tall buildings.

"Eh, Luigi!" Someone laughed. "Do you have a fare in the old woman's gondola? What are we coming to?"

"*Basta!* Enough out of you!" There was a chuckle in Luigi's voice. "Where is Giovanni? The guest of La Vecchia does not remember how to reach her lodgings at the cousins of Giovanni.

So he must give directions. Don't tell me he has gone to bed!" More laughs filled the air.

"How should he go to bed—with his woman scolding him about laziness and his *bambini* making music with yelling and crying! Have patience. He went on a necessary errand and will return in good time." More laughs. Bold bright eyes assessed Allegra. She drew herself small in the scarlet velvet seat, feeling conspicuous.

"There he is," another voice called. "Hey, Giovanni, a beautiful woman wants to see you."

Giovanni came bounding along the quay around the gondola pool. He recognized Allegra quickly. "Good evening, Signorina Brent, *ciao*, Luigi. What is the trouble?"

Allegra rushed into words, apologetically explaining the problem.

"Do not worry further. I will take you home, *signorina*." He leaped down into a gondola and then across it into another, picked up the oar and poled it expertly alongside the di Rienzi craft, then held out a hand to Allegra. Luigi steadied the boat while she gingerly transferred herself into Giovanni's work-worn gondola.

"Better get back, Luigi, before you get a scratch on it." He leered at the di Rienzi gondola.

"Get out of my way then, you loudmouth, or I'll tell your woman you were out paddling around with a pretty girl at a late hour."

Laughter greeted this exchange. Giovanni poled away, and Luigi shot his gondola toward an exit canal. Allegra settled into the threadbare seat of Giovanni's boat. They glided under bridges and down waterways, where only the lapping water and their own breathing broke the stillness. Allegra began to relax a little. She felt secure with Giovanni Fancelli. Out of the silence, he spoke behind her. "You have not visited Venice before, eh, *signorina*?"

"Only in imagination."

"In dreams, is it not so?" he replied. "Many dream of Venice, but we who live in the dream forget the magic, except at night, *signorina*. Then, I believe, Venice lives again the days of her youth. Like a woman, who in the harsh light of day shows her wrinkles but in moonlight recaptures the beauty of her full bloom.''

"You are a poet, Signor Fancelli." Allegra turned to smile at him.

"In my youth," he laughed wistfully, "I wrote poems. I told myself that in this city of my birth, so beautiful, so unique, I should become an Italian Byron, picturing my beloved, my city, in words as shining as her waters, as mellow as the sun on the domes of Della Salute, as carved and curved as the Ca' d'Oro.'' He sighed. "Ah, *signorina,* I am no Tiziano, no Veronese. My words hold no color. I cannot make my city leap into reality with a magic stanza. So here I am . . . a poor gondolier, riding on the breast of my beloved. I can only love her and hope she lives forever.''

"You are a poet, *signore*," Allegra said. "You have just proved it to me, and I have fallen in love with your city, first in my dreams and now forever. Remember what Byron said: 'It was to me always a fairy city of the heart.' ''

The gondola noiselessly moved past a wall ornamented with worn but rakishly smiling little stone lions. They came out on the Grand Canal. Giovanni spoke. "I used to go and sit in front of the Mocenigo over there, in my youth . . . and try to instill in myself the essence of Byron's poetry. See what a foolish boy I was." He pointed to the left where the canal made a wide curve.

"Oh, Giovanni," Allegra said softly, unaware of using his first name. "Could we go there for just a moment, now?"

He looked a little surprised, and she hurried on, "When I was a child in my grandmother's home, I spent hours reading, dreaming of Venice and the Mocenigo Palace."

"So," he smiled, "two dreamers meet, one old and one young. Let us go, *signorina,* for a moment and give our loving respects to one who has given each of us joy."

He turned the boat with an expert motion and set it rushing toward the curve of tall ancient buildings, leaning their elegant shoulders against one another. He drew the gondola steady before one of them. "There are three palaces together, here," he said softly. "See, the family lives here sometimes."

"The family?"

"*Si*, the Mocenigos. They have lived here since the days of the Mocenigo doges."

"All those years," Allegra said in wonder. "Then how did Byron—how was he able to live there?"

"He rented a part of it," Giovanni replied. "They say it is not known which—but I think it is there, where part of the blue awnings are and to the left. Maybe one Mocenigo needed money then—just as sometimes now," he chuckled. "And it would not lower his pride to let his palace to a famous milord." They lapsed into silence, each with his own thoughts, while the gondola swayed with the gentle tide.

Giovanni awoke from his reverie of youth and poetry. "We should go, *signorina*, it grows chilly and I must see you safely to my cousin's home. They will worry if you are too late." He looked at his wristwatch. "*Dio mio!* It is very late."

He set the boat flying in long strokes down the canal again and wove his intricate way to the landing of the Casa Bugelli. She fumbled with her purse, intending to pay him and yet shy, after their shared moments of friendship.

"No," he said firmly. "I take nothing, *signorina*. It was my pleasure." He smiled. "Let us let Byron pay, eh?"

Allegra held out her hand, and he shook it warmly. He jumped down into his gondola and with a great push slid out of the rusted old water gate and sped away from the Bugellis.

"Thank God!" Eleana Bugelli exclaimed, when Allegra opened the door from the inner stairway. "Come in, *cara*, come in; I had fear that you were lost."

The clock on the dining alcove wall said 12:20 A.M. Allegra looked at Eleana wrapped in a flowered bathrobe, the lace of her nightdress showing at its hem. With a pang of conscience she realized that Eleana had been waiting up for her.

Impulsively she held out her hands. "I'm sorry, Eleana. Much has happened today, and I'd better tell you about it. I have to decide something tonight, and I need your advice."

Eleana listened thoughtfully as Allegra talked. Finally she said, "I have often seen *la contessa* in her gondola. She is a relic of the past, but from what I hear, not an unkind woman. She is known for her charities and her good sense, although she is unable to get out much now. In the past years everyone enjoyed seeing her pass, so exquisitely dressed, so very friendly." She paused for a moment, then, "As for the brothers, Renaldo and Guido . . . . They are an example of the new Italy. Even though aristocrats, they have professions. Signor Renaldo is a well-known industrial designer, and his younger brother works with him—but not too hard, I understand."

She paused again, then continued: "Renaldo is famous—but he looks harsh. When his wife died several years ago, he shut himself away for a time. Now he is seen with Contessa Falieri. I have heard from friends who have worked at the palazzo that the child is not a happy one—no playmates. A tutor and the old grandmother are the only ones who seem to care about her."

They both sat silent when she finished. Then Eleana said in wonderment, "You certainly have had an eventful day!" Allegra felt Eleana's eye on her and knew that many questions were being turned in her mind.

Finally the Italian woman said, "The di Rienzis are a very old family—maybe too old. The times change. The aristocracy is loosening hold of itself, fighting a modern world and a middle class that grows more educated all the time." She paused. "Renaldo di Rienzi lives in two worlds. He has the manners of a prince—except that princes have not such a big place in today's society. Still, he is considered one of the most eligible men in Venice. Many mamas invite him to parties, you understand?"

Allegra nodded as Eleana went on, "My young friend, I would only say to you, if you go to stay at the palazzo, keep your heart cool. And this may be hard, for you are warm within. Trust in the old *contessa*; she is honest, I believe. But do not involve yourself with the men of the family. That could be painful."

Allegra put her hand on Eleana's capable one. "Thank you. I do understand. But, Eleana, I have dreamed of Venice for so many years. To live for even a short time in a way of life so different from any I have known—that would be an unforgettable experience. Maybe I'm romantic, but to see La Vecchia is to see backward into time. She is fascinating. I'll just stay long enough to help with her birthday party and then leave."

Eleana smiled and shook her head. "I'm surprised that Aldo di Rienzi agreed, even to please his grandmother. Not that you are not a fine person, but he is very conservative."

"I know," Allegra smiled. "He isn't too pleased. With him, I will stay on tolerance."

"Then enjoy your encounter with the nineteenth century, my romantic young friend. and if you find it is not what you want—the Bugelli family is your family. Don't forget."

For answer, Allegra leaned to kiss the rosy cheek of the kind woman who sat beside her. They stood to clear away their coffee cups and then embraced good-night.

Sleep did not come easily. Disturbing dreams flickered across the screen of Allegra's mind and finally, at dawn, sleep deserted her altogether. She rose in the shadowy room and started to pack. Something was urging her to go to the di Rienzis, even as her common sense told her not to.

She snapped the catches on her suitcase and went to have breakfast with the comfortable, normal, uncomplicated Bugelli family.

IT WAS TEN O'CLOCK, and the resounding clangs of San Marco's clock were fading into the bright air when Giovanni Fancelli slid his gondola up to the water stairs of the Ca' d'Argenti. Allegra could not help feeling pleasurably excited. Luigi opened the door to her knock and eyed the suitcases as Giovanni placed them in the hall.

"Remember," the gondolier said, "if I can serve you, *signorina* . . . ." He did not smile but looked at her seriously—a little anxiously, she thought.

She passed through the doorway and almost ran into Renaldo, who stood observing her luggage. His face was a polite mask. She was glad she had dressed carefully. Her simple primrose yellow dress set off her dark hair, still curling uncontrollably from the Venetian dampness. She did not think of herself as a beauty. Her nose was not classic, her mouth curved too widely. But at least she knew she looked passably pretty, and that gave her a sense of confidence.

"*Buon giorno,* Miss Brent." Renaldo's deep voice saluted her.

He spoke briefly to Luigi, who picked up her bags and started up the stairway with them. She made a move to follow, but Aldo stopped her.

"In here," he ordered. "I wish to speak with you." His firm hand grasped her shoulder and urged her toward a room to the left of the entrance hall. The heavy door was carved deep with decorative squares. In the center of each one, alternating, was either a rakishly horned faun or a smiling cherub. Despite her feeling of trepidation, Allegra was amused by the contrast of expressions on the small carven faces.

Renaldo pushed the door open and stood aside for her to enter. With as much dignity as she could muster she preceded him into a sizable room, whose windows overlooked the Grand Canal. Her first impression was one of mellow warm colors—browns in the well-worn, deep leather chairs, golden ocher in the rug and draperies. A lovely old tapestry covered one wall. A very large desk covered with inlaid wood designs dominated the room.

Renaldo showed her to one of the comfortable chairs facing the desk. For a moment she thought he would sit behind the desk, a position of dominance, but he changed his mind and sat down in another chair near to her.

Allegra tried to appear relaxed, holding a pleasant, attentive face toward him. She smiled inwardly. He was, for the Conte Renaldo di Rienzi, a bit ill at ease.

Abruptly, he began to speak: "Miss Brent, my grandmother has seen fit to hire you to act as companion for Bianca and herself. She was much influenced by your romantic tale concerning her grandmother and Lord Byron."

"I haven't been hired . . ." she began, but he waved her to silence. With an effort she kept her eyes steady on his, curious to discover what was on his mind—*his arrogant mind*, she corrected herself.

"I am sure," he went on confidently, "that you understand how easily forgeries are made. Perhaps some lonely woman of your family in the past conceived a romantic attachment to this poet and manufactured the so-called diary and the story. That, of course, is an uncertain theory. But I find it very difficult to accept all of the story, even though it is true that my ancestress did disappear from Venice. However, if such a thing gives La Vecchia pleasure, it is harmless, I suppose." He looked at Allegra intently to see if she was reacting.

"I do not wish you to believe if you do not want to," she said in a steady voice. "I am not really concerned with proving this strange tale to you. I would like to repay your grandmother for her understanding. If for a while I can help her and have the pleasure of Bianca's company, that would make me very happy. And I certainly would not take pay! To become for a short time part of the life of Venice has been a cherished dream. I believe I can teach Bianca a little English and perhaps something about her own art heritage, before I return to my own world." She stopped; even to herself her voice sounded firm and sensible.

Deep in Renaldo's dark eyes a glint was growing, which could have been amusement in a less dignified being. Then, to Allegra's surprise, a small smile quirked the corners of his sensitive lips.

"Very well. We shall see how much you can help La Vecchia and Bianca. But you shall be recompensed for your time, Signorina Brent." She drew breath to protest, and he made another quick gesture of his long fine hand. "Furthermore," he continued, "I do accept your honesty in believing your own story about my family. But if you think to make use of such a situation to gain advantage in any way—especially with La Vecchia—or to reveal it publicly as a true story, I shall know how to deal with you."

Allegra felt heat rising in her face. Anger flushed through her. "Perhaps this situation should be ended right now," she managed to say. "I should like to have my bags returned, and a gondola to take me back to my pensione." She stood and turned toward the door.

Renaldo rose, moved past her and put his hand on the latch, barring the way. "'Dramatic actions do not solve many problems," he said in a friendly and reasonable tone. "La Vecchia is expecting you upstairs. Maria will show you to your room. I shall be gone for the next three days on business. I am sure that grandmother and Bianca will enjoy having your company. And I advise you to believe nothing my young brother Guido says." He was actually smiling, and it transformed his face into a heart-stopping charm.

He opened the door and stood aside for her to go through into the hall. Allegra felt like a child in the hands of a no-nonsense parent but, strangely, her anger had dissolved, and she couldn't pull up enough shreds of it to take further action.

She had walked a few steps up the stairs when she heard Renaldo call to her. "One moment, *signorina*. I forgot to tell you." He came in long strides across the hall. "Since you have such an interest in Lord Byron—" again he smiled and a flicker of response jumped unwillingly along her nerves "—I have telephoned to my friend, the abbot of the Armenian monastery on the island of San Lazzaro. Perhaps you know that Byron studied Armenian there, and that they have memorabilia belonging to him. I thought you would enjoy seeing these things, and so you have permission to visit the monastery. You have but to telephone, and we can arrange a time. It is only a few minutes to the island by launch or by the *vaporetto* that goes to the Lido in the afternoon." He turned away, his thoughts already intent on business.

Allegra found her voice and spoke to his tall retreating back. "*Signore*—thank you."

She followed the waiting Maria, her mind racing. To visit San Lazzaro! The prospect delighted her. Then the thought of Renaldo's cold warning to her only a few moments earlier swept over the pleasure. Maria's voice roused her from her reverie. "Here, *signorina,* your room." She held open a door.

La Vecchia's rooms were in this wing, but they were not to be neighbors. Far from it. The hallways of the Ca' were endlessly long, and one wing could have held two or three ordinary housefuls of rooms. They had come to a hall that led away from the front of the palazzo, and Allegra entered a spacious bedroom. The bed—high and with a fine needlepoint headboard—was draped with a coverlet of embroidered cascades of tiny flowers.

It was useless to pretend it wasn't the most beautiful bed she had ever seen. Maria smiled at her obvious response to the room. The rest of the furniture was white and gold florentined work. There was a delicate dressing table whose mirror was edged with a wreath of fragile Venetian glass flowers, repeating the colors of the bed. Near it was a chest of drawers with cupid handles. On one wall a plump curved little desk invited use, and at the opposite end of the room, near a small fireplace, a dainty scrolled table with two chairs waited to be tried.

French windows revealed a small balcony outside. Down a little hall she discovered a roomy bathroom, tiled in pale blue and lighted by a Venetian glass chandelier in the shape of a bouquet of wild violets. Allegra couldn't have imagined such a bathroom. A great wardrobe stood against one wall, and thick white towels were draped from long Venetian glass rods on both sides of the marble washbasin.

"I have unpacked for you, *signorina*," Maria said. "When you have refreshed yourself, the *contessa* waits for you."

After Maria left the room Allegra sat down on one of the blue-cushioned chairs and ran her hand along its elaborately worked wooden arm. Her eyes swept the room, getting acquainted with the lovely inanimate friendly things that waited to serve her. She wondered whose room this had been in the past. Was this where the first Allegra had slept, wept and dreamed?

She stood up quickly. Time enough for such thoughts later, when she waited for sleep. She set out to find La Vecchia, the center of energy in this ancient house, where time and memories did their battle with the here and now.

ALLEGRA STOOD before La Vecchia's open door. A scene was going on—she could feel it even before she saw the tense disarray of the old *contessa*'s chambers. Two harassed young servants were dressing her for lunch. Clothes were spread everywhere, and in their midst, impatient, sat La Vecchia upon her pillowed chair, critical of each blouse, dress and glove.

"Ow!" she snapped. "You handle me like a sack of flour, Maria. There you are, Miss Brent . . . come in, come in!" Her voice changed quickly to a gentler tone.

Maria eased the old arms deftly into sleeves while Giovanna, the other maid, brought a white lace summer hat for approval. Allegra felt like Alice in the Duchess's kitchen. La Vecchia announced that she was lunching with Signora Nichelli, an old friend. "Bianca is occupied, Allegra, so you will have the afternoon to yourself." She returned to her problems of dress and said as an afterthought, "But be sure you are here for tea at four."

As she returned to her room, Allegra let her mind start to consider the possibilities for her Venetian afternoon.

CHAPTER SEVEN

ALLEGRA PICKED UP HER PURSE and walked down to the reception hall. It was empty and silent, and her gaze moved thoughtfully over the patterns in the marble floor at her feet. She suddenly thought to check her money. The exchange rate was still puzzling, and she was having to learn to think in terms of thousands of lire. As she counted the large-sized bills she became aware of somebody behind her.

She turned around quickly with her billfold still unsorted in her hand. A young man stood in the doorway of the study, looking at her. He had the beginning of a smile on his round tanned face. Blue eyes looked out from under a thatch of unruly dark blond hair. He raised a hand in greeting.

"Miss Brent?"

Allegra nodded, returning the bundle of bills to her purse.

"I'm Guido." He was dressed in nautical clothes—white duck slacks, navy blue jacket and an open-necked white shirt. Handsome in a boyish way, Allegra thought. But he lacked the smooth maturity of his brother, and the coolness.

"Hello," she said, half pleased with his friendliness, yet cautious. "If you're looking for your brother, he just left."

"I know," he grinned. "My grandmother told me you were coming, so I thought I'd take a chance and wait." He walked toward her jauntily. "I was thinking of going to the Lido for lunch." It was an invitation, and his light blue eyes stayed on her face awaiting a reply.

Allegra thought of the hallway full of serious di Rienzi faces in the portraits upstairs, but she could see very little of the somber di Rienzi blood in this forward young man. "Well," she said, already accepting, "I was thinking of spending the day seeing museums and churches."

"But you'll have to eat somewhere, Miss Brent. I'll make you a proposition: If you go with me to lunch, I'll be your guide for the rest of the afternoon."

Allegra laughed. "I accept—with one warning. I must be back here by four. Your grandmother has asked me to tea, and I shouldn't be late."

"You're going to meet everybody, I suppose. I'll have to give you some brotherly advice about my family and the hangers-on." He winked, taking her hand. "From what I hear, you're the first interesting person to come to the old Ca' in a long time. I'll bet you haven't seen the Excelsior Hotel yet," he said as he opened the entrance door. "I have the keys to the launch while the master is in Milano. Wait here and I'll bring it around."

He left her outside on the landing steps and darted back inside. He had effectively lifted her from any mood of sobriety or contemplation. She gathered that lunch with the exuberant Guido would be a long one, and she tucked away her visions of the museums for another day. She pulled a scarf from her purse and tied it quickly around her hair.

The Grand Canal had taken on a gray blue color since morning. The day was growing humid, with wisps of cloud forming a film over the sky. Not many gondolas were in view. She could hear Guido gun the launch from its water garage on the side canal around the corner, and in a moment he brought the neat little boat snugly against the steps. He helped her into the highly polished wood interior and turned hard into the traffic of the Canal, weaving past slower boats, which were carrying crates of goods for delivery. One had a large potted oleander bush in full pink bloom riding in state to some hidden terrace garden. Guido came up fast behind it, managing to veer off at the last moment, leaving Allegra breathless and the oleander's driver unmoved.

"Slow down a bit," she shouted to him. "I thought you were going to be a tour guide."

"But I'm hungry," he called back, running a hand through his disheveled hair and gunning the engine again. The beautiful

Piazzetta came into view on their left, as well as the outlines of the Doge's Palace, softened by the mist that had begun to settle over the city.

Guido turned the boat away and began a straight fast run across the pool of Venice. The Lido lay ahead, flat and long—a thin finger of land that stretched for miles behind several small turreted islands.

Cold spray pelted her each time the boat slapped the top of a wave. She was starting to shiver. "The island of San Giorgio," Guido shouted back with a gesturing hand, ". . . and Murano, over there. We'll be at the Excelsior in ten minutes. There's a jacket under the seat across from you. You'd better put it on." His own blue jacket was already limp from the sea splashes, and he eased the engine down to a slower speed.

"Thank you," she said, grateful for a return to a relaxed pace. She lifted the cushioned seat and found, among the life vests, a blue Windbreaker, complete with hood. It was almost too late for a waterproof coat. Her dress was thoroughly baptized by the Adriatic, but the coat was at least warming.

Guido gave her a smile. "I didn't think it would be such bad weather. Yesterday was really nice." His coat lapels were sagging, the white shirt clung damply to his chest and he had the look of a child whose sand castle had just been swamped. Allegra returned the smile. "Anyway," he said, "you're going to like lunch."

They had come to the Lido, turned into one of the canals and chugged across the island to the outer shore. The buildings Allegra saw were much more modern than those in Venice proper. An occasional old church softened the views with curves and spires. Cars could be seen on the streets. The island bustled with tourists.

"Do you like to gamble?" he asked as they passed a large low building. "That's one of the casinos."

Allegra shook her head. "Not very much. I'm not lucky that way."

"I'll have to take you someday. I have great ESP with roulette. It's a better investment than the stock market," he laughed.

They drew up in front of a large rambling comfortable-looking complex of buildings. A young man helped to dock the launch. "Signor di Rienzi, what brings you out on this dismal day?"

"A beautiful woman, Tonio. Are you blind?"

Allegra looked down at her dress, hanging soddenly from under the bright blue coat. She must be a pretty picture, she thought. Guido took her hand, and they ran toward the hotel entrance. Inside was a spacious lobby, with inviting overstuffed chairs placed for the ease of its guests. To Allegra's mind at that moment, it was a sanctuary.

"There's a women's lounge down that hall," Guido said. "I'll dry off a bit too and meet you back here. Armando will have a good table for us." His voice had the sure tone of a regular patron.

One look at the face in the mirror of the ladies' room was enough to convince her that she was past the point of a quick repair. She now had a certain Bohemian quality. She frowned, but then concluded this was simply one of the hazards of Venetian life; vanity must retire in favor of reality. She pinned her hair against her head and wound her scarf like a turban. For the dress, some firm pats with a soft towel started the drying process.

Guido was waiting for her in the lobby. His hair was combed, and his shirt had been changed for a dry one. "I keep a locker here," he explained. "I suppose I should keep women's clothes in it, too."

The dining room overlooked the beach, and Armando escorted them to a corner table with a broad view. There was nobody on the sand outside. Several hotel beachboys were busily folding chairs and umbrellas to take to shelter. Dozens of small cabanas dotted the shore, looking to Allegra like the tents of a great Moorish legion, made even more romantic by the shimmery mist of rain that had settled over them.

There were no more than five or six tables of diners in the quiet, informal room. A waiter quickly brought a silver tray with two glasses.

"I thought you'd need some sherry," Guido said. "Unless you want something stronger."

"This is fine," she smiled.

He lifted his small crystal glass and an odd expression came over his face. "I'm happy you came. You can't imagine how awful my days are usually. When Renaldo is around I have to go to the office every day. It's torture." His face was turning petulant. "I never have anything to do except petty work, which the secretaries can easily take care of. And they're all old and ugly. Renaldo saw to that. How would you like to be trapped in a situation like that?" His sudden change of mood was confusing.

"Why don't you do some other kind of work?" Allegra asked.

"Because I think I'd rather take orders from one of my family than from a stranger. I don't like to be put in an inferior position. Isn't that the way you feel?"

She looked into her glass at the light moving deep in the rose of the sherry. "Not necessarily," she responded cautiously, feeling the rush of intensity from him. "I've worked for some very kind and undemanding people."

"Well, maybe," he said, unconvinced. "If Aldo would just let me have some authority in the business. He has already taken advantage of his position as the elder brother. You know, I could handle all the marketing and leave him free to do his designing. But he's too rigid for that. Like a lot of Venetians, he is proud of his industriousness. But it isn't healthy." He drained the last of his drink in a quick motion. "I don't intend to have a heart attack at forty-five, because I had to prove to the world that I worked like a demon. I just read in your *Wall Street Journal* that men who drive themselves have twice as many heart attacks as others who pace themselves more slowly. What do you think of that?"

Allegra was revising her early impression of Guido, whose face was like a chameleon, going from mood to mood in an instant. She began to sympathize with Renaldo. To her immense relief, Armando appeared at the table with menus.

"Now, then, what does the chef recommend today?" Guido said, leaning back in his chair.

"The soft-shelled crabs are unexcelled, Signor di Rienzi. Their season is short; it will not come again for three months."

"Then we should have them. What else?"

"To start with—rice and peas, our Venetian specialty; then mixed salad with fennel. And a good Veneto wine." He finished with an expression of satisfaction.

"It sounds delicious," Allegra said to him.

"We're hungry, Armando," Guido laughed. "And I am still thirsty."

"Right away, *signore,* right away."

Guido's eyes watched Allegra face. "I don't like calling you Miss Brent, especially now that we've already had a drink together."

"Then don't. It's Allegra."

"I didn't mean to get going about my job. I guess I let it depress me. Things aren't all bad. At least I have a little freedom when Aldo leaves town. It's not like I'm the house dog, who has to stay next to the hearth." He laughed again, a short flat burst. A waiter brought him another glass of sherry.

Allegra tried to shake off a growing impatience; she certainly didn't want to become an unwitting tool in whatever family war Guido was fighting. Armando reappeared with the plates of rice and peas. In other circumstances they would have looked delightful, but she was feeling the first warnings of a headache behind her eyes, and she didn't feel very hungry.

It was already two-thirty. She picked halfheartedly at her food. Despite her flagging appetite she found the rice-and-peas dish delicious. "It's really good," she admitted.

"I know," he said, smacking his lips loudly. "I'm going to take you to another place tonight, after we do a little sight-seeing. It's on Torcello. I'll bet you didn't think you'd be going out there today. All the tourists seem to think it's something special."

Allegra's annoyance was growing. "Won't that have to wait for another day? We have to be back by four—your grandmother was very insistent."

Guido's face was petulant again. "La Vecchia has already started working on you, it seems. You should be careful about that." He pointed his fork at her. "She's going to try to run your life if you let her. She still believes in protocol and duties. All those teas are a lot of stupid pretending. Everybody has a role, and you will, too, if you aren't careful. You have to assert yourself."

"But I *want* to go," she said simply.

Guido smiled humorlessly. "You sound like one of her old servants. Where's your sense of adventure?"

She took a deep exasperated breath and said, "I don't get my excitement from breaking promises."

"I heard all about you from La Vecchia," he said, suddenly surly. "You're on your high horse about literary things. She thinks you are some kind of intellectual. Well, I won't ask you again. I guess you have your sights set on bigger game than me."

They sat in heavy silence for several minutes before Allegra decided he was just a spoiled brat, someone who never grew up and probably never would. She wouldn't let him get a rise out of her after this, she promised herself, and began to smile.

It was an unexpected gesture, which disarmed him. He picked up his glass of white wine and drank from it, putting it down awkwardly and spilling some. "I guess I wasn't being very fair to you." His voice was lame.

"All right—peace," she said.

Her eyes were drawn to the far side of the dining room, where Armando was receiving a slender blond woman. She was unusually attractive in a modish way, costumed in a sea-green dress with a silky raincoat over one arm, and tanned to a bronze glow. People at the other tables turned to look at her, and she bore herself as if she expected to be admired. It was a manner that Allegra had always disliked. Guido saw her a moment later.

"Oh, God," he said under his breath. "It's Vera, and she sees us."

Armando was escorting the woman in the direction of their table. She stopped in front of Guido, who rose to greet her.

"Well, brother dear," she smiled, but not enough to wrinkle her smooth tan face. "I've caught you at play again. You shall have to find some out-of-the-way places for your little rendezvous, it seems." She shifted her cool hazel eyes to Allegra. "And this must be Francesca—Renaldo told me you had a new friend."

Guido thrust his hand through his hair. "Vera, I want you to meet Miss Allegra Brent from the United States. She will be staying with us at the Ca' while she pursues some literary research." He said it in the way one volleys a tennis ball back to the other side of the court. And he was pleased with the results. Vera was staring at Allegra now, almost expressionless.

"Allegra, may I present Contessa Vera Falieri, an old friend of the family." Allegra extended her hand. Bianca's sad little face came before her eyes, saying, *Do you know Contessa Falieri? And La Vecchia's voice was saying, . . . that Falieri woman . . . .*

A cold hand took Allegra's in a brief hard grip. It was an unpleasant hand, too thin and brittle, she decided.

The *contessa* spoke to her. "Forgive me, Miss Brent, you are a surprise to me. I did not wish to seem rude, but Renaldo had not mentioned you to me. How long have you been in Venice?" Her clever eyes were rapidly appraising Allegra, noting the points and faults.

"A few days," she replied. "I have work to do here and Contessa di Rienzi has graciously invited me to be her houseguest." She was careful to articulate in the most polished Italian she could summon.

Guido seemed to be enjoying the situation, after his initial displeasure.

"Aldo knew about it yesterday," he said cheerfully. "I was sure he must have told you about Miss Brent, Vera. She's going to be a summer tutor for Bianca, also." He sat down again.

The *contessa*'s handsome high cheekbones flushed beneath the artful rouge shadows. She brushed a wisp of blond curl from the side of her face and attempted another smile.

"That will relieve me of tending the child. It was very thoughtful of La Vecchia to engage a girl to help. Bianca is very demanding, Miss Brent. I hope you will not regret your new position. . . . If you will excuse me, my table is ready."

When she was gone, Guido said, "She's a real bitch. And Aldo is an idiot to put up with her." Allegra might have said it another way, but Guido reflected her own sentiments.

Armando appeared at her shoulder, wheeling a linen-draped

serving cart, from which an aroma of buttery herbs rose deliciously. Her headache gone, and her appetite restored by the soul-warming blend of flavors, Allegra could now honestly feel good about the day. Guido must have felt it, too. His eyes had a clearer expression, not shadowed anymore, and he seemed to have lost interest in talking about Vera and Aldo.

But in spite of herself Allegra looked over to Vera's table. She had been joined by another woman of the same type and coloring, and the two of them were deep in a sober-seeming conversation.

Noticing them himself, Guido remarked, "That's her sister. She's married to a Polish count, but they go their own ways. Vera is a widow. She married Falieri when he was an old man. Now she's prowling—both of them are. I don't know why Aldo is interested. La Vecchia doesn't like her at all, and I just try to stay out of her way. Anyway, she's too thin for a man to enjoy."

Not wishing to become involved again in a controversial discussion, Allegra smiled and said, "Let's change the subject to something more cheerful."

"All right, Miss Brent of America. After Armando brings us a cup of coffee and a little ice cream, let's go home by way of San Marco. There's a little shop under the clock tower that has something I want you to see."

"Only if we won't be late for tea," she said gently, but meaning it.

"Don't worry."

Allegra looked at her watch—already half-past three. There wouldn't be time for dessert, but Guido insisted on coffee at least.

"I can't drive in that rain without something hot inside me first." He started talking about himself again, especially about his problems in the family business, a one-sided conversation that labored on, while Allegra grew more tensely aware of the time. Her good humor was fading as he lingered over his coffee.

"I hate to change the subject, but Contessa di Rienzi was quite definite about tea at four. We really must go."

Guido's face was immovable. "Oh, she won't mind if we tell her we got stranded out here in bad weather. I'll call home in a few minutes and tell Luigi. He knows how to talk to the old woman. Anyway, a small orchestra comes into the lounge at five for dancing. You didn't really want to have tea—be honest with me."

"The rain is scarcely coming down," she said. "Did you ever intend to go back on time?"

He gave a quick laugh. "La Vecchia's affairs are boring. You wouldn't enjoy the people, and it's not worth worrying about. An evening on the Lido is exciting. There are some shows where . . . ."

Allegra picked up her purse and rose before he finished. "I'll have to call a taxi."

Guido stood up too, with a look of disbelief. "You aren't serious?"

"Never more," she replied and turned to leave.

He surrendered without another word, and they left the dining room together. Allegra ignored Vera Falieri's inquisitive eyes as they went.

CHAPTER EIGHT

GUIDO SWUNG UP CLOSE to the water steps of the Ca' d'Argenti and grasped one of the mooring poles to steady the boat. He waved Allegra out over the motor noise. She stepped precariously out onto the dark steps, and he zoomed the launch away and into the side canal.

She stood silently a moment looking down the busy waterway and thinking of the miniature of this scene on the cover of the first Allegra's diary. Turning, she started up the stairs and found the great door already open, with Luigi holding it for her.

"*Signorina,*" he said solemnly, "I am to inform you that *la contessa* wishes your immediate presence at tea in her rooms."

Allegra's hands flew to her hair, where drops of spray still clung. Her dress felt damp and uncomfortable. "I will go to her as soon as I have changed," she said.

"My orders are to bring you as soon as you return." He unbent to give her a commiserating smile. "The old one does not like to be kept waiting. It is now almost half after the hour."

Luigi was already preceding her up the stairs as if he were utterly certain that she would follow him. A sense of rebellion swirled in a dark cloud in her mind. Every di Rienzi she had met so far seemed to expect compliance—if not obedience—from her.

They reached the upper landing, and Bianca rushed down the hall, her voice high with energy. "You're late, you're late! *Nonna* has waited tea and . . . ." She pulled Allegra toward the open door.

Unwillingly, Allegra stood framed in the entranceway, the focus of several pairs of eyes. She felt disheveled and at a disadvantage. La Vecchia sat in state at her tea table, her silk gown reflecting golden shadows on the parchment skin of her throat. Vital life crackled from her sharp brown eyes, now fixed appraisingly on Allegra.

"Come in, child," she said in a strong voice. "I wish to have you meet some of our family and friends." Allegra looked at the individual faces around the room, and they looked back at her. La Vecchia waved her hand to the right. "My cousins, Barretto and Luisa di Rienzi." The middle-aged faces of a man and woman drew themselves into polite and insincere smiles. "Father Tito Fiorenzo—you could call him the family priest if this were a century ago." The deep-set eyes of a man in a priest's dark tailored robe met Allegra's wary ones. His smile was kindly, almost amused. ". . . And Signor Pietro Luigi Maria Mossanato." La Vecchia rolled the name off her tongue sonorously. The owner of the massive name was a tiny man, dressed in turn-of-the-century clothes adapted to modern styling. His thin, rather youthful face was wreathed in complimentary smiles. He leaped to his small feet, adjusting the narrow ruffles at his cuff, and offered Allegra his arm to a chair next to his.

"I am sorry to be late. I was detained unavoidably," she said to the *contessa* over the smooth head of Signor Mossanato, then leaned against the high, brocaded back of her chair while La Vecchia poured out her long awaited tea.

It seemed a very long time while tea was poured and passed. There was no conversation among the guests, but only a kind of expectant silence, which Allegra felt had something to do with herself.

Contessa di Rienzi looked at her warmly. "Signor Mossanato is an expert on Byron," she said meaningfully.

The statement took her by surprise, and she looked again at the little man.

Signor Mossanato turned to her with an ingratiating smile. "I am told, *signorina*, that you have a great interest in Lord Byron. Ah!" His eyes flew heavenward. "What a man he was! Elegant! A true Regency being." He gleamed at her, waiting for her to say something. Some reply must be made, but she had no idea what La Vecchia might have told him already.

"My grandmother," she said slowly, "had a fine collection of Byron material. I used to read it as a child, soaking myself in the mood and imagery of the poetry. Coming to Venice brings me to places where he lived, and naturally I am eager to see some of them."

The other guests were murmuring among themselves, but La Vecchia was watching Allegra.

Signor Mossanato smiled at her beatifically. "Ah, so fortunate a child! To grow nurtured by the dreams of the great past," he sighed. "I, too, have had my dreams. To have lived in the Regency period, to have seen the great Corinthians . . . what a joy it would have been." He broke off to accept a teacup from his hostess. "I am sure you must possess some pieces of Regency furniture." His expression begged her to own at least one piece.

"I'm afraid I own very few things," she replied. "When my grandmother died, it was necessary to sell our home."

The *signore*'s eyes were liquid with sympathy. "I, too, own nothing of the period." He paused, reflecting. "But it is good just to know that it exists." Allegra had to suppress a smile. "If I had my way," he continued, "I would dress as did the eighteenth-century dandy."

It was easy to visualize his neat little figure encased in the tight pantaloons and cutaway coat of the Regency buck. She spoke impulsively, "*Signore*, do you think there could be a way for me to visit the Palazzo Mocenigo?"

He looked a little surprised. "But the palazzo is in the hands of the Mocenigo family still. I can try, *signorina*, to find a way. They are a most ancient aristocratic family, you understand. They have been doges of Venice. One must have an introduction."

La Vecchia interrupted, "What better than to be a friend of the di Rienzis?" Her eyes challenged the right of any Mocenigo to trump such a card.

Signor Mossanato revolved his slight neck uneasily against his collar. "I will try," he promised, "but they are not sure which was Byron's palazzo. There are three together, you may know."

"Surely, the Mocenigo steward cannot have been permitted to be so lax that records of several years of rent could have been lost.

It is only one hundred fifty years since Byron's stay in Venice." La Vecchia held him with proud glistening eyes. "Our own family has records far beyond the Mocenigo doges."

Signor Mossanato withered beneath the stare, defenseless before this attack of genealogical jealousy. "No one has a longer history in Venice than the di Rienzis," he soothed.

"But there never was a di Rienzi doge." Guido's voice penetrated the conversation as he sauntered into the room. He had changed his clothes, and his hair was wetly slicked down. He favored his grandmother with a smile and eased himself into a chair opposite Allegra. She felt irked sitting there in her unkempt state, while he had made himself comfortable.

An uneasy silence had fallen over the room, and when her eyes moved from Guido to La Vecchia, she saw the reason. The old face had drawn into severe lines, and the eyes seemed almost black under down-drawn brows. She stared at Guido with regal dignity, until a crestfallen look crept over him.

"Humph," La Vecchia muttered, releasing him from her hold. "It is true we have had no di Rienzi doges, because of an unfortunate strain in the family that not only breeds men of great responsibility, who must give time to preserving the family security and honor, but also breeds others of little responsibility, who play with life to scant benefit." Guido sprawled out in his chair, ignoring the gibe.

La Vecchia suddenly switched her attention to Luisa di Rienzi. "More tea?" Her words were more a command than an inquiry. Luisa nervously accepted a refilled cup and spilled forth gushing comments on La Vecchi's choice of tea, her impeccable taste in teacups and her extraordinary ability to choose just the proper confections.

"Enough," she snorted, cutting into the saccharine flow of words. "Drink your tea, it may wash some of the excess sugar from your tongue." Luisa subsided a line at a time, like a record slowing to a stop, until her comments became inaudible mutterings fading into her teacup.

"Now," La Vecchia said decisively, "let us return to the subject of Lord Byron."

"I think you should apologize to Cousin Luisa," Guido's voice challenged. The uncomfortable silence fell again, but this time Luisa plunged into it.

"La Vecchia is right. Everyone knows I talk too much." She twittered. "It's I who should apologize."

"Will you stop your public flagellation, Luisa? You can talk as long as you like, if you will only cease your fulsome compliments. They make me itch." A clearing smile lighted La Vecchia's face, and Allegra saw in the flash of it what a beauty she must have once been. Luisa smiled back at her. It was obviously an old beloved controversy between them. La Vecchia eyed Guido again. "If you want to pay me back, my boy, you will have to do better than to interfere in the affairs of two old ladies who understand one another very well."

He continued to sprawl ostentatiously in his chair with a faraway look of disinterest. Apparently, he still held the anger that had begun on the Lido.

Signor Mossanato leaned toward Allegra. "Signorina Brent, I have a most excellent idea. I shall ask permission of the monks of San Lazzaro for you to visit their monastery. It was there that Lord Byron went to study Armenian for a mental pastime." He smiled with pleasure. "They have his desk, his inkwell—many other things. And of course, the portrait that shows him as I admire him most—the great adventurer in his Albanian costume. So vital—ah, I go there to bathe in the energy of his personality. . . ."

"Better watch out," Guido interrupted, "he probably had VD Did you know that, Allegra?" She ignored him, keeping her attention on Signor Mossanato, whose eyes wavered as he tried to regain the momentum of his speech.

La Vecchia set down her cup with a sharp clatter. "You are rude, Guido, very rude. I don't know what circumstances have set you in a temper, but I am sure it was not equal to the resulting state of your mind. There is no certainty of such malicious nineteenth-century gossip. The truth is that he wrote like an angel—he accomplished the goal of true creative fire despite his personal life, which, I am convinced, was not quite so bad as some say."

Allegra turned to Signor Mossanato. "I had hoped to visit the island, but will the monks consider me a disturbance?"

"Ah, *signorina,* they will not be disturbed. They will honor your interest in Lord Byron. They have kind memories of him and of the help he gave to them. If you will give me a suitable date, I will arrange for us to go."

"I'll take you," Guido said. "I've never been to the island. What do you think of that, Allegra? And I'm a native Venetian."

Signor Mossanato drew himself up in his chair, his tiny body managing a touching dignity. "I shall accompany Miss Brent. The monks know me."

"I was only joking," Guido chuckled. "I'm not interested in the monastic life."

Signor Mossanato inclined his head deferentially toward the *contessa.* "It will be my privilege to enjoy San Lazzaro with Miss Brent. It remains but to decide upon a time."

"I have arranged for Bianca to spend tomorrow at her cousin's home on the mainland at La Mira," La Vecchia said. "Miss Brent will be free then. I want her to see some of the Byron artifacts. And perhaps we shall find a way into the Mocenigo by invitation, eh?"

Bianca, who had been quiet in a tall-backed chair, occupied with her plate of cake and cookies, flew to La Vecchia's side. "I will show Allegra the white birds in the big cage, and the pony. We can ride in the cart together!"

"No, no, little one." La Vecchia put a light hand on her bobbing head. "Another time you will take Allegra. She must go with Signor Mossanato to see something very interesting to her."

"Then I will go too," Bianca resisted. "I want to be with Allegra." She began to weep large tears. La Vecchia grasped the silver handle of her ebony cane, which leaned against her blue velvet chair. She was frowning heavily.

Guido's voice cut in: "Why not let her go with you, Allegra? I don't see why she can't go." His smile was sunny and innocent, as La Vecchia turned wrathful eyes on him. He didn't flinch.

Allegra put out her hand and drew the child to her. "Bianca, Signor Mossanato has asked only me to go to San Lazzaro. It is not polite to invite oneself when we are not first asked."

"But I want to go with you! Please, Allegra, please!" Her voice rose with each entreaty.

La Vecchia raised her cane and brought it down with a loud thump. "Enough!" she rasped. "Bianca, you may go to your room." Tearfully, the child turned to go.

Guido pushed out his foot as she moved past his chair, and she came to a halt in front of him. "I'll get you that doll you wanted in the shop near San Fantin." Bianca left the room smiling coquettishly over her shoulder at him.

La Vecchia looked thunderous. "I will speak to you later concerning your bribing of the child," she said in an ominously quiet tone, then turned to Allegra. "You see our problems—the child is spoiled and headstrong." She looked an apology to Signor Mossanato.

The little man rose with a murmur concerning a late business appointment, kissed his hostess's hand and Allegra's. "I shall call for you at ten-thirty in the morning," he told Allegra. He bowed in the direction of the others and left the room.

Silence fell once more over the tea table. La Vecchia looked suddenly exhausted. Despite the tensions in the room, Cousin Barretto was dozing in his chair. Allegra wondered if this kind of teatime battling was normal to the Ca'. Father Fiorenzo appeared to be in patient meditation.

"I must rest," La Vecchia said in a whisper. "I will retire until supper. Allegra, come back later and eat with me. Now, leave me." The assembled family rose and quietly departed, except for Guido.

"You are being selfish, *nonna*," he said with a hurt face. "Who shall *I* eat with? Allegra was supposed to have dinner with me."

"Eat with the devil if he'll have you," she snapped. He laughed and strolled to the door, holding it open for Allegra.

She would rather not have had to pass so close to him. As she did, he said in a low voice, "It has been an insult to me, Allegra, for you to choose to go to the island with that mouse, Mossanato." Astounded, she looked into his angry eyes, then her common sense took over and pushed laughter into her voice.

"I won't argue with you, Signor di Rienzi. You are teasing me, of course." His eyes flickered. "Your grandmother is a wonderful woman. Why would you want to upset her?"

The dark look vanished. "Allegra, I don't know. She tells me what to do, and no one can do that to me." He drew himself up jauntily. "You are finding the family secrets fast. And I have to pay you back for insulting me. How shall I do it?" He quickly pulled the door shut behind them and walked off, leaving Allegra to stare after him. With some weariness she turned to go to her room.

In the wide hall Father Fiorenzo rose from a heavy wooden bench in an alcove. His smile was commiserating.

"I did want to welcome you to this place." He waved aside a reply. "I suppose you are well aware of the energy put forth by that young man . . . a great trial to the household." Allegra nodded. "It is a difficult situation, but he is a good son of the Church. I know you understand." Frustrated kindness poured from him.

"Father, I can see there are problems around Guido, and around this family, if I may speak frankly. But this is a strange experience for me, too, and I'm trying very hard to understand."

"Of course. Let us talk one day. Never doubt that you have friends in this house." He put his hand on her shoulder with a blessing and walked on.

Back in her room a cool breeze was whistling softly through the shutters at the stern old windows. Her mind was crowded with images and thoughts, as she lay on the cool bed. Even the little excursion to San Lazzaro was something to worry about; Renaldo

had already said something about a visit to the island, but he had
made no clear offer to go with her. Would he be offended to find
she had passed over his invitation in order to go with Signor
Mossanato? How could she know if he had a touchy insultable
ego like his younger brother?

She stopped thinking about the difficult Conte di Rienzi and
gave herself up to sleep.

AN INSISTENT TAPPING at the door brought Allegra back from her
blurred dreams. The late dusk light was disorienting, so that she
didn't know which end of the day she had awakened to. Maria's
soft voice spoke from the hallway. "Eight o'clock, Signorina
Brent. You will be taking supper in a half hour."

Allegra lay still, her eyes fixed on the tall French windows. The
amber walls of the buildings across the water were in part shadow,
where stone escutcheons protruded over doors, and awnings
seemed like hooded brows for the windows. She loved the worn
particolored plaster and the decaying water porches that had
stood against centuries of rising and ebbing waters. It was pure
beauty, and it was touched with sadness, too.

She would be leaving Venice soon, she told herself, that self
that was becoming more and more attached to this place, in spite
of the uncomfortable moments. She wondered if the melancholy
in Allegra di Rienzi's diary had all been caused by the loss of her
lover, or whether the loss of Venice might have added its own sad
note of yearning. The old walls were a dusty blend of evening
shadows now, and she forced her thoughts back to the present.
La Vecchia was waiting.

Allegra snapped on the dainty glass lamp beside the bed and
hurried to shed her wrinkled yellow dress, in favor of something
proper for supper. After appearing this afternoon in such an
awful condition, she wanted to present herself on this occasion in
a bit more integrated manner. She dressed carefully in her
lavender summer suit and trapped her dark curls into a low
ponytail with a white grosgrain ribbon.

A smile started on her lips. She was thinking about Signor Mossanato. Before she went to sleep tonight she would reread some of Byron's journals, which she had brought with her, so that the little Regency scholar might have a more knowledgeable companion in his enthusiasm.

As she walked toward La Vecchia's rooms she was more than ever intrigued by the strategies and insights of the dear old autocrat.

"COME," THE VOICE CALLED from within. Allegra pushed open the heavy door. La Vecchia's outstretched hands took hers in a firm grip. "It is good to have a time alone after the busy day. Sit down, here, next to my chair. You look very nice tonight, child; the lavender becomes you."

The Contessà di Rienzi sat in her cushioned wheeled chair. A spray of white oleander mingled with her silver hair in a loose chignon. She was wearing a softly draped long pink silk robe, which extended to her feet. Only the active thin hands and the energetic beautiful face were uncovered.

Allegra wanted to say some compliment but thought better of it. She didn't want to be one of those who fawned for favors, and it might seem that way. "It's been quite a day," she said instead. "But I don't feel I've been of much use to you."

"Don't concern yourself with that, my dear. Tell me, what did you think of our Signor Mossanato?" Her eyes sparkled expectantly, as she raised the silver bell and shook it.

"He's very sweet. It was a wonderful surprise to meet him."

"He loves studies for their own sake. He will be delighted to share his knowledge with you."

"I'm looking forward to tomorrow."

"More than today, I should think. It's a shame you met Guido when he was in one of his moods. I know he was a trial this afternoon at lunch. I tried to dissuade him from asking you, but he was determined."

Maria came in quietly and set up a round table between them.

She turned on lamps to light the area and left the room. "I gathered you both went to the Lido," she continued. "I'll give that boy a scolding if he took you off in the rain to catch cold."

Allegra laughed. "There's no need. I'm fine."

"Well, he's not a bad boy, only thoughtless. I never know where he is, especially when Aldo is traveling and Guido has the launch. He's a charmer, too. But undependable, not like his brother."

"Frankly, *signora,* neither one was terribly charming today."

La Vecchia drew in slightly. "They both become preoccupied at times, and the moon has its effects, too."

Maria reappeared with a large silver tray and began deftly setting the table with covered soup bowls, salad and hot vegetables. La Vecchia was silent for a minute until Maria withdrew.

"And so . . ." she began, as if continuing an earlier thought. "There are many things on my mind tonight . . . things that I wish to tell you about the di Rienzi family." Allegra braced herself, not knowing where the old woman intended to lead her.

As they ate, La Vecchia began to talk. "Do you know why Aldo chooses to reject your story of Byron and Allegra di Rienzi? It is not because he cannot believe. No. There is a special reason. I have told you of his wife's tragic death several years ago . . . and of his doubts about her fidelity. There is a bitterness in him, my child. The story you bring him is about a beautiful young woman, who deceives her husband and gives her love to another man. That is the way he views it. How can we expect him to romanticize about the dashing Lord Byron? Or to sympathize with the woman's vlunerable heart? It is too much to ask. And what must he feel to be brought face to face with a namesake and descendant of this woman? I ask you not to judge him harshly. There are demons at war within his heart."

Allegra felt color rising in her cheeks.

"But, Allegra dear, I am not saying he has a right to nurture his demons any longer. There is a time for everything, and Aldo's bitterness must end soon before it destroys him. I speak to you as a woman who has seen much of life. All I ask of you is to make an occasional allowance for his state of mind. There is a change blowing in the winds around this family, and we must use our highest intuition to work with it. Fate has brought you here at this time. Perhaps for me, perhaps for Bianca, perhaps for . . . I don't know who . . . .'' She rested her head on her hand, her eyes closed in thought.

Allegra was almost trembling from the effect of La Vecchia's words. There was a strange power in them. It was uncomfortable, exciting. The old, sure voice was telling her to be a part of the di Rienzi fortunes, but what did she expect of an unsure young woman in such a complicated situation? She waited for La Vecchia to elaborate on her thoughts, but saw she had fallen asleep. Allegra recognized the pattern of intense energy and then sleep. Strong will could not always command the fragile body. She took a last sip of tea and tiptoed from the softly glowing room.

CHAPTER NINE

THE CLEAR PING of her travel clock woke Allegra at nine the next morning. She slid from the cozy warmth of bed and pushed open the shutters at the French windows. Someone had set a small pot of red geraniums on the balustrade of her balcony; the flowers were crisp and vital with bloom.

Across the canal, the frowning face of another large building seemed to peer back through windows whose panes winked in the sunlight. She could hear muffled sounds of traffic on the Grand Canal around the corner, and the quiet of the small canal beneath her was suddenly broken by a burst of noise. Pigeons flew up protesting from the opposite roof, and Guido's launch roared out in a wake of spray, turning abruptly from the garage below and speeding away.

She sighed with relief. At least she would not have to cope with him this morning. She showered and dressed, excitement stirring in her at the thought of seeing San Lazzaro. It was still cool, and she chose a simply styled jersey dress in soft blue-and-white checks; conservative, but becoming.

Out in the hallway she hesitated, realizing she hadn't the slightest idea what to do about breakfast. No one had mentioned it yesterday, and she hadn't noticed a dining room, although surely there was one somewhere.

"Buon giorno," Giovanna's low voice greeted her. "I was coming to show you where breakfast is to be found. Follow me, please."

Halfway down the hall they stopped in front of a wide paneled door with a button set into a silver backplate to the side of it. At Giovanna's touch the door slid open, revealing a curving staircase and tracks for a little chair lift. Allegra followed her up the green-carpeted stairs and gave a quick start of pleasure as she stepped out into an area of bright light. They were on the roof of the palazzo—but what a roof!

It was a large glass-enclosed room, the windows resting on an ornamental balustrade about waisthigh. The glass ceiling was tall enough for mature shrubs in pots to grow luxuriantly to a considerable height.

Flowered canvas awnings were partly drawn across under the ceiling, and some of the windows were open to the morning breeze. The floor was tiled in a green leafy pattern, and white wicker furniture cushioned in green made inviting circles in the room. At the far end a breakfast service table held silver chafing dishes and a coffee urn. Crystal glasses sparkled with fruit juice. La Vecchia was sitting in state at a round wicker table. Bianca was next to her, holding a large crusty roll sticky with honey.

"Come," the old woman's curiously deep voice called. Giovanna busied herself bringing a place setting for Allegra. "So, you like our roof garden, eh?" She was pleased with Allegra's expression.

"Oh, it's beautiful!" Allegra's eyes drank in the colors of flowers blooming in wide earthen pots and enjoyed the grace of antique marble fauns playing their flutes in front of an espaliered golden rosebush. "What a joy, a garden all hidden away. Your own lovely secret place."

"Not so secret, I fear," La Vecchia smiled. "In summer we entertain here. And even in winter it is warmed. Then, when there is sun, I come to enjoy it. It is even beautiful when it rains and one can watch the clouds and lightning and hear the rain thunder on the glass. That fool of a doctor of mine has forbidden me to come here during storms, says I am too excited by them and will be straining my heart." She snorted. "As if the actions of this household were not far worse than any rain or lightning. But enough, child, let us have breakfast and speak of San Lazzaro."

Giovanna set a dish of lightly scrambled eggs before Allegra. They smelled of sweet basil and thyme. La Vecchia passed a basket of rolls in a woven silver basket. "From the time of the first Allegra," she said, noting Allegra's observation of it.

"How long has this solarium been here?" Allegra asked.

"It was here when the first Allegra was. Not quite as now, but built up with sheets of thick glass made on Murano. The ceiling was not there then. It was open to the sky and used only in summer. When Aldo's grandfather—my dear Leopoldo—was alive, a wind from Dubrovnik, a devil of a Slavic hurricane, blew tile from the chimney pots and shattered the Murano glass." She waved her hand at the strange top-hatted chimneys, which dotted the nearby roofs. "Aldo's father put in the plate-glass wall, and later Aldo installed the other windows and the roof."

For a moment Allegra shivered even in the sun's warmth, as if she felt the shadow of the first Allegra drift by.

"Eat, child," La Vecchia ordered. "It will be cold on the way to the island of the Armenians. What do you know of Lord Byron's association with the monks?"

Allegra explained what she knew of the poet's studies with them, and how he needed some strong mental effort to engage his restless and unhappy mind. He had become great friends with the monks and had helped to compile an Armenian-English grammar. He wrote of worshiping with them in their fine old chapel. She remembered a phrase in one of his letters: "I work," he wrote, "with the Father Superior, a wonderful man with a beard like a meteor."

La Vecchia nodded. "*Si.* I have seen pictures of that one, a saintly face and a white beard flowing to his waist. Wait until you see the garden and the cloister. You will feel a peace there that must have soothed the heart of that confused young man, your ancestor." She let her eyes follow the flight of a small brown bird outside the windows. "Ah, what a man he could have been if only he had learned to use love well! For he was indeed loving. He quietly helped many in this land who were in need. You see, I am not ignorant of the qualities of this Byron. But he let the fascinating dreams start at the sight of any lovely face, and then they faded around him, leaving him empty."

She put a delicate hand on Allegra's. "Do not begin to dream so that you end by not knowing whether the faces in your dreams are real or only as you have hoped them to be." She smiled ruefully. "I have not always taken my own good advice, but Allegra *mia,* I know it is good. My hundred years of observation have shown me that one must take great care in dreaming, and that loving is first given in kindness to the whole of life without thought of self, before we know how to love."

Allegra sat listening to the beauty of the old voice. For a moment the autocrat vanished, and a timeless face looked at her—wise with the suffering and joys of long years. "Thank you," she said, "I will remember. I do know what you mean. I feel the moods rise in me, and the dreams. My own *nonna* said the same."

"Good. I think we would have been friends, she and I. Now, we have lingered too long, and Bianca has eaten all the rolls and honey while we did not watch, and will be sick. Greedy child!"

Bianca started loud guilty protests and was removed by Giovanna.

"I must begin to work with her," Allegra worried.

"Indeed you must. And I shall see to it," La Vecchia said quietly. "But today, child, go with my romantic friend, Signor Pietro Luigi Maria Mossanato, who wishes he was born in the last century but enjoys himself very much in this one."

ALLEGRA WAS READY EARLY, eager for the sight of San Lazzaro. Promptly on time Signor Mossanato called for her. He introduced her to his friend and gondolier, Enrico, who would take them to the island. Not many *gondolieri* now crossed the Lagoon, Signor Mossanato explained, since better fares were to be found in Venice. The Lido and San Lazzaro meant long strenuous rowing, and most people took the *motoscafi*, but Enrico, being very strong, to use his own words, was happy to take them.

The idea had come to Signor Mossanato in the middle of the night. "I think to myself, she will wish to approach the island as did Lord Byron. Not to fly up amid twentieth-century motor noises and wet spray of the *motoscafi*."

"*Motoscafi!* Pshaw!" Enrico spat emphatically into the canal. He reached out and extended a firm arm around her waist, swinging her quickly up and into the long black craft. She sank thankfully into one of the seats, and they slid out to join the canal traffic. The contrast between the two men with her brought a smile to her lips. Signor Mossanato smiled in return and began a kind of lecture as they proceeded. He fell silent when he noticed the abstracted look on Allegra's face. He was, after all, a man of sensitivity.

They passed San Giorgio and glided silently over sparkling sea. The bumpy wakes and noises of the motorboats were left behind. Allegra's mind began to see the scene as it had been in Byron's day. The Lido was there, but not filled with people and buildings. It was low and flat, covered with sand and scrub growth—a place to exercise one's horses or to hold trysts in the moonlight.

She felt a touch on her arm. The *signore* was pointing dead ahead. "See," he exclaimed, "the Isle of the Armenians!"

Her eyes searched the small island. She could see the mellow tones of terra-cotta on the low old buildings.

Enrico brought the gondola around the curve of the island to a stone landing. He offered his brawny dark arm again to Allegra, and she stepped out onto the wide stairs from the swaying boat. Above her was a tranquil garden. Signor Mossanato spoke to Enrico, who laughed and poled quickly away and around the curve of the walls.

Allegra had almost forgotten her escort as she left the landing and entered the garden. She was tracing the limping but purposeful steps of her ancestor—she somehow thought of him as father, not grandfather, several times removed. He was very close now, near these oleanders, which splashed their pink bloom against green hedges.

Pietro Luigi Maria broke the spell by taking her arm, guiding her along flagged paths to a door set into the long side wall of a building. He smiled and pushed a bell nearby. Almost immediately the door opened, and an intent face framed in vigorous curling dark hair and beard looked out at them from brown eyes. The mouth curled into a smile, and the door was pushed open wider to reveal a monk in a well-worn black robe.

"Come in, come in!" he exclaimed in English. "I was expecting you." Allegra felt an immediate rapport with this man whose robe was patched and spotted with traces of old paint and glue. Signor Mossanato introduced him as Father Arkajanian. She suspected by the condition of his robe that he was an artist as well as a monk. He was a man who could put people at ease with his comfortable appearance. He led the way at a brisk pace, apparently well aware of his guests' reason for coming.

Allegra's eyes absorbed everything in the cloistered garden, with its grape-arbored well in the center. At the far end they entered a building through a polished wood door, climbed steps to a wide corridor and were taken to a large room. The room was strangely furnished: straight chairs and small tables, a lamp or two set against the walls and two immense thronelike black chairs, inset with mother-of-pearl designs.

"The room in which Lord Byron used to work at his Armenian lessons," the monk smiled. "Here." He turned to a glass-fronted cabinet near the door, pointing to the bottom shelf. "These were things belonging to him."

Allegra bent down to look closely at the shelf. There was an inkwell with two glass containers, and other small things: a handkerchief, a petit-point coin purse. Little things, kept because he had touched them, used them. The monk watched her quietly, seeming to sense they had a greater than normal meaning for his American visitor.

Allegra could have wept. The little worn purse, the empty inkwell. They looked lonely and abandoned, left floating forlornly on the tides of time. He had known them well. He would recognize them as one knows the faithful little inanimate servers that become part of our lives and somehow come to bear the impress of our needs. She knew she could not pause there too long. No one could possibly know why she really desired to feel the vibrations of these things. She straightened up and looked into the perceptive eyes of the monk.

He smiled at her and started to talk of the monastery and its long history, as he led them on a tour of the museum and its precious artworks. "We are preservers of Armenian culture," he said softly as they walked. He pointed down to a hallway of newer framed paintings and continued, ". . . and we give honor to modern Armenian artists, as well."

He led them downstairs again and through the cloistered garden, ending his tour in a long narrow room, which was lined with glass cupboards. It was a display area for the books that were printed by the monastery's presses. A portrait of Byron was reproduced in color on the cover of one intitled *Lord Byron and the Armenians.* Her black-robed friend gave her the booklet and another one on the same subject.

"I will treasure these," she said and hugged them to herself.

The monk then took them proudly into a large area filled with modern printing equipment, explaining that the monastery had done printing even before Byron's time. Then, laughing, he showed them a wonderful ornate old black printing press, whose well-oiled iron wheels still moved smoothly to the touch.

"These were here in his time. See how good they are. Beautiful."

Suddenly, brisk footsteps echoed in the quiet of the large printing room. Allegra drew a startled breath as down through the aisles of covered machinery came Renaldo di Rienzi. His face was unsmiling. It warmed when he recognized the monk.

"Father Arkajanian! I didn't expect to see you—how long have you been here?"

The father, smiling with pleasure, grasped his outstretched hand. "Only for two days, my good friend. I had intended to call you today."

Renaldo turned to Allegra and the little *signore.* "You are fortunate to have found Father Arkajanian," he said, nodding a greeting to Signor Mossanato. To Allegra his tone was a shade more formal: "I thought that I had arranged to take you to visit here."

Signor Mossanato bristled slightly. "It was my pleasure to escort Signorina Brent, as suggested by Contessa di Rienzi."

"Ah," Renaldo said softly. "La Vecchia, eh? It is strange. When I spoke with her this morning, she seemed not to remember where you had gone. Perhaps it may be that she is plagued by worry over my daughter, Bianca, for whom you are expected to care, *signorina*." He paused to fix Allegra with a stare from his oddly glittering eyes.

Allegra felt anger rising in her, which was not dampened by the amused interest of Father Arkajanian. "La Vecchia gave her permission. And I would have brought Bianca, but she told me Bianca was going to La Mira with cousins." Her cheeks had turned a determined pink, and her eyes were sparkling. She hadn't wanted her next encounter with him to find her at a disadvantage again, and for some reason there was an unfamiliar heaviness around her heart, which only distressed her more.

He regarded her from his superior height. "It was Guido who informed me of your destination," he remarked. Allegra's fingers curled tightly into her hands.

Father Arkajanian broke into the tension, his mouth almost mirthful under his springing black beard. "However it was that you found your way here, *signorina*, it has been my great pleasure to show you our monastery."

Signor Mossanato had been standing nearby like a bright alert bird, looking unhappy with the confrontation. Allegra could sense his relief at the monk's kindly interruption. Polite goodbyes followed, and Father Arkajanian went with them to the landing, where the di Rienzi launch was waiting. It seemed to be assumed that Allegra and Signor Mossanato would return with Renaldo.

Allegra held out her hand to the monk; he took it in a warm clasp. "Thank you, father. It is so lovely here; I hope I will be allowed to visit again."

"Of course, my child," he smiled, pressing a small box into her hand. "A talisman. To remind you that sorrow is the gate to joy." She looked into his face to find a look of amused understanding—but understanding and amusement at what, she wondered.

She sat in the boat beside Signor Mossanato, as the master of the Ca' d'Argenti set the engine into gear. They veered away from the landing in an arc of spray. Looking back, Allegra saw Father Arkajanian still watching and smiling.

The two men talked amiably on the return trip. Allegra put the little box into her handbag and drew into her own silence. She watched the arrogant *conte* at the wheel from her peripheral vision. Renaldo di Rienzi seemed able to intrude on her happiness at will and take away her peace. It helped when she thought of him as just a man named Aldo, instead of the more formal Renaldo. Nothing was quite real, except the distress of her heart, as they sped over the bright sea toward the beckoning beauty of Venice.

Signor Mossanato was dropped off at the Piazzeta quay. He left with a slight frown, disappointed by Aldo's managerial presence. He did say wistfully, in return for Allegra's words of thanks, that he hoped one day to complete the plan he had intended and take her to luncheon or dinner. Under Aldo's severe eyes, she told the *signore* that she would be most happy to see him again—any time he wished.

Aldo gunned the motor impatiently and left the landing with no further comment, driving almost as if he were Guido, down the Grand Canal toward the palazzo. Allegra watched his straight back. He said nothing more and handed her out of the launch at the water stairs in the mooring area under the Ca'. She had not seen this rear entrance yet. He led the way up marble steps and into hallways, which finally brought them out into the kitchen service area and then into the main entrance hall. He turned to her briefly, "I hope you enjoyed seeing the Byron mementos." His voice was almost pleasant.

Allegra smiled, relieved that he had broken the strangeness between them. "Yes. I understand why Byron went to that place. It must have helped to give him some spiritual easing. The atmosphere is so beautiful."

"There are few such places left in the world," Aldo agreed. "Yet, I wonder how one can ease the soul. Not by places alone. There is no way to shut the door on life and its memories."

Allegra looked up at him, surprised. For a moment she saw pain and loneliness. Then the cool curtain dropped again, and he said brusquely, "Tomorrow you will begin your work with Bianca. I want you to remember that she is a child of highly volatile emotions and too much spoiled, expecting to wheedle her own way about things. She needs discipline."

Allegra raised her head with an unconscious gallant gesture, which brought a tiny quirk of a smile to his lips. "I will do my best, Signor di Rienzi."

"All right," he said and turned away from her toward his study door.

Allegra went upstairs to her room, feeling suddenly tired and drained. She dropped her handbag onto the dressing table and then remembered the box that had been pressed into her hand. She opened it with a surge of feeling for San Lazzaro. Inside, on a bed of jeweler's cotton, lay a dainty golden cross, its edges scalloped. In the center was a tiny pink stone. She lifted it by the fine chain and held it to her cheek. Its coolness was comforting.

Maria knocked to inform her that *la contessa* was overtired and had withdrawn to rest for a period of time; Bianca was still with her cousins, and Signor Renaldo was not dining at home. She suggested that Allegra might prefer to dine in her own room. Nothing was said of Guido's whereabouts, and she did not feel like asking.

Someone had thoughtfully set a small fire in the grate to dispel the slight damp chill of the afternoon. She sat down in one of the chairs and looked into the whispering flames, remembering the last fire at home, when she had read *nonna*'s letter and discovered the secret that had brought her to this fairy-tale room, so far away from everything she had known or experienced. Even Larry was like some stranger now. How could it all change so completely in so short a time!

She lectured herself firmly to remember that she was only a visitor here, a person of no particular status or position—not even an employee. And even if La Vecchia did believe her story and was friendly, there were other interests in her life. There was Bianca; in honesty she had to agree with Aldo. The child was spoiled, yet Allegra longed to smooth the tension between father and daughter.

Her mind jumped away from problems to pleasure. For a time she sat picturing Byron working in the island study room. She reached for the pamphlet *Lord Byron and the Armenians* and saw in its pages pictures of the rooms she had just visited. She smiled to find the portrait of a benevolent face framed in a nimbus of white hair, and a long beard, which deserved the word *meteor*. Undoubtedly the Father Superior that Byron wrote about.

Luigi came to her door with a dinner tray. She arranged herself cozily in front of her fire, enjoying the excellent food and reading about Byron. If there were ever two more opposite men than Byron and Renaldo di Rienzi, she didn't know who they could be. The high-handed *conte* hadn't the slightest poetry in his soul, nor the perception to see clearly into the motives of another human being.

It bothered her that her thoughts kept returning to him. She had to be a realist; her only purpose for staying here was to help the *contessa* and Bianca. She had completed her mission of taking the diary of Allegra di Rienzi to Venice, and it hadn't worked out as she'd planned; but that was life. Lots of plans don't work out. It wasn't her business to try to convince Aldo of anything. With a growing resolve to remain aloof from the turmoils of this strange family she banked the little fire and went to bed.

CHAPTER TEN

THE NEXT MORNING was clear and lovely. Allegra woke early and found a breakfast tray waiting outside her door. She determinedly enjoyed every bit of the delicate crisp rolls, the flowery marmalade, the pungent coffee. She must savor and remember every moment of this time, plucked like a dream out of reality.

She watched the pearly light on the water from her window. Somehow she had to convince her emotions that this was only an interlude and that the life destiny planned for her was back in Boston; if not with Larry, then with someone else wholesome and predictable.

Today she would start behaving reasonably, starting with some attention to her duties with Bianca. She dressed carefully in a light blue slack suit. The pale tone made her hair look dark and dusky and flattered her Italian skin. She gathered her hair back into a ponytail, tying it with a pastel scarf. The look she wanted to achieve was businesslike. If Aldo saw her he would have nothing to criticize.

In the mirror her face looked back with a grimace. She laughed out loud. "Why should I care what he thinks?" He probably didn't think about her at all. She never considered herself a raving beauty—she had nothing to worry about.

She spent some minutes being critical of her appearance, but she didn't credit herself with the wistful delicate line of her lips, which was so charming; the lights in her dark hazel eyes; nor the quick lift of her head that was hers alone and caught the attention.

Now, feeling very much like a companion-nanny, she went in search of Bianca. The child was not difficult to locate. The sound of her protesting howls was easy to follow.

Allegra found her in La Vecchia's sitting room, angrily refusing to have her hair combed by Maria. La Vecchia was in her chair, dressed in a pink satin bedrobe. Her face looked old and sallow in the morning light. She was thumping her cane and demanding silence. She turned at the sound of Allegra's, "Good morning."

"I see nothing good in this day, so far." Moving her silver stick in Bianca's direction, she barked, "See if you can do something with this child! *Cattiva!* Naughty one!" she rasped at Bianca.

Allegra went quickly to the child, who bit off a wail in midair at the sight of her. Maria stood frowning helplessly with comb and brush in hand.

"How would you like me to fix your hair the way little girls in the United States often wear theirs?" she said softly. "My own *nonna* used to fix mine for me, and if it pulled a little, she said that people with pretty hair always felt more pull than those who did not have pretty hair—so I could be sure that mine was pretty." She reached out a hand to Maria for the brush and comb. "Shall we try?"

Bianca considered the situation. Tears stood on her flushed cheeks. Allegra waited, looking calmly into the big damp eyes. Bianca wavered. Curiosity won and she nodded.

"No more tears? I can't fix it if you cry. And if your hair is all undone, I can't take you out with me today." Allegra led her to a chair, sat down and drew the child to her side. Quietly she worked the long heavy curls into some smoothness, then braided two thick plaits and tied them over on top of her head with ribbons, which Maria happily supplied. Fluffing out the curly ends of the braids over Bianca's pink little ears, she smiled at the effect she had produced.

Bianca ran to a long mirror and contemplated herself, patting the new coiffure with a tentative hand. She laughed delightedly.

"Go and show your *nonna* how nice you look," Allegra said.

"Bene," La Vecchia approved. "You are excellent with the *bambina*. Now, take her. I must have some peace and quiet if I am to manage the celebration to come." She paused, a tiny ironic smile on her lips. "How I hate being old. My spirit is still wanting activity. And yet I sit here, tied to this foolish chair." She

thumped its velvet arms. "But I am not dead! Not dead yet! I intend to finish a few affairs before I resign myself to earth."

She looked up at Allegra with penetrating eyes. "Go," she said, not unkindly. "Leave me to battle with my years. You may take Bianca to lunch in the city but return in time for tea. I rely on you to improve her mind as well as amuse her." She leaned back and closed her eyes, seeming to fall into one of her quick naps. Allegra and Bianca silently left the room.

Luigi was waiting at the water steps with La Vecchia's polished old gondola. Little choppy waves had sprung up on the Grand Canal and Luigi had to pole strongly to swing the black craft into side canals where the water was quieter. He brought them to the gondola pool where she had been before, but today only a few boats swayed at the moorings. "When you wish to return, please to telephone and I will come," he said, handing her a bit of paper with a number on it.

The two young ladies of Venice set out eagerly to join the activity in the narrow walkways. Bianca wanted to linger in front of a pastry shop, where delightful cakes and cookies were displayed like jewels on glass shelves. Allegra hurried her past, promising sweets for lunch. Very easily, she found the beautiful old wood bridge that led to the Accademia.

"Have you come to the Accademia before?" Allegra asked.

"No. My uncle only takes me to the shops and to luncheon. And my papa takes me to eat once in a while, but then I must sit quiet a very long time in someone's office while he talks and talks about his business."

Allegra made no comment. They went into the old museum, and Allegra drew on all her knowledge of art to gain Bianca's attention. The child was thirsty to learn. She gazed earnestly at the paintings, sometimes asking questions that showed real perception. They came upon a wonderful portrait—an old woman, who obviously viewed life with amused understanding.

"It is called, *La Vecchia*, The Old One," Allegra said.

Bianca's head tilted to the side as she considered the portrait.

"My *nonna*, they call her La Vecchia, too. She's not the same as this one, but maybe just a little. You know—not afraid of things."

Allegra was intrigued by Bianca's analysis. The child continued: "I'd like to live to be one hundred years old, like my *nonna*. But I'm afraid of lots of things. Sometimes I can talk to her about it, but not always, and sometimes I'm afraid of papa—he doesn't listen very well."

She slipped a confiding hand into Allegra's. "It is so nice with you, Allegra. I have someone to talk to. I like to learn things. It's better in winter, in school." She sighed, then in a rush of intensity, her grip tightening, "Please don't go away, Allegra. Please! Please!"

Allegra looked into the urgent face. "I'm here, Bianca, don't worry," she soothed, unable to give the real promise the child wanted. Bianca relaxed and they continued through the museum.

They came out again by the canal, and after a short walk they were in the Piazza San Marco. It was awash with people and pigeons, as usual. "Let's go to Quadri's for lunch," Bianca said.

She ran out through the colonnades along the side of the square opposite Florian's, and found a small table among the many that were set there They ordered pasta with scampi and then cakes and ice cream. The midday hour passed in companionable silence, while they ate and watched the tourists and the strutting pigeons.

Suddenly, Bianca jumped up from her chair to run toward a tall man a distance away, who was coming across the square.

"Papa, papa! Here we are!" she shouted. Aldo looked up, just as Bianca catapulted against him with a flurry of small arms and legs. He picked her up and followed her pointing hand toward the table.

Allegra watched uncomfortably as the confident figure approached her. In the bright sunlight of the piazza, the slight silvering at Aldo's temples gleamed against his sable hair. His eyes looked intently at her, drawing forth an involuntary shiver from within her. She took a deep breath and presented what she hoped was a calmly friendly face to him.

"Have *gelati* with us, papa." Bianca was all smiles as he set her back onto her feet by their table. He drew another chair to the table and ordered coffee from the waiter, then, seeing the remains of their lunch still on the plates, he ordered more cakes and ice cream. Bianca bubbled over with enthusiastic descriptions of their morning at the Accademia. ". . . And there was one called *La Vecchia* but not like our *nonna*."

Aldo looked at Allegra with a more relaxed smile. "She seems to have got quite an amount of information about art this morning. You are well-informed, *signorina*."

"I studied to be a teacher of art history," she answered quietly.

"Then, how is it you have been a secretary and not a teacher?" He raised an inquiring eyebrow.

Allegra looked into his face, keeping her eyes steady with effort. "I was secretary to the head of the art department, and I did some teaching—a senior class, on the symbolism of medieval and Renaissance art."

Aldo did not immediately reply. He watched her for a moment, as if seeing another side of her. His gaze moved away to the piazza. "Strange, with such interest in your special field, that you have not visited Italy before," he remarked.

Allegra tensed as if he had accused her. "I was saving money for a trip." She heard defensiveness in her voice. "That is why, when my grandmother died, I was in a position at last to travel."

"Then you did not come only to seek out the di Rienzis?" The words dropped like ice into her pleasure at his presence.

"I would have come to see Italy, a country I had already learned to love, Signor di Rienzi. Perhaps I should not have bothered your family with the story of its stray lamb. I was naive enough to think that the history of such deep human emotion would be meaningful to you."

She swallowed painfully to maintain a natural voice. "However, your grandmother's kindness has meant a great deal to me. She is a remarkable person, and I feel privileged to know her. And Bianca is a dear. I shall not trespass on your kindness too long, *signore*."

To her surprise, Renaldo's eyes softened, and his firm mouth lifted in a smile of amusement. "Do not fluff up, small kitten, I am sorry. Forgive me. I forget that romance is the joy of women." His smile held her eyes. "We must make sure you see the treasures of Florence, Rome and Verona before you leave us."

Bianca, spooning the last of her ice cream, caught her father's words, and her look of pleasure faded into anxiety. "But she's not going to leave us for a long time! You won't go, will you, Allegra? Please! Please!" Her shrill voice was causing heads to turn.

"Signorina Allegra is not leaving. Control yourself, Bianca," Renaldo said severely. The child shrank into silence. Allegra was torn between pity for the child and irritation with her ability to cause a scene.

Renaldo gestured impatiently for the waiter, paid him and rose to his feet. "Come, I will take you home; my gondola is at the pool." He turned and strode off, hardly looking to see if Allegra and Bianca followed. They went hastily under one of the arcades, back through a short walkway and over the bridge. Luigi was dozing in a gondola, a more sober craft than the one that seemed to be the property of La Vecchia. He jumped to his feet at the sound of Renaldo's voice.

Seated in the gondola, Allegra drew Bianca near her, the child's whole being registering dramatic dejection. Renaldo lounged on one of the side seats, his long legs thrust out in front of him. He watched Bianca with a slight frown and compressed lips. Allegra let her eyes stay on him, although her sensible mind said look away. The late sun touched his fine clear profile with edges of gold. She was unwillingly aware of the grace of his body, the broad shoulders, the long-fingered hands, like those in the portraits in the Doge's Palace. He turned his head, and their eyes locked for an instant, then she withdrew hers quickly, but she remained uncomfortably tuned to his scrutiny. It was an unembarrassed, impersonal stare, as if he were assessing her whole being. A queer shaking energy moved in her nerves, almost like pleasure

She mentally tried to erect a wall between herself and this man whose dark eyes probed at her.

Just as his silent contemplation was becoming unbearable to her, a trim motorboat pulled alongside the gondola. "*Ciao, Aldo!*" Guido's strong voice hailed them with a laugh. The launch idled down and Luigi, muttering, tried to hold the gondola steady. Other voices called out good-humored comments. Bianca forgot her sulk and smiled at Guido. The Contessa Falieri sat languidly posed on one of the blue leather seats of the launch.

"So you have returned, Aldo." She spoke on a light note. "It was a short trip. Did you have success?"

Renaldo smiled. "I will tell you more at dinner, hmm?"

"*Ah!*" she exclaimed, then waved a jewel-sparkling hand toward Bianca. "*Ciao, bambina*, I have a present. I will give it to papa for you." The *contessa* sent Aldo a dazzling smile.

The others in the *motoscafo* clamored to continue on their way, and she laughed, "Impatient buffoons! Let us go, then; we are late for tea at the Lido. *Arrividerlà, Aldo mio.*"

Their boat roared into life and cut against the water, while Luigi fought to keep the gondola from being tossed by the waves. Guido leaned back and blew a laughing kiss to Allegra. She remembered his telling her how much he disliked Vera Falieri. Was everything a game with him?

As they neared home and the boat landing at the rear of the Ca' d'Argenti, Renaldo said quietly, "The child was rude to Contessa Falieri. Not a word of greeting, or thanks for a gift. You will have to see to it that she has better manners, Miss Brent. I will not have her grow up to be a spoiled selfish woman.

"Come," he ordered Allegra, as the boat gently bumped the dock. He held out his hand to her, while Bianca leaped out and ran into the palazzo, calling for Maria. Allegra ignored his hand and stepped forward to climb the tiny step out of the gondola. In a sudden motion his two strong hands came around her waist and lifted her bodily onto the quay. She stood there, breathless with surprise, while Aldo walked away and up the inner staircase. He did not look back.

She found her way up the stairs, annoyed with her weak vulnerable body and its responses to Renaldo di Rienzi—a man whose world could not be farther from her own if it were on the moon.

Maria stopped her at the landing, a look of concern on her face. "*La contessa* is feeling weak this afternoon and will have no visitors for tea," she said in a whisper. She quickly added, "It is not serious. There are often days like this. She is not young, you understand."

Bianca was already at the door to Allegra's room. She had found a note from Guido taped to it. "The sun will be shining tomorrow on the Lido beach. What about another chance?" Bianca looked up at Allegra hopefully. Her face was still puffy from the recent emotional storm.

"I'm sure this is meant for both of us, Bianca. Why don't you write an acceptance note and leave it at your Uncle Guido's door?"

Bianca delightedly skipped down the hallway out of sight, to the wing where Guido had his rooms.

ALLEGRA HAD A DEFIANT URGE to explore the city, to make it hers by right of her ancestry, free of the need to be a part of the Ca' d'Argenti's "protection"—as La Vecchia had said. It took only a suggestion for Bianca to agree to venture out again, and they walked into the narrow zigzagging streets of Venice, hand in hand.

They refused to take a gondola. Allegra wanted to feel the old stones beneath her feet, and she didn't care how long it took to get anywhere. The afternoon was hers and Bianca's entirely. After a time they were heading in the general direction of a restaurant, which Bianca promised served the best pizza in the world.

They threaded through alleyways and over crumbling bridges, until the aroma of the pizzeria drew them to an open doorway. There, they found seats at a small table, and agreed upon something called a *capricciosa*, a combination of tomatoes, artichoke hearts, cheese and olives.

"This is my favorite place," Bianca said in an earnest voice. "Papa brought me here once, before he got too busy." She tried to sound matter-of-fact.

"Then you both have good taste," Allegra responded cheerfully. "I think it will be my favorite place, too."

Bianca smiled a little, as if some of her doubts had lifted. "Let's take the rest of our pizza home for our own special supper."

"Secretly?" Allegra winked.

"And we won't have to let anyone know . . . except cook." Bianca was happy again.

MORNING BROUGHT WARM SUNLIGHT and the sounds of bonging church bells into Allegra's room. She looked at her travel clock: nine o'clock. A strident horn blared repeatedly beneath her window. She looked out to find the disturbance and saw Guido, waving at her from the motor launch.

"Aren't you ready yet?" he shouted up at her.

"You didn't say what time we were supposed to meet you," she shouted back.

"I must have forgotten. How long will it take you to get down here? I thought we'd have breakfast on the island."

Allegra debated for a moment before answering. Guido's face was filled with boyish expectation. She couldn't be seriously put out by his absence of good manners. "Give me ten minutes. And for heaven's sake, turn off your engine and see if Bianca is ready."

She raced through her shower, pulled on her only sun dress, thrust her bathing suit, towel and a yellow scarf into a string bag and ran a brush through her curls. Bianca opened the door as she was picking up her purse.

"Uncle Guido's angry with me, Allegra. He says I can't go if I'm not ready right now, but . . . ." She stood in front of Allegra with her brush and ribbons in her hand. "I don't know how to do my hair."

Allegra quickly made two neat braids with ribbons for the top

of the perturbed hot little head. She and Bianca bounded down
the stairs together to be met at the door by Guido. "They only
serve breakfast until ten," he said, as he handed them into the
boat and roared off toward the Grand Canal.

This time the weather was a friend, the skies pure Botticelli and
the waters warmly blue. The church towers and rooflines stood
out with crisp clarity upon the Lido in the distance.

Bianca was restless to be there. "I want you to see me swim,"
she said to Allegra. "Papa thinks I'm a fish because I like to swim
underwater." Her eyes suddenly looked distressed. "Oh! I forgot
my diving mask. I can't see in the water unless I have my mask."

"I'll buy you one over there," Guido called back.

"I hope someone told the *contessa* that we were going out for
the day," Allegra said.

"Didn't you?" the child asked.

"Oh, God." Guido turned around. "We'll have to call from
the hotel. You'd better do it, Bianca. She'll be angry with me."

Bianca was clearly weighing whether she wished to brave her
great-grandmother's displeasure in order to please her uncle. "I'll
do it," she agreed. "But first I want my mask."

"All right, all right," Guido agreed.

"*I'll* call La Vecchia," Allegra said. They both looked
reprimanded by her cool tone.

"What's the matter?" Guido asked defensively.

"Nothing. Except that you weren't bringing out the best side of
your little niece."

"Oh, God," he said again, and turned back to his piloting,
with an irritated shrug of the shoulders.

"Will I still get my mask?" a worried Bianca asked.

Allegra didn't answer.

Once again, the launch purred to its dock outside the Excelsior.
There were several motorboats nearby, and the hotel dockman
was having a busy morning arranging moorings. Guido pulled in
close and jumped out to secure the launch.

Bianca had run inside already. They walked through the lobby and past the glass-enclosed dining room to the beach. The Moorish cabanas stood facing the water from their rows along the sand.

Bianca was racing ahead, obviously intent upon the di Rienzi cabana. Guido waved at several groups of sunbathers. The beach was already crowded.

"I have some friends here," he said. "I'll introduce you when we've had something to eat."

The terrace was set up with a buffet table manned by an attentive staff. Freshly baked rolls spilled from brimful baskets, and jam pots were set temptingly nearby, with chunks of preserves glistening in the sunlight. Dishes were piled with tempting plump fruit, and in the middle of the table, like a presiding judge, sat a great puffing brass espresso machine, dispensing its well-digested contents conservatively into the waiting cups, a little at a time.

Guido cheered noticeably with the prospect of eating and sent one of the beachboys out to fetch Bianca, who was already in her bathing suit. He found a table in the sun, where he could keep an eye on the beach activities. "Aha!" he laughed, pointing, "there's Aldo. I guess he's not all work and no play either."

Allegra followed his finger to a group of people sunning near the water. A little shock ran through her when she saw Renaldo. His torso was lean and dark, vital even from a distance. His face was in profile, and Vera Falieri clung to his arm.

Guido snorted a laugh. "She's doing all she can to get Aldo. I suppose he'll give in someday. La Vecchia won't have her in the family tree, but then, Falieri can afford to wait for death to come. And Aldo will do as he wishes, anyway."

Bianca's face grew dark at the words. "And I shall run away."

Allegra gave Guido a withering look for his loose tongue. "There must be something cheerful we could talk about. Do you see any of your friends here, Bianca *mia*?"

"Well, Rudolfo's waiting for me to finish so we can dig in the sand." She made fast work of her sweet roll and ran off.

"Don't you know what effect your words have on her?"

Allegra spoke sharply as soon as she was gone.

"Oh, she didn't know what we were talking about. She's all right."

Allegra wanted to strangle him.

Aldo's group was walking toward the terrace in the direction of the bar. Guido called out to them and stood up to motion them to the table. Allegra was uncomfortable in the presence of Vera Falieri, whose charm was so very calculating.

"So, little brother," she was saying to Guido, "I find you here again . . . and so soon." She tapped him lightly on his chest.

Aldo was clearly displeased with Guido's presence. "Is it so easy for you leave your work?"

He shrugged his shoulders. "I thought Bianca might need the attention of the masculine side of the family now and then."

Aldo's lips pursed in response, but he said nothing. Two young men in the group smiled at Allegra with warm inviting Italian eyes. Allegra deliberately smiled back and had the satisfaction of seeing Aldo's eyes flicker with irritation.

Vera was next to Allegra. "My dear," she said casually, "how long did you say you were planning to stay in Venice?"

Guido's face was impish. "Well, Vera, we don't know yet. Maybe she'll become a permanent guest. Bianca is still young."

"And where *is* Bianca?" Aldo demanded.

"You won't find her at the bar," Guido fired back. Allegra wanted to stop the nonsense.

"She's with her friend Rudolfo, looking for shells and things. I think she'd rather do that than sit with the grown-ups and talk."

"Just so someone keeps an eye on her. She's an unpredictable little thing," Aldo said, his voice a bit defensive.

"I'm going to the cabana to change. Guido, you'll have to show me which one." Allegra stood up.

He stepped beside her with his arm over her shoulders. "Also, I hope you and Vera have a nice day. I know *we* will." Aldo's party left for the bar.

"We could have joined them if you wanted," Guido said.

"I don't think your brother would like that."

"Why not? I'd like to see Vera get really upset. It would probably wrinkle her perfect face. She's had it lifted, you know. That would be fun."

"I'm afraid that's not my idea of fun."

"Oh, I was just kidding," he said quickly.

They walked out onto the fine sandy beach to the cabanas. When they had changed, she and Guido went to the water's edge among children and nursemaids and found Bianca kneeling with a red beach pail and shovel. A deeply tanned little tow-headed boy was with her. They looked busy with their digging. Allegra spread a towel farther back and sat down. The sand felt warm, therapeutic. Guido lay down next to her, propped on one elbow facing her.

"You came here at an interesting time, Allegra."

"What do you mean?" she asked cautiously.

"There are going to be a lot of changes at the Ca' pretty soon. If you stay here, you'll see what happens to old pecking orders." He laughed a quick bark.

She wished she hadn't asked. She closed her eyes and let the sun lay its soothing vibration over her.

Some time passed in relative silence before Guido spoke again. "I suppose you want to go back for tea with La Vecchia."

"Yes. I haven't seen her for almost two days."

"At her age, you don't notice time anymore. She's not as sharp as she used to be," he said carelessly.

Allegra sat up abruptly. "Guido! We forgot to call and tell her where we went."

"Well, it's no use calling now. Anyway, the servants must know where we are. They tell her everything. You're too tense about things, Allegra, but if it bothers you, we can go back. Bianca's probably got a sunburn by now, and I know how upset you get when you miss tea."

MARIA WAS WAITING at the rear entrance door when the launch drew up to the Ca'. "Bianca!" she scolded gently, "you are covered with sand."

"Yes, Maria, but see what I brought for you." She held up her bucket of seawater and shells.

Guido pulled it from her sandy hands. "Mmm. These look good. I think I'll boil them for my dinner." He started toward the kitchen with Bianca trailing angrily in pursuit.

"*Signorina,*" Maria whispered. "*La contessa* is feeling better this afternoon and wishes to see you in her rooms. The doctor has left orders for rest—no activity."

"I understand. I'll go to see her as soon as I've bathed and changed."

Bianca's cries from the kitchen took Maria's attention. "I shall see to the teasing. Do not worry," she said.

Allegra used the servants' stairway to the first landing and quickly let herself into her room. It was cool and quiet. Bianca's yellow cat was spread across the bed, like a definition of comfort. It followed Allegra with its eyes as she undressed for her shower. "I'm glad you're a girl," she smiled, stroking the silky hair and down the long back. A soft rumbling purr answered.

Allegra walked out, refreshed, toward La Vecchia's quarters. She had missed the bright clear conversations with the old woman. The carved double doors were ajar, and Allegra sensed activity within, even before she knocked.

"Come in, child, come in!" La Vecchia's voice was impatient.

Gently closing the doors behind herself, Allegra turned to face the room. It was in great disarray with gowns draped over everything. "I need help, Allegra," she said breathlessly. "I've had to sneak about in my own house to avoid my doting physician. I have been upstairs in the old wing, which we used for storage when I was young. What do you think of my little discoveries? I had to pile them into the dumbwaiter shaft upstairs to get them here."

Allegra looked again at the array of gowns. There were voluminous silks and laces, pastel shoes and gloves and extravagant beaded bags, long feathers and sequined tiaras— all scattered about the room in shimmering disarray. "They're too beautiful for words. I've never seen such breathtaking costumes."

"But they're not costumes. I remember most of them quite well. You see, these were mine many years ago, when Leopoldo and I were young and celebrated each new season with a great ball."

Allegra couldn't speak right away. It was such a surprising vision of real and make-believe.

"Did you think I was planning a birthday party for myself to consist of a large cake and discreet congratulations from the family? Too many years have passed since the Ca' d'Argenti was alight with torches at the walls to announce a di Rienzi ball. I probably shall not live to be two hundred, and so I wish the one hundredth celebration to be extravagant." She settled back contentedly, a few last words moving soundlessly on her lips, and closed her eyes.

Allegra picked up one of the gowns and held it up to herself in front of a mirror panel. She loved the heaviness of the layers of rustling blue taffeta. The waist was tiny, the bodice thickly laced but cut low off the shoulders. She whirled around to feel the flow of the heavy skirt. How wonderful it must be to remember a time when you wore this dress and danced, she thought.

"I was sixteen." La Vecchia's eyes were open again. "I begged father for months to let me have my own ball, and that was the gown I wore. There is still some of my youthful joy in its old seams." She smiled at the dress and at Allegra holding it to herself. "But that is not the one I want you to wear. There—see the beige one on the corner bench? Bring it here to me."

Allegra followed her eyes to a satin gown, overlaid with tulle.

Rich beading in lustrous tones of copper cascaded over the full skirt. A beige silk rose filled the deep cleft of the neckline, and clusters of rosebuds caught the soft sleeves into gathers just below the shoulders. A reticule was next to the dress, beaded with the rose pattern to match.

"I think that one suits you, *cara mia*—your coloring, your spirit—would you mind if I asked you to wear it for my birthday?"

"It's exquisite, but it must be too fragile to be worn. It's very old, I know."

"Yes, but it is well cared for, and the fabric is very fine. Do not fear."

Maria entered quietly with a tray and left it on the tea table for them. She didn't seem surprised by the display of ball gowns all over the room. Allegra knew that Maria must have been an accomplice.

"You see—I want it just right." La Vecchia's voice was remembering another time.

"You shouldn't be worrying about the plans," Allegra said. "I know something about organizing and Bianca hasn't enough to do. Let us take the worry from you." She stood in the midst of the gowns, hands on her hips. "To start with, what shall we do with all this?"

"That is indeed a question. I wish you to take that one dress to your room. Maria will bring the petticoats that belong to it after she presses them. If it needs altering, I have a seamstress who will come before the ball. The others I haven't decided upon. I'll find one that won't look too youthful on my aged skeleton and put the rest away. Maybe I'll find something for old Luisa. But Falieri will certainly have some creation of her own to wear, something to show off her face. Good breeding forces me to invite her. Otherwise . . . ." She rolled her eyes expressively.

Over tea Allegra learned more of La Vecchia's childhood. It had been a lonely one, with an aging father demanding her attentions. "He was becoming senile, and I was a very young girl of thirteen. I had scarlet fever that year. It is amusing," she smiled, "everyone thought I would die of the disease. They put me to bed for weeks, and father decided that I was an invalid. He never quite believed I was healthy after that. It was a great event when a cousin was allowed to visit me. I was isolated and, of course, became a voracious reader. Nothing escaped my gaze. When father was napping I ran to the upstairs wings where I had my reading room—a tiny storage loft where I piled pillows next to the window.

"My mother was a gentle lady, but she was more interested in riding her horses on the Lido than in her small family. I suspected she had a lover. My thoughts were mature for my age, and I remember thinking that she must regret marrying papa and having me." La Vecchia closed her eyes and sighed. "But Leopoldo came to me, and soon my life was filled with real happiness. So much is written about foolish love, urgent emotions and consuming jealousies. Ours was none of this. I have had time to think about those beautiful years with Leo. It was as if we had always loved, not just in this lifetime—as if when we met, we were picking up a love that had begun long before, already tested and ripened. And you know, Allegra, we shall continue it again." La Vecchia's words stirred Allegra with a sense of hidden worlds.

"Fate is a friend," the old voice whispered, "although we don't always appreciate what it brings us. Now, I am weary. Damn old age! Tell Maria I wish to rest for a time." Her head dropped forward into sleep again, and Allegra slipped out, taking the beige gown with her to her room.

The rustling sound of the old fabric sent a little yearning sensation through her. And there was the fleeting odor of violets that seemed to come from the contact with her own body's warmth. It was too easy to fall into the mood of distorted time. The faint sound of cellos played in her mind, chamber music impressed into the atoms of these rooms, audible again for those who wished to hear.

Maria and Bianca were coming up the back stairs as Allegra

passed in the hall. Bianca dashed over to her, paying no attention to the ball gown. "We rescued all of my shells, Maria and I," she said. "Uncle Guido makes me angry sometimes."

"But he buys you beautiful things, too, don't forget," Maria soothed. "Now, to your room. You've burned your skin in the sun, and you must sleep while the salve works."

"Allegra! Allegra!" Bianca cried, resisting Maria. "Let me come to have supper with you. I don't want to eat in the kitchen tonight, and I don't want to see Aunt Lidia and Uncle Guido and everybody in the dining room. The priest always lectures me. Let's both have headaches like Contessa Falieri when she doesn't want to do something. Please!"

Allegra looked over the child's head to Maria's eyes. Maria nodded. It was all right. "I wasn't invited anyway, Bianca, so I won't need a headache," she smiled.

"Oh, that's just because *nonna* isn't coming downstairs for supper anymore. They think you are with her. I'll bring our trays up at seven tonight." She squeezed Allegra's hand and followed Maria off down the hallway.

The room was cool and silent and very welcoming when Allegra entered. She laid the gown on the coverlet of her bed and looked at it for a long moment, then shook herself free of the feeling it called up in her.

What could she do with the rest of the day? Such a glorious summer afternoon. Cloudless and hot. She should call on Eleana Bugelli, and she should shop for a thank-you gift for the whole family. Giorgio was probably feeling neglected, after giving his all as tour guide that first day, before she entered the world of the Ca'd'Argenti.

But a sudden picture of Clinton Meserve, so sincerely concerned with her safety, made her sit down at her elegant writing desk and pick up a pen and paper. She should have written when she first came here. Her pen poised for several minutes. She smiled at herself. What could she tell dear old conservative Clinton? "I'm living in a palazzo with a hundred-year-old *contessa* and her two unmarried grandsons. . . . I'm searching out my links to Lord Byron. . . . I'm falling deeper into the dreamworld of Venice and may never want to come home. . . . "

Instead, she wrote about art museums and the Bugellis, her opportunity to be companion to Bianca and her sweet aged great-grandmother, of the very respectable di Rienzi family. She enclosed a postcard photograph of the Piazza San Marco and sealed the envelope. *There, Clinton, you'll feel better about me knowing where I am,* she thought.

Allegra rested her head in her hands, looking out at the water traffic. So few gondolas amid the modern boats. The window was open enough to let in the complicated smells of the city, borne on warm bursts of air, and she began to doze.

Time passed in the warmth of the open window. Allegra woke drowsily to find it almost half past six. She rose and looked at herself in the mirror of the armoire. She looked very young and very American. Reflected behind her on the bed was the nineteenth-century ball gown. How was she going to wear it for La Vecchia's birthday and not look laughably out of place and time?

Bianca's insistent little voice chirped outside her door. She had a cart with supper for the two of them. They relished their food and talked about the grand birthday party. Bianca studied Allegra's gown and announced that her father was having Contessa Falieri's dressmaker design a Victorian child's gown for her. She didn't sound pleased. Allegra asked about La Vecchia's dressmaker.

"Oh," Bianca said, "contessa says that she doesn't know about style. But I don't care. I'd rather have *nonna*'s." She thrust her jaw forward. "Allegra, why is somebody always mad at somebody in my family? It isn't fair."

Allegra took her hand. "Every family has its problems, and they seem the most important and terrible of all. You have to make sure you are as helpful to everyone as possible and not add to the distress."

A loud knock sounded at the door. "It's me, Guido—are you decent?" His hand turned the latch as he spoke. "Everyone's having a good time downstairs. You should come and join us." His voice was a little too loud. Allegra knew he had been drinking.

"I don't feel up to a dinner party tonight," she said as gently and firmly as she could. "Bianca and I have just finished eating."

"But it's just for dessert—and they're all wondering where you are. . . ."

Allegra's suspicions were growing. Something in Guido's face and eyes was baiting her.

". . . Your friend Pietro Luigi Maria Mossanato is asking for you. He hasn't been able to get a conversation about Lord Byron all evening," he laughed. "Luisa, Aunt Lidia and Father Fiorenzo won't stop talking about the Holy Mother, and Mossanato is in a state. Come on, Allegra—get something pretty on and come down. I'll give you ten minutes, then I send your miniature Byron up after you." He wheeled about with another chuckle at his own wit, and closed the door behind him.

The air smelled heavily of wine and cigarettes. Allegra had no wish to join Guido and the others, except Signor Mossanato—the thought of his being merely an amusement to them made her change her mind.

"That's all right, Allegra," Bianca said, "I think you should go downstairs, too." Bianca sounded adult, a small version of a di Rienzi lady giving gracious leave. Allegra had to hide her smile.

"Thank you, *cara mia*. I'll just go for a while. Go to bed now, and we'll make plans tomorrow."

Guido's condescending tone almost made Allegra go downstairs dressed as she was, but she overcame her irritation and changed into her blue linen sheath and draped a white sweater over her shoulders. She could hear the voices of the dinner guests in the distance, as she descended the great curving stairway. She had not yet fully explored the palazzo and did not know where the dining room was, although she was sure it was somewhere beyond the main reception salon. Following the voices, she passed through the blue-and-gold salon.

"Signorina Brent," a solicitous voice spoke from a doorway to the garden. "This way. We are dining on the terrace." Signor Mossanato's immaculately dressed figure motioned to her. "How charming of you to come. How delightful." He pressed her hand to his lips with heartfelt sincerity. Allegra was happy to see her Regency scholar and friend. "You must tell me your feelings since seeing San Lazzaro. We were too soon interrupted by worldly problems that day to share our thoughts." Signor Mossanato talked as he steered her to the far end of the walled garden where torches were set into the ground and a summer canopy extended over a long dinner table.

In the flickering light Allegra could see six or seven people seated around the table. Guido stood at Allegra's approach—then the other men. She recognized Father Fiorenzo and the husband of Cousin Luisa. Aldo stood, too. She hadn't expected to see him here. Guido reintroduced Allegra to everyone and made a point of seating her next to Vera Falieri.

"Vera and Aldo dropped by for dessert. It seems to be fashionable. Where were you going tonight, *signore*?" Guido pressed at him.

Aldo answered in clipped words. "La Fenice. Pennario is playing Beethoven's Fourth."

"That's very fashionable, too."

Allegra was next to the priest on the other side. Signor Mossanato lost out in the seating arrangement and, looking thwarted, took his place next to Aunt Lidia.

"My dear," the priest's kind voice brought her attention away from Aldo and Vera. "You have done well, I hear from *la contessa*. I was afraid, that day we met, when all was pandemonium, that our family would be harsh wine for your young palate."

Allegra smiled at his perceptive face. "I am having to look at life and people from a different viewpoint, father. I know it's good for me." She felt Renaldo's eyes on her. "At least I keep telling myself it is!" she added.

"My dear child." Father Fiorenzo lowered his voice and put a comforting hand over hers. "I am always nearby if you need me. Don't forget that."

"*Signorina*," Vera Falieri's penetrating voice demanded her attention, "I hear you are a reliable nursemaid to the child. It was a great relief to Conte di Rienzi and me. The servant situation is so bad nowadays."

Guido leaned over from his seat across the table. "I'll bet Allegra has friends—attractive girls from America—who'd love to work for you, Vera."

"Fortunately, *bambino*, I shall not be concerned with my domestic problems for long. My *casa* is for sale." She bent her head toward Aldo's shoulder in a little possessive gesture.

Aldo was not pleased with the conversation. "Miss Brent is not a servant, Vera," he said stiffly, looking at his watch. "We can't wait for dessert any longer. The recital starts in a few minutes." He took Contessa Falieri's arm, almost pulling her from her chair.

"Aldo, my pet, what is the hurry?"

Guido grinned at her. "It's time to go, Vera. The master has spoken."

"Be at the office early tomorrow, Guido—if you can! Good evening, Miss Brent, father, everyone." Abruptly they left the garden. Vera's voice could be heard in wounded tones as they walked through the French doors and into the salon.

Allegra's intuition told her that the two brothers were building to a confrontation. Something more than Guido's insulting humor was working at Aldo's nerves.

Signor Mossanato quickly took the empty seat next to her. "Ah, it is more peaceful now," he said with obvious relief. "I have been waiting to tell you about the fine Byron exhibit in Athens next month. It is a celebration of his brave endeavors in the great uprising against the Turkish oppression. I fear it is in part a political exhibition, but, nonetheless, it should be an exciting display. I thought you might enjoy the event with another devotee of Byron." He looked hopefully at her.

"I would love to go, *signore,* you are very kind. But I really don't know if I will be in Venice a month from now. My situation is unsettled."

"Please, don't explain. There is no need. I shall plan to go myself, and I shall be in touch with you as time progresses. I do not wish to cause you distress, dear friend. The event begins on the eighteenth, and if you are still here—then I will enjoy it all the more." He leaned closer. "I have just this morning learned of the existence of a newly discovered item of Byron memorabilia here in Venice. Imagine it! The rare book dealers are all talking about it."

Allegra's heart jumped. It couldn't be . . . .

"A tiny Bible, not two inches square, and a handwritten dedication to Allegra on the first page. That was the name of his little love child by that Englishwoman, you recall. What a coincidence that you, too, were given that charming name," he said. "If I were a man of great wealth, I would take great pleasure in giving you that intriguing Bible, but alas . . . ."

She reached out to touch his hand, as much to steady herself as to thank him. Her heart was still beating fast. "What a generous thought, *signore,* but such a thing belongs with scholars and not with someone like me."

She wondered if the dedication to Allegra had really been intended for Allegra di Rienzi and never presented to her because of his sudden change of heart. Her mind was calculating the possibility. Byron's little child, Allegra, died at a very early age, not more than five or six. How likely was it that she would receive a book to read?

"I would like to see the Bible someday, though," she said to his expectant face.

"Indeed, and just think what else might be waiting to be discovered. I find it fascinating—fascinating. The life of Byron was such a tapestry of human emotions," he mused and gave her hand a final pat.

Dessert finally arrived, and conversation moved generally around the table. Guido was silently staring at his cognac glass, removing his usually heavy comments from the light chatter. Crickets were making a rhythmic counterpoint from under the geraniums, a warm light breeze moved the oleander flowers and a pleasant atmosphere settled at last over the fragrant garden.

CHAPTER TWELVE

THE NEXT MORNING Maria brought a note with the breakfast tray. A spidery decorative script requested Allegra's presence on the roof terrace in an hour. It was from La Vecchia.

Ruefully wondering what the next confrontation would be about, Allegra made her way to the roof garden. La Vecchia was alone, except for Maria. Her chair was drawn up to a table, and she was poring over scattered sheets of paper and notebooks. Her eyes were snapping and alert, vigorous again.

"Good, you're here." She motioned Allegra to the table. "I wish you to help me with this tiresome list of names. I have checked those who have accepted the invitation. There must be a good copy made. Can you do it?"

"Of course." Allegra picked up one of the sheets. "If there is a typewriter in the palazzo, I will make the lists very quickly for you."

"Use one of Aldo's. I will have one brought to the small study next to my sitting room." She reached among her cushions and drew out a leather-bound volume. Its flexible binding and gold leaf edging spoke of another century. "I thought you must have this, *bambina*. It is a reminiscence of Lord Byron done by a man who knew him here in Venice. It has not been translated from Italian, being a private printing, I believe. It shows your ancestor in a favorable light, a man of kindness."

Allegra accepted the book, and her throat tightened. The gift was deeply touching. "Thank you for believing," she said.

"For believing! How should I not believe the evidence of my own eyes and heart?" She looked sharply at Allegra. "It is Renaldo, is it not? Has he again made difficulties concerning your family legacy?"

Allegra denied that anything more had been said. "It's only that I *know* how he feels."

La Vecchia snorted. "Then it is that Guido. Pay no attention to what he says. You will have observed that one of his enjoyments is to stir up trouble and watch the results of it. Do not upset yourself, *cara*. How I wish Aldo would find a suitable wife to give him some joy in life again! This family! Two men, neither of them using the sense they should have. Guido, playing on the surface of life and stabbing out at anyone who tries to bring him to responsibility, and Aldo, carrying a load of bitterness, when he has superb talents and qualities. He walks under a cloud made by himself. Renaldo—the inheritor of the terrible pride of the di Rienzis. To act in such a way!" She stopped, breathing heavily.

A deep voice spoke over Allegra's shoulder. "Did I hear my name spoken by my respected grandmother?"

"People who steal silently upon conversations seldom hear good of themselves," La Vecchia said tartly.

Aldo smiled, but not with his eyes. His gaze swung to Allegra. "Bianca is crying for you. Luisa is having trouble. You were required to see to the child as first consideration!" His voice was hard.

Allegra, startled, stood quickly, and La Vecchia looked from one face to the other. The book was still in Allegra's hand, and his attention fell upon the title: *Un Recuerdo di Lord Byron*.

"Are you still perpetrating this Byron myth? I cannot understand why women are so attracted to a personality like that. Good Lord, he's been gone more than a century. I will not have Bianca's head filled with romantic trash."

La Vecchia held her silence, watching. Allegra's head came up, and she stared at him. A tiny smile flickered over La Vecchia's face and was gone.

"What do you know of Lord Byron?" Allegra flared at him. "He was a genius and much more than the stupid scandalmongers have painted him. This book—" she held it up "—tells of his compassionate actions and virtues. Why shouldn't I care? I have his blood!"

Aldo made a light derogatory sound. "Don't you think scholars would have found your missing link by now? If the material were authentic, it would have brought much money to your family, and someone would have put it into public knowledge. He himself would have told of your alleged ancestress in his journals. He never minded telling of his affairs!"

Allegra's voice was unsteady with hurt and frustration. She wanted to force him to back down. "The world didn't know about your great-great-grandmother because Byron respected her—even loved her. The women in my family have had compassion for her, and I cannot believe that a di Rienzi of this modern day would be so harsh and unfeeling about a woman of his own family."

Aldo's eyes glistened dangerously. "When a woman forgets her vows of marriage, she merits no respect. You are a sentimentalist."

"Enough!" La Vecchia's strong voice interrupted. She thumped her cane hard on the floor.

Allegra, her eyes filled with tears, turned and walked to the edge of the terrace, gazing blankly at the rooftops. She wanted to hurt him until he admitted he was wrong, but at the same time she was sorry. What was wrong with her? If Aldo were anyone else, she would not be standing here so completely off balance. She had never known a man like this one, who brought out these wrenching and frightening feelings from her.

In the dim background she heard La Vecchia's voice. "I gave the book to Allegra, and I will not have her tormented by you, Renaldo. If you would look without prejudice, you would see there is good evidence that the story is true. I give thanks to Allegra that she came to us with this knowledge and did not publish it to the world. She could have had both money and fame by exposing such an unknown facet of Byron's life. She has asked nothing of us, and she has been of real service to me and to Bianca. You have only to observe the child, which you seldom do, to see that she is happier. I am distressed with you, Renaldo. You do not remember the courtesies that are part of the duty of the *conte* of the house of di Rienzi!"

Allegra feared to turn around and would have liked to become invisible and slip away. There was silence for a few moments, then Aldo's deep voice spoke gently.

"*Nonna mia*—you speak truth to me, as always. What can I say? I must not vent my own problems on the innocent heads of those around me. Forgive me." He paused, and there was the light sound of a kiss.

"*Caro mio.*" La Vecchia's voice was full of love. "When will you look to see that despite all troubles, the world is full of gifts of joy? Now, I think Allegra needs some apology from you. Isn't that so?"

Allegra heard Aldo's steps come toward her. She forced herself to turn around. He stopped close to her, his expression grave but gentle. She saw his fine-drawn face, the pride of his bearing. His eyes were probing hers now, softened from the dark flashes that were usually in them. His intimate regard shook her.

"Will you forgive me, *cara* Allegra? Why is it that we always have distress, hmm? I have been ungrateful for the kindness you have done for us. You do a very good job here. Bianca is joyful, and one whom La Vecchia trusts I know to be good . . . even though I may speak rudely sometimes. You see before you a man beset by many things. This is not an excuse, Allegra. I ask your understanding." He reached for her hand, which rested on the balustrade, and holding her eyes with his, he touched her fingers with a soft kiss. A stab of excitement shot through her, and she lowered her eyes quickly, fearful that he would read her emotions.

"Of course; I understand. It is I who should ask forgiveness. When I return to the United States, it will be with the most grateful memories. I truly love Bianca and La Vecchia." She smiled a little sadly.

"If the story *is* true, my child, then you belong here with us, and our house is yours." La Vecchia spoke on a note of quiet fact. Allegra felt Aldo tighten suddenly, then he dropped her hand. Aldo returned his grandmother's gaze, but the sardonic twist was back on his lips.

"We dwell too much on bloodlines of the past," he said

abruptly. "Forgive me, Vecchia, and do not begin to lecture concerning the pedigree di Rienzi." He turned his eyes on Allegra. "And you, little romantic, I hope you will come out of your dream. There are no more Byrons today, thank God. This world is too wise for them."

Both women drew in their breath to speak at once, and he held up his hand, laughing at their faces. "Do not scratch me with your words, my ladies, I will leave you to your enjoyments." He turned away and went swiftly to the stairwell. He opened the door and looked back at them for a moment, then with a salute of his hand he was gone.

The two were silent for a while, their eyes on the closed door. Allegra heard a small stifled sound from La Vecchia. Her mobile thin face was drawn into a deep frown, and tears shone in the old eyes. She held Allegra's startled gaze, not attempting to cover her feelings.

In a rough voice she spoke, almost to herself. "Aldo! Aldo! For a moment I see him as he used to be, then he is back in his prison again. No man should hold to such a burden or should so punish himself for the stupidity of another. I have tried, Allegra *mia*, I have called on all the persuasion of my long years. But I cannot break this shell of pain. I thought that perhaps you . . . ." She broke off there. The old shrewd eyes held Allegra's, probing for response, then she sighed. "I dislike that Falieri woman intensely. She would ruin Aldo and make Bianca miserable, but each man brings his own suffering on himself, and who am I to interfere?"

Allegra nodded some kind of assent. La Vecchia's words had unlocked a whole Pandora's box of thought, and a terrible truth was growing in her: She *did* want Aldo's attention. She *did* want to see that look again in his eyes, as when he kissed her hand. His presence excited her, and when the door closed and he went away, part of her joy went also. *I cannot be in love with him—I cannot!* She almost said it aloud. She found La Vecchia watching her with an oddly knowing look.

"You had better find Bianca, my dear, if she is giving trouble.

Later in the day we will discuss these lists for the ball." She closed her big address book with finality. "Ring for Luigi. The bell by the door there. I wish to return to my rooms."

Allegra left, her mind still in turmoil. Instead of looking for Bianca, she went quickly to her room and shut the door as if to find sanctuary. She sat on the edge of the luxurious bed, feeling sick inside. Maybe she should return to the Bugellis, she thought. Leave Venice. She tried to blot out Renaldo, to be the person she was before she met him. But the ball! To leave now was unthinkable. She sat straighter. She would have to avoid him as much as she could and keep busy. After the ball she would be free. She smiled wryly. Free to carry a burden of remembrance for the rest of her life, like the first Allegra.

She went in search of Bianca, and moments later they were walking to the pizzeria to have lunch. They spent the early afternoon exploring the church of Santa Maria della Salute, then walked around the point of the Dogana, the old customhouse, and looked up at its golden weather vane. It was nearly three o'clock when they returned to the Ca'.

Bianca scampered off with Luigi for a cool drink in the kitchen. Allegra felt better now; her body was pleasantly tired; she had walked miles, and her mind had been able to remove itself from its darker contemplations. She climbed the great stairway, intending to offer her services to La Vecchia. As she neared the *contessa*'s rooms, she heard raised voices coming from within the partly open doors. She hesitated, reluctant to enter into the commotion, and peered quickly into the room. La Vecchia's sharp eyes saw her.

"Come in, my child. You will not be against me as are all these others!"

Allegra wished with all her mind to retreat, but the old woman's challenging face was turned to her. Father Fiorenzo, cousins Luisa and Barretto, Maria and someone obviously a doctor, stood around the embattled figure in her elaborate chair. Allegra shrank inwardly from the many eyes that watched her entrance. La Vecchia's cheeks had spots of crimson on them. The doctor stepped forward. He was a smooth man of middle height with waves of silver hair at his temples. He had the reassuring presence of the professional, along with a cultivated charisma of his own. His voice was mellow.

"*Signorina*, I am Dr. Andrea Nepi. Since you are a friend of *la contessa*, I plead with you to dissuade her from the plan she is making. I cannot be responsible for her health under these circumstances."

Cousin Luisa broke into speech on high nervous notes, her hands making wringing motions. "It is terrible, terrible. She cannot stand it. And just before the ball, Holy Mary! Signorina Brent, tell her it must not be." She turned to La Vecchia: "Don't you want to enjoy your one hundredth birthday?"

Barretto echoed her with, "*Si*, Vecchia, do not be foolish. Listen to reason!"

"Silence!" La Vecchia's voice was loud and angry. Cousin Luisa burst into tears and Maria began to sob in sympathy from behind the thronelike chair.

"Peace! Peace!" Father Fiorenzo implored over the weeping.

Allegra had been able to say nothing in the uproar. She looked at the assembled faces. "What is the matter? What is the plan that is so upsetting?"

Father Fiorenzo answered. "Contessa Amalia wants to go to the farm at La Mira for an overnight visit and *festa*. It is felt by us all that such an effort would be too strenuous for her. She has not been as far as the farm for more than fifteen years. And a *festa* such as she remembers from her youth is not a simple request. It would take weeks to arrange a thing like that."

Allegra's eyes met La Vecchia's. The autocratic old face wore a bright look of willfulness and mischievous delight. "It has come to a pretty pass when my own flesh and blood will not do as I say anymore. Allegra, I want you to help me—order my gondola and some others. We will all go. Stefano will help Luigi as gondolier."

Father Fiorenzo moved toward her. "But, my dear, he is dead twenty years."

La Vecchia stared him down. "Well, no matter. Get somebody. I am going!"

Dr. Nepi leaned over her chair and took one of her hands in his.

He kissed its fingers, gazing into her eyes to exert all of his practiced masculine energy. "*Madonna,* I pray you, for all of us who love you—do not risk this thing. I ask it for our friendship."

Her face crinkled into a shrewd expression. "I am too old for my pulses to leap, Andrea. You will not soften me this way. You may not remember, but I do, how your mother changed your diapers when we visited together in this very room. God rest her dear soul." Dr. Nepi drew back, deflated, and La Vecchia clucked to herself. "Well, Allegra, what do you say to this problem? Is it too much to ask, to see my beloved childhood home once more? It is only at Mira, not more than twenty miles away, and what used to take a day to reach can now be covered in hours."

Allegra found herself in the center of the ring of anxious and angry eyes again. She had to speak. There was no escape. She looked directly into La Vecchia's face. "*Signora,* I have known you only a short time, but I do not think you have lived so long by being foolish." Smiles were growing on some faces, and the old woman's was drawing into a frown. "But I would trust your judgment concerning yourself. If you want very strongly to renew your memories at Mira, and you feel able in yourself to go, then I believe you should do so. We must do in life what is good, not only for the body, but for the soul."

A quiet voice spoke from the doorway. "I agree with Signorina Brent." Renaldo came forward into the room. La Vecchia's face broke into a charming smile. For a moment the shadow of the youthful Amalia was there.

"It will be arranged, then." Her voice had a lilt. "Now, I want some peace. This discussion has exhausted me far more than any trip to La Mira could possibly do. I will speak of the ball with you later, Allegra *mia.* I knew you would not fail me."

Allegra edged toward the door, intent on leaving. She was not sure she had done right, but she had been honest, at least.

Renaldo leaned to kiss his grandmother's cheek, and for a moment she raised her hands to his face and held him close. Cousin Luisa sniffed and left the room with Barretto. Father Fiorenzo patted La Vecchia's hand with a humoring smile, and Aldo turned to Dr. Nepi: "I want to speak with you." They left the old woman sitting in tired triumph.

As Allegra went through the door, Renaldo detained her by a hand on her arm, which made her nerves quiver. *Now* what did he want? "I want you to help plan this excursion," he said. "Please come to my office in an hour . . . and I agree with you, it is necessary sometimes to be considering the needs of the spirit." His smile was gentle as he turned to Dr. Nepi. "Come, Andrea, we will have a taste of a special Lacrima Cristi I have recently found." He steered the doctor toward the staircase.

Allegra stood, astonished, watching his straight back move down the stairs. He had commended her!

CHAPTER THIRTEEN

HESITANTLY, ALLEGRA TAPPED on the heavy door of Aldo's office. She half wished that he would not be there, but he answered, and she went in. He was seated at his big desk surrounded by piles of papers, some of them blueprints. He rose and motioned her to a chair and then sat down again. Her hands were cold.

"Forgive me if I finish this letter," Aldo said. "It will only be a moment." He turned back to a typewriter on the side of the desk and began to type haltingly. Allegra's fingers itched to take over for him, but she sat quietly, holding herself in calmness, glad that he was busy. Deliberately, she examined a large golden glass swan, a triumph of the glassblowers' art, on a table nearby.

His voice startled her from her thoughts. "So, you like my swan, hmm? It was a gift from one of the artisans on Murano, the island of the glass. You must go there one day soon. No one comes to Venice without a visit there."

She replied with an easiness that surprised her. They spoke for a while about the ancient art of glassblowing, so dear to Venice. Then Aldo held her eyes with his. "I want to thank you for your help to my grandmother. I do see more than you might suppose, and I realize that you are honestly her friend. Shall we call a truce, Miss Allegra Brent?" He was smiling with an openness that was hard to fault.

She laughed softly. "If you remember, my own grandmother was Italian, and La Vecchia fills an empty place in my heart." She looked directly at him.

Renaldo smiled again. "You will not be persecuted by me any longer. But you can understand my necessity, as head of this house, to protect La Vecchia." He leaned back in his chair. "So, now, we have this excursion to La Mira," he chuckled. "I have not seen La Vecchia as interested in things for a long time. It is come close, light upon your hand for an instant but quiver to fly away at the least movement.''

He rose, as did she, and walked her courteously to the door. His hand held the knob and she waited for it to open, eyes resolutely on its dark oak surface. Instead, fingers came gently under her chin to turn her face up to his. She mustered her resources and met his brilliant gaze quietly. ''Has it been only a week since you came here?'' He spoke very low. ''What surprises fate brings.'' He dropped his hand and opened the door. ''At eight o'clock, then.''

Allegra heard the door close behind her. She stood bemused, and then Bianca ran toward her, full of a child's urgent talk.

AT EIGHT O'CLOCK Allegra knocked on the door of Renaldo's study. She found him looking distractedly through a sea of papers on his desk.

''These are proposals of designs—packaging ideas for a number of products, as you will see. I will be showing them to an international design conference in Florence next week,'' he said, waving an impatient hand over the various piles. ''Each proposal must be a separate unit, including the descriptions, sketches and recommendations for each.'' He made an attempt at sorting the papers a little, before he handed them to her. It took only a moment for her to see that they fitted together easily in sequence, and she quickly began to arrange them.

A change moved over his tired face as he watched her practiced hands at work. ''Good, good. I see that you know what to do. I have put the typewriter on the small table, and there is a good chair. I will revise and hand you the sheets for copy.'' She returned his smile as impersonally, a little relieved that the intensity of the afternoon had faded, and yet wishing that the cool business voice would hold a more intimate timbre.

He raised his eyes to the ceiling. ''Thank you, God. You have sent me a secretary in the midst of my household.'' The mock solemnity over, he pushed his chair closer to the desk and began a swift editing with a gold pen drawn from his jacket pocket.

She worked steadily. Sometimes, to find something, it was necessary to move close to him, but he remained attentive to his papers. *He does not feel anything,* she told herself, and instantly regretted the silly thought. The proposals were soon in a neat pile back on his desk. She picked up several of his corrected pages and went to the typewriter. He raised his eyes, surveyed his orderly desk and went on with his work.

Several hours passed in silence, except for the noise of keys, the rustle of paper and an occasional word of query or explanation. Allegra felt a sense of companionship. Her back began to tire, and unconsciously, she dropped her hands for a moment and stretched the stiff muscles. Immediately his voice spoke to her.

"Forgive me—I have been selfish. It is past eleven o'clock, and you are weary." He strolled over to her, picking up a page from her pile of finished manuscripts and reading it. "You work well and fast. After you have made arrangements for La Vecchia's outing, could you give me as many hours tomorrow as you can? Do you take dictation? There is needed correspondence, also."

Allegra agreed to work. "But what of Bianca?"

"I will send her for the day to her cousin's," he said briefly and turned back to his desk. Allegra quickly covered the machine and set the papers straight. She turned toward the door, her feet making no sound in the deep pile of the carpet. But his voice followed her.

"Sleep well, Allegra. Good night."

She saw him studying her. "Good night," she said. Her nerves were starting again. She wanted to get to the shelter of her room. And what would she do there, she asked herself, as she mounted the great curving stairway—weep or dream? Or maybe both. "Why did I have to come to Venice?" she whispered, "I should have left the di Rienzis in peace, and myself, too."

The next morning Allegra rose early to do the tasks for the trip to La Mira. Constanza, the old cook, immediately began to plan. Maria and Luigi brought huge basket hampers down from the attics. At Allegra's suggestion, Luigi contacted Giovanni Fancelli.

The cheerful little man was soon at the side entrance to the Ca',
promising his own and other gondolas for the great occasion.

"It will be good to see *la contessa* in her gondola again.
She goes out so seldom now. So—she will be soon one hundred!"
He pursed his lips and blew an admiring breath. "When I think of
the history she has seen, I envy her. But I don't know if I would
want to have so many years. The sorrows grow more numerous
than the joys as time passes." He looked intently at Allegra.
"And you, *signorina,* I think Venice has changed you. You are
more lovely. But your eyes are weary. Are you sure that all is well
with you? Have you seen the Bugellis? They ask after you."

She looked into his perceptive face. "I am all right, but it is
good to have friends. I must see the Bugellis as soon as we get
back from La Mira. Please give them my love."

Giovanni nodded and promised to have all in readiness Sunday
morning. Bianca was sent off, protesting, to her cousin's, and
Allegra went to see La Vecchia before beginning her work with
Renaldo. She found the old lady trying to choose her wardrobe
for the great adventure. Maria threw up her hands despairingly
behind the *contessa*'s back, while La Vecchia sorted through a
jewelry box on her lap.

Pearls, very large and yellow from age, spilled from her fingers.
Clusters of garnets sparkling from pins, bracelets and earrings
were held up for Allegra's inspection. "And what will you wear,
bambina?"

"I have my blue suit—a present from my own *nonna*," she
smiled.

"That is very well for the trip. But what of the evening? There
will be dancing. You will need a dress—have you no evening dress
with you, child?"

Allegra shook her head, smiling. "I didn't expect to need one
on this trip."

La Vecchia's face brightened. "Maria, do you remember the
costumes that Marcella Toroni stored in the upper hall
wardrobe?" She explained: "Marcella is a second cousin on the

side of Renaldo's mother; she is a specialist in folk dancing. A year ago there was a dance conference on Torcello. She brought several dancers from Perugia, and after the conference she asked to store the costumes, as she had exhausted her apartment storage space. There may be something suitable there. Go to see, Maria, quickly!"

Allegra was not sure what to do. She didn't want to appear at the *festa* in costume and draw attention to herself, but how could she refuse La Vecchia? Maria returned, her arms full of billowing skirts.

"Ah . . . spread them out . . . let us see."

Maria began to hold up costumes, some of them very elaborate, full of rich embroidery on velvet. Allegra was grateful, when the old *contessa* shook her head. "No—no—not those. Those would overpower our sweet child. What is that?" She prodded with her cane at the bottom of the pile, pointing to a ruffle of dark green silk. Maria pulled it out, a softly flared skirt with a wide ruffle at the hem. "Good—now there must be a blouse." Maria plunged into the stock of colored fabrics. She looked up in triumph. In her hand was a sheer confection of a blouse, with rounded neckline and full sleeves caught at the wrists. It was the gentlest light green with tiny embroidery of the same dark color as the skirt around the neckline and cuffs. A wide matching sash was fringed with tassels. Altogether it was a beautiful dress, there was no other word.

"Hold it up to her, Maria." La Vecchia laughed like a girl and Maria was grinning. "Put it on, child." Allegra couldn't refuse. Maria helped her out of her own clothes and into the dress. It fitted well.

La Vecchia clapped her hands. "Lovely, quite lovely. You are like a green tree nymph. Wait until you are seen in this. The Falieri would look scrawny in it. But you, *cara*—ah!" She broke off her words as if she had suddenly recalled something, then rummaged again in her big jewelry box and looked up sharply at Maria. "I cannot find my favorite amethysts—they, too, are gone!" She seemed to stop herself and muttered, "No matter—these will do." She drew forth a tangled handful of finely woven gold chain. Two large baroque pearls were strung just above the tasseled ends of the chain. La Vecchia held it out.

"Put it on, child."

"No. Please, I might lose it. It is too valuable."

"Nonsense. I say put it on. The neckline needs exactly that." Allegra put it on. The pearls were cool and heavy against her skin.

"Open the mirror, Maria."

Allegra saw herself with wonder in the carved standing mirror. A speculative look came over La Vecchia's face. "Hold up your hair. Pull it up to the top of your head. *Si*. Good."

Maria spoke breathlessly, "*Mamma mia*. It is like . . . ." La Vecchia hushed her with a glance, and her voice trailed off.

"So. You have your dancing dress, *bambina*. It shall be freshened and pressed. Take the necklace with you. I want to see you wear it, and I shall be angry if you do not!" She began to tire. "Enough for now, Maria. We shall decide on my packing after I have rested."

Allegra changed back to her own clothes, wondering what Aldo would think of all this, while he was slaving in his study with no help. She was nearly an hour later than she had intended to be.

La Vecchia waved away her thanks. "It is my pleasure. Would you deny an old woman her toys?" she chuckled. "Run along to Aldo now. He told me how relieved he was, and what fine work you have done. It will have done him good to wait." She was already falling asleep as Allegra left the room.

She ran downstairs with a sense of elation. She had looked almost beautiful in the green *festa* dress. As she knocked and entered Aldo's study she realized that she still wore the gold-and-pearl chain.

Renaldo looked up, frowning slightly. His eyes fastened on the necklace. Allegra flushed and felt a need to explain.

"Your grandmother has lent it to me for the evening of the *festa*."

"I thought I recognized it. My grandfather Leopoldo gave it to her when my father was born." He looked at her intently. "*La nonna* grows very fond of you. Do not let her become foolish." His voice was cool. "Old people often are too generous with strangers."

Allegra felt as if he had struck her. "I did not want to wear it, but she insisted. She was so happy, planning. . . . I will have Maria put it back with her jewels later in the day. She most probably won't remember." *What a horrid thing for him to say,* she bristled. Her fingers hurried to remove the necklace.

Renaldo's face lessened its severity. "No, she will remember. You must wear it. Now, shall we get to work, hmm?" He indicated a pile of papers by the typewriter. Allegra found his tone patronizing, but she took her seat. She wished she had never seen the green dress. But she was caught between her caring for the *contessa* and her growing desire to leave the di Rienzi family to its accustomed arrogance. Was Aldo just a carbon copy of his ancestor Barretto? She was more and more in sympathy with Allegra di Rienzi's feelings, as she contemplated leaving her husband those long years ago.

After a while he asked her to take dictation. It was as if there had been no problem. He was courteous and considerate. A light lunch was brought in by Luigi, and they continued to work. By four o'clock Allegra was exhausted. Renaldo released her with repeated thanks. He walked with her to the door, and once more the warm look was in his eyes.

"Forgive me, my dear," he said in a voice filled with feeling. "I am a man who has learnéd not to trust life. But I must learn that there is also goodness, eh?"

Allegra went to rest. Confusion compounded what was already in her heart. She had dinner in her room with Bianca. Afterward, Guido passed her in the hall, dressed for an evening out. He greeted her loudly. "Well, Allegra, I hear you are slaving for the big man. Watch out, or he will turn you into an animated typewriter." He preened his silk tie and pulled his well-cut jacket into even finer adjustment. "I'm off on a date with a real beauty. You look tired. All work and no play makes a girl dull. But maybe I'll take you to dinner sometime. If I'm not busy, that is. *Ciao.*" He strode off down the hall without waiting for a reply.

Allegra had to smile. Poor Guido. She had heard nothing more from La Vecchia during the evening. Wearily, she went to bed, trying not to wonder where Aldo was dining or with whom he was spending his evening.

CHAPTER FOURTEEN

THE DAY BEFORE the great excursion Maria brought in the green dress, fresh and beautiful. Allegra observed it as she ate her breakfast tray. Her mood was gray, although the light sparkled into her room from the bright day outside. If she had to go to this *festa*, she wished it could be as a small bird watching unnoticed from some tree.

Bianca interrupted her dour thoughts. "Oh, Allegra, will you wear this?" She ran over to the green dress. "How pretty! Wait till you see the *festa* dress that my *nonna* has given me! But Maria is too busy to pack for me . . . you'll have to help me, and tomorrow before Mass you must fix my hair with ribbons."

The child was glowing with excitement, and they spent much of the day together. Allegra wanted to give Bianca a feeling that she was able to help with the planning of the country celebration, and didn't have to be merely an impediment to the work of the adults. The house itself was noisy with footsteps, sounds of unusual activity, a sense of anticipation.

As Allegra was returning at last to her room, the doors of La Vecchia's suite flew open, and Luigi came out, looking harassed. La Vecchia's voice followed him: "Imbecile! No one ever does as I ask. Just a pack of fools! Maria, can't you do anything right, either?" Luigi made a gesture of resignation as he passed.

Allegra peered cautiously into the room and caught the full force of the belligerent old eyes; then the *contessa*'s face miraculously smoothed itself. "Ah, Allegra, you have packed for Bianca—good." Clothes were strewed about on chairs. Maria, holding a hairbrush, was trying to work with the gray waves of hair. She smiled ruefully from a position behind the *contessa*. A big old portmanteau was open on a table, some clothes packed into it. Allegra talked of the details of the arrangements for a while and left to check on things downstairs. She found the staff eating lunch in the kitchen. She was amazed at the fine food old Constanza the cook was able to prepare from a kitchen that had a minimum of modern equipment. There were trays of delicacies waiting to go into the wicker hampers.

A bell rang insistently, and one of the younger servants ran to the summons from upstairs. The others smiled indulgently. They did not seem dismayed that La Vecchia was in her most truculent mood.

Satisfied that all was as it should be, Allegra approached the door of Renaldo's study. It was slightly ajar. She tapped and there was silence; he was not there, only a great pile of new papers on his desk. On top was the gold pen. She picked it up and on impulse held it to her cheek.

She saw there was much more corrected work. So, he must have worked late last night without calling her. Her heart ached suddenly. She felt impelled to help him, but a part of her hesitated, afraid to intrude and then be criticized. She sat down to type anyway and worked for several hours, forgetting lunch, until she finished. She was alert for the sound of his footsteps, but he didn't come.

She went upstairs to have tea with Bianca. La Vecchia was not seeing anyone for the rest of the day. By evening, after seeing that Bianca was occupied and had had her dinner, Allegra was suddenly very tired. At her request, Maria brought her a small bowl of soup and a salad.

Allegra stood a long time at the window, watching the restless waters lapping against the ancient stones of the building, and the dusk colors deepening into night. All was quiet on this side canal, but sounds blew on the breeze, carrying the energy of the active world. She felt very far away from the world that she knew.

ONE OF THE MAIDS woke her at seven o'clock with breakfast. "In a half hour in the chapel for Mass, *signorina*," she said. Allegra ate and dressed quickly. She went to tie Bianca's hair, but the child could hardly stay still for a moment, wriggling with delight in her sailor dress. She looked like a painting in her white pleated skirt and red middy blouse.

Allegra had not been to the chapel before, and Bianca happily showed her the way. The others came from various areas of the house. Renaldo accompanied his grandmother, who was dressed in a light blue suit cut in princess line, its ankle-length skirt brushing her soft blue suede short boots. Hidden in the folds of the ruffled white blouse, a sapphire set with tiny seed pearls sent out sparkles of azure. A blue pillbox hat was on her head, with a chiffon veil, which could be tied to protect the throat. She wore discreet makeup, and her eyes were snapping with controlled excitement. She seemed to have shed years, and her smile was so wide it was almost a grin.

Aldo was not relaxed this morning and had the look of a man with a thousand problems on his mind. He said nothing to acknowledge Allegra's work. She tried to ignore him and notice other things.

Luigi was dressed in a version of the di Rienzi livery, and Maria looked demure in her full-skirted uniform. Guido was jaunty and carefree in white with a nautical white blazer. Cousins Luisa and Barretto bore expressions of disapproval but were brave in casual clothes for the occasion.

Father Fiorenzo was waiting. Allegra and Bianca sat down on one of the old polished wooden seats, while La Vecchia and Aldo took their places in carved chairs in the front. Allegra's eyes moved around the chapel to the paintings and mosaics. It was a small gem of a place. There was a San Sebastiano in an alcove, mourned over by chubby angels—it could be a Tiepolo—and a Holy Family that had the colors of Veronese. A dark Titian *Ascension* over the altar set her mind to wondering if these paintings were the secret pride of the di Rienzis, unknown to the world of art.

After the Mass, and well blessed, they gathered in the great entrance hall. La Vecchia's harsh old voice was barking orders, until Aldo unceremoniously picked her up in his arms and strode through the open entrance door. Luigi was holding the black family gondola close to the water stairs. He had put fresh pink roses in the silver vase at the prow.

Aldo deposited La Vecchia on one of the red velvet seats and motioned Allegra to sit next to her, where the *contessa* was already patting the cushions for her. Maria skipped into the boat after her, carrying a large basket, and sat on a floor cushion, while Aldo and Bianca settled on the small side seats.

Allegra looked back and saw Giovanni grinning from his gondola. He gave a quick salute. Luisa and Barretto were riding with him, and Dr. Nepi and Father Fiorenzo. A third gondola was piled high with the hampers and suitcases.

The silver lion on the door seemed to grin, as the doors were pulled shut by the staff left behind.

La Vecchia's eyes were alert. "I will see it once more, all of it," she whispered to Allegra. "It is the long way and hard to row, but Luigi's back must bend to my will today."

They moved past the old palaces, whose shuttered windows held their secrets, and came into the area of the Rialto Bridge. The traffic was brisk, but as though on a signal, the motorboats and gondolas moved aside, and the di Rienzi boats went in a majestic flotilla along the Grand Canal.

Voices began to rise from the walkways and the gondolas. *"Brava! Brava, Vecchia!"* A shining white police launch came alongside, and one officer leaned perilously across to hand Aldo a bouquet of roses for La Vecchia. More voices joined the greetings. *Gondolieri* sang out, "Good luck, be happy, our Vecchia!" They doffed their wide-brimmed hats and blew her kisses. A folk tune lilted like the sparkles on the water. The song followed their progress as they moved, new voices taking it up when others stopped. Allegra had never seen such a spontaneous outpouring of loving pride.

La Vecchia sat holding her roses and waving her gloved hand from side to side. She was smiling and beautiful, her face lighted by joy, and yet tears were streaming down her cheeks. Allegra's own throat grew tight. She saw that Luigi and Maria wept, and a suspicious moisture shone under the darkness of Aldo's lashes.

Bianca jumped from her seat, waving excitedly, "She is my *non-na*! She is my *nonna*!" The childish voice broke the spell, and kindly laughter echoed back and forth across the canal.

The procession moved like the progress of some medieval Venetian princess. The greetings continued, but the intensity of emotion declined, and La Vecchia deigned to accept a large linen handkerchief from Maria. By the time they reached the area of the railway station, normalcy had been restored. They drew stares from the tourists at the station water steps. Cameras clicked frantically, as La Vecchia and her roses swept past. Luigi exercised his oar with dramatic dignity. He surged the gondola ahead and out into the smooth water of the Lagoon, then started the trip across to the mainland not far away. They could see traffic on the long auto bridge to their right. Factories and smokestacks stretched out along the shore.

La Vecchia had been silent until now. In a pained voice she said, "How they have ruined Mestre. *Dio mio*—and look at the waters here—it is terrible!" Smoke from the factories hung in the blue sky. The water around them was dirty. La Vecchia brought her hands up to cover her eyes. There were tears, and the coquettish blue hat held pathos. Aldo's face was filled with sympathy.

Suddenly, a motorboat at full throttle came skimming toward them. It seemed to be bearing down on them with no intent to turn aside. Luigi and Giovanni and the other boatman began to shout, and Luisa screamed. Bianca climbed over Maria to hide her head against Allegra. Aldo gripped the side of the gondola, until his knuckles showed white. He was furious. The boat swerved away at the last minute into a wide curve, leaving a jarring wake. Allegra had seen the grinning face of the driver and recognized the di Rienzi motorboat. Guido was at the wheel.

"Son of the devil!" Giovanni shook his fist at the noisy craft, as it roared past them. With a wave, Guido circled again and pulled to a slower pace somewhat away from the other boats. He smiled blandly back at the angry faces in the gondolas.

Renaldo spoke loudly. "Get that launch out of here immediately. How dare you upset her in this way? Have you lost your mind?"

Guido gunned his motor and turned away from them. "Nobody in this family has any sense of humor!" he yelled back.

They were all quiet for a time, while Luigi poled steadily shoreward. La Vecchia put a hand out to touch Renaldo's shoulder.

"*Caro mio,* let us ignore him. I wish to enjoy, and I wish not to see that frown on your poor face, for I wish you to enjoy also."

Renaldo took her hand and held it to his cheek. "It is his supreme lack of consideration for you or for anyone," he said grimly. Then he released his anger and smiled at her. "We are nearly to the landing."

ALDO CARRIED HIS GRANDMOTHER EFFORTLESSLY along the small dock, as Maria hurried ahead to unfold a portable wheelchair. He saw her settled comfortably and turned back to supervise the unloading. Luigi strode across a road toward a parking area for cars. Dr. Nepi attempted to ask his patient if she was all right and was waved away like a buzzing fly. Allegra stood silently next to the *contessa,* letting her shadow shield the old head from the direct sun. La Vecchia's eyes had the distant, fixed look of remembering.

Giovanni walked swiftly up to La Vecchia and bowed gravely to her. "May I wish you joy for your trip, *Eccellenza,* and for you also, Signorina Allegra."

La Vecchia smiled. "Do you know this gentleman, Allegra *mia*?"

"May I introduce Giovanni Fancelli, a cousin of the Bugelli family, with whom I first stayed in Venice."

"Ahh. So that is it!" She looked intently at him. "Our young relative has told me that you and your family were very kind to her. I am grateful."

Giovanni swung a startled glance at Allegra, who was silent in surprise herself. La Vecchia held out her elegant blue-gloved hand to Giovanni, who took it with innate Italian grace and kissed it like a courtier.

"I wish you well, *Eccellenza*, Signorina Allegra. I will meet you when you return." He bounded off with a wave.

Allegra was disturbed. How would Renaldo like his grandmother's public acknowledgment of her as a di Rienzi relative? Surely Giovanni would not be silent over such a tidbit of news.

CHAPTER FIFTEEN

RENALDO DI RIENZI was impatiently scanning the roadway, his hand resting on the pyramid of luggage, just as the motor caravan came into sight and started to form a line at the dockside. The large Venice parking garage was not far away.

A Rolls-Royce limousine of stately age, its black body gleaming with polish, stopped smoothly. Luigi was driving. Guido smiled innocently at everyone from behind the wheel of a Mercedes sedan, and a hired driver brought up a Fiat station wagon at the end of the line.

Guido moved to lift La Vecchia into the Rolls as Maria prepared a place in the car, and between them they settled her with pillows at feet and back. Allegra entered next, at Aldo's insistence, then Maria and Bianca pulled down the jump seats for themselves.

Luggage was being strapped onto the top of the Mercedes and into the station wagon. Father Fiorenzo went in Guido's car, choosing to sit in front next to him, obviously in preparation for a leisurely lecture on courtesy. Guido had not helped with any of the loading and sat playing with the car radio, adding to the disorder of the moment.

La Vecchia dozed lightly with her head against the white leather cushioned upholstery. Aldo sat in front with Luigi; he rolled down the partition between front and back.

As the car started to move, La Vecchia opened her eyes. "Things are going well so far, Aldo, *caro mio*. Thank you for your efforts for me. I do hope Father Fiorenzo has some well-chosen words for your brother, having to do with the sensitivities of frail, elderly ladies!" Aldo caught the smile on Allegra's lips, and his own lips moved slightly in response.

The narrow roads wound gently through farm country. Fields of green corn ripened in the sun. Old square two-story farmhouses sat in the midst of fields of grapes, which grew on supports strung between espaliered pear trees. Through villages and deeper into a green countryside they drove, where canals flowed between wild-flowered banks.

La Vecchia seemed to absorb the scenes around her. Allegra sensed her hunger to take in this experience, maybe the last time she would be able to travel over her beloved land. Allegra looked gratefully at Aldo's straight back in the seat ahead. He had made this happiness possible at a sacrifice of his own priorities.

As they entered a tiny village, La Vecchia spoke up in a loud voice. "Aldo, I wish to stop!" Luigi slowed the car. "There," the thin old hand pointed. "I remember that place. See the tables under the grape arbor. When I was first married, we had wine there, Leopoldo and I. The wine was very special. I want to taste it again!"

Aldo smiled, and Luigi stopped beside the small *trattoria*. An ancient arbor held up an equally ancient grapevine, whose gnarled stems twined around decaying posts, now supported with makeshifts of pipe and wire. Some workmen sat at one of the dusty arbor tables, with a carafe of wine and steaming plates of pasta.

The rest of the caravan had halted, and the doctor hurried to the limousine to see if La Vecchia was in need. She smiled sardonically at his anxious face, peering in at the car window. "Do not bury me yet, Andrea. I only want a small glass of wine."

"But you can have a good wine from your own hampers," he protested.

"I want the wine from this place, and I do not need to explain why!" He withdrew his head from the window, shrugging his shoulders, and went back to the other car. Aldo followed him. There was much talking and moving of heads among the rest of the party.

"This is ridiculous!" La Vecchia exploded. "Allegra, go and see what is happening. I don't want to sit here forever. Tell Aldo to get wine for everyone . . . quickly!"

Bianca jumped from the car and ran up to her father. "Papa, *nonna* wants everybody to have wine, quickly!" Allegra was close behind her.

Aldo hesitated and looked at his watch, then shrugged his shoulders. "Very well. Allegra, will you see what can be done?"

She went into the weathered old building, with Bianca at her heels, to talk to the proprietor. He was impressed, but dignified. He hastily assembled a tray with glasses and a bottle and came outside to serve his wine.

Aldo and the others were standing near the limousine. La Vecchia was served first with much bowing, then the rest of the party. The old lady sat back satisfied, sipping at the wine with her eyes closed in thought, taking her time. Guido was restrained by Aldo from urging her to hurry, and at last she handed out her empty glass. Aldo went inside with Allegra to settle the bill. Bright old eyes watched them as they returned to the car and took their places.

"You make a handsome couple," the *contessa* said. No one replied. "Renaldo," she growled, "have you lost all Italian manners? Allegra is young and pretty—do you forget the duty of a man to make her feel glad of her womanhood?"

Aldo looked back. "I agree that Allegra is very pretty, but why should I flatter her? I had thought her more sensible."

Allegra felt her face grow hot. "Humph!" La Vecchia grunted, by way of ending the matter. She was soon dozing, and the car started back to the roadway. Renaldo held a low-voiced conversation with Luigi, but more than once she saw his eyes on her in the rearview mirror.

The countryside was in full color, and Palladian villas showed themselves in fleeting glimpses from behind high hedges. Luigi slowed his pace and turned off onto a side road. As though she had slept with one eye open, La Vecchia woke up and demanded that Maria fix her hair and hat. They wound up a low hill and came to a long iron fence with tall pillars flanking a great gate. Benevolent stone griffins sat supporting the di Rienzi shield atop the gateposts. The intricate lacework in the iron made beautiful patterns against the deep sky.

Luigi stopped the car. He was poised to honk the horn, when an elderly man rushed to the gate from inside. He moved briskly even though his back was a little bowed, but his shoulders were broad and his white head vigorously erect. He quickly worked the lock at the gates and swung them open with a flourish. Other figures were hurrying along the inner road, but the old man drew attention to himself by his very presence.

He was dressed in a dark corduroy suit with brass buttons, and his white shirt was as snowy as his hair. Still standing in the center of the gateway, he made a beckoning movement, and a child ran out to give him a long-stemmed red rose. He came forward slowly to the limousine.

"Vittorio!" La Vecchia whispered. *"Dio mio."*

Allegra saw his rugged face, tears streaming from dark eyes, which were fixed on La Vecchia. Maria quickly rolled down the window as he approached. He held out his perfect rose, and Maria placed it into La Vecchia's trembling hand. The two gazed at each other. The old man's Adam's apple worked convulsively in his throat. Evidently a speech of welcome was struggling to come out.

Finally, he whispered, "Welcome, *padrona*."

"Vittorio!" Her voice was infinitely tender, her eyes filled with tears. She smiled at him over the great dewy flower, and he drew back as Luigi eased the car through the entranceway. Aldo looked at La Vecchia anxiously.

"Don't watch me as if I would shatter into fragments," she said. "A few more tears added to those I have wept in my lifetime will not drown me."

Aldo smiled and turned to wave at the people who rushed to line the drive. They were holding long poles tied with flowers, and they called out to La Vecchia. The drive ended in a circular grassy area shaded by tall plane trees, and beyond stood a beautiful old farmhouse. Its ocher walls were mellow with age, and blue shutters weathered to a soft mauve color half concealed bright windows. It was solid and rectangular, two stories high. Tall wooden doors were open to show a courtyard and fountains in an enclosing inner wing. They stopped before the open doors. A red banner hung from a central window, and flowing swags fluttered out from the doorposts.

People awaited the arrival of the car and watched as first Renaldo, then Luigi, opened their doors and stepped out. Bianca raced away at full speed toward a knot of youngsters, as Renaldo helped his grandmother from the car. A cheer went up from the people at the doorway, when she walked erect and proud on Aldo's arm.

Her progress was slowed by greetings. Many kissed her hand. She spoke to them by name, and if she did not recognize a face, she asked. Allegra and Maria followed, carrying pillows and shawls. Some of the women ran ahead, pointing the way up a flight of stairs. Aldo swept La Vecchia up and carried her to the landing. She caught Allegra's eyes and showed a satisfied smile. *You see, I have got my way,* it said. Allegra's admiration for the old lady was like pride—pride for one's own.

LA VECCHIA WAS ESTABLISHED in a huge four-poster bed in the main bedroom and was soon deep in siesta. Allegra settled her own things and Bianca's in smaller rooms and went to find the child. She almost collided in the narrow hallway with Luisa and Guido, who were having an argument. He was trying unsuccessfully to persuade her to trade rooms with him, since hers had an outside balcony. "A man has to have a way to come and go," he winked at Allegra. "I don't like to tiptoe down the hall late at night. Too many delicate sensibilities around that could be offended."

Allegra kept walking. The house was larger than it appeared to be from the outside. Allegra searched through a series of high-ceilinged rooms, finally coming into a kitchen, which contained a gigantic iron wood-burning stove. On its vast black top, pots bubbled with savory odors. Food overflowed the scrubbed wood tables, and a half dozen pairs of lively dark eyes gazed at her curiously. Bianca was not to be seen.

She went outside, and hearing faint laughter, followed the sounds. Gardens, trees and grassy places surrounded the house, with a kitchen herb garden growing within protective plantings of hedges. A long row of buildings paralleled plots of thriving

vegetables. Clucks of chickens and assorted animal voices led her
into a courtyard surrounded by stables. Children's delighted
squeals drew her to Bianca and a group of youngsters, who were
gathered around an entrancing sight—a little foal happily accepting the caresses of small hands, while its mother watched from
behind long-lashed eyes.

The oldest of the children, a boy of about fourteen, noticed
Allegra and came toward her. "I am Cesare, grandson of Vittorio, *signorina*. May I help you?" Allegra was attracted to his
pleasant face and natural courtesy.

"I am Allegra di R—" she caught the word back on a breath
"—Brent . . . a friend of the family, from the United States. I was
looking for Bianca. She must come inside now."

Cesare smiled again, remarkably self-possessed. "We have
been watching over her," he said. He didn't seem to notice that
she had almost called herself a di Rienzi, but it shook her. The
unspoken name brought into sharp focus the workings of her sub-
conscious thoughts, despite her efforts to set them aside. It was as
if she were moving faster and faster along a track and couldn't
stop herself.

Bianca looked mutinous, but hunger and promises of more
visits with the children and animals persuaded her to go back with
Allegra.

The house was quiet except for the kitchen, where preparations
were at a feverish pace. Allegra got a glass of milk and a big slice
of fresh bread for the child, then took her upstairs for a nap. On
returning to her own room, she found that someone had unpacked
her small suitcase. The green dress was hanging in an old fashioned wardrobe, ready for the evening . . . and the green slippers,
which La Vecchia had insisted she have to go with it. In her handbag was the gold-and-pearl necklace.

She sat down on the big mahogany bed. A handwoven rug in
blue-and-white flower patterns lay on the polished marble floor.
A small washbowl and towel stand looked sober next to an
elaborately carved dressing table, its mirror misted with age. The
room was pleasant—practical, sturdy and comfortable. The fur-

niture smelled of beeswax, and the bedspread was crisp with the scent of soap and sunlight.

She looked at the old mirror in its wood frame, thinking what emotions it had reflected. Her own face looked back at her, like a pale ghost behind the crackled glass. She wanted to creep into the big bed and sleep until the *festa* was over. The thought of facing Aldo's penetrating eyes, and Guido's cynical ones, and La Vecchia's perceptive gaze made her want to weep. How could she put on the green dress and act joyful, when her nerves were singing with her painful sensitivity to Aldo's nearness? Surely it would show. It was becoming harder to control her eyes, not to let them linger on his face. But she had never been a very good actress.

She dropped her face into her hands and tried to call back the tears that stung her eyelids. She didn't want to give a name to the gathering pressure of feelings inside her. *It can't be love,* she thought miserably. Love was supposed to be sweet.

A light tap at her door brought Maria with a pot of tea and buttered bread. No special tea today. "One must be ready for the great feast," Maria laughed as she turned to leave. "The pasta is enough to build a mountain, and the *torta*—wait until you see it!"

Allegra made a concerted attempt to rest, and to come to some kind of equilibrium. She was surprised to find that, in spite of herself, she had gone to sleep; she woke to the tugging hand of Bianca.

"Allegra, Allegra, wake up. Maria just brought me my *festa* dress, and I want you to put the special ribbons in my hair." She pulled Allegra from the bed to lead her to the dress. It hung in Bianca's room, a mass of blue ruffles and pink bows—the epitome of a small child's desires. Bianca stroked the bouffant skirt. "I shall dance with papa and Uncle Guido and—" her face was suddenly feminine and knowing "—and maybe with Cesare."

Allegra smiled. The warm sun of Italy bred flirtation into the very bones of its women, even six-year-old ones. She tied the hot excited little head with pompons of ribbons at the ends of dark

braids and buttoned the blue dress over the plump little figure.
Bianca whirled around in front of her mirror, posing joyously.
Maria came in, exclaimed with suitable flattery, and took the
child for *la nonna*'s inspection.

Allegra hurried with her own dressing. As she splashed cool
water over her face and shoulders, a sense of unreality possessed
her. This moment she lived in had all the elements of a dream,
and it would surely have to fade. Why could a dream not be enjoyed without pain?

The dress fitted well. She tied the gold-tasseled sash firmly
around her waist. The delicate green silk of the blouse caressed
her shoulders, and the skirt whispered about her ankles. It was a
dress for joy, for moonlight, for dancing, and for the touch of a
man's hand on its softness. She shivered with tension. Watching
herself in the mirror, as if from a distance, she pulled her hair into
a severe dark knot at the back of her head and slipped the
necklace around her throat. She put very little makeup on her
glowing skin, only slightly darkening her eyes with mascara and
using a rosy lipstick.

Putting some necessities into a tiny evening bag, she gave
herself a last look in the mirror. Despite the simple hairdo,
the reflection showed a face whose cheeks glowed with color,
whose dark eyes shone with a hazel light shot with mysterious
glimmers of green, like the emerald of her skirt. She gazed at her
face. She wanted to be beautiful, but if she were, what then?
Would Aldo care, or would Guido or someone else say words she
only wished to hear from one special voice? She hesitated at the
doorway and took several deep breaths slowly, the way her *nonna*
had taught her to calm herself as a child. She would be as unobtrusive as possible and get away from the *festa* as early as she
could.

In the hall she met Maria, gaily costumed and looking for her.
La Vecchia was demanding her presence. They found the old lady
adding a small gold locket as a last touch to the resplendent Bianca.

La Vecchia herself was like a portrait from the past. Her dress was of dusty purple, full and gay, the tiny waist pulled tight to her figure. The bodice was cut low with puffed sleeves over the shoulders. Soft lavender chiffon filled in the neckline and buttoned into a high straight collar. Long chiffon sleeves ended in points over her delicate hands. Ruffles and intricate braid trimmed the bodice. Her hair was dressed high, and garnets sparkled from her ears and at her throat. A beautiful pale lavender shawl, fluffy and furry, was over her shoulders. She looked up smiling when Allegra entered.

Allegra caught her breath at the picture of the child with her great-grandmother. Suddenly the tableau dissolved, as Bianca rushed forward, and La Vecchia's face became displeased.

"What is this, the hairdo of a matron?" She pointed at Allegra's head. "Sit down over there." An imperious hand waved her toward the dressing table. "Maria, take out those pins—dear God! It is a sin to pull back your lovely hair. Are you not young? It is a time of *festa*!"

Allegra had no choice. Deftly Maria brushed out her hair into heavy dark waves and drew part of it back, fastening it with a gold clasp, which La Vecchia gave her. She fluffed the hair into a cloud of soft long curls.

"That's better." The old woman allowed herself to smile again and ordered Allegra to stay seated. "Put some shadow around her eyes and a darker color on her lips," she ordered.

Allegra murmured dissent but was ignored. She saw herself coming into a focus of beauty, and felt elated and fearful.

"That's better," La Vecchia said at last. "Let us go out now. It is almost seven. The evening will have some hours of twilight yet. Call Aldo, Maria. I will not sit in a wheelchair tonight. He must carry me down, but I will walk outside."

She grasped her silver-topped cane and sat straight, seeming to be speaking to herself. Allegra thought she said the name Leopoldo. Maria opened the door, to find Aldo about to knock.

Allegra's heart made a sudden leap at the sight of him. He was wearing a black velvet jacket with gold buttons over a ruffled white shirt. The neck was open to show the glint of a gold medal-

lion on his tanned throat. Narrow dark trousers were tucked into
short boots, which were stitched around the tops in red. A red silk
sash was fastened with a heavy gold buckle around his waist.
Maria moved aside from his gaze, leaving Allegra directly in his
line of vision. Their eyes met and held, then he looked her up and
down with a strange smile curving his lips.

He made a sweeping gesture with his hands. "Is it indeed
Allegra? Exquisite!"

"My Allegra, is she not pretty? And papa, look at me!" Bianca
twirled her skirt and stopped in front of him, flirting with her
eyes. Aldo's expression was suddenly somber, but he caught
himself and complimented her, lifting her up to kiss the flushed
face.

"So! Age dooms me to be without compliments," La Vecchia
laughed. She stood and held out her arms to Aldo.

"But you are the beauty of them all," he said, gently enfolding
her.

"How good it is to have a grandson so handsome, no matter
how unobservant." She tapped him with a small ivory fan, which
hung from her wrist. "Come, take me to my party!"

He lifted her with ease and strode down the stairs.

CHAPTER SIXTEEN

"*BRAVA, BRAVA LA CONTESSA!*" Voices called out from the open area in front of the house. A group of musicians began to play—an accordion, a violin and a mandolin.

"Put me down, Renaldo *mio,* and give me your arm." La Vecchia began to walk toward the tables. They were alight with candles and flowers. Young Cesare bounded up to her, bowing, and led her to a flower-decorated chair. The music swelled into joyous vibrations, filling the warm air, bringing people together in songs and dancing. The *festa* became a kaleidoscope of changing color and shapes.

Bianca was beside herself, not able to decide between the tables of tempting sweets or dances with the children. Allegra became the target for light-hearted stares from the expressive eyes of some of the local male guests. Aldo devoted himself to his grandmother, bringing supper and staying near her chair. Allegra vainly tried to keep Bianca under some control, but Aldo saw the uselessness of it. "Let her go. She will be sick tomorrow, and it will teach her."

La Vecchia nodded. "I wish you to enjoy also, Allegra *mia.* The child will come to no harm."

Dr. Nepi was fine looking in his dark trousers and white shirt and bright red neck scarf. He was enjoying his wine, having shed his professional manner, and was watching Allegra speculatively. He caught her eye and raised a brow in invitation, but she smiled and pretended not to understand and turned away. A vigorous country dance was in progress, and she was aware of his intentions. She really didn't want to have to dance with people and act carefree and festive.

A few moments later she was carrying a plate of steaming pasta back from the long serving table. She sat on a stone bench near La

Vecchia. The *contessa* leaned over to her and hissed, "Look at Luisa. She's like a hen about to cackle over an egg." Allegra followed the glance to see Dr. Nepi turning his charm upon that poor lady, as she simpered and fawned like a nineteenth-century belle. "Ha! That Andrea Nepi thinks he will outlive me. I'll show him a few things yet."

The farm people danced close and showed off their steps for La Vecchia, who laughed and applauded. Allegra was worried about the frail body, but Amalia di Rienzi was in full control. Bright spots of color burned on the finely wrinkled cheeks, but there were no sudden little naps. Her eyes brimmed with life.

She was silent a moment after the music stopped. "Do you see these flowers? They are exactly like those Leopoldo brought to me on the first week of our honeymoon. Vittorio—may God bless his dear heart—he sent them to me." Tears were in her eyes once more. "Age does not alter love, *bambina,*" she whispered. "Do not think that an aging body ends the warmth of feeling. The spirit does not age, it only grows. Remember what I say and look to see where the reality of love is."

Allegra could only nod. A creeping pain entered her heart and spread. The reality of love? Aldo was her reality! As much as Italy was real, and this bench where she sat. Whatever bound her to Aldo had nothing to do with his angers and strangeness. It simply *was.*

Cesare broke the spell. He was wheeling a cart with a cake that was the model for all cakes. It was mounted high with fruit and thick whipped cream. Behind him came several young men carrying trays with many small glasses of a golden liqueur.

Vittorio came last, straight and proud. Balanced on his white head was a glass filled with wine, and he moved in time to the music. Steadily he approached until he stood before his *contessa,* holding out his hand to her with an inviting gesture. She rose, impatiently pushing aside her lap robe, and her hand went into his. Voices hushed on indrawn breaths as the music played in a slower, even rhythm. The old man held her hand high in his, and she began to move around him with delicate steps, while he turned in time to her movement. The glass of wine reflected shafts of ruby light.

Looking into each other's eyes they moved to full circle, then slowly Vittorio went down on one knee before La Vecchia, who lifted the glass from his head, held it up and sipped from it. She gave it to him, and he, too, drank from it. Slowly, and with great ceremony, she raised him to his feet, and he finished with a stately kiss of her hand. Then she started to sway, and Aldo's arm came quickly around her, and he eased her back into her chair. She sat down straight and regal, but the bodice of her dress rose and fell with rapid breaths.

A shout went up, and applause. Many eager hands took the glasses from the trays, as Aldo raised his for a toast. "To the health of the woman who is the true House of di Rienzi!" More shouting, and the music played furiously in response.

"You must cut the cake for me, Allegra, I cannot," La Vecchia's voice was a whisper. "They expect the first cut to be made by a woman of our family. Do it," she urged. Allegra looked up, confused.

Aldo nodded toward the cake. "Yes. Do it." She knew his thoughts: *Cut the di Rienzi cake, but don't take your role seriously. It is only for La Vecchia's sake.* His face was a mask.

She was aware of Luisa's gaze from hurt eyes, but she took the big silver knife Cesare held out to her, and with a little bow to La Vecchia she plunged it into the billows of whipped cream.

Cesare said close to her ear, "I will take care of the rest." She turned in relief from the cake cart. The trio was playing a waltz, Vittorio was being congratulated by his cronies, Cousin Barretto was sitting apart, looking sour, and Father Fiorenzo was running his beads silently through his fingers. Her body urged her to get away, but Dr. Nepi stood in her path.

"*Signorina,*" his voice was soft. "You have not danced. Come, waltz with me. You are beautiful and you must dance." He slid his arm around her waist and drew her back into the dancing area. As they moved she caught Guido's knowing smile, as if to say she had done well to make a catch of the doctor.

"You do not speak, little one?" He held her closer. "Are you shy? What a joy to find a woman who is not giving invitations with the eye. It is like a rosebud to be unfolded." His voice purred in her ear. She felt his breath and a light kiss on her cheek.

Desperately, she looked for a way to free herself, praying for the music to end. Aldo watched her expressionlessly from his place beside La Vecchia, and she felt suddenly guilty. Why, she thought angrily, *what had she done?* The dance finished, and she escaped her partner's urgent plea for another.

"I must find Bianca and put her to bed. . . . It is very late for her and she is probably sick from all the sweets."

"I will help you and see if the child is well," he smiled.

"No, you must stay with La Vecchia!" She pulled her hand from his and fled.

She found Bianca, flushed with excitement, and there was struggling and crying when Allegra tried to take her into the house. Allegra sat with her until she was asleep, then slipped downstairs again, leaving a young maid in charge.

She had need to go out into the night, out into the glow of the shimmering moon. To run through the dark shadows and luminous brightness. How good it would be to lay her hot cheeks against cool grass, or the rough kindly trunk of a tree—something that would accept her love and return it without questioning. Her painful heart needed soothing—some balm for its aching hopelessness.

She went out a side door, past roses nestled between low hedges. She walked along moon-white paths, stopping to draw a flower to her face and delight in its perfume. A sound startled her. Guido was coming across the grass unsteadily.

"So, this is where you have gone to, eh? Who are you waiting for, Dr. Nepi, or the incomparable master of the house of di Rienzi!" He approached her and stood staring. His eyes had a blank unpleasant look, and she backed away, feeling his energy flowing toward her. His hand seized her wrist.

"What's the matter, Allegra, what's wrong with *me*? You look hot enough for other men. Maybe you just need persuasion." He dragged her against him with a painful grip and forced his lips against hers, but she turned her head away, struggling to release her hands.

"Let me go—you're drunk, Guido!" He pressed her body against his again, and she slapped him hard, the sound echoing in the quiet garden. She ran from him, and he followed. "You're just a common tease, but you won't get away from me. You love it, Allegra!"

She scratched her arms on the rosebushes, as she stumbled away from him. Thorns caught on her long skirt and tore at the gold fringe of her sash. While she frantically tugged her skirt free from entanglement, Guido's voice went silent. She looked up from her struggle in time to see Aldo's hand seize Guido's shoulder, pulling him off balance.

"What do you think you're doing, Aldo—get your hands off me!"

"I saw no effort on your part to get yours from Allegra when she requested it."

"God, Aldo! I thought you were a man of the world. Can't you see that all she wants is to get one of us to marry her? Do you think I'm here without invitation?"

Aldo's face was harsh and shadowed. He shoved Guido toward the house. "You're a drunken boor and a fool. Get out of my sight before I thrash you, as I long to do."

Guido moved off but turned to fling one more angry attack. "I won't forget the insult by both of you. *You're* the fool, Aldo!"

"Enough!" Aldo's voice grated. "Go to bed!"

Allegra watched Guido disappear into the house, then anger and shame, fear and love burst in her heart. She pulled her skirt free and fled down one of the moonlit paths into the pinewoods nearby. Her feet slid on the smooth needles. She plunged onward distractedly until she stopped, breathing hard, beside a stone pine tree. Her arms embraced its earth-warm trunk, and she leaned her body against its benevolent being. The grove was silent. Then tears came, and all the misunderstandings, loneliness, yearnings—and disgust at her own frailty—poured through her.

A soft sound made her raise her head. Aldo had stopped several feet from her and was watching. The moonlight etched his face in brightness. Then suddenly he was close. His arms reached out to hold her. She let herself rest against him, and comfort flowed over her in waves.

"My poor Allegra." His voice was close to her ear. "We have treated you badly, the men of di Rienzi. Can you forgive?"

She stood very still, her cheek against the softness of his shirt, feeling his strong heartbeat. She was afraid to move. "I shall see to it that he will not disturb you again." He paused. "I know you have asked little of us and have given much. Would it help if I said that I have come to accept your story? Do not run so hard from me. . . ."

His hand moved in a caress over her cheek and lightly traced her lips. Lights shone in his dark eyes. He drew in his breath quickly and pulled her closer. Something made her try to turn her face aside, but she could not avoid his eyes and the fine lips that sought hers. For a moment his cheek rested against hers, then his hands, gentle but insistent, turned her lips to his. She held them as steady as she could beneath his warm explorations. Then her will failed and she responded, pressing herself against him. With a murmur he kissed her again, and for a long moment they stood enfolded in the strange rare magic that can exist between a man and a woman. His kiss grew more urgent, and Allegra ceased to think; all the dreams of romance in her soul rose up to answer the call of her body and her heart. She heard him whisper, almost to himself, "I shall not forget this kiss." But the next moment his hands were on her shoulders, roughly thrusting her from him. His eyes probed hers.

"So, you do not push me away as you do my brother or Dr. Nepi. What, then, do you offer to me, Allegra?"

Beyond speech, she could only look up at him, her eyes wide with emotion. Again his face softened. "Do you at all know what you want, little Allegra? What would you do if I exerted my will to take you? You, who are almost a child? What can you know about a heart like mine . . . its dark places . . . its memories?"

His hand moved slowly over the lines of her face, while he watched her with eyes that had become black in the shadows of the moon. Suddenly he bent to her, covering her face with swift kisses, which sent sweet shocks through her body.

Then his hands dropped away and he stood back from her, straight and formal. "Come, Allegra, we must return."

She couldn't make herself move for a moment, and he looked at her with an odd smile on his lips. "A man could think you were not much used to kissing. I apologize. I am not a good one to bring comfort, who have so little of it myself." His hand urged her to move. In the silence the crackle of their steps on the pine needles sounded terribly loud, and even louder was the crunch of their feet on the gravel paths of the garden.

He opened the side door of the farmhouse and stood aside for her to enter. Head bowed, she went in. His voice spoke behind her. "Forget this, little Allegra, it is better so. Romance is a happier word in books than in life. When it comes off the page, it has thorns like the roses in this garden. I have no desire to hurt a woman. Go and dream of your romantic ancestor. When daylight comes, *bambina,* one can see far better than in moonlight. *Addio.*"

She walked on leaden feet to her room and shed the green dress and La Vecchia's necklace—shivering into her nightdress even though the night was warm. Slow, wrenching tears blurred her eyes. *What a shameful fool you have been, what an obvious beginner at this game,* her mind repeated incessantly—while her heart explored and remembered each touch and kiss, examined each word.

In the morning Bianca woke her, looking at her curiously. "What's wrong, Allegra, don't you feel good?" Allegra dressed with some care, trying to minimize the darkness beneath her eyes. She could not eat breakfast past the lump in her throat and the knot in her stomach.

Outside in the courtyard they found La Vecchia getting ready for a drive around the farm in a small fringe-top horse-drawn carriage, with Aldo and Bianca and Dr. Nepi. The *contessa* was remarkably alert after the past night's excitement. Allegra avoided looking at Aldo, glad not to be included in the proposed ride.

After they left, she put her energies into packing. Guido was not in evidence, and the old farmhouse was silent, even though life moved in it.

At noon La Vecchia called Allegra to her room for luncheon. Bianca was going out to have one last look at the animals in the stable, and Maria was busy with the homeward preparations. La Vecchia's shrewd eyes watched Allegra over her teacup, making her feel nervous and exposed. The old lady chatted about the farm, but her eyes were searching.

Allegra was relieved when the farewells were over, and the whole caravan full of flowers and fruit and gifts started down the road to Venice. Aldo sat silent in the front seat by Luigi. La Vecchia dozed, and Bianca played word games with Maria.

Everything appeared normal. Aldo inquired concerning their needs from time to time. He seemed pleasant and completely without emotion. Allegra could not read past his words; it was as if there had been no last night. She had never before thought herself naive, but now she wondered. This kind of thing obviously meant nothing to a sophisticated man like Renaldo di Rienzi, she thought. At the same time, she yearned to be close to him and to hear his voice whisper softly to her.

After an eternity they crossed the long bridge and approached the Lagoon of Venice. Giovanni was waiting with his gondola and with La Vecchia's elegant one, which Luigi would command.

After the unloading and reloading of baggage, they were moving along the network of waterways to the Ca' d'Argenti.

CHAPTER SEVENTEEN

IT WAS LATE AFTERNOON, and the di Rienzi boats jammed the small side canal, taking turns unloading passengers and cargo at the water garage of the Ca'. Luigi eased La Vecchia's gondola up to the steps. He and Aldo made a chair of their arms to lift her out and through the kitchen entrance. Bianca hopped along beside her, laughing to see her great-grandmother trying to look dignified in so makeshift a vehicle.

"Silence, naughty one!" Aldo scolded her in mock anger, "or you will have to ride in on a round of cheese."

Dr. Nepi followed La Vecchia inside, very seriously. He was profoundly relieved that the folly was ended. Maria and Luigi stayed behind to tend to the luggage and the cases of wine from the family vineyards. Huge cheeses were rolled on planks from the boats, freshly made at La Felicita. The kitchen staff were delighted to see new provisions coming into their domain. Guido was of no use to Luigi in hoisting the cases of wine, except to give a monologue on the quality of this year's crop compared with last year's. Allegra picked up as much as she could hold and followed the others inside.

In her room, her treasured room, she flopped down on the bed, kicked off her sandals and looked up at the ceiling. A tiny flesh-colored cupid was painted among the flowers in the center medallion above her. It extended a fat childish arm down toward her and grinned. She hadn't noticed it before.

Giovanna brought up a tray of fruits and cheeses and said the household was retiring for the evening. Was that all, Allegra wondered? Was Aldo going to continue his withdrawal from her? It wasn't fair to bring her this far and then pretend nothing had happened between them. She took a long fragrant bath and settled into bed with the booklets about Byron, which the dear Armenian father had given her.

She began to think of the past ten days. What an upstart she was to be so very much at home in so short a time! Ten days ago she had only heard of Renaldo di Rienzi. Eleana Bugelli had told her in no uncertain terms what a distant world he lived in, how dangerous it was to extend a hope toward it. And she was right.

But what if Allegra had not met him, if she had stayed with the Bugellis and explored the glorious city in peace and composure, with no one to ignite her senses? Even then, she told herself with assurance, she would call Venice her home. *I belong here no matter what Aldo does with his life. Even if he marries Vera Falieri . . . if I never see the Ca' d'Argenti again.*

She looked up at the painted cupid on the ceiling, and a heaviness closed in around her heart.

A quick soft knock at her door pulled her from her thoughts. "Allegra, I'm sorry." Aldo's rich voice begged forgiveness for disturbing her. She reached in confusion for her robe and tied it around her, smoothing her hair as she turned the door latch.

Aldo stood before her in a dark red silk dressing gown. His face was tired and drawn. "I have been in my office attempting to finish my work for the Florence conference, but I am so far behind schedule—Allegra, if you could give me perhaps an hour. If you are not too tired from the long day . . . ."

He looked at wit's end, and Allegra wished she could reach out her arms to him. She found her voice. "I was only reading."

"I know it is late, but I have no time for the amenities. There are revisions to be made." His eyes held hers intensely, searching for a response. He couldn't know that hers were seeing a man who needed her, came to her. She didn't look away this time.

"Let me put something else on," she heard herself say. "I'll be downstairs as soon as I can."

His face relaxed into a smile. "I assure you, I am grateful." He took her hand in a quick fluid motion and brushed it gently with his lips.

Allegra pressed the door closed again as he walked off down the hall. As quickly as she could she put on the yellow cotton dress and threw a sweater over her shoulders. The face in her mirrored wardrobe door was glowing with a natural rouge, her eyes

clear and intent. Minutes later she was pushing open the paneled
door to Aldo's office.

The orderly stacks of paper, which she had taken such care
with, were scattered again all over his desk and piled upon the
chairs nearby. Aldo looked up when she entered and motioned
her to the typing table. "These proposals will have to be changed.
One of the largest American producers of cosmetics is coming to
the conference expecting to see my designs, and I have only this
evening received the message. I am doing several new renderings
for the American market, and time is breathing heavily on me. La
Vecchia's little outing has caused me serious delays. It was unwise."

"I'll stay here as long as you need a secretary." She was already
straightening the papers near her table.

"I have made notes where the changes go, but use your judgment with the wording." He picked up his ruler and pen and turned
to his drawing board.

Allegra watched him work for several minutes. She wanted to
prove to him that she wasn't part of the "unwisdom" of the trip
to La Mira. She observed the fine disciplined hands, which could
touch with tenderness. She could still feel his warmth against her.
She knew he could love, but what could she do if he refused to let
himself? She shrugged and turned away to her table. Enough.
Byron's blood was painful.

The proposals were in English and Allegra quietly corrected
and smoothed the sentence structure and vocabulary. She approved
of his revisions. Aldo had a good understanding of the psychol-
ogy of selling, even though the designs would sell themselves. He
had chosen the special adjectives that caused one's interest to
spark.

Occasionally her eyes would go to his deeply concentrating
face, in profile near her. Sometimes a half smile would be at his
lips, as if from satisfaction with his work. Allegra understood that
special kind of joy that comes when one pulls an idea out of
nebulous thought and concretes it into lines and form. But he
would never know she knew.

Three hours passed before she finished with the proposals. She reread her work for mistakes and felt satisfied with the finished product. Aldo's drawings were really good—practical designs hidden within beautiful flowing shapes. It was almost midnight. She turned to Aldo but saw that his head was resting on the drafting board. He was asleep. She put the papers on his desk and walked quietly from the office.

"Good night," she whispered at the doorway, "my dearest love."

BIANCA AWAKENED ALLEGRA EARLY to tell her that La Vecchia and her papa were expecting them for breakfast in the garden terrace, and they should hurry. "I think papa has a surprise for you," she said breathlessly. "I heard him talking about it to *nonna.*" She watched impatiently as Allegra dressed. "What do you suppose it is? Papa always tells me he hates surprises."

Allegra's busy mind was questioning Bianca's secondhand information. She couldn't imagine Aldo in a playful mood dispensing surprises. At best he probably appreciated her work last night and was going to try to press money on her again. Maybe a gift, instead, since he knew she would refuse payment.

She and Bianca went down the fairy-tale staircase hand in hand, and she debated whether to accept a gift. Aldo rose as they came out on the terrace. He smiled warmly and held out a chair for Allegra.

La Vecchia was smiling cheerfully. "Well, *cara mia*, I hope we didn't call you away from a well-deserved rest. Aldo has been telling me of your extended working hours. You really shouldn't let him bully you like that."

Allegra turned to Aldo. "Was it satisfactory? I didn't want to wake you when I left."

"More than satisfactory," he said. "You made my words sound better than they were."

Allegra found it difficult to be so near to him. There was a flow of energy between them.

La Vecchia took a sip of tea and looked at her grandson. "What were you telling me about your secretary earlier, Renaldo?" she prompted.

He turned to face Allegra. "I have a further crisis, Allegra, if you are not already weary of my problems." She felt his frustration tangibly. "My secretary was to go with me to the conference tomorrow. I was counting on her. She is familiar with my work. But her husband insists she is not strong enough from the operation. And so—"

"And so—" La Vecchia's voice echoed crisply, leaving the sentence poised in midair.

"Allegra, I need you to go with me to Florence. *Nonna* has released you with her blessings, and I need only your decision."

Allegra's heart was pounding. She knew her face had suddenly blushed. "And Bianca?" she said, forcing order back to her excited thoughts.

"Bianca shall be my temporary secretary and help me arrange costumes and make decorations for the tables," La Vecchia said. "We shall both be quite occupied for the next few days."

"Oh, Allegra, say yes, say yes!" Bianca begged. "I want you to go with papa."

Three faces turned to her for an answer. They couldn't know how her blood raced with the desire to go to Florence with Renaldo, to be alone with him and be indispensable. "I'd be happy to go with you, Aldo." Her voice was almost a whisper.

Bianca grasped her hand tightly. "We'll both be secretaries, Allegra! You and me."

Aldo looked at his watch anxiously. "I must go to the office for the rest of the day. It is a great relief to have this thing settled." He pushed back his chair abruptly and stood.

"No breakfast, Aldo—only coffee?" La Vecchia scolded.

"Tomorrow comes too soon. I will see you at tea, hmm?" His eyes included them all in their sweep, and he left. At the doorway he stopped and turned back as if remembering something. "Oh, Allegra—thank you," he said and walked on.

She met La Vecchia's smile. "He is grateful, little one. He cannot tell you how much because of his damnable pride. But that will ease, my intuition assures me. Now, we must talk of your trip to Florence. It is a more formal city, even in summer, and you will want to make a good appearance, for Aldo's business. I wish you to do me a special favor, since there is so little I can do to compensate you for coming to us. Allow me the pleasure of outfitting you for the trip. You will need a good dinner dress and some silk frocks for afternoon. Do not refuse me, *bambina,* my health won't stand for it."

"But you have done so much for me already. And I have enough clothes, really. . . ."

The old woman thumped her cane. "I don't hear you." Her eyes were clamped shut. Allegra suddenly burst into laughter. She was defeated.

"All right," she said. "Tell me where to go. I don't know the places to shop."

"I shall give you a list. They will put the charge to my account, and I shall be very angry to learn that you used your own money." She set to scribbling a few swift words on a small piece of paper. "I almost forgot. Be back by two-thirty. My hairdresser comes then, and I know he can do something very nice with your hair."

"Let me go too, *nonna*," Bianca said. "I know what to wear in Florence."

"My worldly pigeon, you have your piano lesson at eleven this morning. Signorina Lucca expects more practicing than you have done. Now come," La Vecchia said, "let us enjoy in silence our breakfast and give thanks for the beautiful day we have been given."

Allegra was uncomfortable about the arrangement. It ate away at some of her independence, eroded just a bit the dignity she so carefully guarded; but she couldn't be rude and refuse the offer of the new clothes. Aldo and La Vecchia in one morning had drawn her more deeply into their world. She wanted it, yet resisted. She hated those weak women who accepted gifts and favors until they had no choice but to accept the terms of the men who gave them.

She set out with La Vecchia's list, looking for the shops that would make her well dressed for Florence, the city of flowers and the heart of the Renaissance. She vowed to think less of her precious pride and enjoy the opportunities to learn that were opening all around her.

She found two very small intimate dress shops, which were on the list. The proprietresses of both were expecting her, having already brought out several appropriate costumes. The prices had been quietly removed, frustrating Allegra's wish to purchase modestly priced dresses. La Vecchia's hand was evident in this, and she bowed to the greater will. She chose carefully, rejecting what she considered radical styles. She just wasn't the type for the black sequins and the Oriental narrow slit skirt . . . or the long clinging flowered jersey halter gown, which had no back.

At the first shop she found an evening dress in sky-blue chiffon, which looked very Greek. Long, soft and flowing, it draped gracefully across the bodice, caught at one shoulder with a dolphin clasp. She almost didn't choose it for fear of looking too conspicuous for just a secretary, but she allowed the shop's owner to convince her otherwise. "What reason have you to conceal a good figure, *signorina*? You will be elegant, yet modest—irresistible!"

Minutes later she walked from the little boutique, dress box in hand and sought out the next place on her list. It was not far from the Piazza San Marco, back under the arcades and down a narrow lane. By lunchtime she had selected three simple pastel silk dresses for day and was persuaded to take a broad-brimmed white straw hat and matching straw purse. And for a dash of color, flowered pastel scarves were tied around the crown of the hat.

Allegra was delighted with her new wardrobe. She felt colorful and fresh, and she had a nagging suspicion that everything in her slim clothes boxes was enormously expensive. But uneasy peace had already been made with her conscience, and she happily found a small round table at Florian's and ordered a light lunch. She basked in the sun and activity of the piazza. She felt like a native, amused at the array of tourist groups, trying to guess where they had all come from. She was certain she was not noticeable as a tourist herself.

A leisurely walk back to the Ca' d'Argenti brought her home at almost two-thirty. Bianca met her at the front door and demanded to be the first to see the new dresses. They ran up the stairs together to Allegra's room, and Bianca fell upon the packages with relish. She seemed disappointed to find just four dresses and looked up from the wrappings, puzzled. "Where are all your gowns?"

"I won't need gowns in Florence," Allegra explained.

"But Fiona Barducci's mother always takes lots of beautiful ones when she goes there. Did papa tell you not to get any?"

"No, my little crow. I bought just what was proper for what I shall be doing. Now, tell me where your *nonna*'s hairdresser will be. I have an appointment right now."

Bianca's instructions led her past La Vecchia's door and down a side hall to a cheerful sunny room, which had once been a laundry porch but now was outfitted for Maestro Bruno, the hairdresser. He was waiting for her, dressed in a pink-and-yellow smock, thin and serious, standing in silent vigil over his one chair and sink. Allegra fought the overwhelming urge to laugh. Signor Bruno had a small waved head, a hairline mustache and he held a comb poised in one delicate hand like a conductor awaiting his orchestra.

"Signorina Brent," he bowed slightly and kissed her hand. "Please sit down. I have been waiting." With a flourish he shook open a folded pink linen cloth and pinned it around her shoulders. Just a hint of displeasure was at his lips as he slowly walked around her, studying her hair.

Allegra closed her eyes and let Signor Bruno wash, curl and work with her hair. She planned to comb out anything too outlandish as soon as she left his little salon. Right now she was thinking of Aldo's business needs. She wished she were familiar with his methods of procedure. No new dress or hairstyle would compensate for errors of judgment. She wanted to be more than competent for him.

Maestro Bruno suddenly turned her chair around, so that she faced him. It was a shock to be thinking of Aldo, and the next instant to be face-to-face with a triumphant little man in a striped smock. "It is a masterpiece—a classic style, *signorina*." He presented her with a golden filigree hand mirror. She tentatively glanced at her reflection in the larger mirror. Her hair was softly waved over the temples and drawn up into a smooth twist in back.

She looked more mature, more interesting; she saw that at once. Bianca was right about her surprise, only there had been more than one today.

She thanked the hairdresser warmly, and he saw her to the door. As she walked away down the hall she heard a strange noise behind her—Maestro Bruno was standing in the bright doorway, a satisfied grin on his face, applauding lightly.

She hurried back to her room to study herself in privacy and to try on the dresses once more, to be sure they were right for her. She chose the flowered pink shirtwaist for this afternoon's tea and knew she was dressing for Aldo. It occurred to her she should be keeping a diary, but the idea was too close to the feelings of the other Allegra. It almost frightened her to think of the parallel.

THE GLOW OF LIGHT coming from La Vecchia's sitting room reached into the hallway. Allegra's heart quickened as she approached, feeling conscious of the eyes that awaited her within. She felt like someone else with her elegant new look, as if more would be expected of her now, even though she was the same Allegra underneath the expensive styling.

"Come in, *cara mia*," La Vecchia beckoned her closer. Warmth stole over her as she came fully into the room. She was aware of the dozens of fragmented reflections of herself coming from the ancient mirrored panels on the walls. Guido was there, Cousin Luisa and Dr. Nepi. Maria was preparing the tea cakes and gave her a wide approving smile.

Guido stood up to her and planted himself. "Well, Allegra, I can see you're too elegant for me now," he said. "Luisa, what do you think of her? Looks like one of the family, when we used to have some good-looking women."

La Vecchia put out a hand to Allegra. "You did well, my child. I want you to show me everything after tea." She looked toward the doorway, at the figure who dominated the space with his presence. "Aldo—good afternoon."

Allegra held her breath. He breezed past her and kissed his grandmother's hand. Impatience and time pressure came in with him. "Good afternoon, everyone," he said crisply. "Forgive me if I do not stay, *nonna*. A courier is on his way here from Milano, and I must arrange a packet for him immediately.'' He accepted a cup of tea from La Vecchia and quickly drank it. Then he saw Allegra.

''Oh—there you are. I was going to leave a message for you. We leave at six tomorrow morning. I hope you can be ready then.'' He looked at her with eyes she couldn't penetrate. She tried to hold his attention, but he wasn't to be held. She nodded to him, unable to speak. Behind him, grinning like a perverse faun, was Guido, reveling in her discomfort.

Bianca burst into the room from an inner door of the apartment, clutching a handful of hair ribbons. ''Allegra!'' she cried. ''Oh—you look beautiful!'' She rushed forward.

Allegra's emotions hung on a fine thread, and Bianca's words brought a rush of tears to her eyes. She couldn't stop them, and she was furious with herself. She let Bianca throw her little arms around her in a hug. She took the ribbons from her hand and put herself to the task of tying the child's hair, fiercely fighting to regain composure.

La Vecchia was watching her closely, then motioned Dr. Nepi to her side. He took her hand, inclining his head to her, as she whispered into his ear. He stood erect again and signed to the others to leave. All except Allegra. Cousin Luisa looked concerned. She hurried to La Vecchia, and was dismissed with the wave of a weak hand. ''I am tired. Even family takes its toll on my strength,'' she managed to say. With the last words her head went forward, and she was asleep.

Dr. Nepi stood at the door, hurrying everyone out with professional authority. Bianca didn't want to leave, but the doctor was stern-faced. He turned back to Allegra. ''I fear the worst, *signorina*,'' he said in a low voice. ''She cannot continue pretending she is sixty. And I have done all I can.'' His eyes rolled up resignedly, as he pulled the doors closed behind him.

Allegra stood for a moment, feeling tired herself. As she came back into the room, she was met by two sharp eyes and the canny face of La Vecchia.

"So, Allegra," she said, "you are feeling forlorn and sorry for yourself. Do you think it does not show?" She pointed to a chair across from her. "Sit down, my child. I want to say a word to you."

Allegra obeyed. "I speak to you as I think your own grand-mother would. Perhaps you asked yourself why, on that first day when you appeared at my door, I received you with interest. No doubt you know I rarely see uninvited visitors. But I have a sense, a faculty for seeing more than the surface of things. And I sensed that afternoon a strength, honesty and dignity in the young woman from the United States.

"I felt that she had something to give to the house of di Rienzi that it had not known for a long time. You will forgive me if I seem to scold, but I cannot be silent about the things I see. You have been letting go of your emotions, my dear child, at a time when you need to guard them. I understand the pressures you are under now. My eyes are acute to human nature. So I tell you, from the experience of a very long lifetime: hold yourself steady. Your best qualities are being tested by the foolishness of the people around you. You have much to teach them, and you cannot if you are unsteady."

Allegra listened, surprised her distress had been so apparent. "I don't think I'm strong enough," she said shakily.

"Stronger than you know, *bambina*. Listen to my words, Allegra Brent. They come from the clear sight—understand?"

"I'll try," she answered, still not accepting La Vecchia's prophecy. When she lifted her eyes, the *contessa* was asleep again in her silken throne, small amid the upholstered luxury. This time she was not pretending. Allegra quietly drew a wrap over the thin knees and regarded the dear old face for a moment. The will burned so fiercely yet, and the wisdom. She loved the Contessa di Rienzi.

ALLEGRA WENT TO HER ROOM. She wasn't hungry for dinner. Bianca poked her beribboned head in once to say that Uncle Guido was taking her to see a cowboy movie from America. And then the hallways of the Ca' fell silent. Happy to be alone and quiet, to digest what was happening to her, Allegra began to pack for Florence, thinking and questioning herself as she moved about the beautiful room.

Had she really lost the dignity and honesty of the Allegra Brent of two weeks ago? She couldn't be doing what Clinton Meserve feared the most—being led astray by her own unsophistication!

After she carefully tied a scarf around her hair to preserve the set, she went to bed, her eyes focused on the ancient walls outside her window. Bits of moon reflection jumped and shimmered on them from the narrow canal below. She wanted to find strength and steadiness, but when her thoughts drew pictures of Aldo as he held her, and again as he disregarded her today, her nerves flared into response. It was a long time before sleep came.

THE NIGHT WAS FILLED with dreams and voices. She awoke several times, disturbed and restless. It was still dark when a soft tapping at the door awakened her. Someone had left a breakfast tray at the threshold and was gone before Allegra found it. The aromas of strong coffee and honeyed rolls blended to clear away the dullness in her head. She took the tray back to bed with her and tried to pull herself into a better mental state.

She cursed the genes of her wayward ancestors with a rueful smile and began earnestly to prepare herself for the secretarial duties that lay ahead. At least she had confidence in that area of her life, she thought, and drained the last delicious reviving drop of coffee from her cup.

She heard the noise of a small motorboat in the canal below and looked down from her window, expecting to see Aldo, but instead she was witness to a peculiar scene. A white launch was idling at the side entrance to the Ca', while Guido was in animated disagreement with two other men in the boat. Their voices were low, but an angry pantomime made it clear that Guido was having trouble getting away from his companions. He finally broke from them and sprang onto the quay and into the protection of the building. The men watched for a moment, then turned their launch into the canal and left.

Allegra turned away from the window. She wouldn't mention it to Aldo. It probably wasn't the first time Guido brought troubles on himself. But still, she felt very uneasy about the scene below.

CHAPTER EIGHTEEN

SHE WAS WAITING in the main hall a few minutes before six, a suitcase at her feet, and carrying her new straw hat and bag. The hairdo had survived her thrashing about in the night, and she felt fresh and colorful in her pink-flowered dress. She wore it again this morning, knowing Aldo had not noticed it yesterday at tea.

The great front door was ajar, letting in the smells of Venice, and Luigi pushed it open farther. "This is all, Signorina Brent?" he asked as he thrust her bag under one arm. Allegra nodded and followed him outside. Aldo was on the water steps arranging his materials in the freshly washed blue motor launch, glistening with beads of early morning moisture.

"We'll need a plastic cover for this, Luigi. Ah, Allegra—you're here. Good."

She took her seat in the middle of the boat. Aldo wedged into the seat at the rear with briefcases, drawing boards and luggage all around him. He looked a little like a mother hen with her precious brood. Their eyes met for the first time as Luigi steered them out into the canal, and Aldo smiled.

"Well—the grand adventure, eh?"

She allowed herself a guarded answering smile. She wouldn't want to be too grateful for the slight warmth he offered. She began to notice the morning life around them. Venice was busy, but not with tourists. Small boats of all descriptions passed, heaped with produce for the market stalls. In an hour the canals would be empty of them, and the other Venice would be awakening to its day's activity.

Pearly light bathed the walls on the Grand Canal. Umbers and gilts and mossy stones pleased the eye of a lover of art in all its variations. Luigi drove their launch in the wide sweep around the perimeter of the city to the landing near the parking complex on the mainland.

Allegra waited with their luggage while Aldo brought the Alfa around. "We're going to have to go by way of Verona—cursed inconvenience," he said. "But the regional office neglected to send me certain papers with yesterday's packet. Everything has gone wrong that could go wrong."

He turned the small sports car onto the causeway road. His jaw was set. It would mean an extra hour and a half before they got to Florence, and Allegra pulled her emotional shield close about herself and tried not to look at him. It was going to be a warm day. Mists of humidity blurred the outlines of the nearby hills. Signs along the highway said Mestre, Padova, Vicenza and, finally, Verona. It was just after seven-thirty when they drove under old Roman arches and into a large piazza.

Verona was a beautiful city, architecturally in struggle between Roman and medieval styles. Jagged high walls of both ages stood within view of the lovely circular piazza. Aldo drove past the old Roman arena and parked in a narrow one-way street behind the piazza, leaving Allegra to sit alone while he let himself into a locked doorway. She briefly glimpsed an interior courtyard beyond and hated being left in the car between two rows of high brick walls.

Aldo reappeared with his package, and they roared into the square and out past the archways again. Her face must have been a picture of disappointment. Aldo reached his hand out to touch hers in a sympathetic pat. "When there are no time pressures you should see Verona. The art in the Castel Vecchio is very fine, and I'm sure you will want to stand on Giulietta's balcony. Next time."

Allegra wondered if "next time" for her would be when she was on her way back home, for good.

They drove south on the Autostrada del Sole. It was still humid and overcast. Cornfields high and ripe for harvest were on all sides, divided by long rows of espaliered pear trees, like living bountiful fences.

Aldo was quiet, except to point out certain old hill towns on the distant peaks and to offer her an apple and slices of yellow cheese in lieu of stopping somewhere for refreshments. She did not intrude upon his silence, happy at the very least that he was not emanating irritation any longer.

This part of Italy, over the spine of the Apennines, was so vital with natural force, so offering of its energies to the traveler. As the highway left the hills and tunnels, Allegra gazed down into the valley of the Arno. The river looked cool and gentle far below. She knew it had its moods and rages, but the picture from the hilltop was serene. The red-crowned buildings of old Florence were a soft blur yet, as the car descended into the city.

It had been raining for the past few miles, and now the sun was sending shafts of gold through the clouds, making a breathtaking backdrop for their arrival. Part of a rainbow hung over a far-off hill, where the rain still fell.

Aldo was preoccupied, and they couldn't share this moment. As they neared the center of the city, she began to feel a pressure in her head, behind her eyes—not a pain but a kind of vibration or energy intensity. She knew that fully half the artistic treasures from her long and loving studies were here in Florence. Just beyond the next turn or two would be the Duomo—Giotto's Tower—the Baptistry. The pressure increased, fed by her educated imagination, and when they approached the crowded famous intersection she gasped with pleasure.

The streets were packed with tourist buses and cabs. Police were standing on little podiums attempting to make order where none could possibly be. Allegra turned her head for a view of the Duomo in the middle of the congestion of traffic.

"I can't believe I'm really here," she said.

Aldo was caught in a series of one-way streets, which led them in a roundabout pattern toward their hotel. After countless digressions from any straight path, they came to a stop in a little square next to the river. The Grand Hotel was here, an old solid-looking building, whose length ran along the Lungarno.

Aldo had arranged adjoining rooms overlooking the river. The desk clerk was impeccably courteous to the Conte di Rienzi and his young secretary. Allegra had a moment of discomfort. She didn't want the hotel staff to assume anything about her relationship with Aldo, and she attempted to appear businesslike. Happily, she didn't see the desk clerk's smile, as she fumbled in her purse for her passport.

"Welcome to Italy," he said smoothly in English, as he looked at her brand-new passport and even more recent date-of-entry stamp.

"Thank you. I am delighted to be in your beautiful country." It was as near to flawless Italian as she could manage. And it served very nicely, she thought, to place her dignity back where it belonged.

Aldo took her arm with a small pressure of acknowledgment and led her through the paneled lobby to the bank of elevators. "I think you'll like the accommodations," he said as the bellman opened the door to her room. "I can sleep better here than in most hotels."

The bellman quickly opened the wardrobe and bathroom doors and drew open the curtains. Daylight flooded into the lovely French Provincial room, warm with dark wood tones and natural fabrics. It was more sedate and solid, more restrained, than her heavenly Venetian bedroom.

Aldo tipped the porter. "I can let myself into my room," he said in dismissal.

"Allegra, my friend, we are in a somewhat difficult situation. . . ." He turned to face her, his forehead wrinkled from an apologetic half-smile. Her nerves tensed in response. "I do not quite know what to do with you now, since I must attend a luncheon in a few minutes with business friends. If you were strictly a hired office person, I would have no feelings of responsibility for you—but . . . ."

"Signor di Rienzi," she smiled, "put your conscience to rest. I am at your disposal if you need a secretary, but I am also very independent."

His face was still in tension. "I wanted to say something to you because I never can tell what a woman is really feeling. Be frank with me, and then I shall not wonder."

"My mind is already exploring the Pitti Palace, and I intend to follow it immediately." Her voice was gentle and open, and Aldo relaxed his expression.

"You are easy to please. But I must have you back here in time to prepare for this evening. It will be cocktails and dinner with the representatives of the largest cosmetics houses. It is rather formal. I will knock at six-thirty, hmm?''

He let himself out, and Allegra went to the window to orient herself. She already knew Florence by heart from her studies and was delighted to look down to the left and find the Ponte Vecchio just where it belonged. The Pitti Palace and the Boboli Gardens were on the far side of the river, a short walk from the bridge. But first, she was achingly hungry for lunch. It was the simplest thing to order room service, which she did, with a mental note to herself to repay Aldo for the extravagance later.

Before setting out, she unpacked and laid out her blue evening dress. She caught herself thinking how nice it would be to have Maria put her things in order while she was out. ''Aren't you suddenly an aristocrat?'' she said to her reflection in the mirror and made a face at it.

A fresh wind was blowing along the Arno, and an occasional droplet of rain touched her as she walked out into the city. There was a golden light here, too, as in Venice, but with its own signature for the eye that could perceive. She looked at the low arched bridges, which crossed the river at short intervals. The Ponte Vecchio looked burdened with the shops that bulged out of its side.

She joined the press of pedestrians crossing the old bridge and quickly became absorbed in the magnificence of the jewelry displays in the shop windows. There must be something for a person of modest means, she thought, scanning past the diamond and gold bracelets and pins, pearl-encrusted goblets and baskets woven of gold threads. And then she found it. A dainty gold ring with three round cut garnets across the top, nested on a black velvet tray with other garnet jewelry. She almost didn't enter the closed door of the tiny store, but a woman's face looked up from behind the display and smiled at her encouragingly, and she went in.

''Seventy-five thousand lire, *signorina*,'' the proprietress said. ''Do you wish to see it?''

Allegra computed rapidly. It would be sixty-five dollars, more or less. *Nonna* had told her of the great collars of garnets that

ladies of wealth wore when she was a young girl in Venice. The
stones spoke to some kind of sweet memory in Allegra and made
sixty-five dollars seem a fair price to pay to pursue it. The ring felt
warm on her finger. It brought her another step closer to the
essence of Italy. What she tried not to think about was that she
now had something tangible to hold to when it was all over.

It was one o'clock, and the skies had been blown clear again.
The sun was making an intense pattern of light and shadow
through the central archways of the Ponte Vecchio. There was a
fragile fragrance in the air, and Allegra wrapped herself in the invisible cloak of the mood of Florence. Automobiles encroached
on her as she left the bridge and walked the rest of the way to the
Pitti. It looked dour and stolid. Tour buses were parked near the
entrance, letting out streams of people. She sighed at the sound of
many voices and waited until the others had gone ahead before
approaching the old building. She wanted to explore quietly.

In gallery after gallery she strolled and paused and studied,
sometimes smiling in sudden recognition of a well-loved painting.
She could never have been a true student of art history without
the experience of standing before the real things.

It was midafternoon when Allegra emerged. She hadn't
thought of Renaldo or anyone else in all that time. It was cumber-
some to fit back into the muddled little container of Allegra
Brent, but she had to give some thought to her duties. Six-thirty
would come quickly. A busload of Japanese sightseers was just
pulling away, and cameras were clicking from every window.
Allegra crossed the old bridge again and returned by the narrow
congested streets to the hotel.

The desk clerk called to her as she entered the lobby. There was
a message. He gave her a small envelope, and she recognized the
fine wavery script.

Dearest Allegra,
You left me too early this morning for me to wish you a
joyful visit in Firenze. I am with you in spirit as you climb
those accursed stairs of the Uffizi. Remember.

Affectionately,
Amalia di R.

Allegra looked up with a question on her lips. The deskman's face was most respectful. "A special messenger brought the messages. There is also an envelope for the *conte*."

She let herself into her room and lay down on the quilted muslin coverlet. The room was cool and silent, and she felt La Vecchia's presence intimately. Her nets extended far.

Allegra showered and dressed at a leisurely pace, constantly pulling her thoughts from Aldo. She didn't want to bring to life again the times of warmth: the great unbearable feeling of being part of him—the pain of the embrace. She needed to withdraw from the heat of her own nature for a while. It was alarming to be so vulnerable to his touch or a whisper. It seemed like the hardest thing in the world right now, to rein in the flaring energies of love. And La Vecchia saw it all.

She stood before the long door mirror and looked at her image. She was afraid she looked too well-groomed, maybe too much like the polished Falieri. She picked up a small stenographer's pad from her suitcase and felt more functional. It was the most comfortable role she knew at the moment—without it she was disarmed.

At six-thirty she heard Aldo's door close and steeled herself for his knock. She opened her door to him, avoiding his eyes. She felt conspicuous in her elegance.

"You honor me, Allegra. Not only are you quite a beautiful woman, but you do not keep a man waiting." He appraised her with frank approval and kissed her hand. Allegra snapped shut her purse with the notebook inside. She showed no feminine response to the compliments.

"I wouldn't be a very good secretary if I made you late." She looked at his face for the first time and saw that her words had been too cool. He drew back and she regretted her masquerade.

They drove out of the city into the hills of Fiesole. Cypress trees marched in single file back to distant villas off the road. Aldo hadn't spoken at all. Allegra made herself ask where the dinner would be.

"Angelo Bardo has a villa here. He has invited certain of the

American cosmetics executives to have a first look at the Italian designs. It is not a part of the conference agenda, but business is usually done this way. While the wives and mistresses are chattering, the men are in an airless room making commitments. I do not like to mix cocktails with business, but . . . ." He made a shrugging gesture as if to say, that's how it is and I can't change it.

He turned the car into a narrow lane. The high pink walls of the villa were on a rise, with terraces of flower beds banked against it. The scent of flowers grew stronger as they approached. Aldo parked on a level area near the entrance.

"A word of warning. Bardo is a ladies' man—*un damerino*."

Allegra turned to him. "That won't be a problem."

He looked at her for a moment. "I shan't worry about you, then," he said flatly.

The villa grounds were meticulously tended, commanding a view over the valley of the Arno. Aldo offered his arm, and they were shown to a large balcony terrace off the formal sitting room. It was a lovely setting. Several couples stood near the balustrade, looking like an advertisement for an expensive liqueur. The scene came to life when a smartly dressed vigorous older man stepped toward them and heartily embraced Aldo.

"My old friend! Why can I only entice you to my lair on the pretext of business? It is not right for you to rot among the antiques of Venice—human and otherwise!" He exploded into a loud laugh.

"Because, Angelo, I have a devil of a demanding profession, which chains me to my desk. Otherwise I would be a man of leisure, like you."

The man fixed Allegra with a practiced eye. "*Signorina* . . . may I have the pleasure?"

"Allegra Brent—Angelo Bardo. Signorina Brent is my secretary and assistant."

"Hmm. In business there is yet pleasure. Well, why should it not be?"

She acknowledged the introduction as gracefully as she could, aware of what his words implied.

"I wish you to meet Paolina," he went on. "She was fearful there would be no young women near her age to talk with tonight. Paolina! Come here!" A snap of his fingers brought a fragile beauty to his side. She looked no older than sixteen or seventeen, with shy eyes and soft brown curls around her face. Signor Bardo put his arm affectionately around her waist and kissed her cheek. "We shall all sit together at dinner, eh?"

Aldo and Allegra moved on to greet more new arrivals.

"Is there a Signora Bardo?" Allegra asked.

"She goes for summers to their country house on Lake Garda. The children are with her there."

"Except for Paolina," she said. "She seemed very timid. Not at all like her father."

Aldo took two glasses from a servant and gave one to Allegra. "He is not her father."

Allegra couldn't stop a look of surprise. Aldo took a sip of sherry and said almost apologetically, "It is the old Italy. Angelo is no scoundrel, but he is one of those men who can only love a child-woman. Paolina is the daughter of a poor Catania family. She would probably be married to a village boy by now, with a couple of *bambini* in the cradle. But a wealthy man has become her sponsor, and she goes to a fine Swiss school for young ladies. It is not to my taste, but it is an old and accepted form of social advancement."

"It wasn't my business, anyway. I guess I'm not much of an Italian."

"I beg you not to change," he said quickly. "Now let us meet some of the Americans who have just come in."

He guided her to a pleasant-faced couple. The man was design coordinator for one of the most expensive lines of cosmetics. He was intent upon drawing Aldo aside into a private conversation, leaving Allegra and his wife to make small talk. It was easy to find light words to say about the sunset and the glowing clouds. But Allegra's eyes were always searching out Aldo. She had a feeling of pride in seeing him as a respected and sought-after artist. It was unwise of her to allow it, but there it was. This was his world and she loved being a part of it. She saw him go into another room with the man.

Angelo Bardo put his hand on her shoulder. "Your man has stolen one of my guests, *signorina*. Would you lovely ladies care to meet my other friends?" He was a good host, not one to allow a slack in the party if he could help it. "I love American women. . . ." he was saying. "They are so candid, you know? It is refreshing. Life would be dull if there were no varieties of experience."

He deftly arranged to leave the executive's wife with another American couple and then excuse himself with Allegra. "Aldo is a genius—you know that, of course," he said as he let his arm slide around her waist. Allegra managed to turn in a way that disengaged his arm but was not clearly a rebuff. She decided to ignore his approaches if she could.

"I think he is a part of the rebirth of art in Italy," she said quietly, facing him with cool but cordial eyes. He didn't seem put off.

"Genius can be boring if you still have passion in the blood. If you are a person unfulfilled." He stared at her for a dramatic moment. She expected him to beat his chest for emphasis or let a tear fall from his dark glistening eyes.

"A true genius is an exciting person, *signore*. I can think of nothing sadder than playing always on the surface of life and its small pleasures."

"Ah," he sighed. "I bow to an intelligent American woman. A beautiful creature concealing so much seriousness." He stepped away from her as if to go, then stopped, shaking his head. "I do not disapprove—no. I think my friend di Rienzi has at last found a female to challenge him. You are a strange woman, but interesting . . . a great loss for the rest of us." He bent low over her hand.

Allegra was disturbed by her own intensity in replying to him. Why did she feel she had to defend Aldo?

The exuberant host announced that his guests should come now to the dining room. A young man, one of the other designers, came to Allegra's side with a courteous offer to escort her to dinner. Since Aldo was still closeted with the cosmetics man, she accepted him as a temporary escort. His name was Ernesto, and this was his first experience with the large companies. He was unsure of himself in this setting, having known the other designers only by their reputations. Angelo Bardo had taken a liking to him and wanted him to have a chance to become acquainted with the buyers before the formal presentations tomorrow. He was a cheerful dinner companion, easy to talk with and grateful for her conversation.

"I see you are taken care of, *signorina*," the host smiled over her shoulder. "I shall not worry that you are lonely, even though your man could be jealous." He laughed at his own humor and seated himself at the head of the table.

Aldo entered the dining room a few minutes later. He was seated several places away from her, next to Paolina. The American cosmetics man was across from Allegra. Aldo acknowledged her with a brief nod.

Ernesto wanted to talk with her, asking her nervous little questions to fill up any silence around him. She became aware of Aldo's eyes on her and looked up to see a hard disapproving light in them. It disturbed her. She wasn't doing anything except waiting for his call.

The American leaned across the table with a broad smile. "Miss Brent, I'm borrowing you for a few minutes after supper. Your generous boss tells me you take fast notes, and I want to draw up a preliminary contract for his designs. I hope you won't mind."

She felt Aldo's energies again, hitting at her composure. "Not at all," she said quickly. "That's the only reason I'm here."

"I find that hard to believe, Miss Brent. Don't sell yourself short."

The rest of the meal had very little flavor for her. She was being more than ignored by Aldo, and the attentions of Ernesto were tedious.

Aldo came to her side as the guests were leaving the table. "I realize that it is not to your pleasure to work this evening, Allegra, but I have a request to make of you."

"I already know," she said.

"Are you sure you won't be missed?" he snapped.

"You damn well better miss her, di Rienzi!" the American's voice broke in. "If I weren't here with my wife, I'd carry her off myself." He laughed heartily, but Aldo's face was stony. "I'll get her back to you as soon as I can. I know a possessive boss when I see one."

He took Allegra's arm and drew her into a small library study. She didn't look back. Once inside, he was all business, to her great relief. When he finished dictating he called for Aldo to read the agreement. It was a generous commitment, and it left Aldo considerable artistic freedom. Allegra smiled as he read it. She could rise above the surface tension between them to be simply happy with his good fortune. The men shook hands cordially after signing the paper.

"I just want to add one thing," the American said, "that when we come to Italy again next year, you'll have the same lovely secretary."

Aldo looked momentarily at a loss.

"I'm only a substitute," Allegra said. "Really just a tourist like everyone else. I don't expect to be here very much longer. My old job is waiting for me back home." She surprised herself with her words.

They left the villa within minutes. Aldo said rapid thank-yous and rushed them both out to the car. Allegra didn't resist his urgency but felt that something was quickly flaring to a climax.

He whispered roughly, "We must talk." The car doors opened and slammed shut, disturbing the shadowy quiet of the villa grounds. They drove back down the hill and along the Fiesole road. Allegra's thoughts were racing to anticipate what he might say. She knew he had judged her guilty of something during the course of the evening, and she was already defensive.

He turned the car off the road and stopped the engine. It was dark and silent, except for their measured breathing. Aldo lighted a cigarette tensely and turned in his seat toward her. "I must have an explanation."

She waited for him to continue. Her heart was beating unevenly.

"You seem to be amusing yourself at my expense, and I find it intolerable." The words were spoken in a low tone, but they cut into her. He went on, looking directly into her eyes. "I have seen how you work to attract men, to encourage their attentions."

Allegra almost laughed, the accusation was so idiotic. But in truth, she was angry. She was not caught off guard as before in the rose garden at La Mira.

Her voice was steady. "If I didn't care for you, I would call you a fool, Aldo."

"You are playing with me. Teasing me with the ways a woman learns. Your gown, for instance—what makes you want to display yourself for all the men to leer at? Maybe you are just another American tourist as you said, imagining romantic Italians will sweep you off your provincial feet!"

"Don't be insulting!" she snapped. "You're acting like a child! And you have no cause to berate me. Who are these men you see me enticing into my nets? Your brother, who should be spanked for his spoiled behavior? Dr. Nepi, a decent man who had too much to drink at the *festa*? Who else? Signor Bardo? A man who would press himself upon anything in skirts. And what about my dinner partner—a young man who would have made conversation with a lamp post to hide his nervousness. Oh, yes—the tryst in the library over my stenographer's notebook! You came in too soon. I was just getting him warmed up. . . ."

"Enough!" he shouted, grasping her shoulder. "You are mocking me!"

"Renaldo—look at me. Am I really so provocative? Is my dress such an invitation?" she said quietly. "What do you want me to look like?"

His hand loosened, and the intensity suddenly left him. He looked beaten and sad. "I do not know. I do not know. Forgive me. I think I am not fit company for gentle people. I cannot truly trust anymore." He took her hand in his. "I wish with all my heart that I could." Tears glinted in his eyes as he pressed a gentle kiss into her palm. Allegra put her cheek against his dark hair and drew his head against her. The moment was sweet and innocent.

Wordlessly they drove back to the hotel. Allegra knew that she was moving deeper into the dangerous territory of love and commitment. At the door to her room he pulled her into an embrace, but they did not kiss. He smiled solemnly down at her. "With all the words I spoke tonight, little one, I neglected to say thank you. Now, rest. I shall call for you again at noon."

As she lay trying to sleep, the work "trust" went round and round in her mind. It meant so much to Aldo.

She thought of the note Byron had pressed into the first Allegra's hand. It said "trust me." The Byron crest declared its motto: Trust Byron. It was a convenient word for seducers. She could feel Aldo's bitterness around the word. She wondered if the house of di Rienzi had a motto. Maybe it was Doubt Everyone. She smiled ruefully to herself in the darkened room, and when the waves of response to his touch finally eased, she gave her mind up to sleep.

CHAPTER NINETEEN

SHE WAS AWAKENED in the morning by a knock at the door. The hall porter wheeled a breakfast cart inside and drew open the curtains at the windows. She hadn't ordered breakfast for herself and was grateful to Aldo for the indulgence. A small florist's box lay next to her plate, with a note:

"I dare to hope you understand," it said, and then in English: "The first step of error none e'er could recall." A single yellow rose rested in the tissue of the box. *What an odd thing an apology is,* she mused. A flower and a quickly written line—fragile things themselves, but with the strength to blot out harsh memories. What had made him send her a line from Byron, unless he did truly want her to know the depth of his regret?

She quickly put caution around herself. Aldo would do exactly what he wished, and she was not yet invited into his private world. She had come to the conclusion that she had not the strength nor the right to force an entry. If she didn't want to be battered by Aldo's sudden turns of emotion, she would have to learn to expect nothing from him. Then, a loving crumb or two would be a gift to cherish. It was an unsatisfactory arrangement, but it assured her own survival. At least on the surface she would maintain her dignity.

She picked up the half-opened rose and smelled its honeyed fragrance. So—he was familiar with Byron's poetry. She did not miss the fact that he had selected a passage from a poem on the infidelity of women.

There was a silver bud vase with straw flowers on her bureau, perfect for her rose. It was not yet nine o'clock, and her window framed an intensely bright and clear view of the river and its bridges. She had time to explore before the business meeting at noon. She put on her blue pantsuit with a silk scarf to protect her hair and carried a string bag for any baubles she might collect on the way. It would be good to walk, this time to the Uffizi, in honor of La Vecchia. She had a small map of the city for a guide.

She walked the back streets toward the Piazza della Signoria. The jutting stone tower of the palazzo was in view much of the way. It looked solemn and intimidating, as if the need for dominance and fortification were permanently impressed into the mortar.

Allegra blended into the flow of tourists in the square. The statue of Cosimo the First looked unpleasantly over the crows from atop his bronze horse, to remind the uneducated visitor that this was unquestionably the seat of temporal power. She walked among the pigeons, who followed children with packets of corn in sudden flurries of activity.

A few steps farther brought her to the entrance of the Uffizi. The stairways were there, as La Vecchia had said, several stories of them. The first room of paintings was hung with early Florentine and Sienese works. Vibrating with gold in their backgrounds and frames, virgins sat enthroned with angels and saints. The spare images of Giotto, seen as if for the first time, threw out their energy to Allegra. She lingered, surprised by the immediate personal aura of the artist. The paintings almost tangibly projected a feeling of spiritual devotion.

Something in the simple vital power of the early masters made a connection in her mind with Aldo. It was what she had seen in his face the first day in the Ca' d'Argenti, when she walked alone down the hall to La Vecchia's apartments. It was the old and the new, yet within the new still the impelling force of what was.

After an hour she realized the Uffizi could not be seen and appreciated entirely in one quick tour. And a restlessness was growing in her to return to the hotel to prepare for her afternoon with Aldo.

She let herself into her peaceful room, happy to kick off her shoes and lie back on the cool coverlet of her bed. *I shall expect nothing from him,* she prompted herself. *It is possible to love and not need a return of affection.* Heroines of romantic novels did it all the time. She smiled at her own melodrama. "It is a far far better thing I do . . . ." She laughed aloud and started to undress for her shower.

At noon exactly, Aldo knocked at her door. She was ready, her mood light, and she felt cool and fresh in her new sea-green shirtwaist dress. Aldo appeared relaxed, too, handsome as always, with a large black portfolio tucked under one arm.

"Today we work, my friend," he said. "Last night's contract was easily done, because the man knew what he wanted, but with these people today—who can say? Much talk, much pressure to go one way or another. I need you close at hand to take notes, so that I do not forget what has already been discussed. This is the part I dislike, playing the games of the business world. I wish I had a brother whose judgment I could trust. Can you imagine Guido with a cool head, negotiating contracts for my designs? It is what he wants most to do."

They took the elevator to a private dining room. A buffet was set up along one wall, and waiters were circulating with trays of drinks. Maybe fifty people, mostly men, and well dressed, were standing in the high-ceilinged room. Allegra could hear English, Italian, French and German. Here and there groups were gathered tightly around display easels. Aldo greeted a number of people familiarly, fellow designers and businessmen for whom he had done work in previous years. Allegra was introduced as his assistant. There was none of the social byplay of the dinner at the villa. And in Aldo, too, there was no tinge of that uncomfortable shadow. The atmosphere was stimulating.

At one point, as Aldo was attempting to explain a design concept to several interested cosmetics packagers, he suddenly deferred to Allegra for an opinion. "You represent the woman's point of view," he said. "How does the shape and texture affect you?"

"I don't know if I'm qualified to speak for all women," she said cautiously, but seeing several pairs of eyes ready to take her seriously, she continued. "We have been beaten over the head with things labelled 'New,' but where is the lingering warmth in

New, after the first impact wears off? I am attracted by the best of what *was*. I don't mean the old and dusty, but there is such life and grace in the classic styles. I believe many women are looking back again to find the lyric voices of the old masters. It is just beginning. Perhaps we want a Renaissance again after such a long time of functional cold designs." She looked at Aldo, not sure if she had overstepped, but he was smiling.

"This is what I wished to express exactly, gentlemen. The beauty of the old, expressed through new hands. Why should it not take its birth in Italy, where it lived so well before?"

"So—you'd take us right back to the Medicis?" one Englishman chuckled.

"Back to Pompeii, my friend, if you'll go. These vials and perfume pots were used by some of the most sophisticated women who ever lived. I have been researching Egyptian designs lately . . . ."

"Enough!" the man laughed. "Let's have a spot of food, and I'll put myself in your hands."

For the rest of the afternoon the discussions were brisk and fruitful. Allegra was thoroughly happy. She felt the pace of Aldo's mind and moved with it. She listened and took notes and consulted with him until five o'clock, when the conference dispersed. There was to be a concert later in the evening, in the Pitti Palace courtyard. "To honor the distinguished international representatives and designers," the civic director of tourism announced.

"We can finish work over dinner," Aldo said, as he arranged his portfolio to leave. "My room has a good writing table. We can order food brought in." He held the door to the elevator for her. "And then, *amica mia,* I give you an outing at the Pitti. Small reward for your services."

He stood close to her as they ascended to their floor. His hand enclosed hers in a warm and steady grip. It felt natural to be standing there, satisfied with a day's work together, sharing a moment of calm.

She rested in her darkened room for an hour. Larry's pallid image floated past in weak contrast to Aldo's. The memory of Larry was being wiped to nothingness . . . erased more completely with every small awakening with Aldo.

She stopped her mind's wandering. More thought would lead to visions of the future, and that was unwise. She picked up her notebook, slipped back into her sandals and left her room.

The door to Aldo's room was open. A waiter was arranging a dinner table near the windows, and Aldo was at the telephone. "I was just calling you," he said. "Come in. I took the liberty of ordering for both of us."

He pulled up a chair for her and poured some white wine into their glasses. "Just a little," he smiled, "to celebrate. We are a good team, Allegra. I am grateful." He touched his glass to hers.

"I am happy to have helped a little."

"More than that, Allegra, much more. But I'll not make you a slave to work. A letter to *Candide Freres,* confirming the changes, and a memo to the Milano office, can go out tonight by special messenger. Then you can dress up, and I shall take you to hear beautiful music under the stars."

Their dinner conversation ranged from Aldo's studies of Egyptian art to the silly-looking French buyer whose bad hairpiece listed to one side. And then Aldo spoke of Byron. "I'm not comfortable in the role of ogre and cynic. If you wish, I shall find some university experts on Byron. Maybe one can authenticate your letters. There was a small poem, too, was there not?"

"I'm not sure they belong to the world," she said.

"You mean you won't put your story to the test?" he goaded gently.

"No. Not to satisfy the skeptics. That isn't why I came to Italy."

A silence settled between them. Allegra looked out over the river, knowing there weren't words sufficient to explain. "It doesn't seem to matter very much, Aldo. Not now," she said finally.

He smiled slowly. "My dear, I wish I understood. But that is not your fault. It is only mine. Now, let us write those letters, hmm? I promised myself not to intimidate you." They both laughed and moved to the large oak desk where they quickly finished their work.

Back in her room to change for the concert, Allegra held the light blue gown up to herself. The guilty dress. Anyway, it was too formal. Perhaps he would have a better response to one of the new pastel silk dresses. She showered and dressed quickly and put a small flowered comb in her hair. She was ready when Aldo came to the door.

He was, as usual, very handsome, in a dark gray silk suit and deep maroon tie. At his shirt cuffs were fire opals set in gold.

"I hope you will accept a compliment, *signore*," Allegra said.

"In Italy you must always allow the gentleman to notice the lady first. But I shall overlook custom. I am known to be a very traditional man," he chided, smiling as he bent to kiss her hand.

They walked along the Lungarno and across the Ponte Vecchio. A soft evening air moved gently over them with the last glow of dusk light. The palace front was bathed in light, as people and cars and small horse carriages drew close to the entrance. They joined other concertgoers, walking through the reception hall and into the central courtyard. Renaissance fountains made a shimmery backdrop to the stage. Chairs were arranged in rows facing the small orchestra. It was to be an evening of baroque and classical music.

The lights dimmed around the court and the orchestra went silent from its energetic tuning, when the conductor entered. Allegra let herself blend into the eighteenth-century atmosphere. She was aware of the clear starry night above her and the faint light at the top of the terraces of the Boboli Gardens beyond. Then the first passionately restrained measures of a Brandenburg Concerto pulled along her nerves, forcing them to the surface. She was painfully alert to her own emotional fragility, and she couldn't find the will to continue fighting it. Her eyes clouded, and she closed them in an effort to deny the tears of fatigue and love.

"What is it, little one?" Aldo took her hand.

She managed a smile. "It's Bach. His music affects me."

"So I see. I sincerely hope that Mozart can make you happy again. For a moment I thought I had done something beastly to you."

She put her other hand over his. "You haven't done a thing," she lied. He kept her hand in his for a long time and kissed it when he finally let it go.

After the concert Aldo thought it would be pleasant to go home in one of the open horse carriages. He told the driver to go past the Duomo and the Piazza della Signoria. He sat close to Allegra and took her hand again, in a natural gesture of companionship.

"Do you know that I have never done this before? Never relaxed to play the tourist." The hooves of their chestnut horse were loud on the bridge, and both banks of the Arno were bejeweled by lights. Aldo smiled then and said, "One misses much that is beautiful in life by being a busy man. Sometimes I feel very stupid, running and pressing. For what? My grandmother is so disapproving of my life." His eyes looked straight ahead. "And she is right. It is the life of a man who does not want to see."

"I think you have had much pain, Aldo," she said. "And you have a sensitive heart. I know what it is to lose someone you love."

"I wonder if you do, little one. For instance, what happens when you see something that brings memory of one you loved? Your pretty garnet ring is such a thing. I noticed it last night when you looked so lovely at the villa. I said nothing, but the memories cut into me. I couldn't stop reacting to them."

Allegra turned the dark stones into her hand and closed her fist over them.

"When Bianca was born, I was beside myself with happiness. I had everything a man could desire—a beautiful wife and the start of a houseful of children. I gave her a small token of my joy: a garnet ring very much like yours. I thought it would please her with its simple beauty, perhaps be handed down to Bianca when she was old enough. But she never wore it, and one day I saw one of our maids with the ring on her hand. These are the memories I have of love. And when I hear Bianca begging thoughtlessly for baubles, I hear my wife's voice demanding amusement. That is what love recalls to my heart. I know it is not right, but there is no way for me to change it. I am what I am.''

"And that is that, I suppose," Allegra said crisply, turning to face him. "That is your excuse for making Bianca feel unloved. Do you expect her to understand all your complicated emotions at her age? How in heaven's name will she grow up to be the kind of woman you respect unless you teach her? Your grandmother won't live forever!''

Aldo stared at her. "All this from you, Allegra? La Vecchia has found a younger tongue. I think I should thank you for your frankness. And, yes, I am aware of what Bianca needs, yet I cannot help reacting harshly to her childish ways. There is so much impatience in me with female deviousness. I fear she has it in her blood.''

"That is absurd, Aldo, just another excuse for avoiding your duty to her. What do you plan to do as she gets older and reminds you even more of her mother?''

The driver half turned his head to hear better.

"I am not sure I like your tone, *amica*," he said with a smile of surprise and admiration stealing over his lips. "I should be insulted, but I am not a complete idiot." He kissed her hand, the one with the garnet ring, and gathered her close into an embrace that left her breathless.

The cab came from the shadowy narrow streets out into the Piazza della Signoria. The faces of the buildings and the areas of statuary were lighted like a great stage setting. The horse stopped in front of the Loggia, and the driver jumped down to fasten a bag of oats over his friend's long face. He grinned up at Aldo and Allegra. "We wait a minute here so you can enjoy the most perfect square in all Italy. It is an inspiration for lovers, *signore, signorina.*"

Allegra leaned close to Aldo's ear. "It's also a good place for a Dutch uncle." He looked baffled. "It's an American expression, for a friend who takes it upon himself to do plain talking when it's needed."

Aldo laughed. "You are a Dutch aunt, then?"

"No, there's no such thing."

"Hmm. I feel very odd sitting in a *carrozza* with an uncle, but I am very happy to be with my honest friend."

The driver unstrapped the feedbag and climbed into his high seat. "The Duomo next," he announced, flicking his whip for show over the head of the horse. The animal had already started his slow walk.

Aldo's face was relaxing. "I am not accustomed to having a woman for a friend, and I am not a man who tolerates such frank criticism from anyone, but Allegra, I confess that you are an exceptional person. La Vecchia's obsession with fate may have its merits. You have dropped into our lives when we needed you . . . I needed you. I do need you, Allegra *mia*. I think you know that."

The energy between them lightened. Aldo spoke of Bianca with more ease. He never mentioned Vera Falieri as a potential stepmother. They spoke eagerly about art and design. It wasn't the usual conversation for an evening carriage ride in Florence. He reached out to her with his ideas and was just as quick to criticize himself. Aloofness, brittleness and sardonic smiles were suddenly not part of his personal armor.

In her joy she didn't notice they had come again to a halt, this time between the magnificent Duomo, Giotto's Tower, and the venerable Baptistry. The coachman looked frustrated with their lack of appreciation for his tour. "Please, *signore*," he begged, "take the *signorina* to see the Baptistry doors—they are world famous."

Allegra laughed. "I must see Ghiberti's doors, Aldo."

They returned to the hotel near midnight. His kiss at the door to her room was very gentle. "I will not forget this day with you, Allegra, and I will not forget your words. It took courage to speak as you did, and that is a quality I treasure. I am almost sorry that we must go home tomorrow."

Allegra's mind was racing as she prepared for bed. She wanted to believe she had broken through the shell. It did seem that way, even though she knew that the progress could be as quickly reversed by a casual word on her part. She feared the delicate balance of their relationship. She had no way of knowing where all the dark places in Aldo's memory lay.

She looked at her ring, such a small thing to have the power to shake Aldo so. Thank God she wasn't keeping a diary of all this, she thought. She wouldn't want one of her descendants to read what a mess she made of a simple trip to Italy.

IT WAS ALREADY VERY WARM early in the morning, and Aldo had the top down for the drive back to Venice. Allegra twisted a silk scarf into a narrow headband and wedged into her seat with Aldo's portfolios around her. He drove fast along the Autostrada. It was exhilarating to be so close to the fields and trees in the open car. The wild herb smells flowed around them in sensuous bouquets of aroma.

Aldo turned his tanned face to her and spoke loudly against the hot August wind. "I suppose this is ruining your hair—I'm sorry!"

"I don't care!" she shouted back, her face partly hidden in swirling brown tendrils that the headband couldn't contain.

"Dio mio!" he laughed. "A natural woman!"

As they drove through the hills north of the city, his hand took hers from time to time.

For lunch they found a little restaurant in Bologna not far from the university. From there Aldo called ahead to Venice, to make sure Luigi would have the launch at the landing to meet them.

Allegra began to feel less joyful as they neared Venice. There was a strange heaviness around the thought of the Ca' d'Argenti, even though La Vecchia and Bianca would be there to greet her with love. She analyzed the uncomfortable feeling and decided

that her poetic ancestor's sense of melodrama was leaking
through the veils of time onto her imagination. One last disturbing thought blew through her mind before she caught it: who
would Aldo have on his arm at the great birthday ball?

She managed to juggle her inner doubts with a flow of easy
conversation as they drove. He was as pleasant and uncomplicated as any woman could ask for. But deep within her,
she was not at peace.

CHAPTER TWENTY

Luigi swung the motor launch into its berth under the Ca'. He tapped lightly on the horn, and one of the younger serving boys clattered down the marble stairs to the dock. Aldo made the line fast and gestured to the bags, then held out a hand to Allegra. She put hers into it, delighting in its strength. He pulled her up and out of the boat, holding her for a moment.

"So, we are returned to our usual pursuits, eh? I am grateful for your help. Shall we face the ancient one in full preparation for the birthday? I have a feeling things will not be as usual."

He kissed her hand and then urged her toward the entrance stairs. He seemed tense, already anticipating what was inside.

In the entrance hall a scene of confusion was in progress—stepladders, small gold and velvet chairs, drop cloths over the marble floor. The great glass chandelier was lowered, and Maria was supervising its cleaning. A pair of large doors opposite Aldo's study was wide open, and Allegra looked into a room that took her breath in surprise.

It was the ballroom, its walls paneled in soft red velvet brocade, and its ceiling seemingly held up by dozens of fat golden cherubs. Around the edges was a painting of sky and clouds so real that the eye was drawn into infinity. Across one side the rising sun sent out streaming rays of light, from which drove Apollo, his golden chariot and fiery horses flaming with color.

Allegra had stopped at the doorway, bemused by the impact of color. Now she was drawn suddenly back to reality by a small voice crying her name, and seconds later a little body hurtled against her. Automatically, she bent down to enfold Bianca in her arms.

"Oh, I'm so glad you're home! I've missed you, I've missed you! *Nonna* missed you, too!"

Disentangling herself from the child, Allegra looked up to see a strange tableau. La Vecchia sat in her wheeled chair in the midst of paint cans, ladders, bolts of cloth and gold swags. Next to her chair stood Vera Falieri, her face taut under its exquisite makeup. She looked past Allegra and exclaimed, "Ah, Aldo *mio*, how we have missed you! *La contessa* did not wish to decide entirely on decorations without you. So we progress slowly." She spread out her hands with a frustrated shrug. "I am trying to be of service as I promised."

La Vecchia had been silent, her eyes on Aldo and Allegra. Then she spoke irritably. "It's about time you came home! Come here, Allegra, I want you to see this material. Do not hang on her, Bianca—can't you see that you are being a nuisance?" Allegra squeezed the small hand lovingly, and Bianca released her tight grip.

Vera Falieri moved possessively toward Aldo, reaching up to kiss his cheek. She ignored Allegra entirely.

La Vecchia announced her plans for the decoration of the hall and swags for the orchestra alcove in a very decisive voice, and Aldo agreed with a smile.

"It is not done anymore," Falieri said under her breath, but no one paid attention.

"You must be tired, Allegra *mia*!" La Vecchia's face broke into its enchanting wrinkled smile. "We will have tea. Tell Maria—I have had enough work for today." She turned to Vera Falieri with a courteous nod of her head. "Thank you for your advice and help. I think most things are well in hand now. You also must be weary, so I will leave you. Maria, will you wheel me to the lift?" Allegra followed behind the chair, with Bianca dancing at her heels. Passing Aldo, La Vecchia said, "Do not be long—I have much to say to you!"

Maria established her in the chair lift, and while it rose in a slow curve the old lady's lips moved in silent dialogue with herself. Allegra was glad to escape to her room, promising to return for tea. She shut the clamoring Bianca outside the door, as one of the young maids bore her away.

Poor Bianca, she thought sadly. *Each of us cries for love and attention and is rebuffed so often.* She stood for a few minutes at her window, looking out at the rooftops. Her common sense said, *go, before your roots grow any deeper.*

She sighed and turned to freshen her face. Love lay like a heavy knot in her breast, a measurable physical sensation like a weight or pressure. She shook herself mentally and combed her hair, then on impulse she shed her clothes and put on one of the dresses from La Vecchia that she had not yet worn. It was a soft mauve-pink sheath, bound with an equally delicate blue. The color reflected a gentle flush on her face and made her hair seem dusky with shadows.

She asked herself why she should be trying to make herself attractive. Would Aldo care? Even now he was with Falieri. He had not drawn back from her welcoming kiss. Even after the sweet companionship in Florence, suddenly he seemed to have left Allegra in spirit, to have gone back to Falieri and business as usual. Was it only friendship he felt for her? Had she misread him so completely? Her heart twisted achingly at the thought.

She opened her door to a quiet hall and went toward La Vecchia's rooms. Her hand was raised to tap on the slightly ajar door, when voices made her catch her breath and stand silent.

"I have no obligation to that woman, Aldo," La Vecchia's tone was harsh. "So she complains that I am difficult, eh? I have had to endure her patronizing advice and if I do not take it, in my own house, she uses the knife dipped in sugar to cut at me."

Aldo spoke gently. "But, *carissima,* I asked her to try to help you, since I must be away. She only tried."

La Vecchia snorted. "She had Bianca in tears, bringing out the worst in the child. You will oblige me, Aldo, by not pressing this woman upon me. I have some privileges from age, and one is not to deal with such a personality."

There was a moment of silence, then Aldo said coldly, "She said you were overwrought, and I must agree. This ball is perhaps too much effort for you. I find Vera anxious to be of service. She has a kind heart."

"I thought better of your judgment, Renaldo! I see that argument is fruitless." Her voice suddenly was weary. "I will not let this come between us, my dear. Now you are home. There is no necessity for outside help. Come, I am so glad to see you. Tell me, how was the conference?" Their voices lowered into a more pleasant murmur.

Guiltily, Allegra tapped on the door. Aldo's deep voice told her to enter. He was sitting close to his grandmother's chair on a low stool. Her delicate old hand was resting lightly on his shoulder. Peace was obviously restored. Allegra flushed under their steady gaze. She felt very much outside the di Rienzi circle. The discomfort was broken by the arrival of tea. Aldo rose and placed a chair for Allegra, and Bianca rushed in to glue herself to Allegra's side, while La Vecchia poured tea and gave Allegra an especially welcoming smile.

Aldo said nothing, abstractedly looking into his teacup. Allegra had to drag her eyes from his face. She looked up to find La Vecchia watching her.

It was a relief when La Vecchia began to talk about the preparations for the ball. Allegra was drawn into the web of plans, and Aldo excused himself to go to his office. The old lady made no inquiries of her concerning the trip to Florence.

Allegra settled into work after tea, ordering cases of champagne, writing orders for food, confirming plans for a suitable small orchestra. Dinner hour came, and she ate with La Vecchia. Finally, the guest lists were complete.

"Go to bed, Allegra *mia*, we have done enough. There is tomorrow." She beckoned her close to place soft lips on her cheek. "Do not be sad, child," she said gently. "My nearly one hundred years have taught me some things. One is that whatever at the moment seems very bad, may change. The other is that we must be honest with others in relationships. If we love people, we should let them know, because if we do not we are wasting a precious thing that should be shared." She paused and patted Allegra's hand with a comforting touch. "And so, *cara mia*, I wish to tell you that I have love for you. It is a joy to have you with me. Now, sleep well."

SHE DID SLEEP WELL. To her surprise, things appeared less difficult in the light of a bright morning. One of the maids brought her breakfast tray, asking her to join La Vecchia in an hour. On her tray was mail, which had come for her while she was away in Florence.

Clinton Meserve's businesslike envelope lay on top. She began to open it and barely noticed that part of the seal had been torn and then pasted down again, for she was curious to read Clinton's news. A small letter dropped from the folds, an envelope addressed in Larry's handwriting. She drew a sharp breath at the sight of it. How long since she had seen Larry? Only a month?

She read Clinton's letter first. His kindly worried voice spoke from the page. Why had she not written more often? He had been contacted by Larry, who felt that she was in some kind of shock reaction to *nonna*'s death. Larry seemed such a solid dependable young man. Hadn't she seen enough of Italy by now? Wasn't it time to come home and build a real life for herself? He had heard that aristocratic old families in Europe, like the di Rienzis, were decadent. Allegra could hear the echoes of Larry's attitudes and was angry. Poor old Clinton should not be made to worry like that.

Reluctantly, she opened Larry's letter. It was brief:

I'm concerned about you, Allegra, but I'm trying to understand how you feel. I can see that you wanted to get something out of your system, from all of the romantic ideas about Italy that your grandmother taught you. I imagine that the reality has made you realize that the good old U.S.A. is a lot more comfortable. Clinton seems to think you are working as some kind of a servant or nurse. You don't have to do that, Allegra. Just come home and I'm willing to get married. You have hurt me, but I'm ready to build a new life for us. If it would make you happy we can honeymoon in Venice. Let me know when you will be back, but you'll have to understand that I can't wait forever.

Love, Larry

Allegra sat with frustrated tears in her eyes. Poor Larry. She hated to hurt him, but his ego was so unshakable. She let the letter drop from her fingers; its vibrations were distasteful. She drew her stationery from the desk drawer and wrote a hasty reassuring note to Clinton.

She was happy in Italy. She would let him know soon when she would return. She asked him to contact Larry and tell him that she would not be renewing any relationship with him. "Quite simply," she wrote, "I do not love him and I will not marry only for security." She tore Larry's letter into small pieces and threw them away from her balcony. She had a feeling of relief watching the pieces float on the wind to light on the canal waters and disappear.

She spent the morning working with La Vecchia. The chair lift grew hot with the old *contessa*'s journeys up and down it. Finally, somewhat weary, Allegra went to her room for an afternoon rest.

She was lying fully dressed on her bed, gazing out her balcony window at the rooftops across the canal, when a knock sounded at her door. She was tempted not to answer, but it came again. Luigi was there with a note in his hand. He waited while she read it.

I regret disturbing you, but I am in need of your help for several letters. You have the materials in your notebooks, not yet transcribed. Forgive me, but will you come to my study for a short while?

Aldo

She looked up at Luigi. "Tell Signor di Rienzi I will come in a moment." She turned back into her room with her heart pounding hard. They would be close again—he wasn't with Falieri. A stream of images rushed through her mind.

When she left her room, Guido was standing at the top of the stairs. He grinned at her. "Well, well, Allegra. How was Florence?"

"Very pleasant," she said noncommittally.

He fell into step beside her as she went down the stairs. "You're going to work for the lord and master, eh? He always gets service with no trouble. You should see the secretaries at the office run to help him. Guess you're like all the rest of them. Somehow I thought you wouldn't fall so easily." He put a heavy hand on her shoulder and gave what could be considered a commiserating squeeze. "Listen, Allegra, I don't like to see you hurt. Maybe I should have advised you earlier, but you overreact so, it's hard to help you."

She shrugged his hand away. At the foot of the stairs he favored her with a sympathetic smile. She longed to wipe it away with some stabbing retort. Instead, she said, *"Ciao,"* and turned toward Aldo's office.

To her irritation, Guido followed her, opening the door for her with a flourish and coming in after her. She marched stiffly ahead of him toward the typewriter desk. Aldo looked up in surprise to see his brother.

"Ciao, Aldo," he said, grinning at Allegra, "I'm just dropping in for a minute. Your secretary is in a bad humor. Maybe her letter from her fiancé in the United States upset her. What kind of a fellow is he, Allegra? He's either impatient, very patient or he's a fool—better not play with him too long or he'll find another girl."

She turned to find him staring at her, his face bold with a look of satisfaction. Aldo's full attention was on them now, his eyes hooded and cool.

"So you opened my letter! I thought it had been tampered with! What a rotten thing to do!"

"Don't get all righteous, Allegra. Your letter was unsealed, and when I picked it up, part fell out. I just put it together again. Of course I couldn't help seeing a few sentences," he chuckled. "Everybody knows I'm curious."

Suddenly, she was defeated. She turned back to the typewriter, picking up her transcripts from Florence to stand waiting with the impersonal expression of a well-trained office worker.

Guido had more to say. "Too bad, Aldo, you're going to lose

your little secretary. He wants her back, you know, and it's my guess she's satisfied, now he's crawling again. That's women for you." He laughed on a derisive note.

She spun around, stung. "He is not my fiancé. I gave him no reason to assume that." She addressed herself to Aldo, frightened to see the dark glitter back in his eyes. "Please tell me what parts of the reports you need."

He drew a deep breath. "Of course. Guido, I suggest you leave us in peace to get some work done. We all haven't your good luck to do nothing."

Guido smiled at them both. "It's time for me to go anyhow. I'm meeting Adeline Specchi for tea. Work hard." He walked out, slamming the door shut with a careless thrust of his hand.

Aldo's lips shut into an austere and irritated expression. In a quiet strained voice, he instructed Allegra on what he wanted to have transcribed. She turned back to the typewriter and started to work. It was hard to concentrate with the knot in her solar plexus. Her hands were clumsy on the keys, and sometimes the symbols of her shorthand blurred through tears. The silence was taut with unspoken words. Aldo rustled his papers, his correcting pen hovering over sheets of figures.

Finally she finished what was needed and rose to take the completed sheets to his desk. He received them without comment, setting them aside.

"Have you more for me to do?" she asked in a small voice.

His eyes were distant. "I am surprised, Allegra, that you did not consider me enough of a friend to honor with the knowledge of your engagement. You were happy to listen to my confessions so recently; I assumed there was trust between us."

She stood staring at him. "But I'm not engaged; I never was. Larry took too much for granted. He couldn't believe I was only a friend. He wouldn't take no for an answer." She heard her own voice protesting too frantically.

"I see," Aldo said in a heavy, unbelieving tone.

"You don't see at all. How could you?"

"Women are women the world over, is it not so? No real loyalty, nothing cherished . . . you almost convinced me otherwise. I was beginning to dismiss my doubts. No matter that Guido was wrong to read the letter.''

Blood rushed into her face, and anger exploded in her. "*Signore*, I am glad I have so little of your blood in my veins. The unreason of the di Rienzi males is amazing!''

"Are you so proud to have the bastard blood of a licentious poet, who was the laughingstock of Venice!'' The fire between them changed to ice suddenly. "Surely,'' he rasped, "it will be impossible for you to stay at the Ca' any longer. You will wish to leave as soon as the ball is over. La Vecchia must not be inconvenienced by this unpleasantness.''

She was stunned, wanting to say something to hit out at his insanity, but unable. He looked at her as at a child. "We will not argue.'' He picked up his pen to work again. The chill of his feeling engulfed her, and she turned away toward the door. As her hand touched the latch something made her look back at him. His head was bent over his work. The light glowed behind his coin-fine profile.

"I feel very sorry for you, Renaldo. Good night.'' .

He did not seem to hear. The energy behind his words was punishing, and Allegra was confused and angry . . . frightened by the intensity of her own emotions.

In what way was she guilty of anything? It was all upside down and crazy.

She didn't want to see any of the di Rienzis. She went immediately upstairs and tried to arrange reservations by train to Milano and from there home by plane. She wanted to go now, today, but it was August, and all of Europe was on vacation—impossible to buy a ticket to anywhere. She would have to wait until the morning after the ball, four days from now.

She shut herself into her room, sending word that she had a headache and wanted no dinner. She refused to answer the light knocks that she knew were from Maria. She was lying in the dark, exhausted, when she heard the faint sound of a key in her door lock. She rose up on one elbow, pushing her tear-dampened hair away from her face. The light in the hall revealed La Vecchia's small upright figure. Her hand found the light switch.

"So," she said, closing the door behind her. She moved quietly to the bed and sat down on its edge. Her soft fragile hand smoothed the dark mass of curly hair. "It is Aldo, is it not?" Allegra could only nod. "Is this the way you intend to face this problem, Allegra *mia*?" The old face was warm with a smile. "Tell me what has happened."

Bit by bit the story came out: Larry's letter, Guido's revelations and the episode in the rose garden at La Mira with Guido and Aldo. La Vecchia looked thoughtful with a faint smile upon hearing the last part. The tale of friendship blooming in Florence made her shake her head and mutter, "Poor, poor Aldo!"

"I've made a botch of it, I know that," Allegra ended her recital. "And I didn't want you to have one more thing to worry about. I expected to keep it all to myself. I'll be going home after the ball, Contessa Amalia. It will be best."

La Vecchia looked deeply into her eyes. "Is this Aldo's suggestion?"

Allegra was silent.

"Ah, then you want to marry this Larry . . . ."

"No, of course not," Allegra said quickly. "I will never marry him. I'll get my job back and find an apartment. Maybe I can save enough to come back to Italy one day and study."

"You feel there is no possibility that Aldo might soften to you?"

"None. If he did feel anything toward me, it's dead now. You saw him with Vera Falieri. That's what he needs, a wife to be proud of . . . to be another accessory to his station."

"That is a matter of opinion. Falieri chose him—he did not choose her." La Vecchia said the last with a hint of anger.

"I'm not a teenager. I'll get over him." A rush of bright tears invalidated her words. With a sympathetic murmur, La Vecchia put her arms around her. For a moment the two heads, old and young, rested close to each other.

"It has been my experience, as I have told you, that what seems impossible one day may not be so at all. I would advise you not to be hasty, *cara mia*. Aldo is in a struggle with his own soul." Her hand began to stroke Allegra's hair, and comfort flowed from the touch.

A feeling of deep love toward her welled up in Allegra. She took one of the small hands with its flashing rings and held it close to her cheek. She couldn't control the emotion in her voice. "Even if I have been so foolish as to let Aldo disturb me, I am so terribly grateful for the privilege of knowing you. Your kindness has been wonderful. I'll never forget you—and I love you. I only wish I were truly a di Rienzi."

"Nonsense. My dear child, you belong with us through the blood of Allegra di Rienzi. As far as I am concerned, that is settled." She nodded for emphasis and rose from her place on the bedside. "It is late, *cara*, and I will go. I simply was worried about you. I am not too old that I forget how the heart can hurt. Do not plan to leave after the ball. Give life time to act for you. The young are so hasty, when it is the old who have reason for it."

Allegra released her hand. "Will you tell me one more thing?" she asked in a low voice.

"What is it, my dear?"

"Was this . . . was this her room? The first Allegra's? I have to know."

The *contessa* stood for a while before answering. She bent to place a light kiss on Allegra's cheek. "Of course it was. I thought you must have known it from the first day, but I was waiting for you to ask." She smiled lovingly and walked from the room. In the soft light the illusion of youth was around her.

Allegra lay looking at the closed door for a long time. She thought of the courage of the small woman, whose aged back was still straight to meet whatever the future could bring, and she felt ashamed for her own weeping. But misery washed over her again. Would she ever be able to fill this empty place in her heart? Would this painful ache be with her always?

She slept fitfully, swimming through disturbing dreams where she ran about in room after room in what seemed to be the Palazzo Mocenigo, searching for Byron . . . hoping to be eased by his understanding. There was no one else to turn to now. But she couldn't find him. He had already gone away with another woman.

CHAPTER TWENTY-ONE

IT WOULD BE FOUR DAYS until the ball—long days, which Allegra would have to fill with activity to distract herself from thought. Workmen, decorators, seamstresses moved feverishly about the Ca' as the tension of anticipation grew strong. Bianca had to be forced to take her afternoon naps, and Maria assumed increasing responsibility, as di Rienzi relatives and their attendants arrived. She tried her hardest to keep the kitchen and upstairs staff in order and happy, in spite of the added burdens on them.

Allegra buried herself in lists and bills, finding in the impersonal accounting work a little respite from herself. The preparations were going well, Bianca was busy, everyone was occupied, but she was restless. She had not seen Aldo, and he had not joined the family for meals. It was understood that work and Vera Falieri kept him away. The servants were quietly aware of everything that went on in the great house.

A picture of the Bugelli family moved into her mind, and she decided to visit them. It would probably be the last time she would see them, she thought sadly. She set out in the morning to walk, checking to make sure she had written down the right address. She had a street guide of the city and wanted to find the house herself if possible. There were a few hours to spare before the fitting session with La Vecchia's seamstresses. It wasn't really necessary, since the gown already fitted adequately.

She found herself pleasantly lost in the mazes of walkways between the Ca' and the Casa Bugelli. Here and there at the corner of a building a stone was carved with the name of the lane. At last Allegra came into the street she sought, feeling a desire to run for the serenity of the Bugellis' front door.

Eleana answered her knock and stood speechless for an instant, before throwing her arms wide to embrace Allegra. "I think of you every day, my friend!" she exclaimed. "And we all miss you.

Giorgio wonders if he was such a bad guide that you decided to leave Venice right away. Come in, come in!''

Eleana's warmth was irresistible. It stole over Allegra's tired nerves like a comforting balm, and she returned the good feeling with gratitude.

"Tell me everything!" Eleana insisted, as she put a dark old teakettle on the stove. "I am so happy to see you." And then her perceptive eyes saw what Allegra was trying to conceal—but she said nothing.

Allegra started to talk about her past busy weeks, with emphasis on what a bright child Bianca was, what a fine woman the *contessa*. There were few words for the *conte*—too few—and Eleana began to see what was going on in the heart of her poor young friend.

"I will be going home in a few days," Allegra said. "I just had to see you before I left."

"With no regrets?" the older woman asked. "Has it all been the happy adventure that you hoped?"

Allegra knew what she was asking, and her eyes puddled with a bank of tears. She was weary of tears. She wanted to tell her but couldn't. It would be selfish to burden this kind loving woman with her tale of woe. "I'll never forget Venice," she whispered, then in a stronger voice: "I did a lot of growing up here."

Eleana poured tea for them and brought a plate of cheese and bread. "Yes, *cara*, I know. I hope you will remember, when you are back in your own home, that you have a family in Venice that loves you."

Allegra turned her face away, and Eleana put her arms around her firmly and held her until the tears stopped. "I know," she said again softly. "It will be better."

They finished their small lunch, as the cat, Neroni, wound himself around their legs under the table. Here in this island of peace and sanity, Allegra gathered the energies she needed to return to her remaining duties in the di Rienzi household. She and Eleana parted with love and promises never to forget their brief time together.

She walked to the Piazza San Marco for a farewell to the heart of the city. Her eyes were not as eager now to seek out the enticing window displays in the shops under the archways. The sounds of human activity washed over her like waves on a distant shore. She knew what was happening but she couldn't bring herself into focus, and turned to walk slowly away from the square to keep her appointment with the seamstress.

On the stairway of the Ca', she met Dr. Nepi. He had caught the festive mood of the ball. "I want you to reserve the first waltz for me," he beamed. "There is no doubt that the *contessa* will live to see her birthday and perhaps even more, and I intend to relax myself and have a celebration. They should give special awards to physicians who kill themselves for their patients." He walked on, chuckling at his own joke, while Allegra tried hard to appear pleasant.

In her room she saw the ball gown hanging expectantly, almost alive. She didn't feel like putting it on. She walked out to find the seamstress in the sewing room. The small middle-aged woman was almost lost in the billows of fabric around her. Two assistants were bent close over their work, oblivious to Allegra's entrance. She explained that she would not be needing a fitting, since the gown was exactly her size. The seamstress smiled in relief to have one less chore to accomplish and thanked her from her heart.

Strangers passed Allegra in the hallways now—people with di Rienzi faces. Some too self-important to raise their eyes to greet her, others warm and friendly. The Ca', too, was changing.

La Vecchia was dining alone under orders of Dr. Nepi. Luigi presented Allegra with a small envelope, as she stood outside her room. "It arrived just now, *signorina*."

She reached hesitantly to accept it. Her hands felt awkward, as she quickly opened it and drew forth the parchment stationery. "My dear Miss Brent": the writing began. It was not Aldo's spare rapid script. Her eyes raced to the bottom of the paper to read the signature—Pietro Luigi Maria Mossanato, and a smile broke the solemnity of her face. That sweet little gentleman, with his elaborate handwriting, was inquiring with the utmost politeness and tact, whether she might still be in Venice in two weeks to attend the Byron festival in Greece.

In a postscript, he put himself at her service should she feel the necessity for protection—she smiled at his words, so incongruous to his benign appearance. She had completely forgotten his earnest invitation. How selfish of her to neglect such a kind heart as his! She immediately sat down at her writing desk to compose a letter to him.

ON THE MORNING of the day before the ball, Allegra opened unwilling eyes to a dark dawn. No shafts of sun fingered the rounded chimney pots in view outside her window. Clouds moved in windblown patterns across a dull sky. It was drizzling lightly, and her mood matched the day. Not so long ago it had been joy to wake up in her pretty room. But now Aldo's words echoed acidly back to her, and she hated to face La Vecchia's concerned face and speculative watchful eyes.

She wrapped herself in her robe and set to work checking out the lists of guests and the hand-inscribed cards to be placed with La Vecchia's gifts for her friends. There were beautiful cuff links for men and lovely earrings for the women, all with variations of a scroll pattern entwining the dates of La Vecchia's century of life—designed with the di Rienzi colors in jewellike enamel and gold.

Allegra finished and went over to the window to look out at the dreary sky again. A sound attracted her attention to the canal below. A small motorboat was easing out of the water gates of the Ca'. In the boat were two men, one of them Signor Mossanato. The little man was bundled up in a trench coat against the weather. It was strange, almost like a scene from a detective movie. The faces of both men were grim, and the boat went quickly down the canal, with the motor barely purring. What was Signor Mossanato doing at this early hour at the Ca'?

While she dressed, she thought again about Florence, and the moments when Aldo had seemed so close. She remembered the glowing spark that had lighted deep in his eyes. Now it was gone.

And at the Ca' . . . she had tried to pretend that all was well, yet it was not. A growing density of atmosphere, a brooding tension was unmistakably here. Allegra di Rienzi's long ago misery in the Ca' d'Argenti lay like a film of dust over everything, too easily roused from its sleep.

She thought about the diary. She hadn't looked at it since the day she arrived. There was too much intensity in its emotion, which reached out, defying time, refusing to become part of the dead past. Could it be that the opening of the ballroom and the resurrecting of the old gowns from the attics combined with the diary to stir up the lingering energies of the past? La Vecchia's outward actions covered anxiety, no matter how much her hundred years of self-control had trained her.

She finished dressing and went to the desk in a small annex room of La Vecchia's suite. There she began methodically to attach name cards to the jeweler's boxes, which were stacked on a large table.

Maria found her there and shook her head. "You have been working since early hours . . . and you didn't touch the food on your breakfast tray. This is not good! You must eat." She brought a tray of cheeses and freshly baked crisp rolls, with orders to eat it all. Allegra's spirits rose a little under the loving services.

Several hours passed. The waking house stirred outside her door, and the bustle of preparation began to rise in tempo. Guido opened the door without knocking and came in uninvited. He leaned on the table and grinned at her.

"Well, Allegra, you're hard at work, eh?"

"Yes—I'm busy," she said, going on with her work. His mere presence was irritating, although on the surface he appeared pleasant enough. He regarded her with an appraising stare. "You look tired. Don't let La Vecchia work you too hard."

She pulled her patience together. "I'm fine, Guido. There is just a lot of work to complete, that's all."

He still stared with a commiserating smile. "You're a good worker. No one can say that isn't true."

"Thanks."

"Don't be so grumpy. I just thought I'd try to cheer you up a little. You've been looking like a poor little orphan lately. . . . Oh, sorry, I didn't mean to say it that way. You are an orphan, aren't you?"

She shuffled the cards impatiently and ignored his last remark. "I guess I'm just too busy to be chatting."

"Hmm." He still leaned nonchalantly by the table, idly picking up the boxes and looking into them.

"Please don't get the boxes out of order," she begged, seeing him set one down on the wrong pile.

"You certainly aren't much fun this morning, Allegra."

"Do you really think that I should act toward you just as if nothing had happened?" He looked tolerant, and her indignation got the better of her. "Haven't you made enough trouble? Please go away."

"I suppose you are still mad that I told Aldo about your fiancé. I didn't think it was a secret, especially since the fellow wants to patch things up and all that." He gave her a brotherly look. "Really, Allegra, you should be glad a man with good prospects wants you. You aren't getting any younger, and you're not the type of woman who can get men easily. I think you should go home and get married. You'd make a good wife." His unctuous voice savored the words. "I hope the old lady survives the ball," he started again.

She cut in, "Will you leave my room, please! I have to finish this work."

"Your room! This is a di Rienzi room, and you should remember it." She said nothing, continuing to work. "All right," he said, "let's forget it. I don't want your last days here to be unpleasant, Allegra, but it's hard trying to be friendly when you react so badly. Don't be mad." He had the effrontery to pat her shoulder with the last irritating words "See you later. Hope you feel better." He went out.

He is sick, she thought, *but the sickness is dangerous.* She sat still, trying to control her nerves. It wasn't her business anyway, and she would soon be gone from here.

It was nearly noon, and no one disturbed her again. Then a knock came on the door. It was Luigi, looking serious. "Signorina Allegra, will you come to the study? Signor Renaldo wants to speak to you immediately."

She followed him with a terrible feeling of dread. Something was very wrong. Vibrations of it reached out beyond the study door.

Aldo was standing by his desk, drumming his fingers impatiently and frowning. An older man sat in one of the chairs facing the desk. As Allegra entered she heard him saying, ". . . believe me, my dear *conte*, I do not need extra proof. If you do not want to sell this material I will, of course, return the facsimiles to you." His voice was very British. Two faces turned to watch her enter. Aldo's heavy frown did not change. The other man had a look of polite curiosity.

Aldo broke the uncomfortable silence. "Allegra Brent, Mr. Haversham-Bing." The Englishman rose, bowed and stood waiting. "Signorina Brent, Mr. Haversham-Bing has come to offer to buy the Byron papers, of which he has partial copies. They appear to be the ones in your possession, which you showed to my grandmother. Mr. Haversham-Bing came to me because of a letter purportedly signed by me. . . . But I have informed him that the desire to put these dubious Byron papers up for sale does not come from my family."

His formal voice chilled her. Her mouth felt dry. How could copies of her precious papers be in the hands of this total stranger?

She found a small voice. "But I don't understand."

"Surely Mr. Haversham-Bing's name is not new to you. He is a very well-known dealer in rare manuscripts. Have you contacted others, also?" Aldo's voice was caustic.

"I have contacted no one." Her head was up now, and she looked Aldo in the eyes.

"That is difficult to believe, since this gentleman has copies of part of the material."

She turned to the man, who was watching with interest. "Sir, I regret that you have come on false information. I do have certain old letters handed down in my family. However, they have no interest to anyone except myself and the di Rienzis." She turned intense eyes on Aldo. "I have never had any thought of selling them, and I do not intend to do it now."

"Then perhaps you can explain how these copies came into the hands of Mr. Haversham-Bing?"

Allegra addressed her remarks to the old gentleman. "I have no explanation of this situation. However, I can tell you that I will destroy the papers rather than sell them." She knew that she sounded dramatic, but she didn't care.

"My dear young lady, please accept my apologies. I will not continue to trouble you, but I beg you, do not destroy these manuscripts. If they are genuine, they are of inestimable interest to Byron scholars all over the world. You must realize that there may be episodes in the poet's life, which are as yet unknown to us. He left an autobiography to be read upon his death . . . but, alas, well-meaning relatives and friends burned it. So you see how important your papers might be—the only reports, perhaps, of certain parts of Byron's life. You hold something very valuable in trust." He sounded sincere, and Allegra felt that he did indeed care, in a certain practical way. She softened to him a little.

"Nevertheless, I will never sell or publish the papers."

He sighed. "I don't suppose you would tell me how they came to your family?" He watched her with a look that was not unkind.

"No—I do not want to circulate the story."

He spoke again with a slight smile. "And you would not gratify an old scholar's curiosity? I have been a collector of Byron since I attended Harrow as a boy. I used to go to the old cemetery and sit on the stone where Byron used to dream. I would imagine myself to be linked to him in some way." He paused a moment. "Foolish little chap, wasn't I?" Again he smiled. "Would you at least let me see the papers? I believe I could attest to their authenticity, and it would be a privilege to see them."

She felt the freezing energy of Aldo's silent presence, and her nerves were starting to quiver. "I'm sorry, sir, I do not wish to show them to anyone."

He shook his head. "I am defeated, my dear lady. But if one day you should reconsider . . . ." He held out a card to her with a slight bow. She took it without looking at it.

He turned to Aldo. "I hope, Signor di Rienzi, that I have not intruded at an awkward time. It is my business to follow such leads to valuable material."

Aldo tried to arrange his face into a polite smile and failed. "As I have said, I think their authenticity is dubious." He began to walk Mr. Haversham-Bing to the door, voicing regrets as he shut the door on the gentleman's inoffensive back.

He strode back into the room. "So," he hissed, "this is how you repay La Vecchia's trust and kindness! You are a good actress, Allegra, but your innocent denials do not fool me. What do you want? Should I have offered to buy your little diary to protect the family name? How much shall I pay? Do you have any valid explanation for this?"

He was trying to hold his anger in check, but his sarcasm clawed at her. What was the use of argument? She started to turn away and felt his hand spin her roughly around to face him. "Haven't you anything to say?" He held her in a tight grip.

Suddenly her own anger flared. "Let me go, Conte di Rienzi, you are insulting!" His hand dropped away. "I don't need to explain to you. But you had better explain to me how copies of my private and personal papers were tampered with and copied without my knowledge. I'm tired of being treated like a culprit. You have done that ever since I came to this place. Do you think I would hurt La Vecchia? If you do, you are simpleminded!" He was watching her with raised eyebrows, and the glitter in his eyes was steely.

"If you think righteous anger will change my mind, you are wrong."

"Use your common sense," she snapped. "If I were to sell the papers, would I do it this way? If I wanted secrecy, would I be such a blunderer? But there is no use arguing with you. You are sure of your false judgments and they cannot be changed." She drew an angry breath, "My friends warned me . . . ." She stopped, halted by the fury in his face.

"Get out," he said in a low voice. "I should have heeded my feelings of distrust when I first saw your so innocent face."

"I will be glad to go, Conte di Rienzi. I have reservations to leave the day after the ball." He stared at her. "Now I suppose you will decide that I was going to go as soon as I had sold the Byron papers. That is your kind of reasoning, but I suggest you take more care with the affairs of your own house. Much of the burden lies on a woman one hundred years old, who should have some peace and joy around her. The Ca' d'Argenti is full of pain and anger and you are blind!"

She turned and ran to the door, shutting it behind her with a heavy thud. No one was in the hall, and she reached her room before the flood of tears broke from her. She buried her face in the comforter on her bed and sobbed until she was empty and exhausted.

She started to pack, slowly, automatically, trying hard to construct around herself a permanent wall of indifference toward Renaldo. Her anger helped her. Beneath her room were sounds of activity from the workmen in the ballroom. Echoes of hammering told her that they hadn't finished building the dais for La Vecchia's celebration throne. Allegra prayed it would be a happy birthday for her.

She finished packing, except for the clothes she would wear to travel. The Byron box would stay in the drawer of the beautiful desk. She wasn't going to take it home again to be reminded of old passions. She could almost smile now at her naiveté to think she could step blithely from her old life into this one of *palazzos*, *contes* and uncomfortable shadows.

CHAPTER TWENTY-TWO

THE MOST DIFFICULT THING remaining was to write to La Vecchia, who cared so deeply about this unhappy family and had come to the end of a long life without arranging things to her satisfaction. She would have Vera Falieri after all.

How could everything have got so muddled and misunderstood? She tried again to probe the mood of the Ca' d'Argenti. Beneath the surface was something irrational . . . unsettling . . . but not from La Vecchia or even Renaldo, in spite of his temperament.

It was Guido, and something more than Guido, too. She knew it was he who had copied the Byron papers. She should hate him for what he did to her, but she only felt apprehension.

Someone knocked gently on her door. She didn't want to see anyone, but the knock came again. "Allegra?" It was Renaldo. A sharp pang hit her heart, and she opened the door to him. He looked at her and then to the dressing room where the luggage stood.

"La Vecchia sent me," he said, as if wanting to get a distasteful chore over with. "She feels I have been unfair with you, and she wants you to stay. I think it would be wise if you did not leave immediately."

Allegra searched his face. "Don't say this for La Vecchia's sake, if you are going to change your mind again tomorrow. I don't have the strength, Aldo. I can't stay in a house where I am thought to be dishonest. I'm sure Guido has told you worse already."

"Damn Guido! I have allowed myself to be too much with my work to notice what is happening in my own house. I do not like what I see." He offered a faint smile. "I have been told that I should apologize for my treatment of you. Perhaps it was not my business to condemn you . . . or bring sadness to my grandmother. She needs you right now. As for me, I shall reserve judgment until I have made some sense of things.'' His face was pale and set.

Allegra looked away from him. ''That won't be necessary. I am still planning to leave the morning after the ball. I only regret that we will never completely understand one another.''

He turned to leave and said as an afterthought, ''Then I will say thank-you for tending to Bianca. She loves you very much. My grandmother asks if you will join her for the evening meal. So . . . I will say *addio*. I trust that you will take your Byron with you when you leave us. Good fortune, Miss Brent. I doubt we will have occasion to speak again.''

It was an inelegant farewell, nothing like the words she might have hoped to hear from his fine lips. He left her with a sense of the finality of it all, but she wouldn't allow him to subdue her pride.

La Vecchia obviously knew about the visit from the Englishman. There must have been a scene when she found out, Allegra thought; she wasn't looking forward to dinner with her. She was too tired to talk about Renaldo anymore; nothing La Vecchia could say would change things. Right now, she wanted to get out of the Ca', to take a walk and lose herself among the narrow back streets of Venice.

The outside air was still and moist and very warm. At least it was a change from the rarefied atmosphere of the Ca' d'Argenti.

Unexpectedly, she found herself in front of the elaborate little church of Santa Maria Zobenigo, where the first Allegra had prayed in her despair over her passion for Byron. The little secret room of their brief love—the place where the scrap of wallpaper came from—was very near the church. She looked around the small *campo*, wondering where it was, until tourists encroached on her thoughts and she turned half-heartedly to go back to the Ca'.

As she walked up the great curving stairway, she heard Guido and Aldo arguing hotly from behind the partly open doors of the study. It wasn't difficult to hear everything: two men had come to

Aldo's offices that day to see him about Guido's gambling debts. They frightened the secretaries with wild threats. Guido laughed and said that Aldo was too sensitive and his secretaries were prudes. If Aldo gave him a decent salary he wouldn't have to be in debt. . . .

Aldo shouted his words down. "Get out, and don't drag your dirty affairs to me again!"

Allegra quickly climbed the stairs to the landing and let herself into her room. Even one more day here was too much, she said almost aloud. When she ventured out again it was to go to La Vecchia's apartments for dinner.

The drawing room was filled with flowers from well-wishers. The *contessa* sat in their midst, listening while Maria was already reporting the argument in the study. Kitchen staff were upset, she added, because they felt great affection for the *conte*, and they didn't approve of Signor Guido's activities. Allegra understood now how La Vecchia could know so much about the affairs of her family, without leaving the seclusion of her own quarters.

Maria left to bring their dinner, and La Vecchia put out her hand to Allegra. "My dear child . . . we haven't made it easy for you, have we? I know you plan to leave us, and I don't blame you. The Fates did not do well this time. But we were all very close to a happy ending." She sighed, watching Allegra closely. "If we just had a little more time . . . ."

Maria entered with a dinner cart. She had a note for her mistress from Signor Mossanato, which was read swiftly and crumpled in the thin white hand. "Just a little time . . ." she repeated under her breath.

Dinner conversation was all concerned with the ball. "Guido has promised to spend the morning with Bianca on the Lido. So we'll have no squealing while we prepare. He can do that much, at least. Well, my child," she smiled from weary eyes, "I have brought Dr. Nepi to the edge of collapse, but I have lived to see my hundredth birthday to spite him. I'm really quite proud of my own endurance.

"It is you I am worried about. I have scolded Aldo for his unforgivable rudeness to you. Of course you did not come here to sell the Byron material. It is so strange how he wants to find you false. His old wounds have not healed enough for him to believe in goodness. And so he has lost you, and I think I am the saddest of all, even more than you. For you will mend, and I can only mourn that what should have been was not." Her voice trailed off into a whisper. There were tears on both faces. The meal was finished in silence.

It seemed to Allegra's tired mind that truth and fiction were all the same in the Ca' d'Argenti . . . a mixed-up jumble of episodes and emotions that had no real solution, no final clearing-up. La Vecchia loooked at her quietly and steadily—perceptively.

"But I *am* leaving," Allegra said.

"Of course, my dear child. We will talk about that, too, but not tonight. There has been too much talk today, and I am tired."

ALLEGRA WENT TO BED but couldn't find sleep. When it came, finally, it was deep, and it carried her far away from the Ca' d'Argenti—the House of Silver—the cool and shimmering half-reality that would never be hers.

She awoke early to sounds of the preparations and hurried to dress for the day of work that lay ahead. As usual, a linen-draped tray of coffee and sweet rolls had been left outside her door. A golden yellow rosebud, still dewy from the garden, lay on top of the parchment-colored cloth.

She thought for a moment of the rose Aldo had sent her in Florence, when he had asked forgiveness. She still remembered the line of the Byron poem written in the note: "The first step of error None e'er could recall . . ." Where had she made her own first step of error? In coming to the Ca' that long-ago afternoon? In carrying the restless blood of her ancestor? Maybe the first step was really taken the night Allegra di Rienzi dared to raise her eyes to those of the dangerous English lord.

It might have been easy to sink into self-pity, if there were not so much work to be done before the ball. Downstairs little round tables were being set up in the foyer and draped with silvery cloth. Maria was working with the florist's staff to arrange the hundreds of snow-white roses in silver and crystal bowls.

Allegra spent time arranging the boxes of favors on a small gardenia-swagged table near the entrance to the ballroom. The most pressing jobs were nearly done, the guest book was opened on the table, the dance cards entwined with ribbons. The scene of greatest activity for the rest of the day would be the kitchen. Allegra would next make sure that all the receipts for deliveries had been properly recorded.

She had not even taken a moment to find La Vecchia and wish her a happy birthday. It was nearly noon when Maria called to her from the first landing with a hastily written message from *la contessa*. She read it in a glance: "Allegra, my dear—Maria will tell you what has happened. I can trust you. A thousand thanks, Amalia di R."

"It is Signor Guido," Maria said quickly. "He took Bianca to the Lido, but he left her with some children, and now he cannot be found. It is unthinkable! *La contessa* is furious and is asking you to please go for the child. Luigi is ready with the motor launch."

"Tell her I am going right now. Is there someone who can watch Bianca until I can get there?"

"Si. Signor Mossanato is with her now, but he has a business appointment soon and cannot stay. It was he who telephoned us. He is a good man, *signorina*."

Allegra reached the back landing, just as the launch pulled into place beside it.

"Good morning, Signorina Brent," Luigi said, extending his tanned arm to help her inside. "Signor Guido has given La Vecchia a fine birthday gift, eh?" He gunned the motor and started out into the canal.

"I don't understand his behavior at all," Allegra said.

"It is not my place to wonder, *signorina*, but it angers me to see his actions. Someday he will have to answer to God . . . and then I pity him." He concentrated on his driving until they were slowing to enter the Lido canals. "Please allow me to say, Signorina Brent, that you are a kind woman. We are all sorry that you plan to leave the Ca'." He stopped the boat at the Excelsior dock. "I wanted you to know that, no matter what else is said to you by others." He looked suddenly embarrassed. "I talk too much, but it is from the heart, *signorina*."

"I know, Luigi, and I am grateful." Behind her smile, she was again resisting the thought of leaving, but there was no choice. She had been pushed out and dismissed by the *conte* of the old and honorable house of di Rienzi. It didn't matter who else cared for her.

The hotel dockman lifted her from the boat and placed her back on to her feet in one swift motion. She was greeted in the lobby by the worried face of Signor Mossanato. He took her hand quickly.

"My dear, dear lady—how good of you to come. What an inconvenient moment for all of us! The child is changing into dry clothes. It seems that Guido was angry with his grandmother for giving him this duty, and he simply left. Probably at the Casino, if I may venture a guess. Bianca wanted to return to the Ca' to prepare for the ball, and her uncle was nowhere to be found. The manager knew me as a friend of the family, and I was called. But, alas, I must stay here for business."

Bianca rushed into the lobby with urgency in her little body. "Allegra! We have to go home *now*! I don't want to miss anything, and it takes Maria hours to make my hair pretty!"

Signor Mossanato put his hand on her sandy head. "Bianca, Luigi is waiting for you outside. Tell him that Signorina Brent will join you in five minutes." There was a certain authority in the gentle face of the *signore*. Then he turned to Allegra.

"Dear lady, if you could spare the time from your very busy day . . . we may not have another quiet moment to speak again, and I wish you to know certain things before you leave Venice."

She nodded, puzzled by the change in his manner. They sat in a corner of the lobby area, and Signor Mossanato ordered coffee for them. He was intent on his purpose, whatever it might be. He pressed the tips of this fine small fingers together.

"I received your gracious letter," he began, "and I was most unhappy to read that you plan to leave us. For some time I have known you were in a difficult situation here. Contessa Amalia counts me as a close friend, but I also hold a position that you are unaware of. . . . *La contessa* contacted me over a month ago, because of the disappearance of several pieces of her jewelry. She wished a discreet inquiry to be made. It seems our thief is Guido."

He took a sip of coffee and looked at her almost apologetically. "Signorina Brent, I don't wish to alarm you, but I am an agent of the police." Allegra looked at him, not alarmed, but genuinely surprised. "Amalia di Rienzi is a woman of courage and sacrifice," he continued. "She has asked us to keep surveillance over Guido, and I have been able to recover most of her jewels. She insists on buying them back from the jewelers involved. There will be no arrests. A very painful choice for her, you can imagine." His eyes reflected the pain he spoke of.

"Does Aldo know?" she asked.

"Not yet. You see, Contessa Amalia fears his reaction. She will find her moment to tell him. He is not entirely blind, and I have advised her to tell him immediately, especially in light of the latest developments." He reached to take Allegra's hands to emphasize his words. "My dear *signorina*, I most earnestly wish you to think well of the di Rienzi family. You have been a lady of great forbearance. It would be a tragic loss to us all were you to leave."

"Signor Mossanato, I love the *contessa*. Nothing will change that."

"Yes. And your love is returned. Allow me to tell you one thing more, and then you must go to your business and I to mine. I am informed that you have been accused of offering your Byron papers for sale by unethical means. I wish to make you my promise to prove the accusation wrong and bring the proof to the *conte* himself."

Of course he was aware of everything, she observed. Why shouldn't he know about Aldo, as well as the Byron papers? "You are most kind to care, *signore*," she managed a smile, "but it is too late. I will be gone tomorrow."

"I prefer not to see the dark side, only. Remember, I have made my promise." He stood, and with a little bow, took her hands again and raised one to his lips. "I beg permission for a waltz this evening. It would give me great pleasure."

Allegra's voice wavered slightly as she tried to remain cool. "Signor Mossanato, I will always remember you as a true friend. And of course we will waltz tonight. That is my promise to you."

He escorted her to the dock, where Luigi had already started the motor and Bianca was looking pained and impatient. Allegra watched the churning water move past her. It seemed that every time she returned from the Lido it was at high speeds through drenching wakes.

She felt like telling Luigi to take her to the Casa Bugelli, rather than to the Ca' d'Argenti. The thought of waltzing within a few hours seemed impossible. The waltz was a dance for happy people, for lovers. And she felt quite empty of those emotions, and completely outside of the events swirling around the great celebration. She contemplated having an attack of the flu in her room and being indisposed until she could quietly take her leave the following day.

At home, when she could face things again, she would write to La Vecchia and Bianca and Signor Mossanato and tell them how grateful she was for their love. She couldn't find the right words now, and face-to-face would hurt too much. But they would know someday the depth of her love for them.

The boat was delayed at the landing of the Ca', because several delivery boats were blocking the access. Cases of champagne were stacked by the doorway with mounds of ice piled on top and dripping slowly onto the ground. The hum of activity reminded her of the time she had lost in going to the Lido. She went directly to La Vecchia's apartments to report Bianca's return and was met by Dr. Nepi. La Vecchia had become too agitated and would have to rest until time for the ball, or else he could not guarantee that she would have any strength to celebrate her own birthday. Allegra left her message with him, knowing that it would have a soothing effect on La Vecchia's nerves. At least she would know that Bianca was safely home.

Maria had been working steadily since Allegra had last seen her. The foyer was a confection of silver and pink; candles were everywhere in sconces and on the tables, waiting to be lighted. From beyond the closed doors of the ballroom, she heard the crisp sounds of harpsichord music. The musicians had asked to come early in order to test out the acoustics and rehearse together. There was to be light chamber music as the guests arrived, and then La Vecchia's entrance, followed by dance music. La Vecchia knew exactly what she wanted.

Allegra gathered together a sheaf of receipts and invoices and found a quiet place where she could organize the accounts, so that after tomorrow everything would be in order. Her pride would not let her leave her responsibilities for others to finish. There was a small office alcove between the pantry and the back stairs, and she could still be available in case someone needed her.

She didn't realize how long she had been sitting at the cluttered little desk, until one of the young kitchen servants told her it was growing late. Allegra closed her account book and stacked the papers. It was five-thirty, and she knew she needed to rest before starting the evening. She felt drained and unable to cope with much more.

The foyer was nearly empty, and the chamber music could be heard in the distance. Allegra stood in the midst of the elaborate decorations, as a costumed member of the staff began to light the dozens of candles. Why had destiny chosen her to come to this place? What was she supposed to be learning from the experience? *Nonna* had said that all things in life have their gift to offer to you. But what gift was here for her?

She was partway up the curving staircase when she heard the penetrating voice of Vera Falieri from below. Aldo was with her, and they were walking arm in arm toward his study. Vera's head

was leaning close to his, and she was laughing. It was a picture of
intimacy. They closed the study door behind them. Allegra made
herself continue up the stairs, but she could feel the hot flush
burning on her cheeks. She was glad to be in her room—to shut
out the things that upset her.

The ball dress hung waiting on the wardrobe door. She turned
away from its shimmering presence. It wasn't her dress—someone
else had been its real owner. If only she could get past the ball. If
only she didn't feel so weighted down by everything that had happened here . . . if her heart were not so heavy. She could feel it sitting like a cold stone in her breast.

She lay on her bed with the intention of resting, but it proved
futile, and she slowly set about her preparations for the evening.
A long fragrant bath took away some of the numbness and lifted
her spirits a little. She put on her robe and sat down at the dressing table.

A light knock startled her, as Maria flew in, her face pink with
haste. "Ah, Signorina Allegra, you are ready for the gown?"
Allegra nodded. "Now let me do your hair. La Vecchia has said
how it should be. Then she requests you come for a light supper
with her on the roof."

While she was talking, she had whisked the gown from its
hanger and was holding it ready for Allegra. Reluctantly she took
off her robe and slid her arms into the satin sleeves.

The dress rustled down around her, enveloping her in a cloud
of faint perfume from its many petticoats. She shivered as though
cool damp air had suddenly blown around her. She felt sad—very
sad—yet it was not entirely her own emotion.

Maria was busy fastening the hooks and tying the golden satin
sash. She urged Allegra back toward the dressing table chair with
a gentle push, and she sat down gingerly, unused to the many
layers of skirts. She watched as Maria swiftly went to work on her
hair. An antique style began to emerge, with soft waves on the
sides and one long dark strand curled over the shoulders.

"It goes well with the gown," Maria said with a satisfied pat.
Her fingers were sure and subtle, as she turned her attention to

the makeup on the dressing-table trays. Allegra watched with fascination as her own face was transformed into a shadowy beauty from which her dark eyes shone out, large and full of dreams.

This is not Allegra Brent, she thought, and then Maria's face in the mirror next to hers drew her back to reality. "Come, we must hasten. The *contessa* will be waiting."

Allegra stood up with difficulty; the gown seemed heavy, but with a little adjusting she learned to move with it. Maria urged her from her contemplation of her new self in the long mirror. Who was this woman who looked back at her, she wondered. Her heart was beating loudly in her ears. The gown almost had a will of its own, determined to carry Allegra along on its strange and lingering mood.

There was no one in the hall, and Allegra was relieved. She was fighting against the disorienting sensation that still had her in its grip. Maria had hurried ahead and was standing waiting for Allegra to catch up. She pushed the button to open the door at the staircase, and they climbed the narrow flight of steps to the roof garden.

La Vecchia was seated at the table, wrapped in her favorite cream satin robe. Candles glowed softly in the dusk light. The roses were blooming in their big pots. It was a tranquil eye in the storm. "Allegra, *mia.*" The old voice called gently.

Allegra moved from the shadows.

"Dio mio!" La Vecchia said under her breath. She turned to Maria. "You have done well. She looks lovely, our Allegra. Come, child, sit down. Don't worry, the skirts will adjust themselves," she smiled. "Wait until you see Bianca in her ball gown. I remember well my first ball gown. What airs and graces I put on! I must have been near to Bianca's age." She shook her head. "Bianca will be one of the determined di Rienzis, I think. It is strong blood, Allegra, but from time to time we have our problems.

"Guido!" Her face drew down into harsh and sad lines. "I am sorry, Allegra, that Guido has involved you in his quest for money. I know about Mr. Haversham-Bing and the Byron papers. . . . Guido does not look at things in a normal way. He has lived with his fears and angers too long. I plan to speak to Aldo about this. We will have to find help for him. He cannot continue to disturb the household." The weary old eyes filled with tears. "I pity his struggles. But Renaldo . . . he is an unhappy man for other reasons. I will not be able to watch over the house of di Rienzi for too much longer . . . I had hoped . . . ." She trailed off, seeing the distress on Allegra's face.

"Oh, *cara mia*," she put a light hand over Allegra's. "I know your deep love for Renaldo. No—do not deny. I remember when my Leopoldo and I had our misunderstandings . . . how it hurt! But no matter now. Before long I shall be with him. It has been a terrible time of waiting for me. God teaches me about patience and the endurance of love for more than thirty lonely years." Candlelight flickered over her face.

"I will not deny it to you," Allegra said softly. "I only hope I have the courage to live as you have."

"You are just beginning, *cara*. There is no reason why you should not find happiness."

Allegra was on guard. She knew La Vecchia's manipulative mind. She said pleadingly, "Please don't tell him! I will leave as soon as possible, and I want to go with some pride."

"Pride, eh?" The old woman frowned. "I begin to think you are as foolish as Aldo." She chewed with pleasure on a large strawberry drenched in sugar. Suddenly she became alert, listening—a small expectant smile on her lips. Footsteps sounded on the stairs.

Allegra froze. She was afraid to look up. Her heart twisted, and she fought to keep her face calm. Aldo was coming through the door. He, too, was already dressed for the ball, and he looked elegant. Buff satin knee breeches covered his long well-formed legs above creamy silk hose. On his feet were brown satin shoes with fine silver buckles, and over a lace-ruffled waistcoat he wore a perfectly fitted coat of leaf-brown moiré silk, the long tails lined with beige silk. The lace at his wrists sparkled with diamond studs, and his high-collared shirt was tied in wide silk in the Regency style.

"Oh, my dear!" La Vecchia exclaimed. Tears welled into her eyes. "You are so like Leopoldo. I am proud, so proud!"

He bent to kiss her hand. "I am glad to please you, *carissima,* on this most important of nights."

La Vecchia chuckled suddenly. "Now that I have my hundred years, you must work to please me, *caro.*" She patted his cheek with her delicate old hand. "But where is your courtesy, Aldo . . you have not greeted Allegra. Does she not look lovely?"

Allegra wanted to disappear. Instead she had to bear the impersonal gaze of his dark eyes. He turned and reached to take her hand, touching her reluctant fingers with his lips. His formal manners were perfect. "That dress becomes you, Allegra. It could have been made for you." He looked questioningly at his grandmother. "Is it one of the old ones?"

"Yes. One of those that I found in the old trunks. . . . How are things downstairs?"

Aldo smiled. "All is going according to plan, Vecchia. I believe you will be pleased." He bent down to kiss the soft old cheek. "Happy birthday. You will be the loveliest lady at the ball. There is no one like you."

"Save your compliments for the younger ladies, *caro.*" She chuckled again. "I want you to open the dancing with Allegra. . . . It is a request not to be denied my hundred years."

Aldo raised quiet eyes to Allegra's face. "It will be my pleasure," he said, but the tone was cool and calm. "I will see you both very soon, my lovely ladies. *Ciao.*" He left abruptly.

La Vecchia sighed. "Now I, too, must dress. Aldo puts us to shame with his elegance. You might tell him that, my child. The Falieri flatters him . . . a thing to remember." She put a caressing hand on Allegra's cheek. "My hundredth birthday is not as yet what I have planned. But we shall see. I have a surprise or two left in me."

Maria came bustling in and helped Allegra maneuver her rustling skirts down the stairs. Only when she was back in her room,

sitting again before her dressing table, did she realize that she had
not wished happy birthday to La Vecchia.

She smiled ironically to herself. Aldo's impersonal courtesy was
impeccable. He had got away from an uncomfortable situation
gracefully. She hoped that her exit from the Ca' d'Argenti would
be with as much dignity.

CHAPTER TWENTY-THREE

MARIA KNOCKED AND ENTERED at the same moment, rushing in with a heavy string of pearls. They were like large drops of gleaming yellow cream. "*La contessa* says that you are to wear them—so!" She looped the double strand around Allegra's throat and fastened them together with a clasp that sparkled with yellow diamonds. "Ah, that is the final touch. It is just correct." Maria flew out on her last words, and Allegra lapsed into thought.

She sat looking at herself in the ornate Venetian glass mirror. The pearls glowed with light and moved on her breast with each breath she took. They felt heavy with memory, more memories than her own. Voices from the past whispered from the crisp satin sounds of her skirts and stirred from the pearls.

The small clock on her dressing table showed that the appointed hour had come for the arrival of the guests. Without joy or expectation she picked up her small reticule and left the room. People were entering the great foyer through the wide open doors of the Ca'. Already there was a scent of women's perfumes mingling with the softer odors of flowers.

She walked down the stairs and began to check the table that held the boxes of favors. Servants were intent on their duties, and nobody paid special attention to her. A steady hum of voices came from the ballroom.

She entered that great room, dazzled by its beauty in the glow of hundreds of candles. She smiled. La Vecchia had got her way in this, too. The chandeliers were filled with tiny flames, reflecting a multitude of polished cut crystals. The glowing light seemed to set time in a different dimension.

Allegra drew in a trembling breath. Once more she had that strange wavering feeling, as thought centuries spiraled inside one another, and time was only an illusion. Whoever had worn the dress she now wore stood very close. A wave of urgent thought enveloped her. . . . *Happiness cannot be lost again, Allegra, find it!* She started and looked around, so real was the whispering woman's voice at her shoulder. She stood entranced with the energies that moved in the old palazzo.

"I think the ghosts wake tonight. The di Rienzis of the past have come to this celebration. The house is alive, it is watching." Allegra turned to see Luigi's serious face. His voice was low. "I have a grandmother who has the power of sight. Sometimes in these old places the thoughts of the past are roused by present-day emotions. I have felt it many times." He responded with kindness to the strain in her face, and smiled at her. "You look very lovely, Signorina Allegra."

"Thank you, Luigi." She saw concern in his strong face. Tears were very near the surface, and she tried to gather a smile together.

"If you need anything, let me know," he was saying. "All of us regard you as of the family." He turned away before she could answer.

Luigi had responded to her thoughts. Those loving Italian hearts below stairs understood. "Of the family," he had said. How she wished it were true.

She was now standing with many other guests. She looked toward the dais, where a number of handsomely carved Renaissance chairs were placed beside an imposing high-backed scarlet-cushioned chair inlaid with silver. Flowers were everywhere. Swags of gardenias and carnations hung from the small curved balconies, and great pots of maidenhair ferns and tall silver vases of white roses and gladioli decorated the dais.

The orchestra was seated on a platform at one end of the ballroom, the musicians richly costumed in the style of the nineteenth century. Guests were moving about and talking . . . the women's gowns almost like flowers in the soft light. It was far more a dream than reality.

What am I doing here, she said to herself.

The sounds of the music and the movement of the guests gradually ceased, and heads turned to the great doors in expectation. Aldo stood at the entrance holding a bouquet of white roses tied with silver ribbon. From just outside the doors, part of La Vecchia's wheeled chair could be seen, and Aldo stepped forward to meet her. The harpsichord began with an enchanting air, as Aldo gave his arm to La Vecchia and helped her from her chair.

She was standing now, her fine face serene, her hand resting on Aldo's arm. A sigh of admiration was audible from the guests. She was wearing a creamy gown, the color of candlelight, with deep ruffles of delicate lace covering the full skirt. Her tiny waist was tied in with narrow silver ribbons, and the satin bodice and sleeves had falls of lace at throat and wrists. Diamonds glinted in her high-piled hair, where russet streaks showed dark against the white waves. She was carrying Aldo's white roses.

People made a path for her, as she and Aldo walked the length of the ballroom. *"Brava la contessa, brava!"* voices called out, amid clapping, and one voice penetrated above the other, saying, *"Una sposa"* . . . a bride.

Allegra agreed. She looked like a bride. Maria had done magic with the old face. It had the illusion of youth. To live so long with such will and courage and to be able still to outshine all others—that was accomplishment. "By God," someone said, "the old one is a true woman."

Aldo escorted his grandmother to the great chair on the dais. Maria, in the dress of a last-century lady's maid, and Luigi, proud in the di Rienzi livery, took their places behind her. Maria handed her a white fan sewn with diamante. She sat making a delicate play with it in the manner of the ladies of her youth. Cousin Luisa was seated nearby, looking frumpy despite her finery, and other older and elegant ladies were given seats of honor on the dais. Bianca, dressed in pink, perched in a chair, her legs dangling. She looked miserable, and Allegra wondered why, since her gown was surely a wonderful thing to her. What had happened to the child?

She noticed a large covered object, like a panel, standing behind La Vecchia's chair. It was draped in brocade and had a draw cord. Was this one of the surprises that had been promised?

She was watching the scene the way a child would watch an enchanting show.

Aldo opened the ball formally with a brief and loving speech, accompanied by flurries of hand clapping. The dignitaries of the city spoke, detailing La Vecchia's many charities, and the guests streamed toward her in twos and threes to congratulate her. Some embraced her, some kissed her hand.

Aldo mingled with the crowd, and Allegra lost him for a moment. She sighed. Just to watch his dark head moving in the crowded room was a painful joy.

She looked around her, and the figure of Vera Falieri stood out from the crowd. Her dress was emerald green, Empire style, cut very low on the breast and slit to the hip on the side. Her hair was dressed à la Josephine and a large emerald flashed on her hand. She made her way to the dais with a satisfied smile. La Vecchia watched her approach with a rigid face. In a rush Falieri bent to kiss her cheek and was given a solemn nod in return. Falieri moved off to join others in the room, acting as if she were a privileged and important guest.

Aldo came to the dais again and held conversation with his grandmother. She gestured at him, and from time to time a frown moved over her face. She shook an admonishing finger, which he caught and kissed. The earnest conversation continued, while La Vecchia hid part of it with the flutter of her fan. Allegra was fascinated watching the expressions on Aldo's face. She saw deep sadness one moment and hopeful urgency the next. Finally he kissed La Vecchia, and she tapped his shoulder lightly with her fan in an old-fashioned gesture.

A familiar voice spoke beside her, making her nerves jump. "It's quite a show, isn't it? I guess you'll never see anything like this again. They don't know how to do this in your America." She turned to see Guido, handsome in the dress of a Victorian elegant.

"You're quite right, Guido; only Venice could produce this kind of beauty."

He looked her up and down. "That dress is most becoming,"

he said condescendingly. "It looks like La Vecchia did her best, but this is one time the old fox is beaten at her own game." He had a smug, satisfied smile. "*Dio!* What a scene she and Aldo must have had when he told her his news."

Allegra felt prickles of apprehension begin, and her hands quickly grew cold and clammy. He was truly relishing whatever bit of gossip he had. He was silent a moment, mentally baiting her then looked up at the dais.

"They even got out old Principe Renaldo's silver-decorated chair. Fifteenth century. And those six-foot silver vases are made from part of the loot the sharp old trader brought back from his travels. He was too busy buying and selling to get to be a doge. It's quite a family, eh?"

He paused and Allegra moved to leave his side, but he put a detaining hand on her arm. "Don't run away, Allegra." He pulled his face into a serious but sympathetic expression. "I like you." He patted her arm. "So I decided I'd better tell you the news; you'll know soon enough anyway. I guess the others don't suspect how you feel, but I understand that things have been hard for you here."

He smiled benignly, but his eyes were watching her curiously, expectantly. A horrid feeling slowly ached into her heart. La Vecchia's tense conversation with Aldo just now—the earlier picture of Aldo and Falieri going into the study—all came together in evidence.

"Yes. Falieri will be the next Contessa di Rienzi. They intend to make the happy announcement later tonight. What a bitter pill!" he chuckled, then drew his face into seriousness. "Sorry, Allegra, but it's funny to see La Vecchia finally outsmarted. She'll get used to it. After all, how much longer can she live . . . she's had her own way for such a long time."

He looked at Allegra intently. "Aren't you upset? Bianca was, when I told her. I thought you had a thing for Aldo, but maybe you've got more sense. You go home and marry that Larry and forget the di Rienzis, where you don't belong anyway." He patted her arm again.

Allegra drew on all her strength. "Yes, it will be good to go home. I . . . hope they will be happy." She pulled away from him. "There are some things I must attend to." She was in turmoil. Somehow she had always hoped—but now the sound of the accomplished fact hurt unbelievably.

Poor La Vecchia, no wonder she looked so pained! How could Aldo have done this! And Bianca sitting miserably on her velvet chair! That was why she had not come to show Allegra her finery before the ball.

She pushed through the crowd blindly. She had to get away. Then she saw Aldo moving toward her through the clusters of guests. Of course, the dancing was about to begin, and he was honoring La Vecchia's request and looking for her. The thought of dancing in his arms under Falieri's smug eyes was too much. She skirted the edge of the ballroom and came out into the foyer. She had a terrible impulse to escape. The doors of the Ca' stood open. Guests were still arriving. From the ballroom came the joyful surge of a Napoleonic waltz, with violins and the sound of the harpsichord. She stopped to listen, feeling suddenly lightheaded. She knew she was hearing what the first Allegra had heard.

It's the dress, she clings to it still, she thought. *I know it was hers! And these are her pearls. . . .*

In some way her own anguish was united with that of the Allegra of long ago. Time dissolved and moved. Was this ball happening now, or was it from another time—1819? Allegra di Rienzi's presence enveloped her.

She felt a stab of panic. She must get away or Aldo would find her, and then she would break down in front of him, and he would have proof she was a spineless fool. Someone else's voice wept in her, *I'm a fool!* She fled out the wide doors, her mind screaming to her, and ran along the wet narrow walkway at the side of the Ca'.

Late guests arriving in gondolas looked curiously at the figure in the beautiful gown, hurrying so desperately away from the scene of the festivities.

One pair of eyes was not so curious as worried. Giovanni Fancelli, carrying a load of guests, had recognized her. He hastened to deposit his passengers at the Ca' and quickly poled his gondola down the side canal in the direction Allegra had taken.

She heard him call her name, and she turned a distraught face toward him. He drew his boat to a landing and held out his hand to her.

She climbed down into the rocking craft and sank into its worn velvet seat. Tears came faster, despite her will to stop them. Giovanni made murmuring sounds of comfort and sent his boat shooting through the narrow canals. "We will go to Eleana Bugelli," he said, "so, do not weep, *bambina*."

She shivered, hardly feeling the swift motion of the gondola. In some way she wept not just for herself but for the other Allegra, too. For a time their spirits were joined in grief.

Then another deep force flowed into her mind. It was still the energy of Allegra di Rienzi, but it was purposeful. A rush of love enfolded the being of Allegra Brent, and a far-off tiny whisper spoke in her brain. *Wait! Wait!* it said, *I have not finished.* Again a cold shiver shook her, but the voice had brought with it an easing. Her tears had stopped, and she was Allegra Brent, but she was not alone—she knew this.

They went through the familiar broken iron gates of the Casa Bugelli. Giovanni helped her up the inner water stairs and pulled the bell, setting off an ear-jarring clangor. The door opened to show Fiorenzo Bugelli, and behind him, Eleana.

"*Guarda!*" Giovanni's voice intoned. "Behold! I have brought our little *signorina*,. There is a problem that is for the arms of a woman, the heart of a mother . . . ." He urged Allegra ahead, and Eleana drew her into the house.

"Come, little one." Eleana's arm linked with hers, and they went to the little bedroom that had been hers that first night in Venice. They sat together on the bed, and Eleana looked curiously at the antique gown. She said nothing but held Allegra's hand in her warm sympathetic grasp, as the story was agonizingly revealed.

There were tears in Eleana's eyes. "By all the saints," she

shook her head. "I heard a voice, as though from the Holy Mother herself, to tell me you should take caution with the family di Rienzi. I should have talked with you more often, *cara mia.*" She shook her head. "It is best you go back to America. The familiar things of your homeland will wipe away the romance and pain of the Venetian air." Allegra nodded and turned her white face toward the gentle woman beside her.

"Yes, *cara*, I know," Eleana went on. "Words do not cure love. Even friends can only put a little soothing balm on a sore heart. Stay here until you go home. We ask nothing but to help you. Come—maybe we should take off the gown. It makes me feel strange to touch the material. It is haunted, I think, by someone's tears. You came with nothing? No matter—Giovanni will pick up your luggage tonight when the grand party is finished."

"I just have to be quiet, alone for a little while. I promise not to impose on you. I'll pull myself together now, and leave for home in the morning. Oh, Eleana, I didn't think I would ever tell another person about this, not even you. . . . But you are like part of my family; I had to tell you." Eleana's arms enclosed her silently.

A knock on the door made them draw apart. Giorgio stood in the doorway, his round brown eyes full of importance. "Signorina Allegra, I am to say that the Conte di Rienzi is here. He begs to speak with you."

"No, no. I can't!"

A slow smile spread over Eleana's face. "But, Allegra, is it not better to show him a composed face? After all, he has left his obligations at the ball to come to speak to you."

"La Vecchia sent him," she replied tonelessly.

Eleana clicked her tongue in disbelief. "I do not think a Conte di Rienzi goes on such an errand without some reason of his own. It is only courtesy to a man who has given you employment." She stood, obviously expecting Allegra to make a move.

There was war in Allegra's heart. A force stronger than herself made her say, "All right," and she started toward the door. What did it really matter, the cost to her pride? Pride was something that had already been used too much.

"Wait." Eleana took a tissue from the bedstand and wiped the tearstains around Allegra's eyes. "Your hair needs fixing, too."

Allegra shrugged, "I don't care."

Eleana smiled again knowingly, and they walked without further words down the little hall. The gown whispered and rustled against the walls.

They entered a room beyond the kitchen and dining area, which Allegra had not seen before. It was the *salotto,* a living room filled with carefully brushed plush furniture of nineteen-twenties vintage, with family pictures standing on every available flat surface.

Two men rose from the big armchairs. They seemed to have been speaking together easily. Fiorenzo's perceptive face smiled at Allegra. She could not force her eyes to Aldo. She saw his satin shoes, the ruffles at his wrists and the large cameo ring on his fine hand.

"We will leave you," she heard Fiorenzo say in his pleasant firm voice. There were sounds of departing feet, and a scuffle as Giorgio was bodily removed by his father from his fascinated regard of Aldo. The door closed and there was silence.

As though he were commanding her, she looked up into his face. His brilliant eyes penetrated her defenses. The love in them startled her. Never had she expected to see such a look from him. His voice was low, almost a whisper.

"Why do you stare at me, *cara mia*? It is that you see before you a man who loves you and has been blind to it? A man who has been fighting with his demons . . . forgive me, my dearest." His voice grew rough. "When they told me you were gone, I thought I had lost you. I knew in that moment what emptiness really was!"

He held out his arms, and the power vibrating between them drew her to him. His heart was beating hard next to hers, and she clung to him with all her strength. He bent to kiss her, gently, another more deeply, with a sense of full possession.

He sighed and held her a little away from him. "Can you forgive my blindness and my abominable pride? I can only pray that you will understand. Before you judge me I must tell you what has been eating into me . . . what made me bitter toward you.''

He turned his face from hers for a moment and then met her eyes fully. ''I am ashamed to honor my stupidity with words, but you must know. Guido sensed my growing affection for you. He taunted me and said you planned to have a good nest egg with the sale of the Byron papers and were going home to your fiancé.'' Allegra shook her head in denial.

''Yes, my love, of course, but all I could feel then was betrayal. You were correct about the blood of a di Rienzi. There is some madness. He also said you had laughed with him over La Vecchia's attempt to make a match between us. He was amused that with all my caution I was being taken in by a good actress. And he said more—that you had told him I was too old, a dull sour man, and that even the Ca' d'Argenti and my title would not satisfy you. He was very convincing.''

Allegra's face filled with color. She would never forgive Guido. But could she forgive Aldo?

He looked at her steadily. ''Allegra, love and jealousy make a mockery of reason. Someday I'll tell you everything about my marriage, and why I am the way you have known me to be. I couldn't offer my heart again and have it held up for ridicule by the woman I loved. It happened to me once, and I would rather die without love entirely than go through it a second time. That is why some part of me believed Guido. I didn't want to play the clown again.''

Her eyes melted into tears, and he drew her close. ''My treasure, I would not blame you if you sent me away. How much I have hurt you!''

She pulled away to look at him. His words were faintly registering in her mind, and her heart was racing. She knew she loved him, but she didn't know what she would do about it. Loving him was too painful.

He continued to speak. ''Allegra, let me tell it all. Tonight at the ball La Vecchia warned me about Guido, more strongly than she had ever done. He has been doing great harm to the family.

His influence is not going to be tolerated further. And immediately after this I went to look for you, to dance the first waltz as La Vecchia had wished. When I realized you were gone, Signor Mossanato advised me in most respectful tones that I was an idiot to suspect you of anything dishonorable—and that my ignorance was most extraordinary if I continued to misjudge you. He implied that I could not recognize sincere feeling even if it were in front of my face.''

A smile stole across Allegra's lips as Aldo went on. ''Mossanato is kind but also very shrewd. His appearance is a good disguise. He told me that Guido's room had been searched and evidence uncovered of his correspondence with Haversham-Bing. Guido was going to him posing as the Conte di Rienzi to sell the Byron papers. He never thought the dealer would come directly to me. Guido is a poor planner, as you know. Of course, he intended to blame you, and with the papers gone, how could you defend yourself? Signor Mossanato has found other evidence of Guido's activities, as well, and I am sickened to think that I did not see the truth.''

Her heart ached for his painful confessions. She put her hand lightly against his cheek. ''Oh, Aldo, I'm so sorry about Guido . . . about everything that has happened to us.''

He turned his head to kiss her fingers gently. ''So you do understand! I thank God!'' He pulled her closer into his arms. His lips moved in light kisses over her face, touching her eyelids, the tip of her nose. He felt response in her body. Then his lips were on hers. Suddenly there was a sense of wonder and joy, which swept away all thought.

He looked deep into her eyes. ''So, my little Allegra, can you ever again say I do not love you?'' He smiled with a wry twist of his lips. ''Now we must come out of paradise for a little time, *cara*. La Vecchia will be impatient for news—and the ball is still in progress. She was beside herself when she found you had gone. She said it was my fault and called me names under the edge of her fan that I did not even think she could know. But I agreed with her. They were deserved! Are you satisfied, beloved?'' He watched her with the assurance of a man who was again the master of his situation.

She couldn't speak to his question. Was she satisfied? The nagging thought of Falieri prickled in her mind. His dark eyes were waiting for her answer. Reluctantly, she said, "You don't really know why I left the ball, Aldo. Guido told me you intended to announce your engagement to Vera Falieri. I couldn't stay to hear it. It was too much to bear, and I had to get away."

He swept her close with a low sound in his throat, his cheek to hers. "My poor sweet . . . how thick I have been! Vera was only a companion, whose motivations I knew very well. She never had a place in my heart, believe me. I think that is why I continued to see her . . . she never threatened the part of me I wished to protect. That was for you to do, my love." There was a deep exciting vibration in his voice—teasing and passionate all at once. "Allegra, I love you."

A silence fell between them. He was waiting for her to say she loved him, and for some reason she could not say it. He still held her hand between his own. He raised it to his lips, and she felt his searching gaze on her down bent face. "Must I ask?" His voice was low. "I have tried to answer all the questions your heart might ask. Will you not answer the one most necessary to me?"

She looked up into his eyes. His face was strong, his fine mouth serious. She trembled and the blood blushed into her face. With a comforting sigh, he drew her close to him. Her head rested against his firm shoulder, and it was easier for her to say the words from the shelter of his strength.

"Yes, I love you, Aldo. I think I have always loved you, only now I have found you." His hand stroked the line of her cheek and brought her face to his. She saw the joy and the force of love that moved within him, and it was an unguarded, trusting, completely giving love. He kissed her again and again, as if in reassurance of his heart.

His voice was softly urgent next to her ear. "Allegra, will you be my wife?"

"Yes, yes," she said in a whisper and closed her eyes, afraid that more tears would fall. His kiss spoke for him and Allegra let her whole body respond to his passion.

She could only remember afterward that Eleana and Fiorenzo had embraced her at their parlor doorway, and that there were kisses for everybody. Giovanni was smiling in his gondola at the water stairs. "We will see you soon, Allegra," Eleana said with glistening eyes.

"If you don't visit us at the Ca', my grandmother will be disappointed," Aldo said.

"We will visit her one day, if she will ask us," Eleana smiled.

Aldo helped Allegra into the boat. As they moved through the dark canals, she was beyond thought, in a state of blissful unreality. Yet Aldo's hand was there holding hers, and above them Giovanni swung his long oar and sang a timeless song of love into the warm night.

"We must forever thank our friend, Giovanni. He came to me, Allegra, and told me where you had gone." Giovanni grinned down at them and made the sign with his fingers that everything was all right now.

Aldo drew something from his pocket. It was wrapped in a yellowed silk handkerchief. "Maria found this in a pocket of the petticoats that belong to your gown. She took it to La Vecchia some days ago. It was to be part of her surprise."

Allegra unfolded the silk and brought forth a small diary. For a moment she thought it was the one from her Byron box, but then she saw that the picture on the cover was different. This one showed the ballroom of the Ca' d'Argenti, with many figures dancing, and in the space in the center a man and a woman were waltzing. The woman's dark head rested close to his shoulder, and he held her lovingly, protectively. "It is the earlier diary of Allegra di Rienzi. In it she has written of the events leading to her marriage, the birth of her son—La Vecchia's father—and the first year of her life at the Ca' d'Argenti . . . before she met Byron. It is proof, *cara mia*, proof that your papers are authentic. The writing is the same, and the diaries are a pair. La Vecchia was going to give it to you tonight, but you changed her plans. Oh, Allegra . . . ."

"I know, my dearest, and there is nothing more to forgive." She leaned up to kiss him. The small dancing figures in the miniature were the two of them, as if the future had been painted in the past.

She touched the little diary and thought with pity and affection of the first Allegra. What had truly happened to the lonely, lovely woman in the years after she fled from Venice? And what had her love child been like? If Allegra Brent still felt Byron's energies in her own blood all these generations later, how much more must it have moved in this earlier child? It was tantalizing to have another chapter of Allegra di Rienzi's life in her hands; at least now she could come to know her better from these yellowed pages.

But the most insistent thought of all was a hope that the sweet lost *contessa* had found a haven of love, a deep and wonderful happiness like the one her namesake was experiencing now. Allegra said a silent prayer in the midst of her joy for that other Allegra who was still so strangely near.

They glided swiftly while snatches of music and voices came from open windows above the quiet waters. It was all so beautiful. She found it hard to believe she was the same woman who only a brief while ago had wept, huddled and without hope, in this same gondola. It could be a dream. She put out her hand to touch Aldo's firm knee. Yes, he was real. She felt his hand take hers in a protective clasp. Again, the wonderful sense of comfort and belonging—rightness—flooded over her.

"What is it, my Allegra? Do you feel it, too?" His voice was very low. "I thank God we have not lost this most precious treasure that moves between us." They were silent, as the smooth surge of the gondola made music of the lap of the water against the old stones as they passed.

Aldo released her hand to reach again into his breast pocket. In a caressing motion he slipped a ring onto her finger. It slid on easily, and she drew a quick breath when she saw the moonlight bring fire from the many facets of a cluster of diamonds, set on each side with a large glowing pearl. Her hand went to the pearls at her throat.

"Yes," Aldo's voice said, "they match. It is the set given by my grandfather Leopoldo to the woman he loved, on the day of their engagement. It has been in the family since the first Allegra." He gave a deep quiet laugh. "La Vecchia took it from her own hand and said not to return without you . . . and wearing the ring." His eyes held hers for a long moment. In them was a wordless promise that made her tremble. She needed no more proof of his love.

His mouth lifted into a smile. "Bianca will not speak to me, and she will not come back to the ball without you. She weeps in her room. She loves you, too. You see, your family cannot do without you." He kissed her for a long enfolding time. It was more than she thought she could bear. And then he laughed, as he held her close against him. "Do you know what disturbed me most about Guido's little lies? I must tell you because it is so amusing to me now. He said that you considered me too old for romance . . . that older men were not exciting to you."

She was still glowing from his kiss, but she laughed with him. "I am Italian, Allegra *mia*, and jealous. Remember it," he teased. "But I am not worried. I will love you so passionately you will never want to look at another man."

The sounds of waltz music spread a wide aura around the Ca' d'Argenti, and light streamed in glittering shafts from the windows to the Grand Canal. Gondolas danced on the tide, waiting for the guests within. Giovanni left them at the water stairs. He embraced Allegra and clasped a strong grip with Aldo. When Luigi saw them come into the foyer, his face spread into a beaming smile of pleasure and relief.

Aldo drew her hand onto his arm, and they entered the crowded ballroom. From her enthroned place of honor, La Vecchia saw them and motioned to the musicians, who fell silent. All eyes followed La Vecchia's gaze. A path was opened for Aldo and Allegra as they progressed across the room, the intensity of their happiness emanating from them.

La Vecchia rose to greet them, strong emotion moving on her wonderful face. They stepped up onto the dais, and Aldo bowed formally to his grandmother. There was laughter in his eyes. His voice was strong in the silence.

"Contessa Amalia, may I present to you my fiancée, Signorina Allegra Brent."

A stir rippled from person to person around the room. Allegra looked into the wise old eyes and saw a film of tears. She felt herself drawn into a gentle embrace, to be kissed most lovingly. La Vecchia whispered into her ear with playful chiding, "I will speak to you later about your unforgivable conduct, Allegra *mia.*" She motioned to Maria, "Go and bring Bianca. Tell her Allegra is home."

She turned away to face her guests and gestured to Aldo that she wished to speak. Raising her strong voice so that all could hear, she began: "You have all heard of the lost Allegra di Rienzi of the past. A few weeks ago, this lovely young woman came to tell us of a family secret of her own. We now have proof that Allegra di Rienzi, under stress of deep emotion, ran away to the United States.

"She remarried and gave birth to a daughter, naming her Allegra. She left the record of her life to be handed down to her female descendants." She put her hand on Allegra's arm. "This is Allegra Brent, the last of the descendants. Even if she had not brought me proof, I would have known her. *Guarda!* Behold! This was my grandmother!" She turned to Luigi, who stood holding the cord of the covered object behind the dais. A spotlight flooded the cloth drapery, as it was drawn aside, to reveal a large, richly painted portrait of a woman.

A gasp of surprise greeted the unveiling. Allegra felt her heart pounding. The young woman in the life-size painting was smiling, but sadness lingered in her shadowy eyes. She was in the gown that Allegra was wearing. Her hair, dark and curling, swept into waves, was the same as Allegra's own. The resemblance was startling.

The old woman spoke close to Allegra. "My dear, the first time I saw you I was sure. I had often stood before this portrait, which my father banished from sight, and I wondered. Surely my young grandmother was a sweet woman; her face told me so. But her sadness puzzled me. I longed to know her. Then you came, *cara*. I had to find out if you were more than just an outside semblance of her. I found that you were an honorable woman, who faced your life with courage, as she did."

La Vecchia looked around the room, once more raising her clear voice. "Allegra di Rienzi has come home."

She took Allegra's and Aldo's hands and held them close in her strong grasp. "My birthday is complete. It is as I have prayed, and God has been merciful. You will take Allegra to dance your first waltz together, Aldo. Did I not ask you to do this earlier?" She smiled to herself and sat down in her great chair, raising her champagne glass to them.

The woman in the portrait gazed out over the crowd. Allegra looked back at her and thought the smile had lost its sadness now. Aldo's hand steadied her as they reached the center of the ballroom. The orchestra was playing the same haunting melody that had been La Vecchia's entrance music.

She looked up at his fine face, and nothing else existed to her. He took her into his arms, drawing her into the rhythm of the dance. It was the picture on the old diary cover, alive again. As the music flowed around them, Allegra thought of her own grandmother, her *nonna*. She was very near, very happy.

Then another face moved across the screen of her inner vision . . . penetrating, masculine eyes looked into hers with a smile, at once loving and world weary. In her mind she heard the tones of a man's deep beguiling voice: *You have taken the best of the Byron blood, my little Allegra, child of my love. . . .*

SHE CAME BACK TO HERSELF with a start. Voices were calling out, *"Bravo! bravo!"* Hands were clapping and faces beaming. Aldo whispered into her ear, "You were very far away, *carina*—where?"

She smiled. "I was thinking of my *nonna* and the Allegra from the past . . . and Byron."

Aldo drew her closer. "All right, I will share you with your grandmother, but with no one else. Let the past have its peace, my love.''

Allegra nodded and rested her cheek against his. Those haunting hazel-gray eyes and the resonant voice would have to remain her secret and the secret of the other Allegra.

Gentle laughter started around them as Signor Mossanato, in the dress of a Regency dandy, led an entranced Bianca onto the ballroom floor. She suddenly left his arm to rush into Allegra's tight embrace. Her little face was transfigured with pleasure, and her high child's voice carried around the room. ''Maria says you'll stay! Oh, Allegra, I'm so happy!''

Signor Mossanato winked at Allegra, as if he were delighted with his part in this grand ending, and he drew his young partner into the dance. With enthusiastic applause encircling them, the two couples led the rest in the grand waltz.

Aldo whirled her around and around with him, until the ballroom was a blur of dazzling color and lights. He pulled her tightly against him, his voice speaking for her ears alone: ''I know that other Allegras have danced down the corridors of time, my darling . . . but for me this one Allegra is enough!''

APOLOGY

Fragments from Lord Byron's *The Corsair* and "She Walks in Beauty" were quoted in this book. But the other "Byron verses" herein cannot be laid at Byron's doorstep. Any efforts to identify them will lead only to the pen of Catherine Kay.

The author wishes to apologize to devotees of Byron's writing for presuming to imitate his poetic style. Also, apologies to Byron himself.

The bestselling epic saga of the Irish. An intriguing and passionate story that spans 400 years.

FIRST...

The Defiant

Lady Elizabeth Hatton, highborn Englishwoman, was not above using her position to get what she wanted ...and more than anything in the world she wanted Rory O'Donnell, the fiery Irish rebel. But it was an alliance that promised only ruin....

THEN...

The Survivors

Against a turbulent background of political intrigue and royal corruption, the determined, passionate Shanna O'Hara searched for peace in her beloved but troubled Ireland. Meanwhile in England, hot-tempered Brenna Coke fought against a loveless marriage....